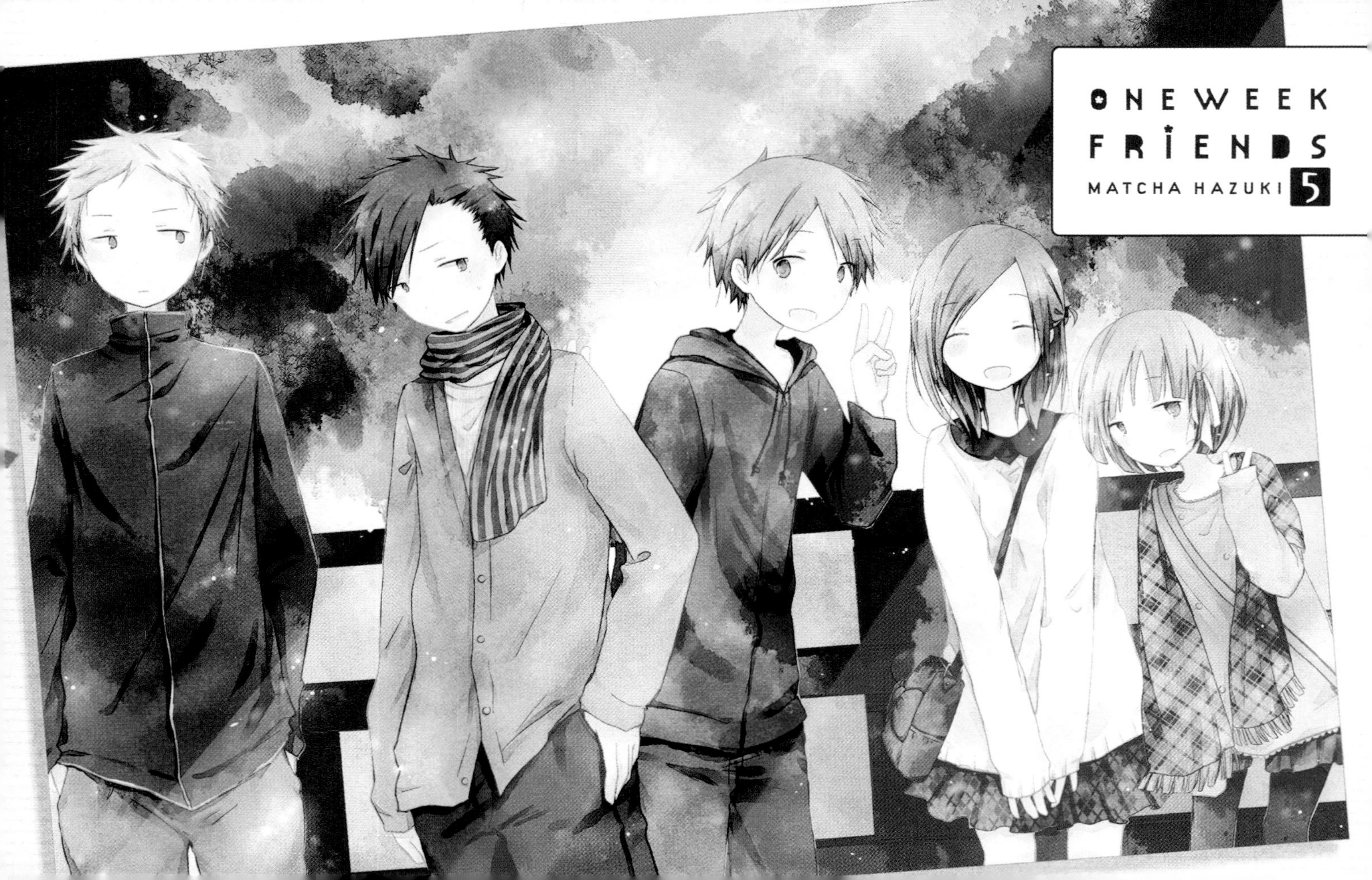
ONEWEEK FRIENDS
MATCHA HAZUKI 5

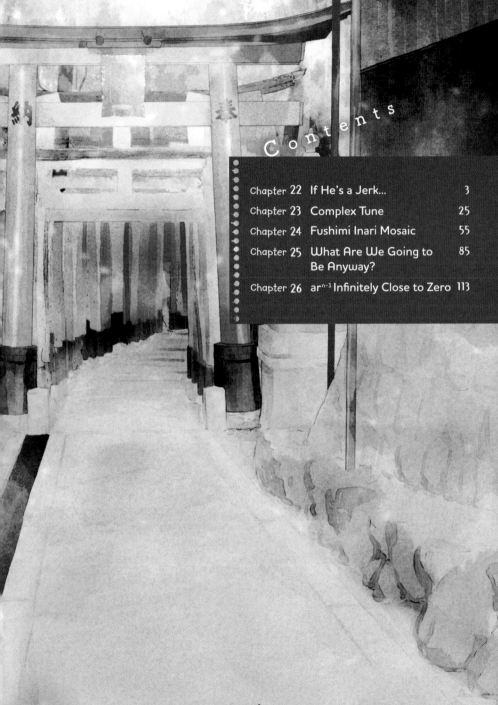

Contents

Chapter 22　If He's a Jerk...　3

Chapter 23　Complex Tune　25

Chapter 24　Fushimi Inari Mosaic　55

Chapter 25　What Are We Going to　85
　　　　　　Be Anyway?

Chapter 26　ar^{n-1} Infinitely Close to Zero　113

ONE WEEK FRIENDS 5

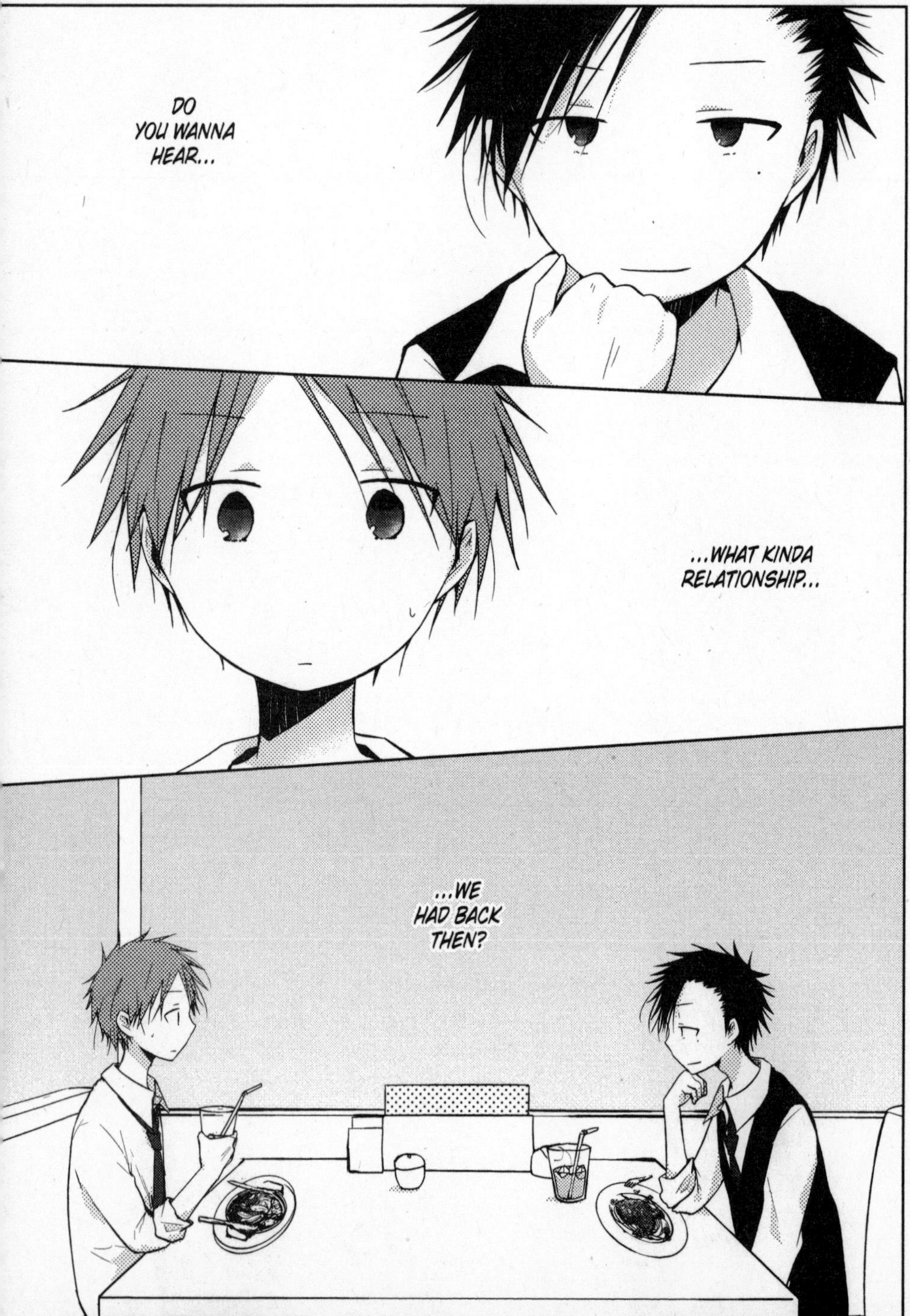
DO YOU WANNA HEAR...
...WHAT KINDA RELATIONSHIP...
...WE HAD BACK THEN?

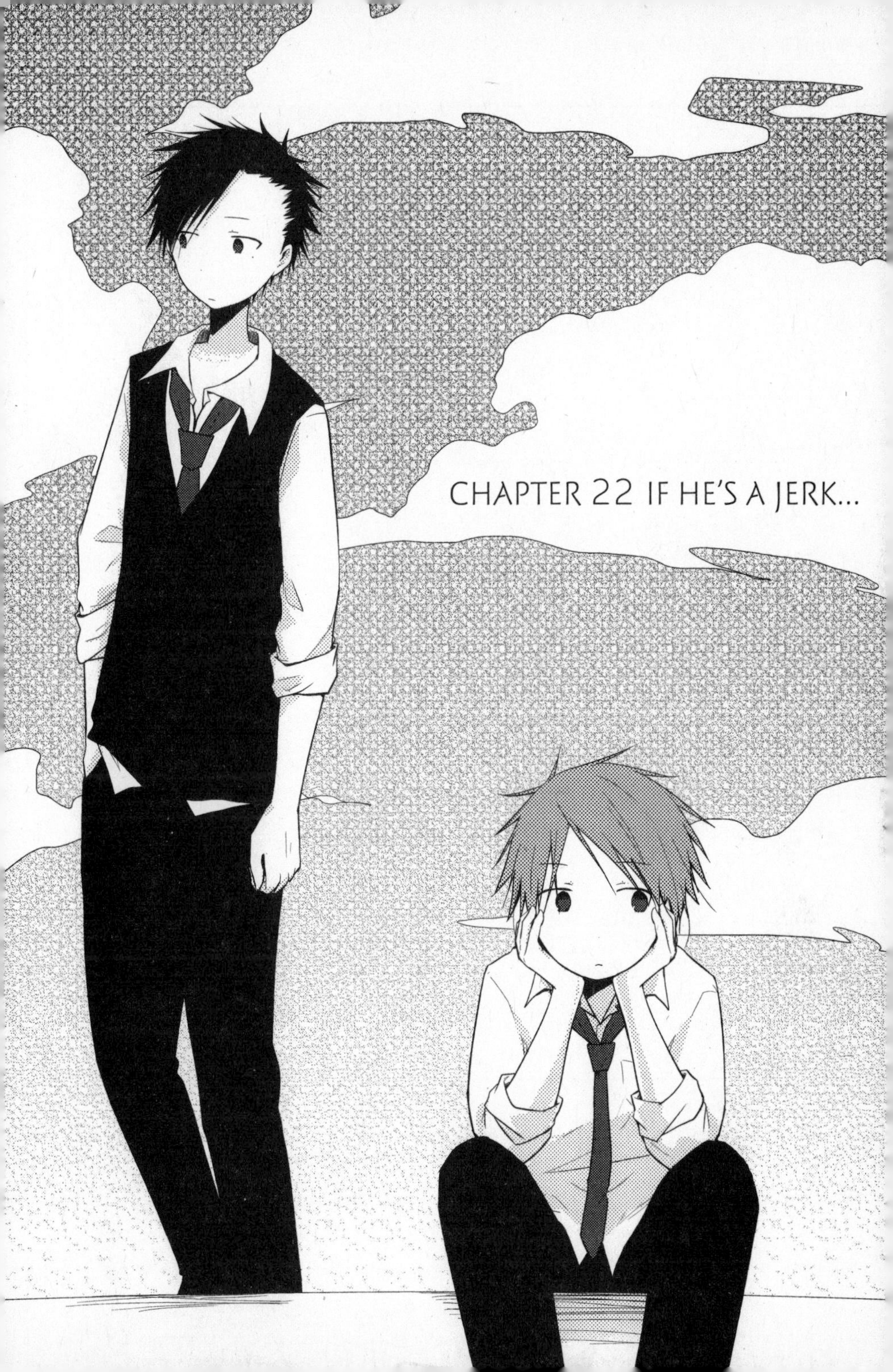
CHAPTER 22 IF HE'S A JERK...

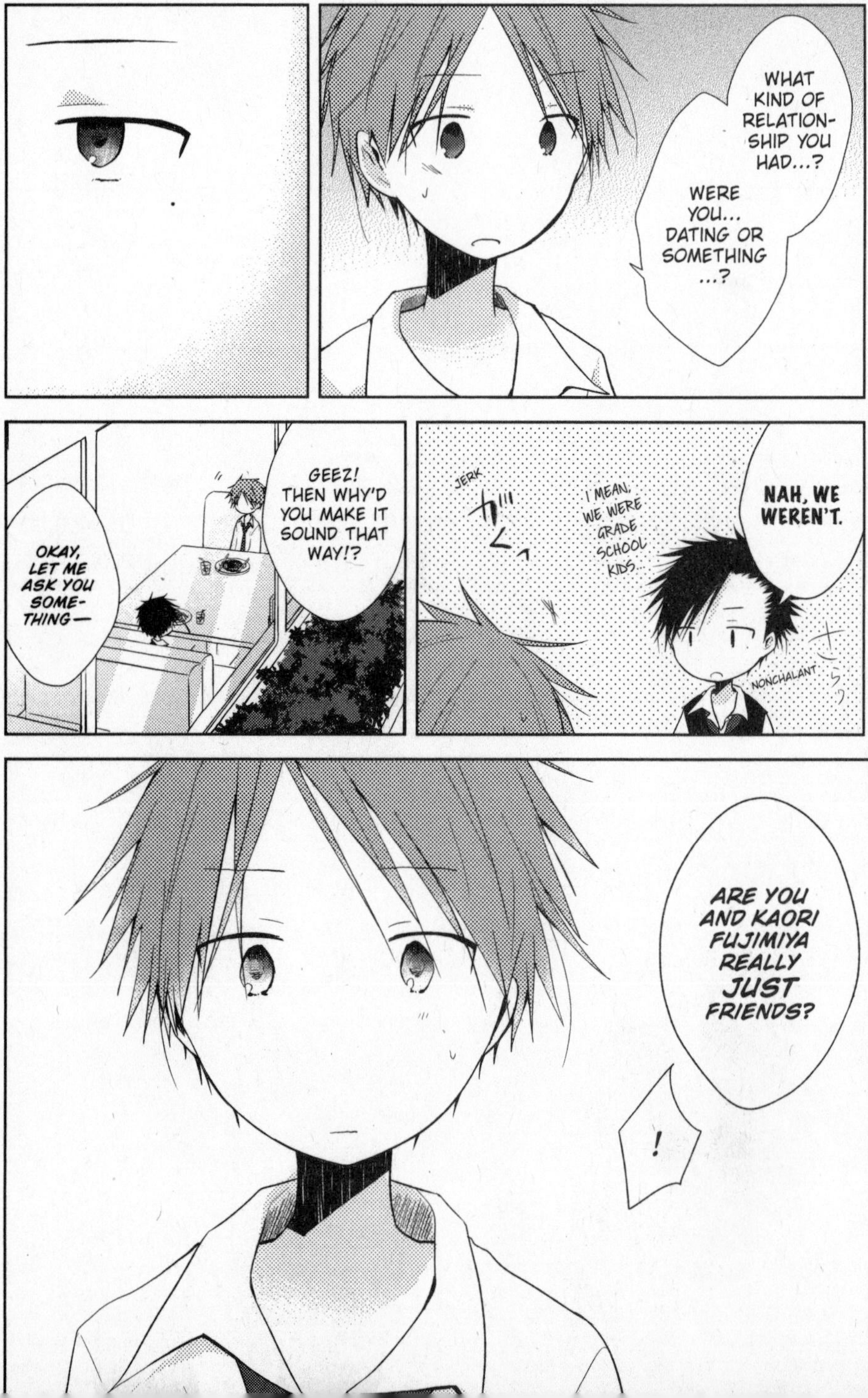
WHAT KIND OF RELATIONSHIP YOU HAD...?
WERE YOU... DATING OR SOMETHING ...?
NAH, WE WEREN'T.
I MEAN, WE WERE GRADE SCHOOL KIDS...
JERK
NONCHALANT
GEEZ! THEN WHY'D YOU MAKE IT SOUND THAT WAY!?
OKAY, LET ME ASK YOU SOMETHING—
ARE YOU AND KAORI FUJIMIYA REALLY JUST FRIENDS?
!

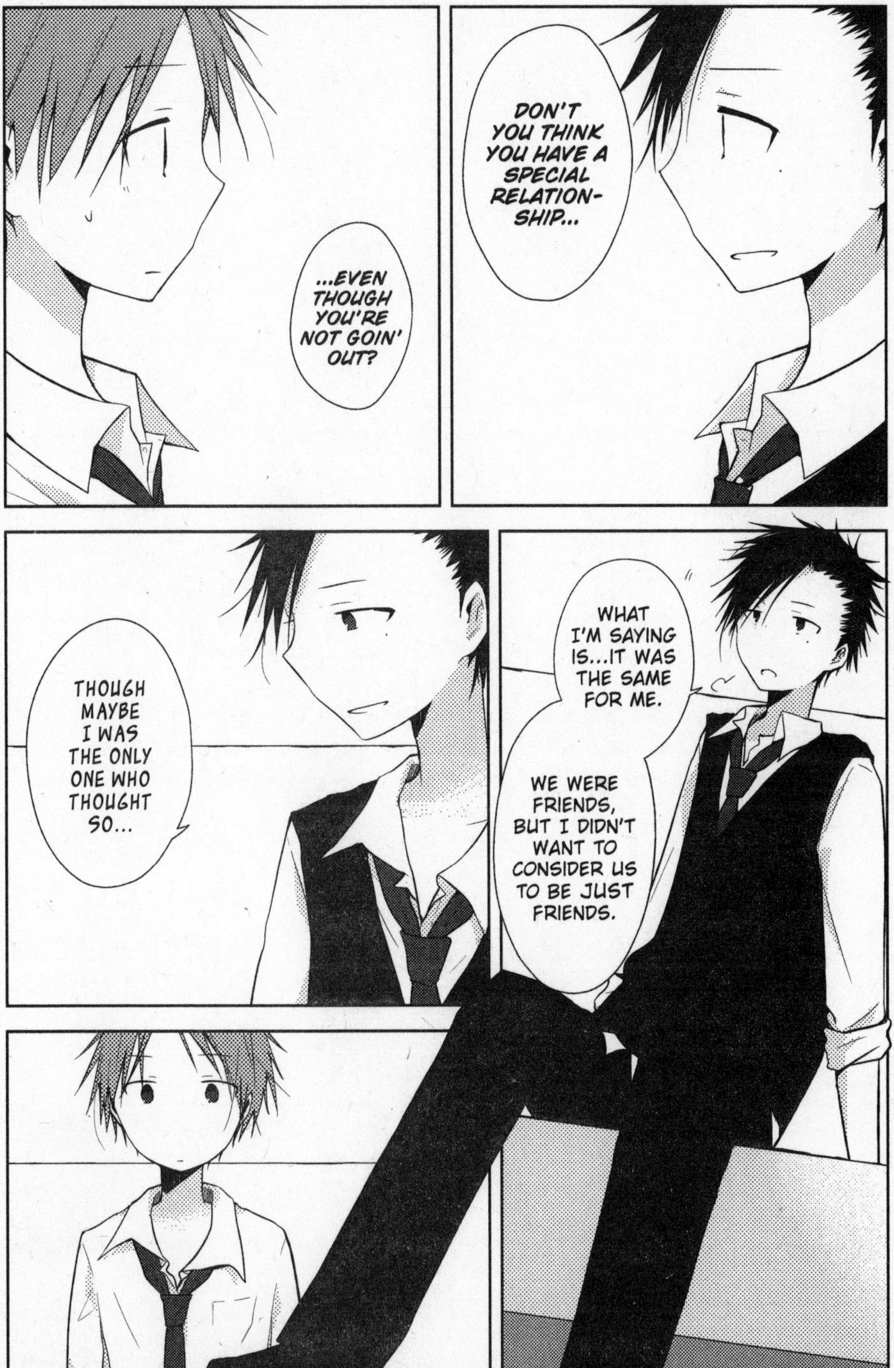
DON'T YOU THINK YOU HAVE A SPECIAL RELATION-SHIP...
...EVEN THOUGH YOU'RE NOT GOIN' OUT?
WHAT I'M SAYING IS...IT WAS THE SAME FOR ME.
WE WERE FRIENDS, BUT I DIDN'T WANT TO CONSIDER US TO BE JUST FRIENDS.
THOUGH MAYBE I WAS THE ONLY ONE WHO THOUGHT SO...

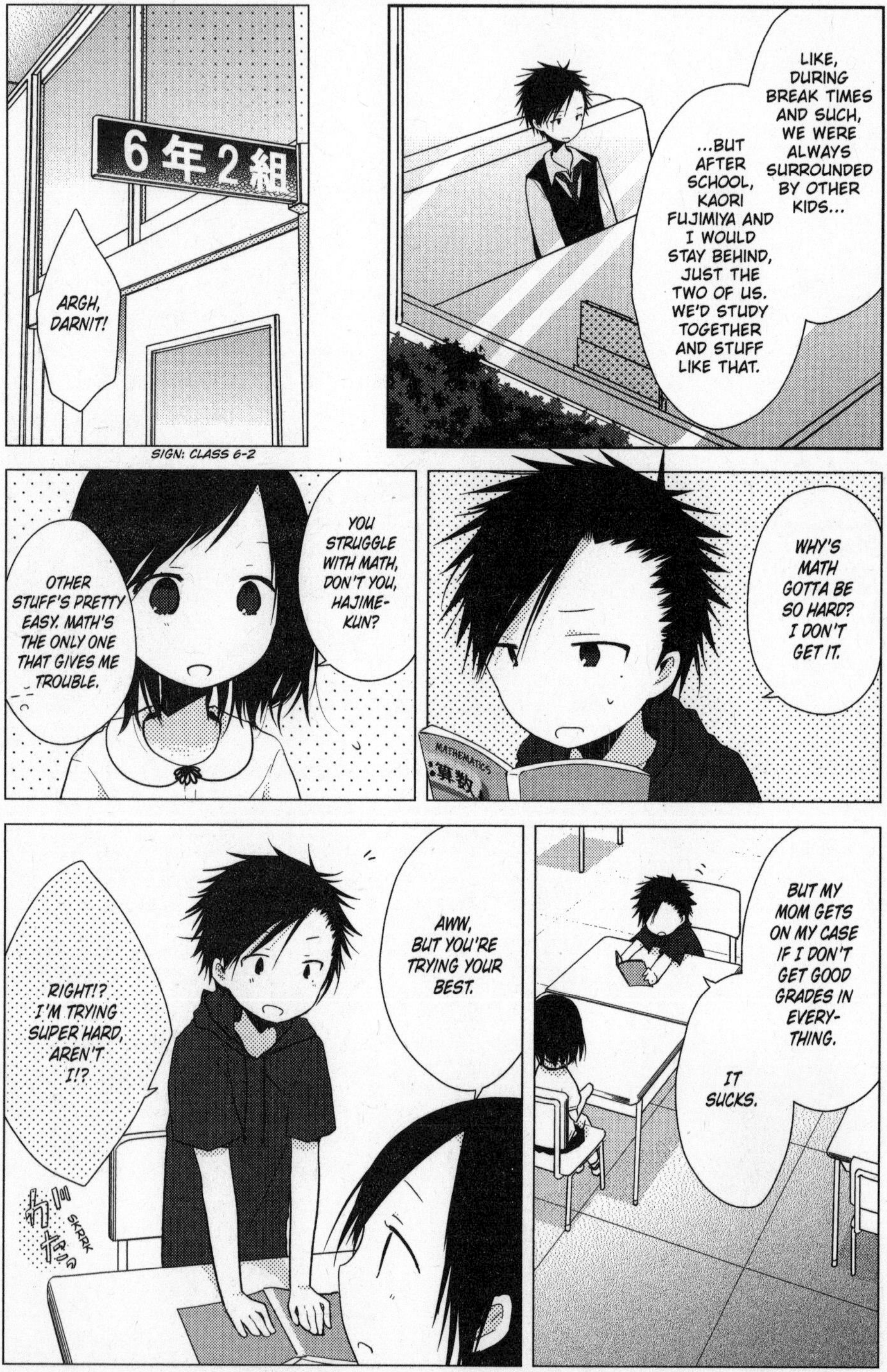
LIKE, DURING BREAK TIMES AND SUCH, WE WERE ALWAYS SURROUNDED BY OTHER KIDS...
...BUT AFTER SCHOOL, KAORI FUJIMIYA AND I WOULD STAY BEHIND, JUST THE TWO OF US. WE'D STUDY TOGETHER AND STUFF LIKE THAT.
6年2組
ARGH, DARNIT!
SIGN: CLASS 6-2
WHY'S MATH GOTTA BE SO HARD? I DON'T GET IT.
MATHEMATICS
算数
YOU STRUGGLE WITH MATH, DON'T YOU, HAJIME-KUN?
OTHER STUFF'S PRETTY EASY. MATH'S THE ONLY ONE THAT GIVES ME TROUBLE.
BUT MY MOM GETS ON MY CASE IF I DON'T GET GOOD GRADES IN EVERY-THING.
IT SUCKS.
AWW, BUT YOU'RE TRYING YOUR BEST.
RIGHT!? I'M TRYING SUPER HARD, AREN'T I!?
SKRRK

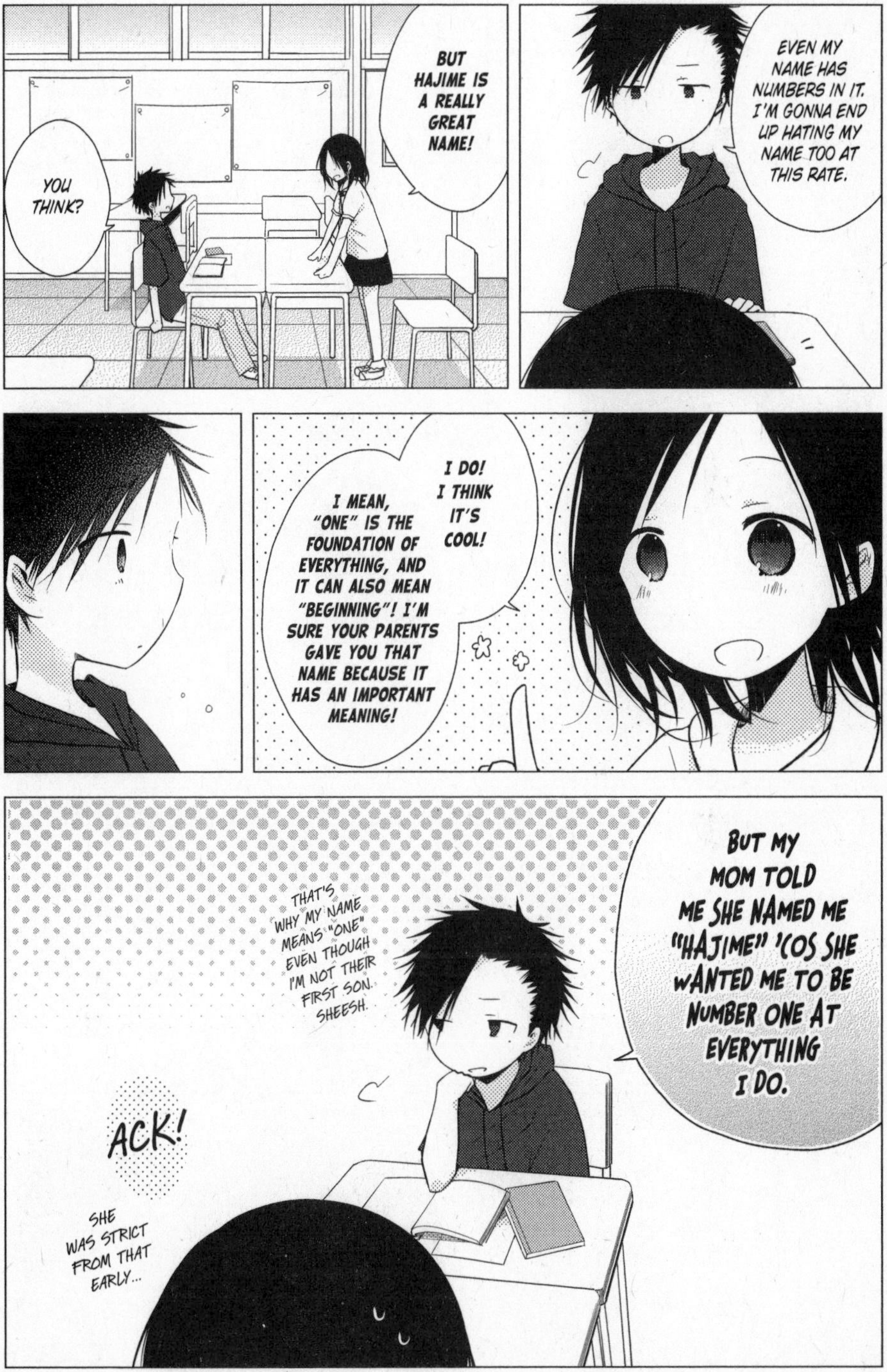
EVEN MY NAME HAS NUMBERS IN IT. I'M GONNA END UP HATING MY NAME TOO AT THIS RATE.
BUT HAJIME IS A REALLY GREAT NAME!
YOU THINK?
I DO! I THINK IT'S COOL!
I MEAN, "ONE" IS THE FOUNDATION OF EVERYTHING, AND IT CAN ALSO MEAN "BEGINNING"! I'M SURE YOUR PARENTS GAVE YOU THAT NAME BECAUSE IT HAS AN IMPORTANT MEANING!
BUT MY MOM TOLD ME SHE NAMED ME "HAJIME" 'COS SHE WANTED ME TO BE NUMBER ONE AT EVERYTHING I DO.
THAT'S WHY MY NAME MEANS "ONE" EVEN THOUGH I'M NOT THEIR FIRST SON. SHEESH.
ACK!
SHE WAS STRICT FROM THAT EARLY...

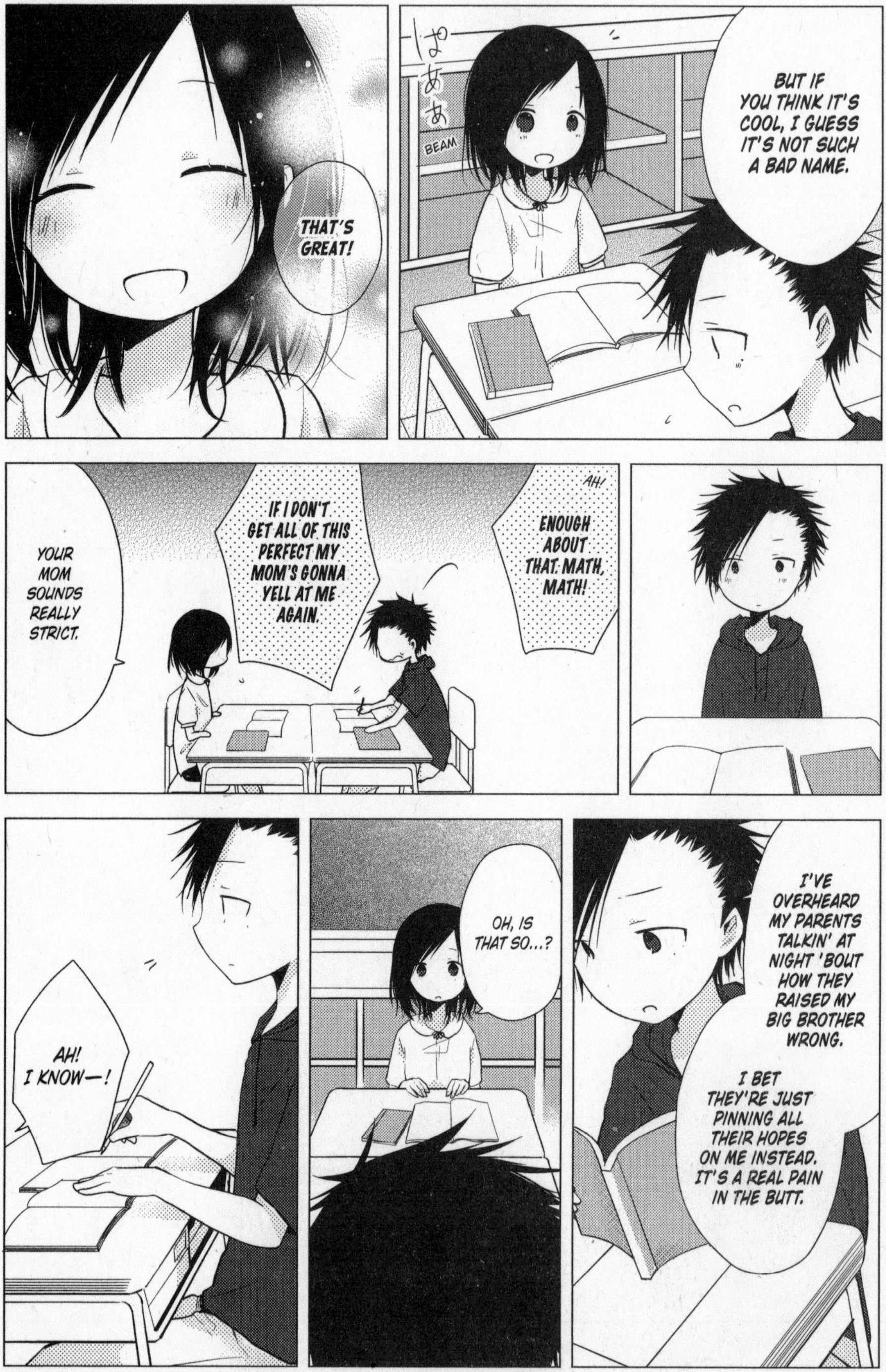
BUT IF YOU THINK IT'S COOL, I GUESS IT'S NOT SUCH A BAD NAME.
ぱあぁ
BEAM
THAT'S GREAT!
AH!
ENOUGH ABOUT THAT. MATH, MATH!
IF I DON'T GET ALL OF THIS PERFECT MY MOM'S GONNA YELL AT ME AGAIN.
YOUR MOM SOUNDS REALLY STRICT.
I'VE OVERHEARD MY PARENTS TALKIN' AT NIGHT 'BOUT HOW THEY RAISED MY BIG BROTHER WRONG.
I BET THEY'RE JUST PINNING ALL THEIR HOPES ON ME INSTEAD. IT'S A REAL PAIN IN THE BUTT.
OH, IS THAT SO...?
AH! I KNOW—!

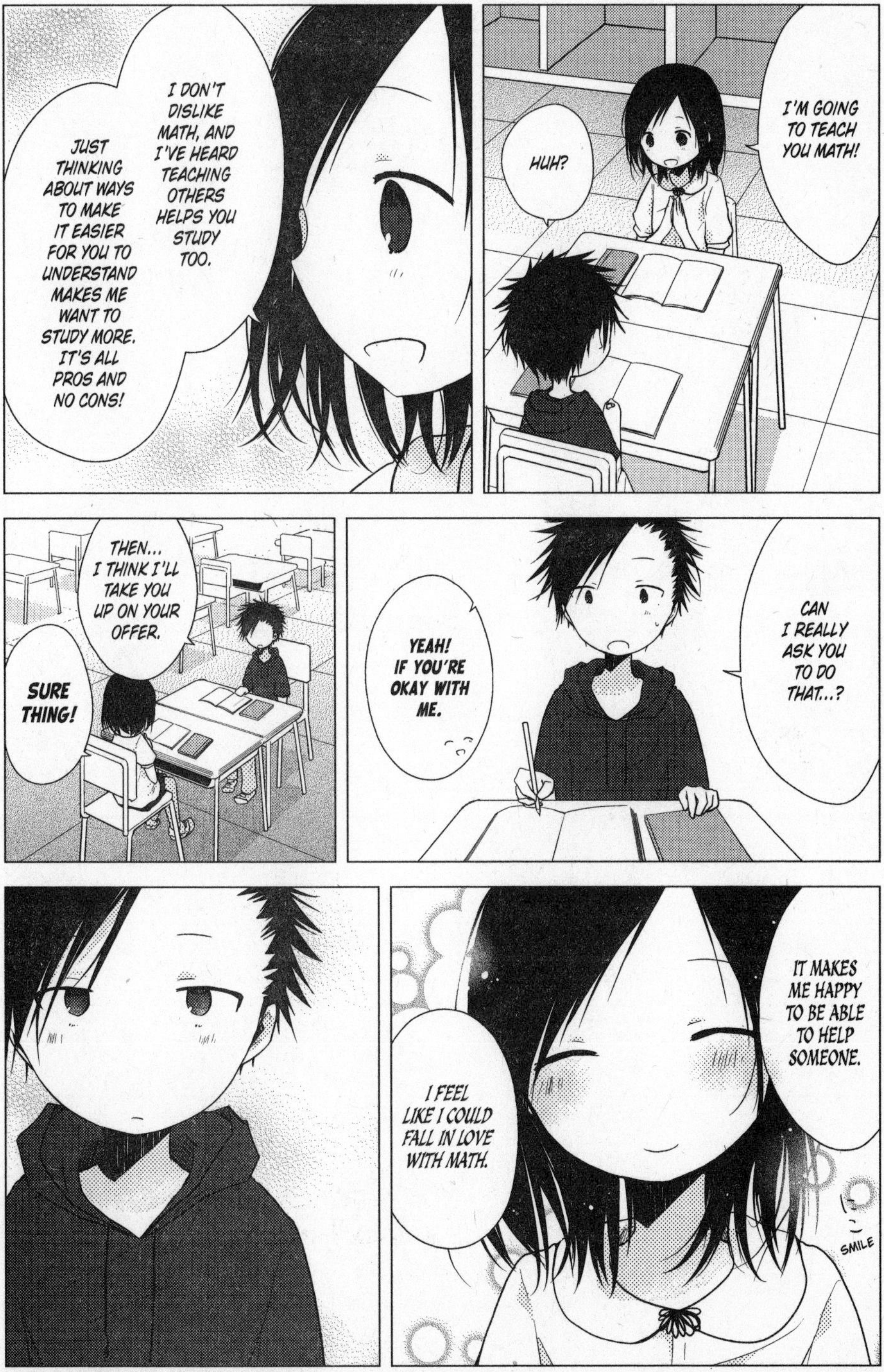
I'M GOING TO TEACH YOU MATH!
HUH?
I DON'T DISLIKE MATH, AND I'VE HEARD TEACHING OTHERS HELPS YOU STUDY TOO.
JUST THINKING ABOUT WAYS TO MAKE IT EASIER FOR YOU TO UNDERSTAND MAKES ME WANT TO STUDY MORE. IT'S ALL PROS AND NO CONS!
CAN I REALLY ASK YOU TO DO THAT...?
YEAH! IF YOU'RE OKAY WITH ME.
THEN... I THINK I'LL TAKE YOU UP ON YOUR OFFER.
SURE THING!
IT MAKES ME HAPPY TO BE ABLE TO HELP SOMEONE.
I FEEL LIKE I COULD FALL IN LOVE WITH MATH.
SMILE

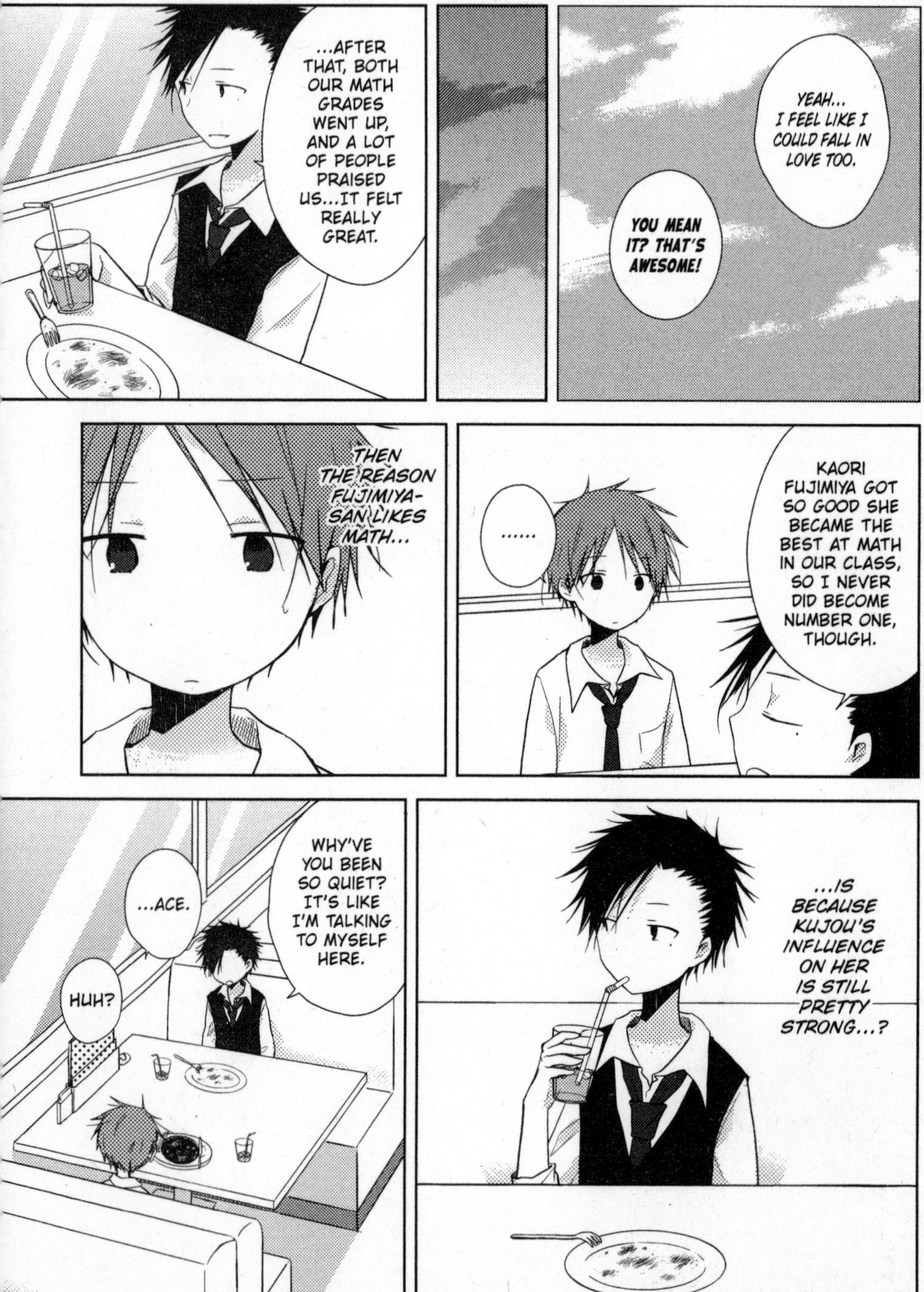
YEAH... I FEEL LIKE I COULD FALL IN LOVE TOO.
YOU MEAN IT? THAT'S AWESOME!
...AFTER THAT, BOTH OUR MATH GRADES WENT UP, AND A LOT OF PEOPLE PRAISED US...IT FELT REALLY GREAT.
KAORI FUJIMIYA GOT SO GOOD SHE BECAME THE BEST AT MATH IN OUR CLASS, SO I NEVER DID BECOME NUMBER ONE, THOUGH.
......
THEN THE REASON FUJIMIYA-SAN LIKES MATH...
...IS BECAUSE KUJOU'S INFLUENCE ON HER IS STILL PRETTY STRONG...?
WHY'VE YOU BEEN SO QUIET? IT'S LIKE I'M TALKING TO MYSELF HERE.
...ACE.
HUH?

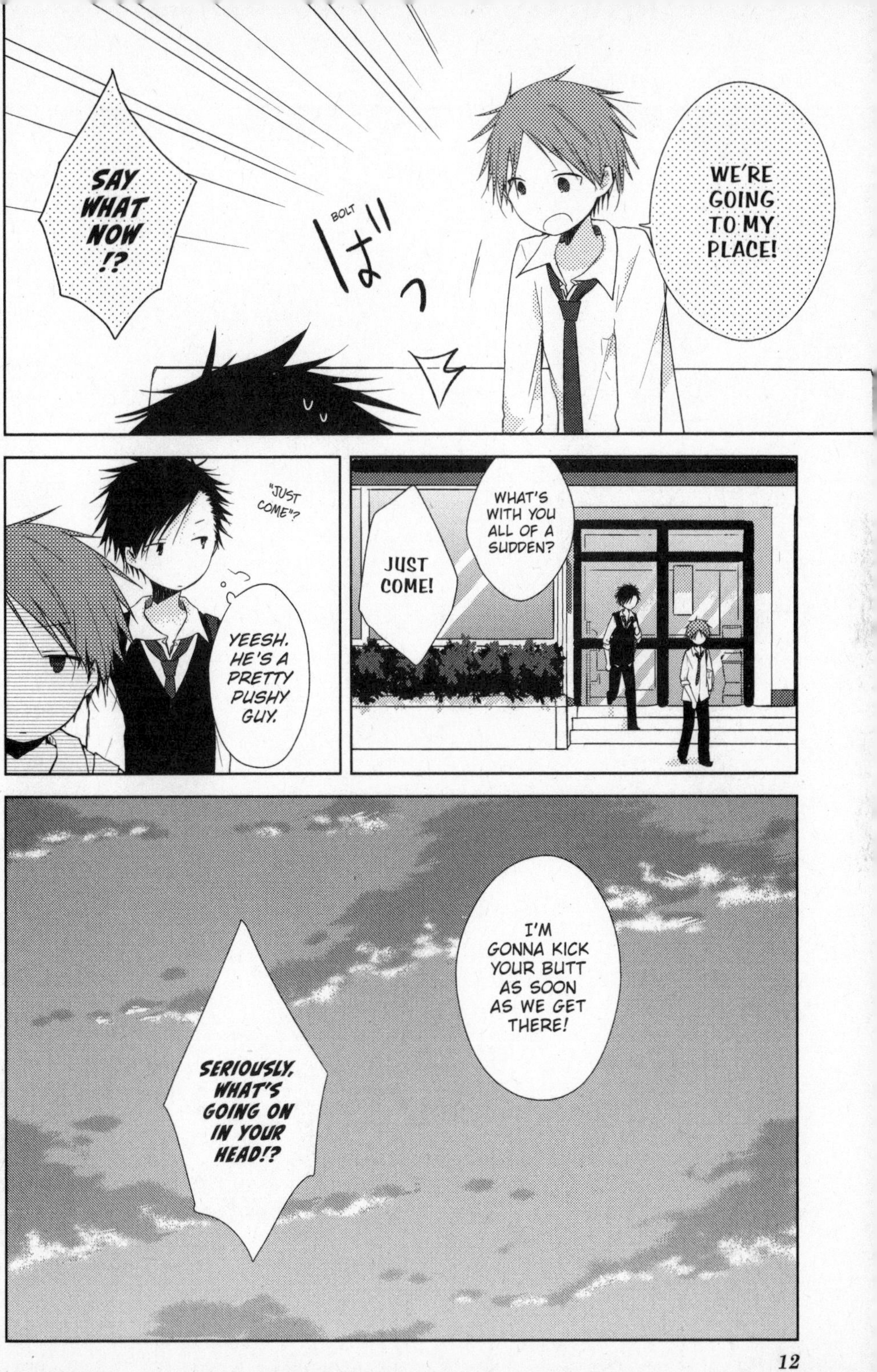
WE'RE GOING TO MY PLACE!
BOLT
ばっ
SAY WHAT NOW!?
WHAT'S WITH YOU ALL OF A SUDDEN?
JUST COME!
"JUST COME"?
YEESH. HE'S A PRETTY PUSHY GUY.
I'M GONNA KICK YOUR BUTT AS SOON AS WE GET THERE!
SERIOUSLY, WHAT'S GOING ON IN YOUR HEAD!?

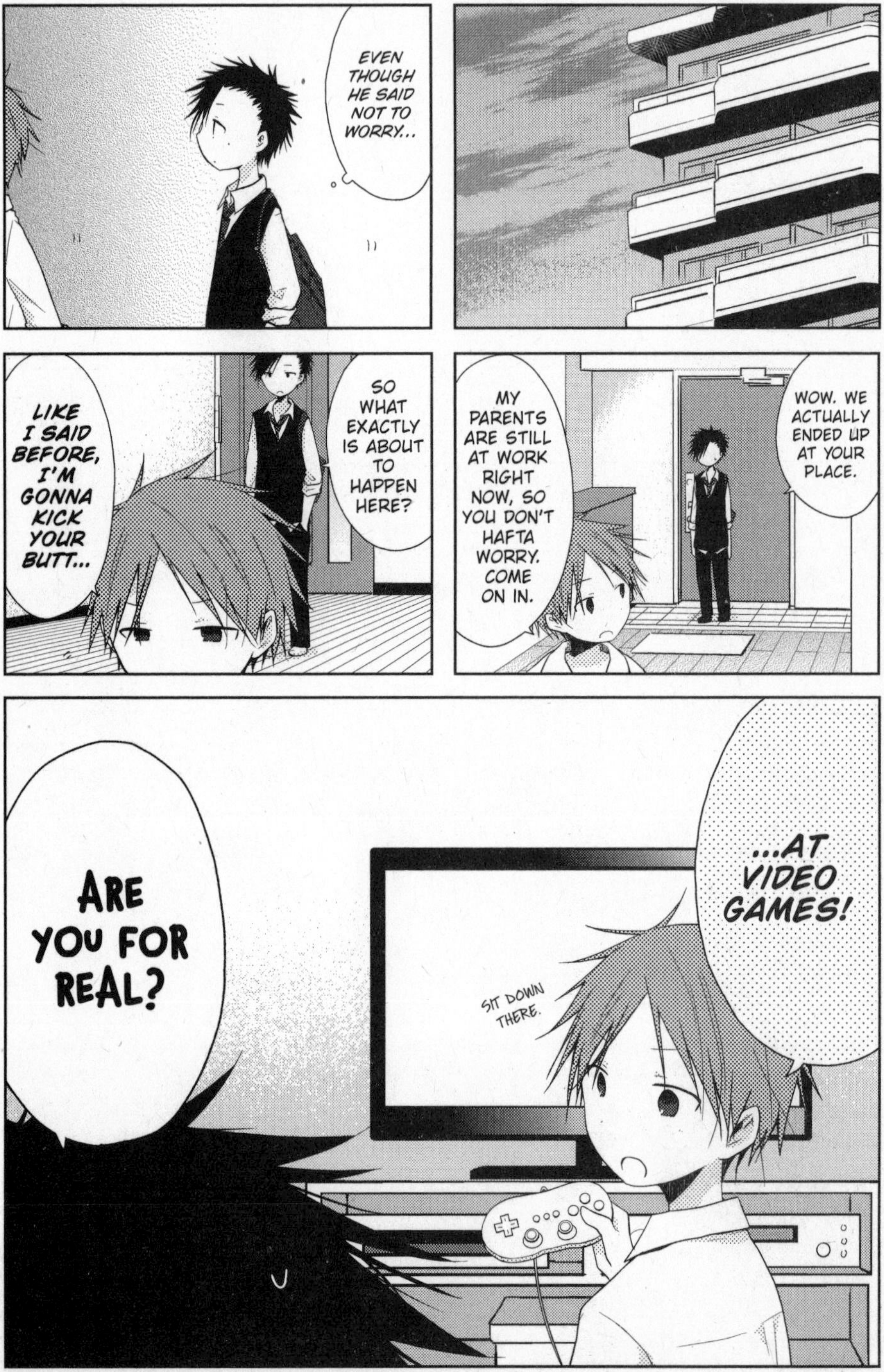
EVEN THOUGH HE SAID NOT TO WORRY...
WOW. WE ACTUALLY ENDED UP AT YOUR PLACE.
MY PARENTS ARE STILL AT WORK RIGHT NOW, SO YOU DON'T HAFTA WORRY. COME ON IN.
SO WHAT EXACTLY IS ABOUT TO HAPPEN HERE?
LIKE I SAID BEFORE, I'M GONNA KICK YOUR BUTT...
...AT VIDEO GAMES!
SIT DOWN THERE.
ARE YOU FOR REAL?

RACING GAME

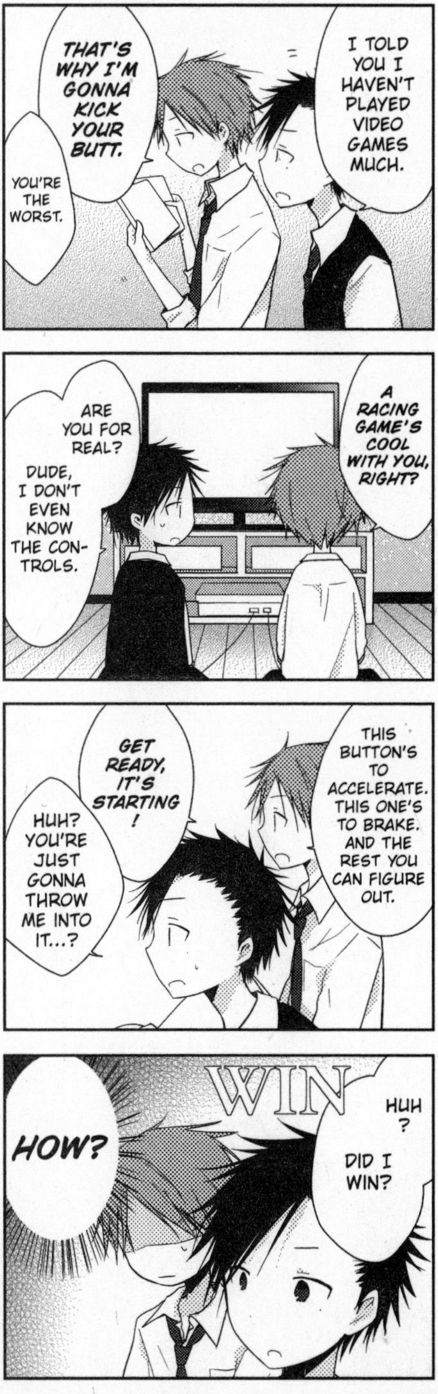
I TOLD YOU I HAVEN'T PLAYED VIDEO GAMES MUCH.
THAT'S WHY I'M GONNA KICK YOUR BUTT.
YOU'RE THE WORST.
A RACING GAME'S COOL WITH YOU, RIGHT?
ARE YOU FOR REAL?
DUDE, I DON'T EVEN KNOW THE CONTROLS.
THIS BUTTON'S TO ACCELERATE. THIS ONE'S TO BRAKE. AND THE REST YOU CAN FIGURE OUT.
GET READY, IT'S STARTING!
HUH? YOU'RE JUST GONNA THROW ME INTO IT...?
WIN
HUH?
DID I WIN?
HOW?

THAT'S ODD

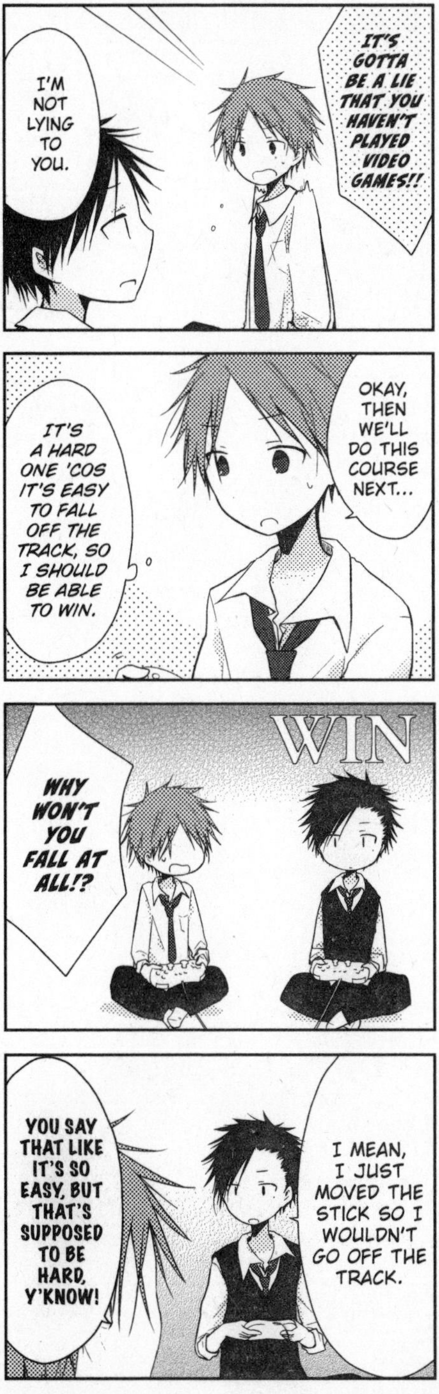
IT'S GOTTA BE A LIE THAT YOU HAVEN'T PLAYED VIDEO GAMES!!
I'M NOT LYING TO YOU.
OKAY, THEN WE'LL DO THIS COURSE NEXT...
IT'S A HARD ONE 'COS IT'S EASY TO FALL OFF THE TRACK, SO I SHOULD BE ABLE TO WIN.
WIN
WHY WON'T YOU FALL AT ALL!?
I MEAN, I JUST MOVED THE STICK SO I WOULDN'T GO OFF THE TRACK.
YOU SAY THAT LIKE IT'S SO EASY, BUT THAT'S SUPPOSED TO BE HARD, Y'KNOW!

FIGHTING GAME

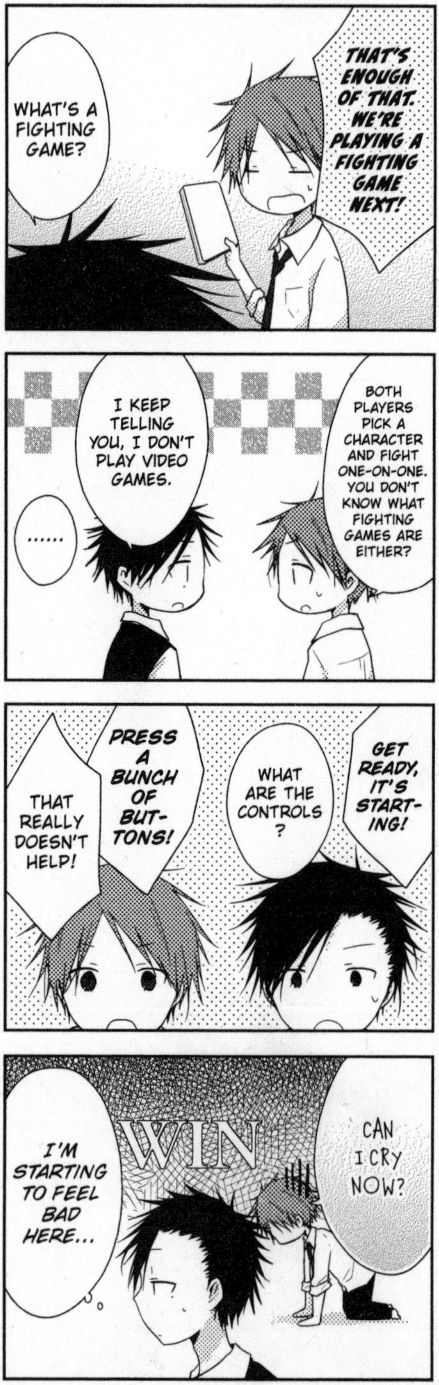
THAT'S ENOUGH OF THAT. WE'RE PLAYING A FIGHTING GAME NEXT!
WHAT'S A FIGHTING GAME?
BOTH PLAYERS PICK A CHARACTER AND FIGHT ONE-ON-ONE. YOU DON'T KNOW WHAT FIGHTING GAMES ARE EITHER?
I KEEP TELLING YOU, I DON'T PLAY VIDEO GAMES.
......
GET READY, IT'S STARTING!
WHAT ARE THE CONTROLS?
PRESS A BUNCH OF BUTTONS!
THAT REALLY DOESN'T HELP!
CAN I CRY NOW?
WIN
I'M STARTING TO FEEL BAD HERE...

SERIOUS

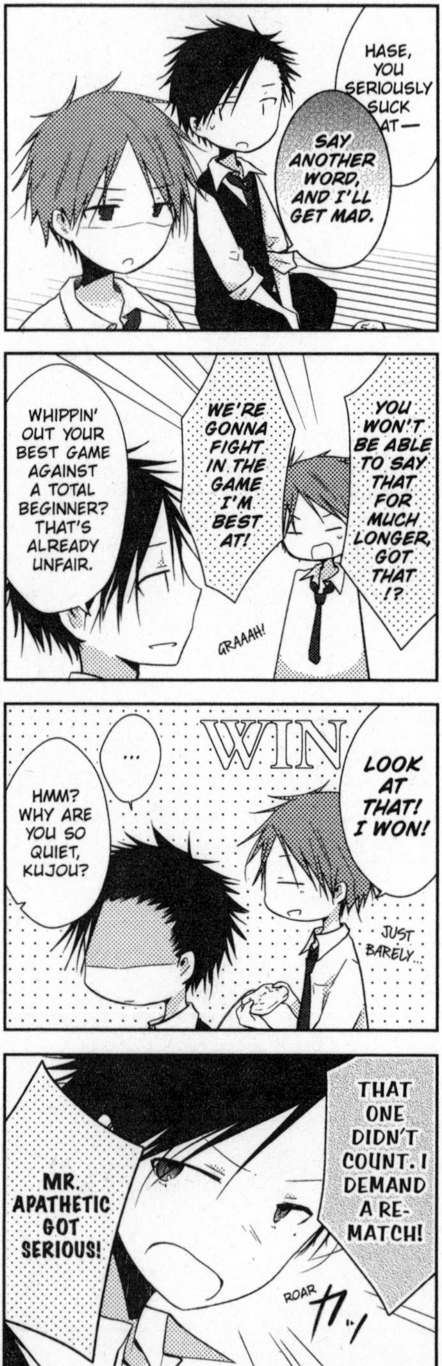
HASE, YOU SERIOUSLY SUCK AT—
SAY ANOTHER WORD, AND I'LL GET MAD.
YOU WON'T BE ABLE TO SAY THAT FOR MUCH LONGER, GOT THAT!?
WE'RE GONNA FIGHT IN THE GAME I'M BEST AT!
WHIPPIN' OUT YOUR BEST GAME AGAINST A TOTAL BEGINNER? THAT'S ALREADY UNFAIR.
GRAAAH!
LOOK AT THAT! I WON!
WIN
JUST BARELY...
...
HMM? WHY ARE YOU SO QUIET, KUJOU?
THAT ONE DIDN'T COUNT. I DEMAND A RE-MATCH!
MR. APATHETIC GOT SERIOUS!
ROAR

HEATED

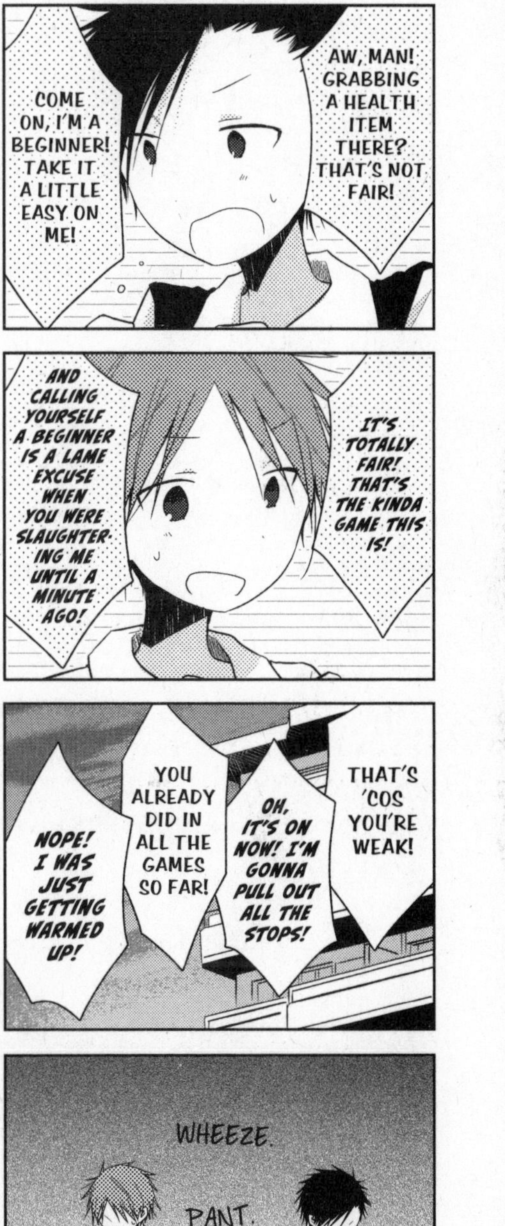
AW, MAN! GRABBING A HEALTH ITEM THERE? THAT'S NOT FAIR!
COME ON, I'M A BEGINNER! TAKE IT A LITTLE EASY ON ME!
IT'S TOTALLY FAIR! THAT'S THE KINDA GAME THIS IS!
AND CALLING YOURSELF A BEGINNER IS A LAME EXCUSE WHEN YOU WERE SLAUGHTERING ME UNTIL A MINUTE AGO!
THAT'S 'COS YOU'RE WEAK!
OH, IT'S ON NOW! I'M GONNA PULL OUT ALL THE STOPS!
YOU ALREADY DID IN ALL THE GAMES SO FAR!
NOPE! I WAS JUST GETTING WARMED UP!
WHEEZE.
PANT.

THE SCORE

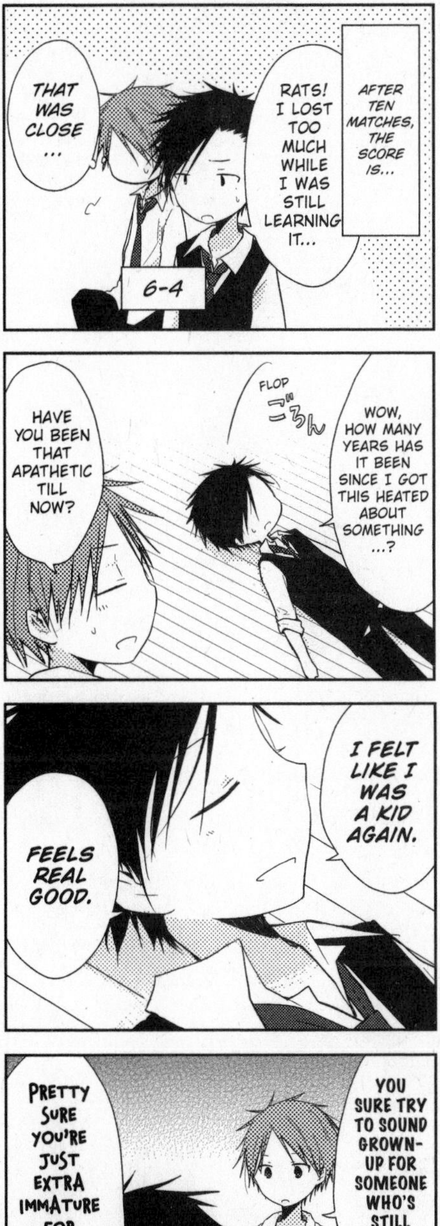
AFTER TEN MATCHES, THE SCORE IS...
RATS! I LOST TOO MUCH WHILE I WAS STILL LEARNING IT...
THAT WAS CLOSE ...
6-4
WOW, HOW MANY YEARS HAS IT BEEN SINCE I GOT THIS HEATED ABOUT SOMETHING ...?
FLOP
ごろん
HAVE YOU BEEN THAT APATHETIC TILL NOW?
I FELT LIKE I WAS A KID AGAIN.
FEELS REAL GOOD.
YOU SURE TRY TO SOUND GROWN-UP FOR SOMEONE WHO'S STILL A HIGH SCHOOL KID.
PRETTY SURE YOU'RE JUST EXTRA IMMATURE FOR SOMEBODY IN HIGH SCHOOL.

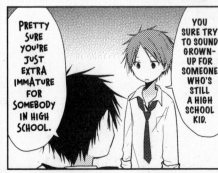

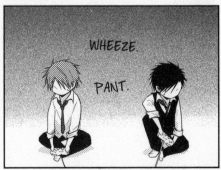

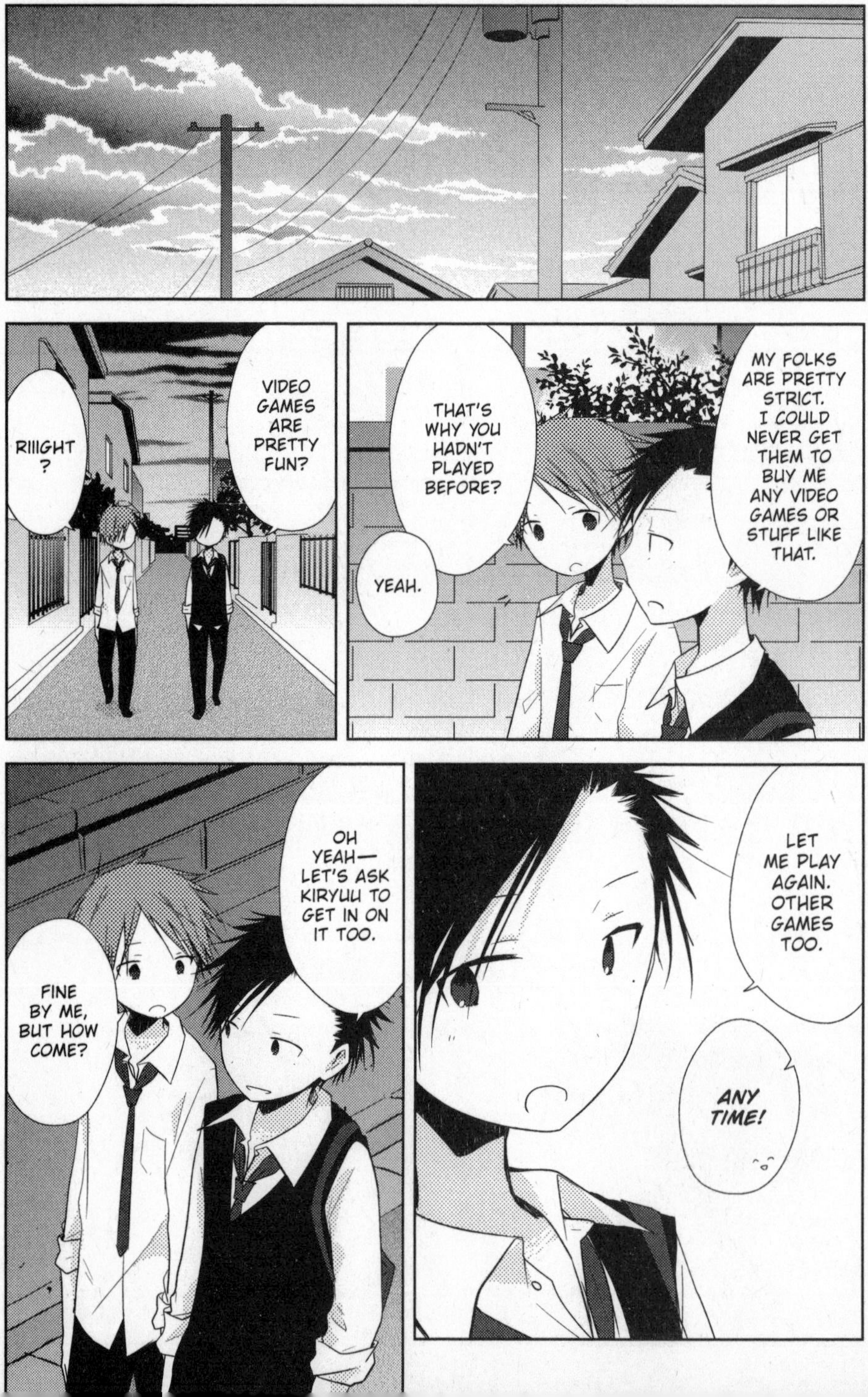
MY FOLKS ARE PRETTY STRICT. I COULD NEVER GET THEM TO BUY ME ANY VIDEO GAMES OR STUFF LIKE THAT.
THAT'S WHY YOU HADN'T PLAYED BEFORE?
YEAH.
VIDEO GAMES ARE PRETTY FUN?
RIIIGHT?
LET ME PLAY AGAIN. OTHER GAMES TOO.
ANY TIME!
OH YEAH—LET'S ASK KIRYUU TO GET IN ON IT TOO.
FINE BY ME, BUT HOW COME?

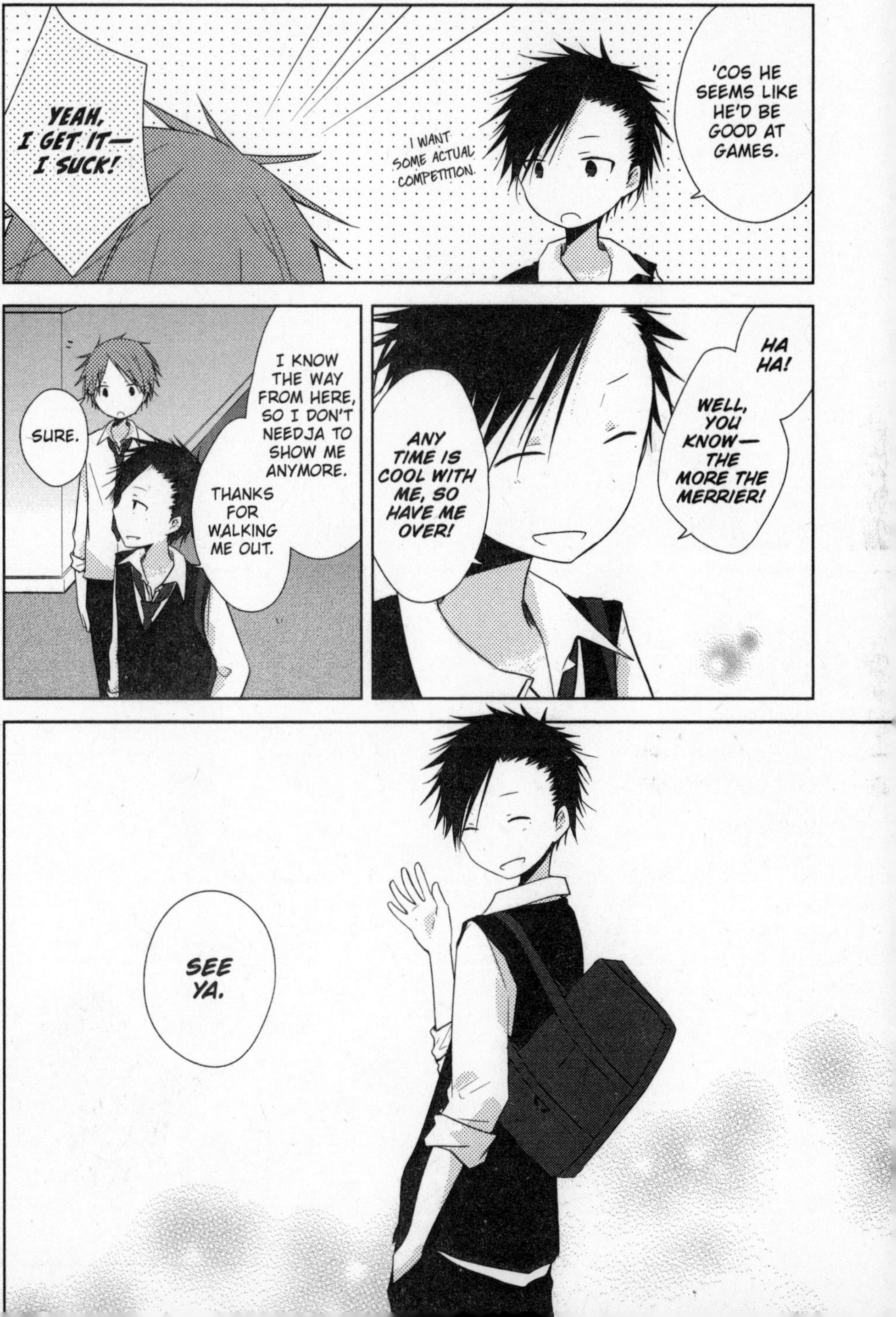
'COS HE SEEMS LIKE HE'D BE GOOD AT GAMES.
I WANT SOME ACTUAL COMPETITION.
YEAH, I GET IT— I SUCK!
HA HA!
WELL, YOU KNOW— THE MORE THE MERRIER!
ANY TIME IS COOL WITH ME, SO HAVE ME OVER!
I KNOW THE WAY FROM HERE, SO I DON'T NEEDJA TO SHOW ME ANYMORE.
THANKS FOR WALKING ME OUT.
SURE.
SEE YA.

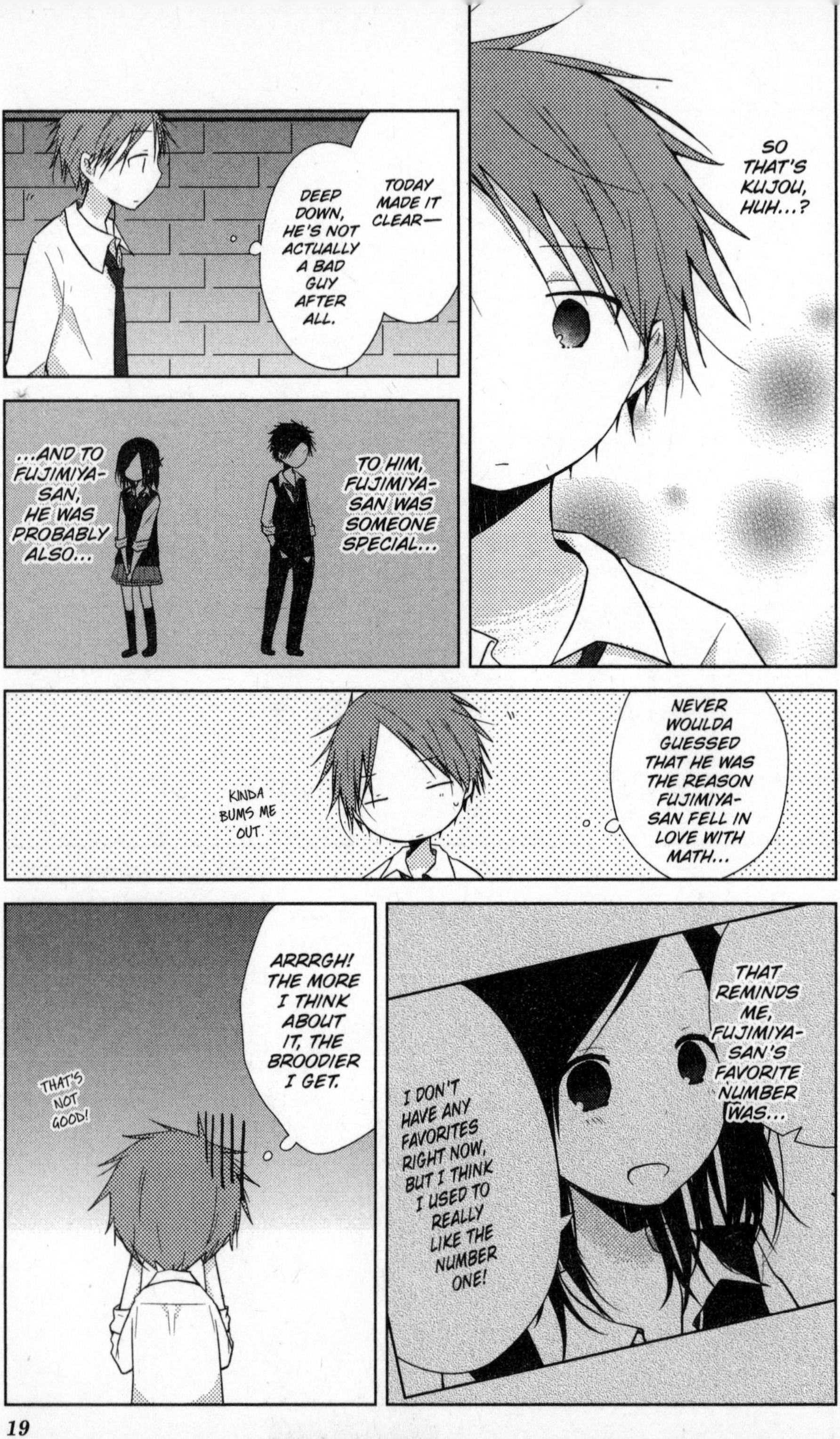
SO THAT'S KUJOU, HUH...?
TODAY MADE IT CLEAR—
DEEP DOWN, HE'S NOT ACTUALLY A BAD GUY AFTER ALL.
TO HIM, FUJIMIYA-SAN WAS SOMEONE SPECIAL...
...AND TO FUJIMIYA-SAN, HE WAS PROBABLY ALSO...
NEVER WOULDA GUESSED THAT HE WAS THE REASON FUJIMIYA-SAN FELL IN LOVE WITH MATH...
KINDA BUMS ME OUT.
THAT REMINDS ME, FUJIMIYA-SAN'S FAVORITE NUMBER WAS...
I DON'T HAVE ANY FAVORITES RIGHT NOW, BUT I THINK I USED TO REALLY LIKE THE NUMBER ONE!
ARRRGH! THE MORE I THINK ABOUT IT, THE BROODIER I GET.
THAT'S NOT GOOD!

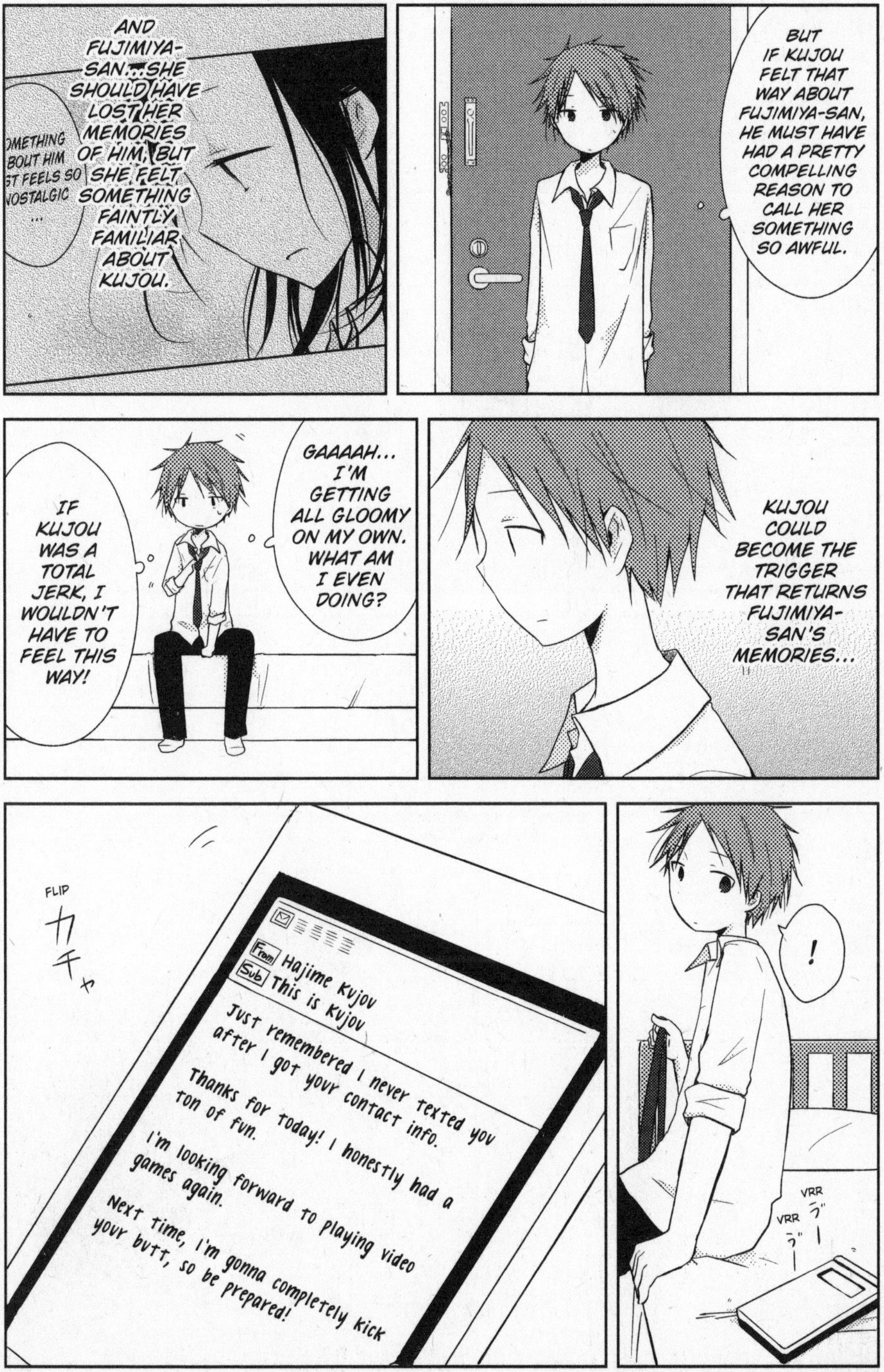
BUT IF KUJOU FELT THAT WAY ABOUT FUJIMIYA-SAN, HE MUST HAVE HAD A PRETTY COMPELLING REASON TO CALL HER SOMETHING SO AWFUL.
AND FUJIMIYA-SAN...SHE SHOULD HAVE LOST HER MEMORIES OF HIM, BUT SHE FELT SOMETHING FAINTLY FAMILIAR ABOUT KUJOU.
OMETHING BOUT HIM ST FEELS SO NOSTALGIC ...
KUJOU COULD BECOME THE TRIGGER THAT RETURNS FUJIMIYA-SAN'S MEMORIES...
GAAAAH... I'M GETTING ALL GLOOMY ON MY OWN. WHAT AM I EVEN DOING?
IF KUJOU WAS A TOTAL JERK, I WOULDN'T HAVE TO FEEL THIS WAY!
!
VRR
VRR
FLIP
From Hajime Kujou
Sub This is Kujou
Just remembered I never texted you after I got your contact info.
Thanks for today! I honestly had a ton of fun.
I'm looking forward to playing video games again.
Next time, I'm gonna completely kick your butt, so be prepared!

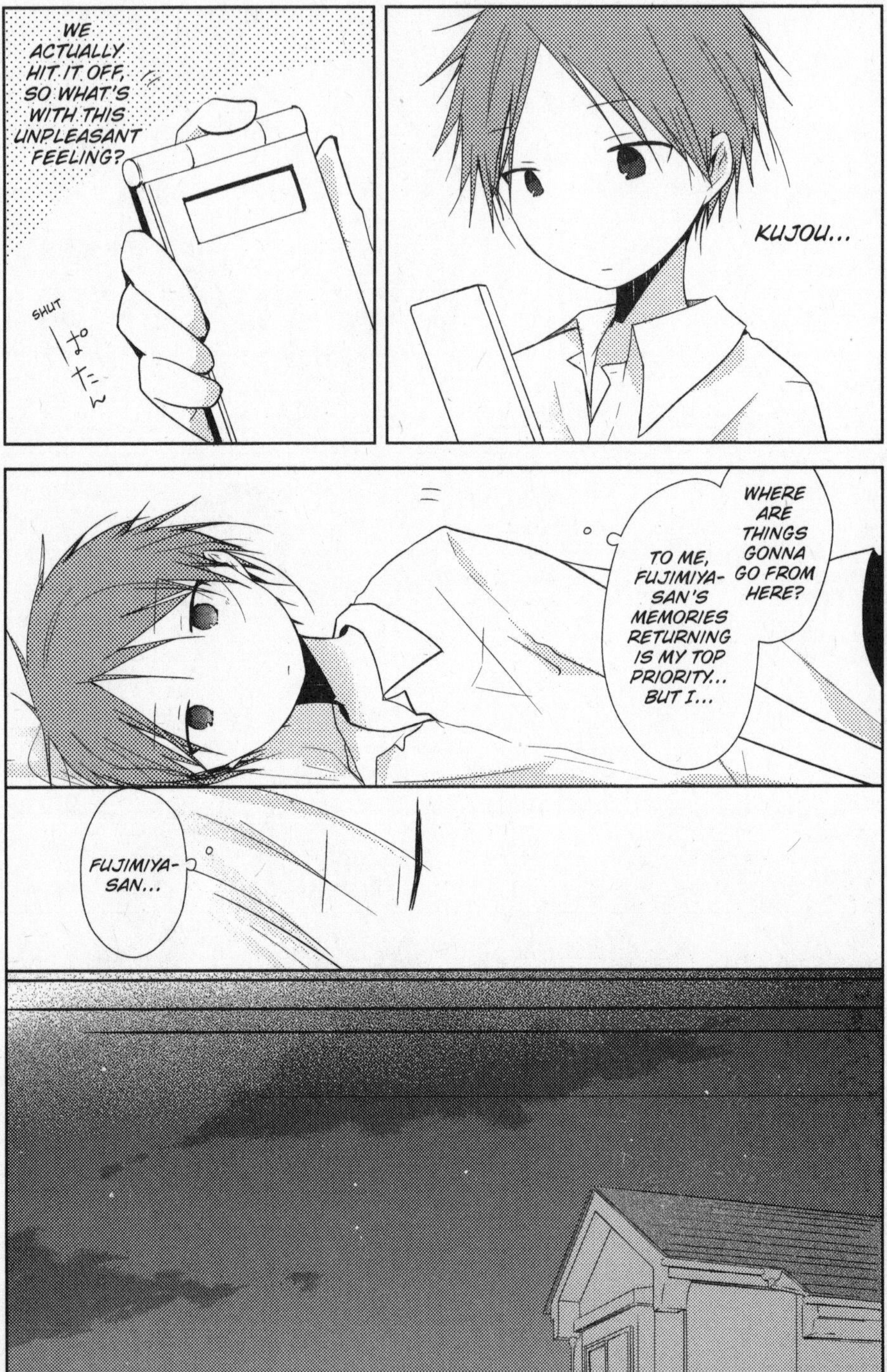
KUJOU...
WE ACTUALLY HIT IT OFF, SO WHAT'S WITH THIS UNPLEASANT FEELING?
SHUT
ぱたん
WHERE ARE THINGS GONNA GO FROM HERE?
TO ME, FUJIMIYA-SAN'S MEMORIES RETURNING IS MY TOP PRIORITY... BUT I...
FUJIMIYA-SAN...

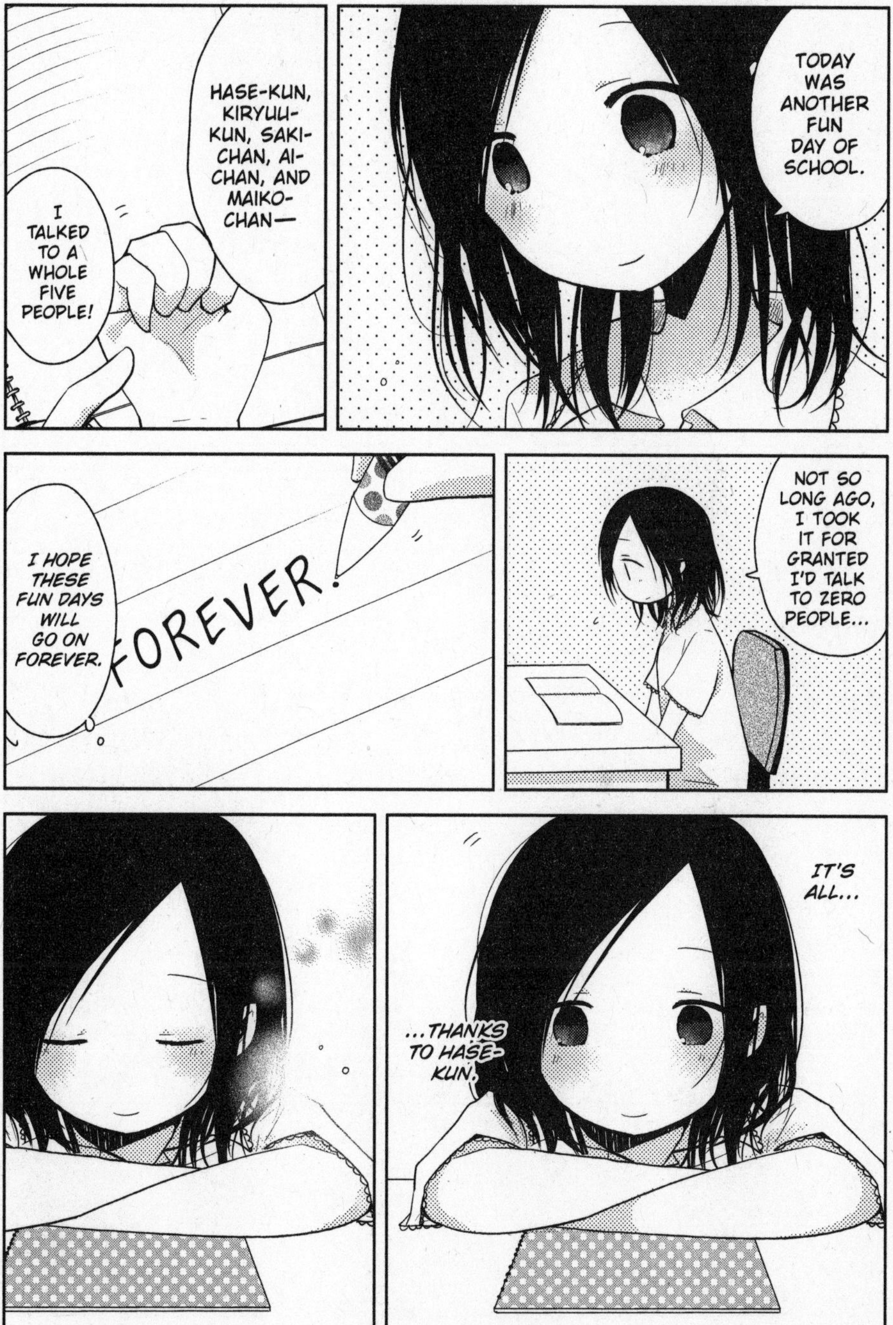
TODAY WAS ANOTHER FUN DAY OF SCHOOL.
HASE-KUN, KIRYUU-KUN, SAKI-CHAN, AI-CHAN, AND MAIKO-CHAN—
I TALKED TO A WHOLE FIVE PEOPLE!
NOT SO LONG AGO, I TOOK IT FOR GRANTED I'D TALK TO ZERO PEOPLE...
FOREVER!
I HOPE THESE FUN DAYS WILL GO ON FOREVER.
IT'S ALL...
...THANKS TO HASE-KUN.

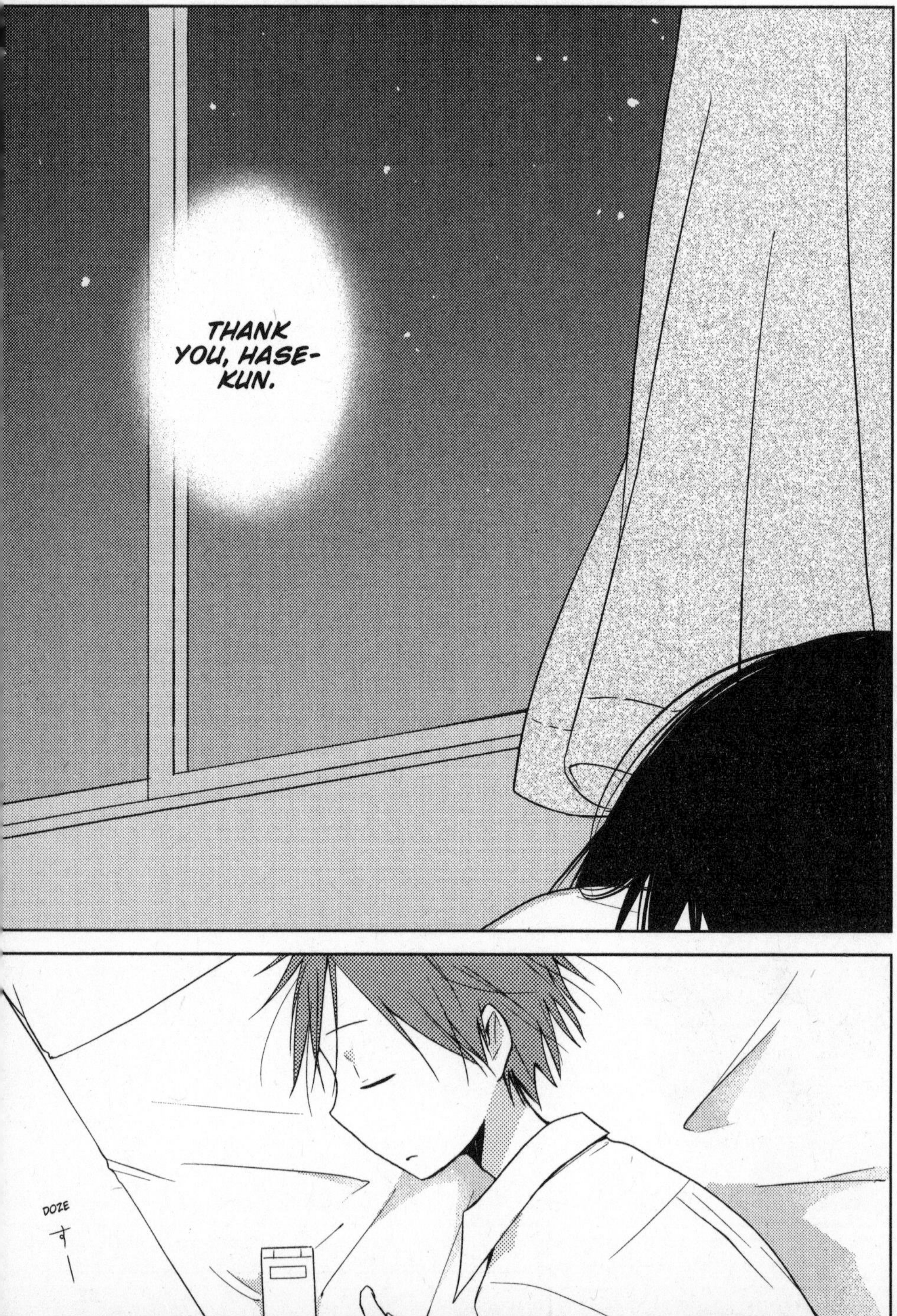
THANK YOU, HASE-KUN.
DOZE
す ー

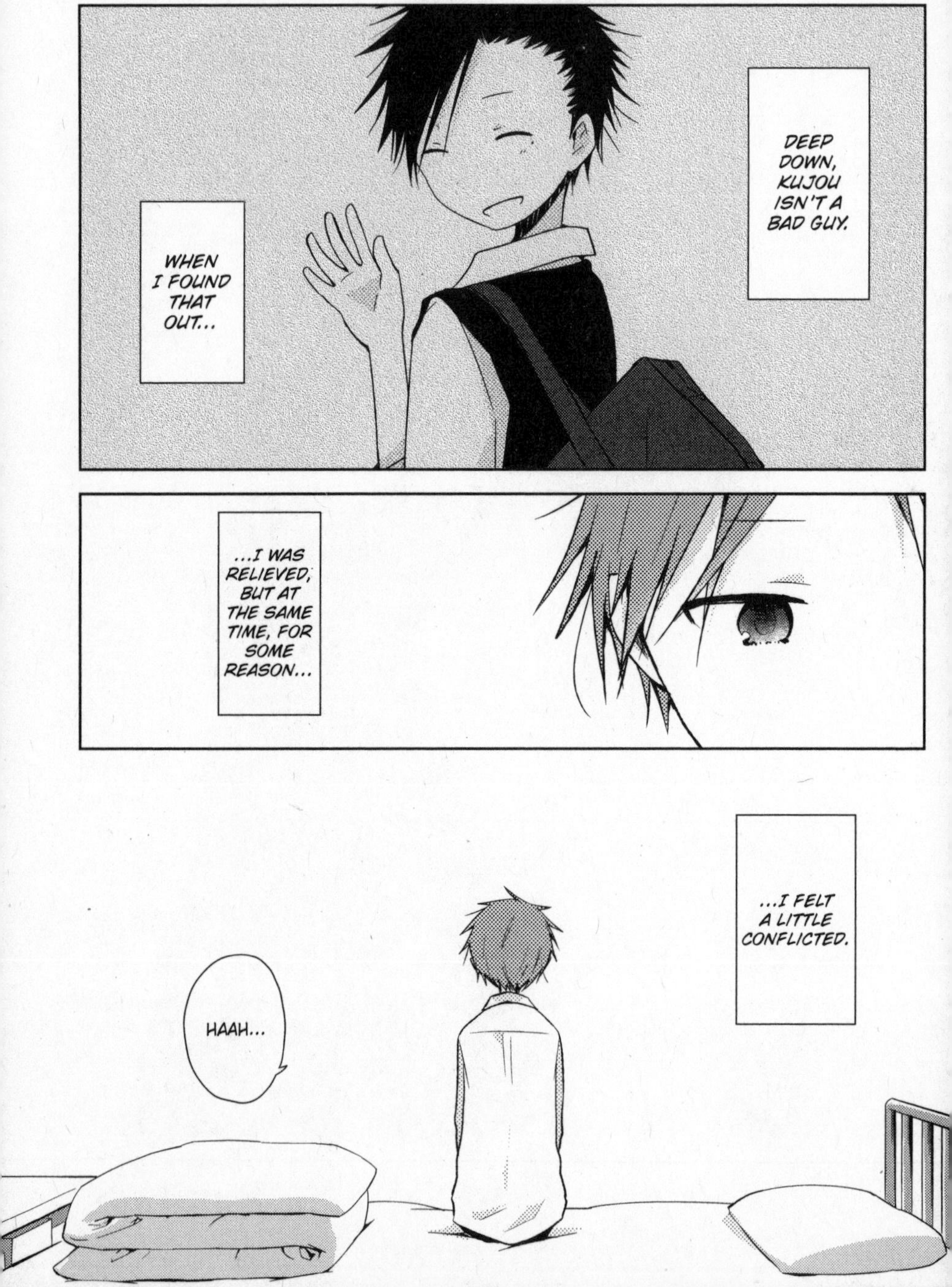
DEEP DOWN, KUJOU ISN'T A BAD GUY.
WHEN I FOUND THAT OUT...
...I WAS RELIEVED, BUT AT THE SAME TIME, FOR SOME REASON...
...I FELT A LITTLE CONFLICTED.
HAAH...

CHAPTER 23 COMPLEX TUNE

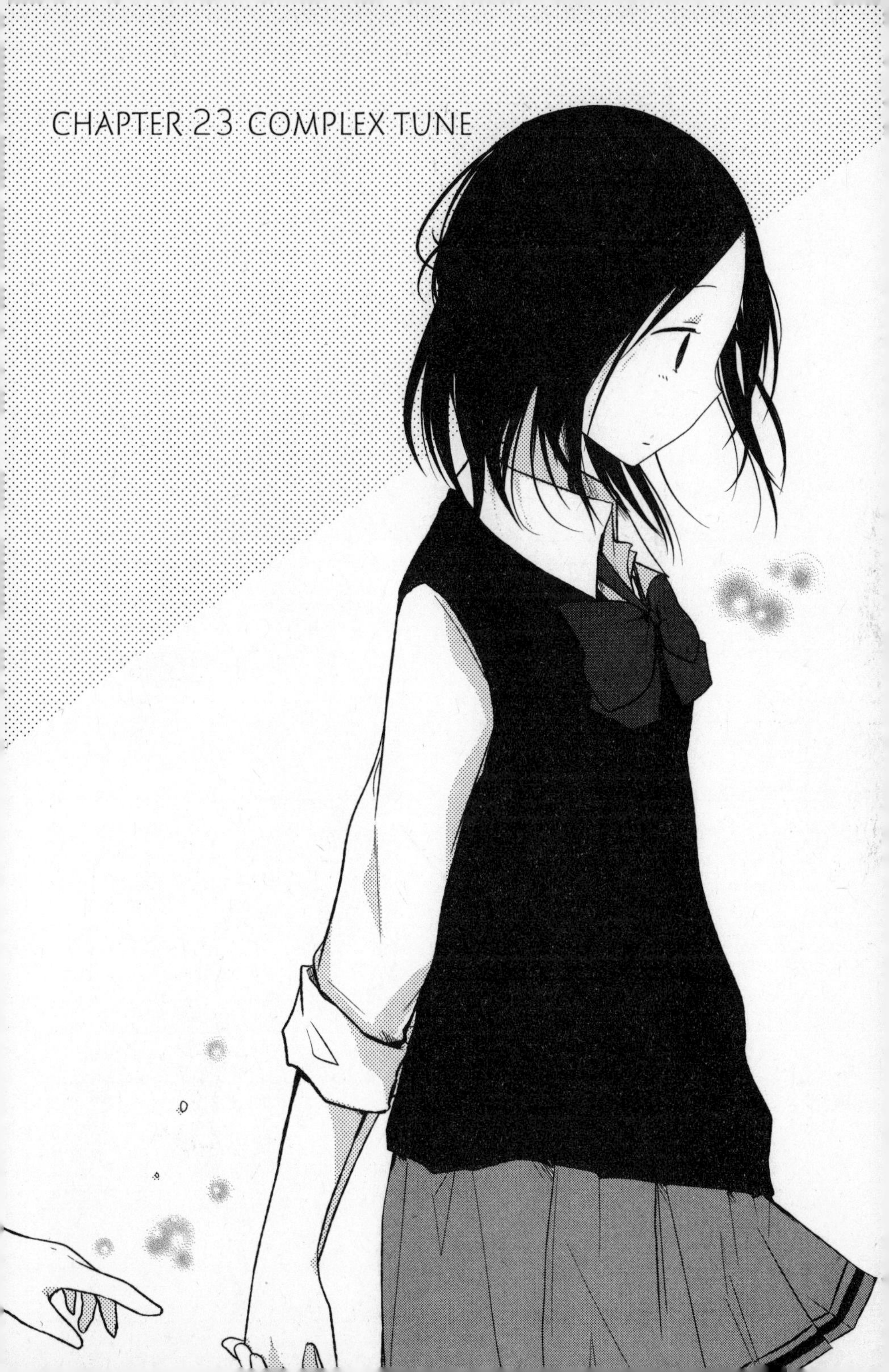

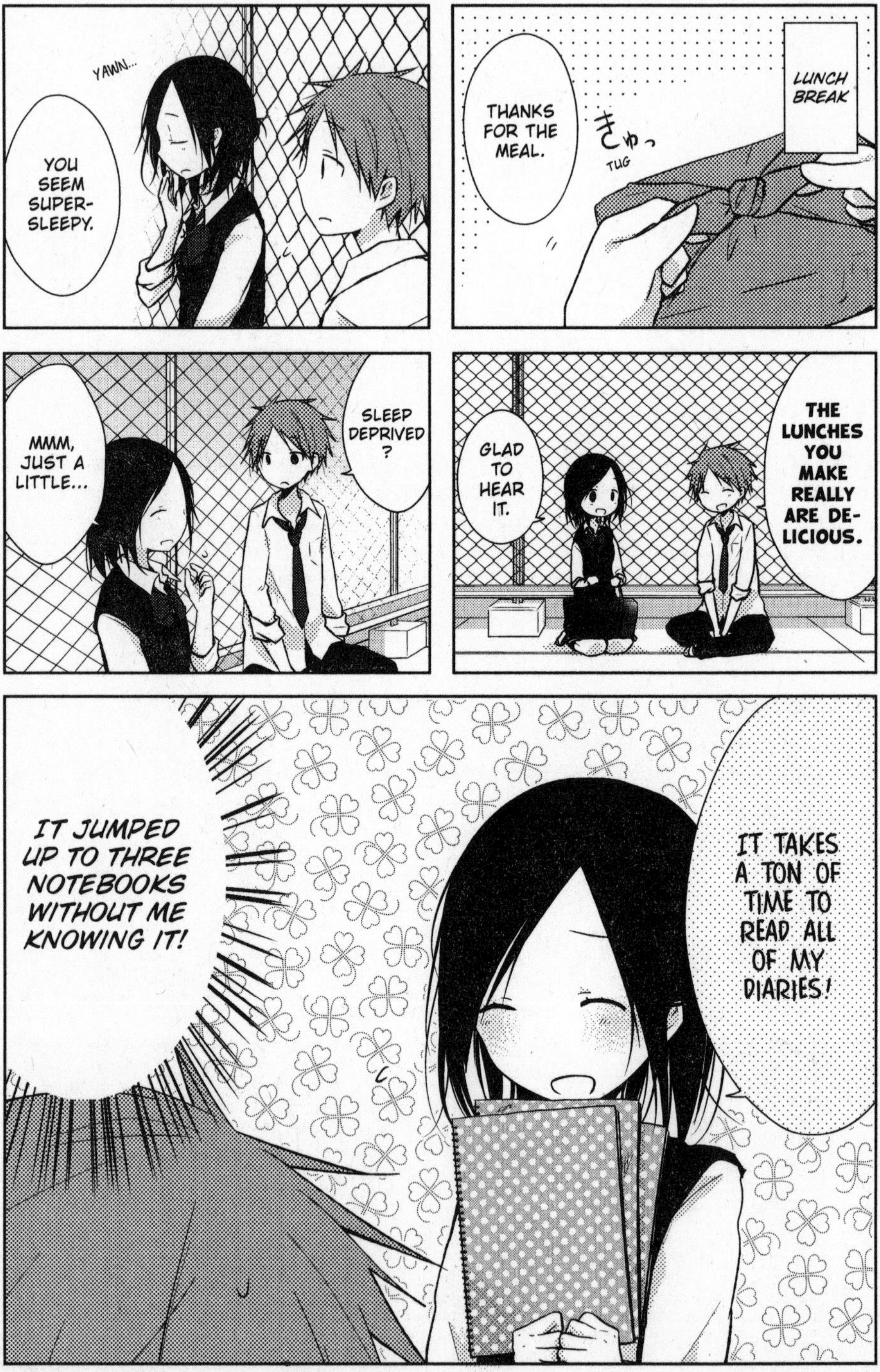
LUNCH BREAK
THANKS FOR THE MEAL.
きゅっ
TUG
YAWN...
YOU SEEM SUPER-SLEEPY.
THE LUNCHES YOU MAKE REALLY ARE DE-LICIOUS.
GLAD TO HEAR IT.
SLEEP DEPRIVED?
MMM, JUST A LITTLE...
IT TAKES A TON OF TIME TO READ ALL OF MY DIARIES!
IT JUMPED UP TO THREE NOTEBOOKS WITHOUT ME KNOWING IT!

STAYING UP LATE

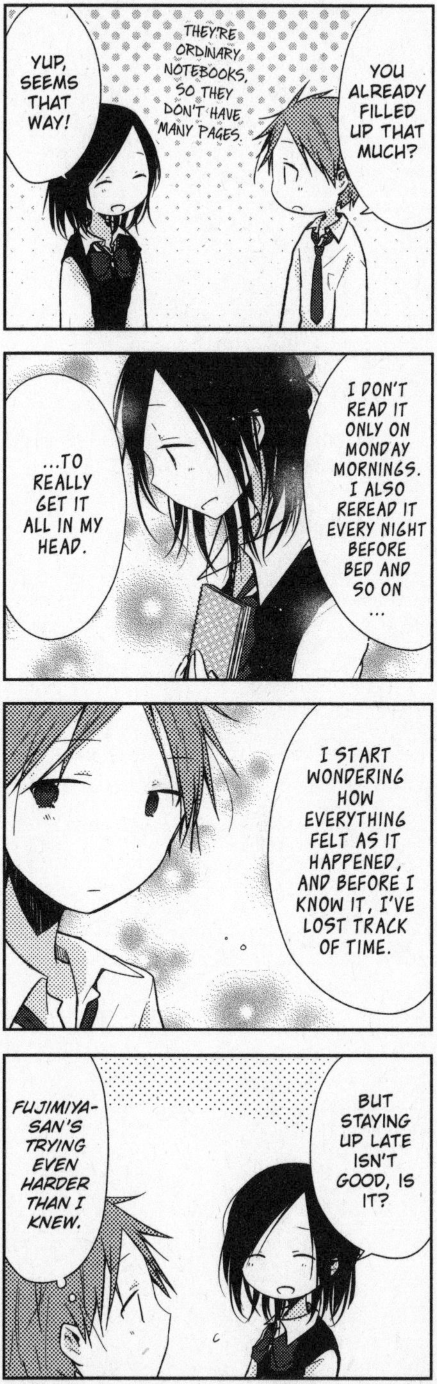

YOU ALREADY FILLED UP THAT MUCH?
THEY'RE ORDINARY NOTEBOOKS, SO THEY DON'T HAVE MANY PAGES.
YUP, SEEMS THAT WAY!
I DON'T READ IT ONLY ON MONDAY MORNINGS. I ALSO REREAD IT EVERY NIGHT BEFORE BED AND SO ON ...
...TO REALLY GET IT ALL IN MY HEAD.
I START WONDERING HOW EVERYTHING FELT AS IT HAPPENED, AND BEFORE I KNOW IT, I'VE LOST TRACK OF TIME.
BUT STAYING UP LATE ISN'T GOOD, IS IT?
FUJIMIYA-SAN'S TRYING EVEN HARDER THAN I KNEW.

HAPPINESS

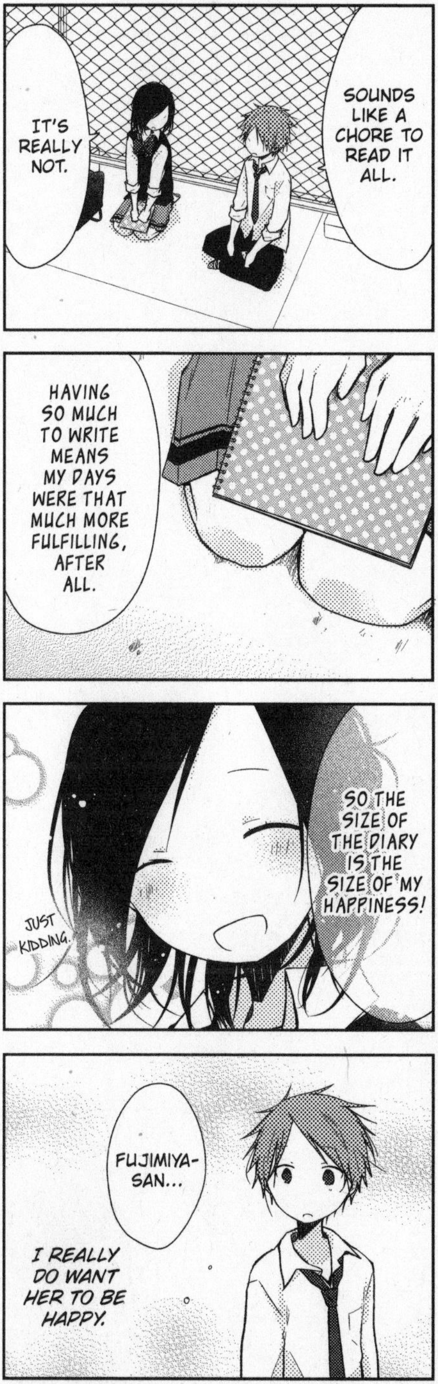

SOUNDS LIKE A CHORE TO READ IT ALL.
IT'S REALLY NOT.
HAVING SO MUCH TO WRITE MEANS MY DAYS WERE THAT MUCH MORE FULFILLING, AFTER ALL.
SO THE SIZE OF THE DIARY IS THE SIZE OF MY HAPPINESS!
JUST KIDDING.
FUJIMIYA-SAN...
I REALLY DO WANT HER TO BE HAPPY.

ABOUT KUJOU

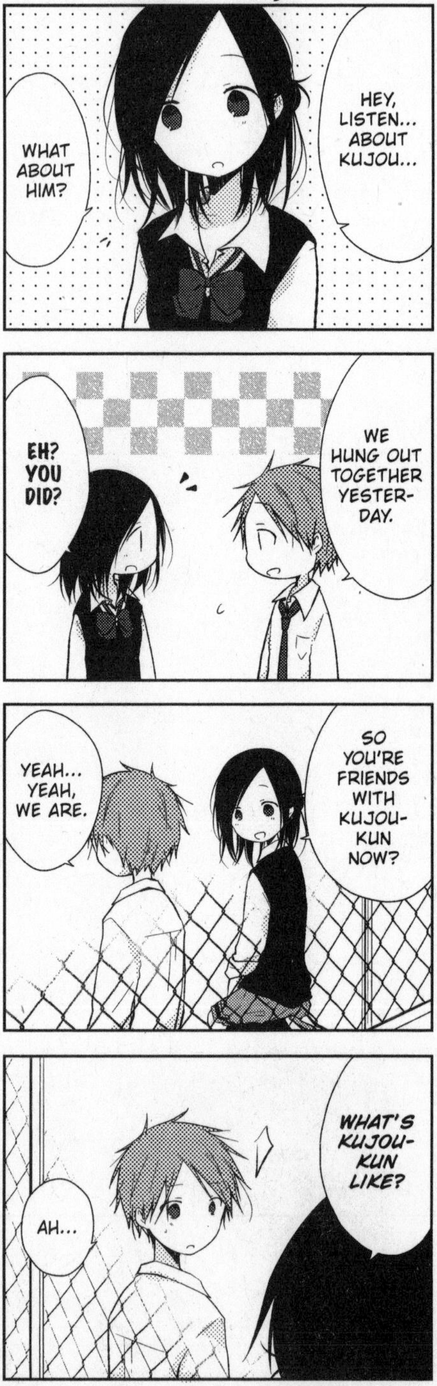
HEY, LISTEN... ABOUT KUJOU...
WHAT ABOUT HIM?
WE HUNG OUT TOGETHER YESTER-DAY.
EH? YOU DID?
SO YOU'RE FRIENDS WITH KUJOU-KUN NOW?
YEAH... YEAH, WE ARE.
WHAT'S KUJOU-KUN LIKE?
AH...

DECISION

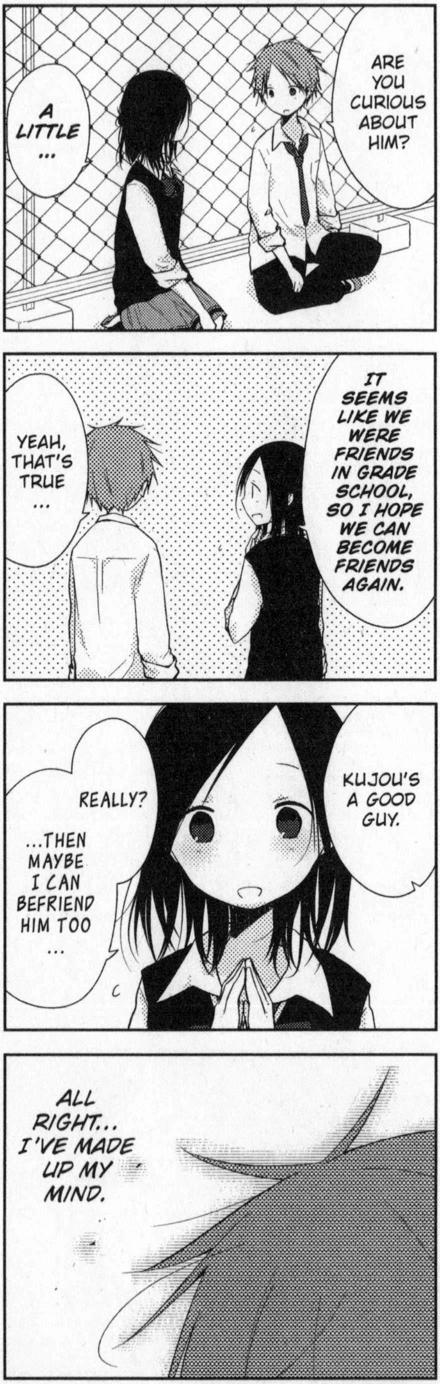
ARE YOU CURIOUS ABOUT HIM?
A LITTLE...
IT SEEMS LIKE WE WERE FRIENDS IN GRADE SCHOOL, SO I HOPE WE CAN BECOME FRIENDS AGAIN.
YEAH, THAT'S TRUE...
KUJOU'S A GOOD GUY.
REALLY?
...THEN MAYBE I CAN BEFRIEND HIM TOO...
ALL RIGHT... I'VE MADE UP MY MIND.

PROPOSAL

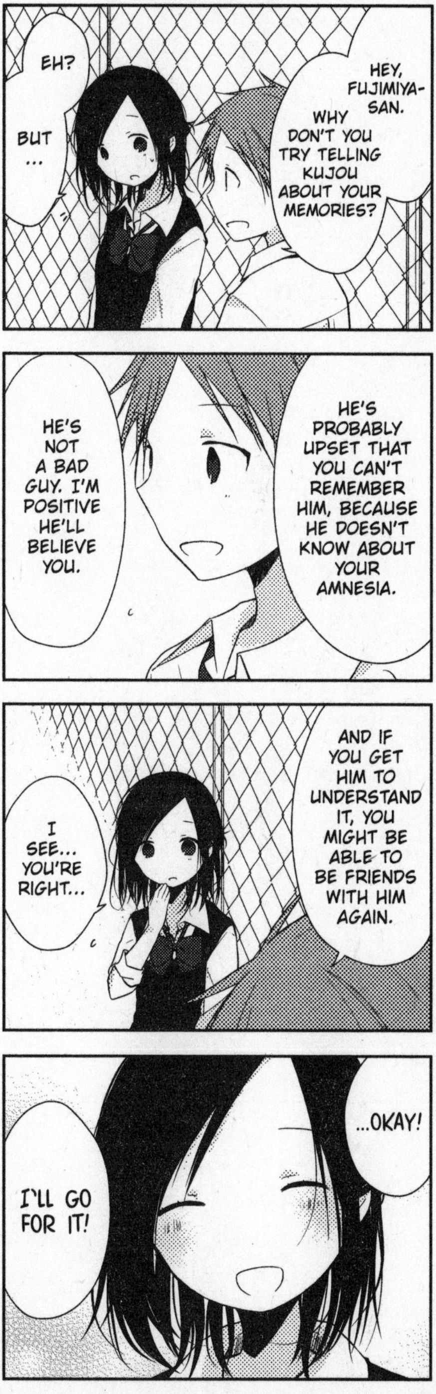
HEY, FUJIMIYA-SAN. WHY DON'T YOU TRY TELLING KUJOU ABOUT YOUR MEMORIES?
EH?
BUT ...
HE'S PROBABLY UPSET THAT YOU CAN'T REMEMBER HIM, BECAUSE HE DOESN'T KNOW ABOUT YOUR AMNESIA.
HE'S NOT A BAD GUY. I'M POSITIVE HE'LL BELIEVE YOU.
AND IF YOU GET HIM TO UNDERSTAND IT, YOU MIGHT BE ABLE TO BE FRIENDS WITH HIM AGAIN.
I SEE... YOU'RE RIGHT...
...OKAY!
I'LL GO FOR IT!

BECAUSE YOU'RE HERE

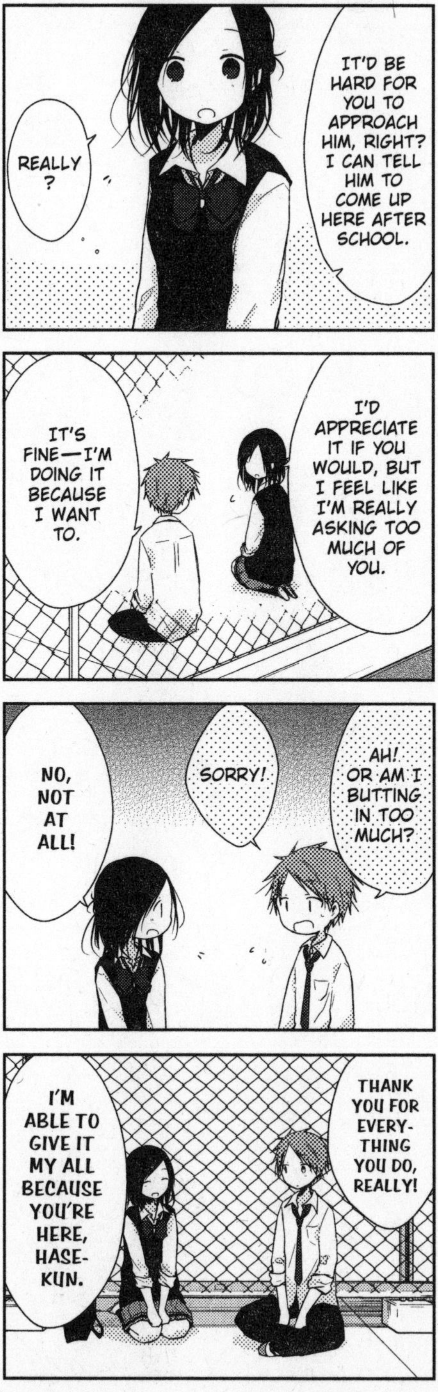
IT'D BE HARD FOR YOU TO APPROACH HIM, RIGHT? I CAN TELL HIM TO COME UP HERE AFTER SCHOOL.
REALLY?
I'D APPRECIATE IT IF YOU WOULD, BUT I FEEL LIKE I'M REALLY ASKING TOO MUCH OF YOU.
IT'S FINE—I'M DOING IT BECAUSE I WANT TO.
AH! OR AM I BUTTING IN TOO MUCH?
SORRY!
NO, NOT AT ALL!
THANK YOU FOR EVERYTHING YOU DO, REALLY!
I'M ABLE TO GIVE IT MY ALL BECAUSE YOU'RE HERE, HASE-KUN.

TO THE ROOF

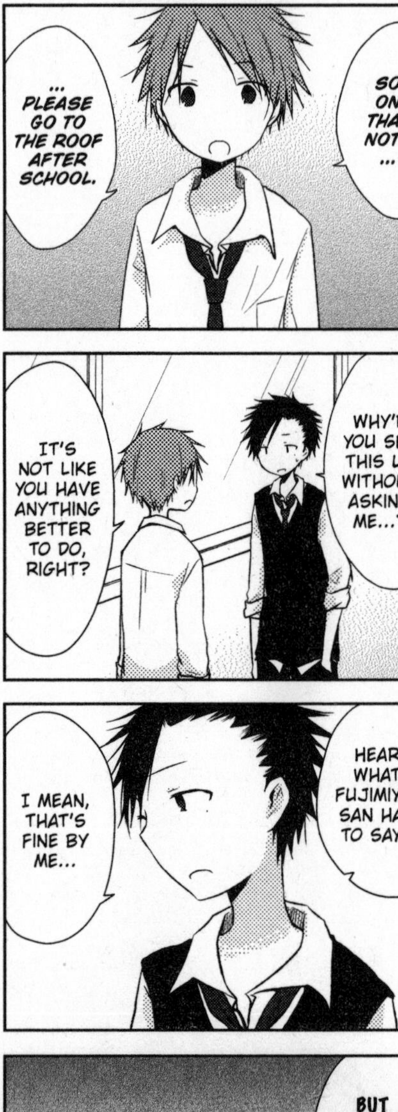
SO ON THAT NOTE ...
... PLEASE GO TO THE ROOF AFTER SCHOOL.
WHY'D YOU SET THIS UP WITHOUT ASKING ME...?
IT'S NOT LIKE YOU HAVE ANYTHING BETTER TO DO, RIGHT?
HEAR WHAT FUJIMIYA-SAN HAS TO SAY?
I MEAN, THAT'S FINE BY ME...
BUT WEREN'T YOU ALL LIKE "STAY AWAY FROM FUJIMIYA-SAN" UP UNTIL NOW?
URK...

I'M WORRIED

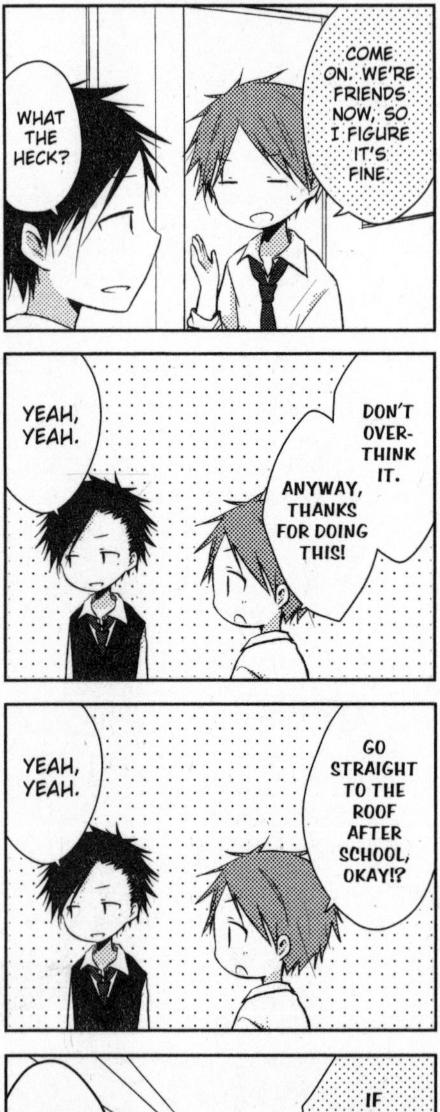
COME ON. WE'RE FRIENDS NOW, SO I FIGURE IT'S FINE.
WHAT THE HECK?
DON'T OVER-THINK IT.
ANYWAY, THANKS FOR DOING THIS!
YEAH, YEAH.
GO STRAIGHT TO THE ROOF AFTER SCHOOL, OKAY!?
YEAH, YEAH.
IF YOU DO ANYTHING TO MAKE HER CRY, I'LL NEVER FORGIVE YOU, GOT IT!?
WHAT ARE YOU, HER DAD?

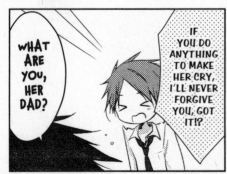

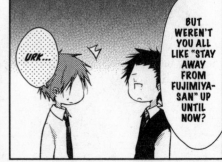

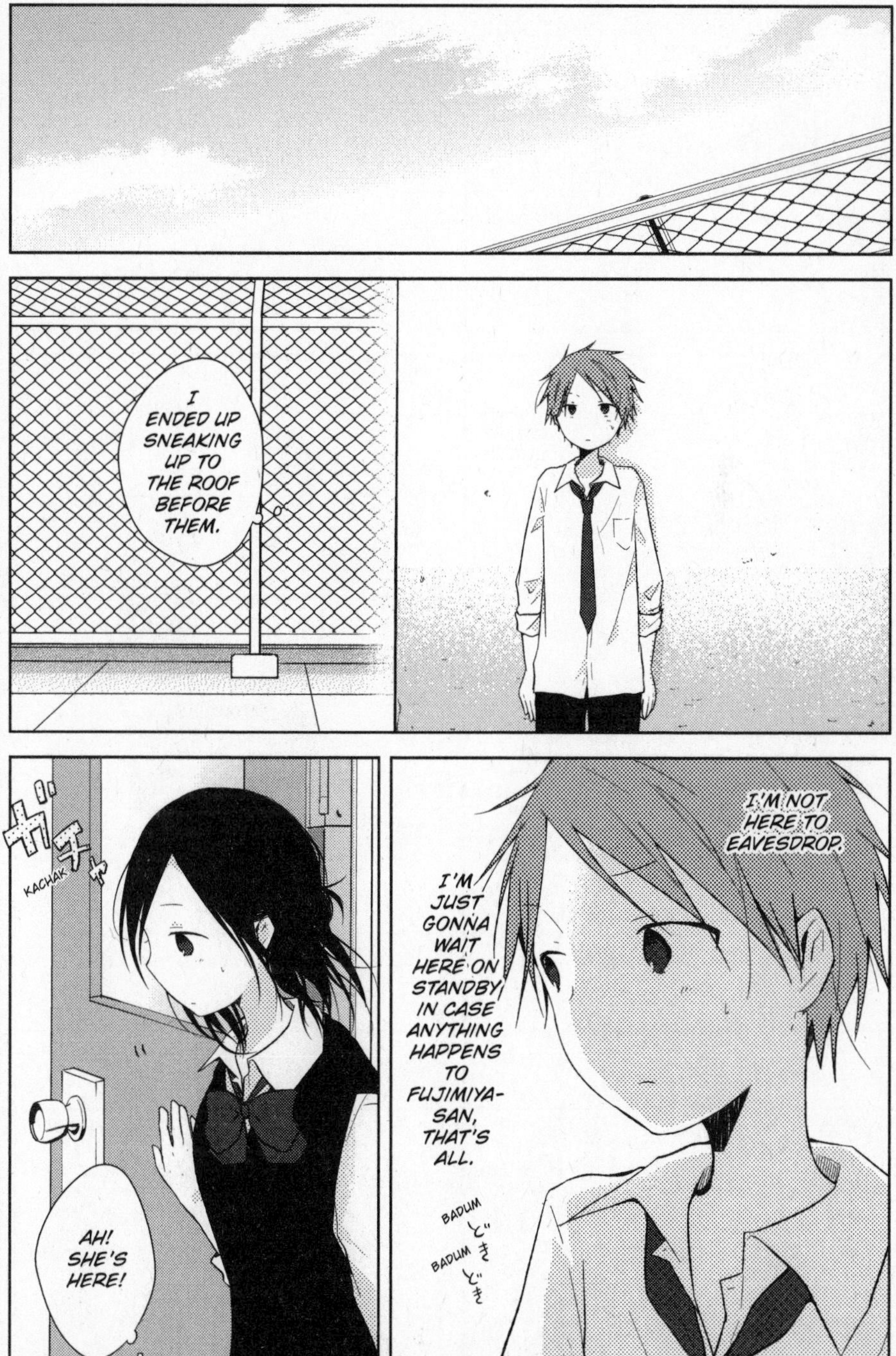
I ENDED UP SNEAKING UP TO THE ROOF BEFORE THEM.
I'M NOT HERE TO EAVESDROP.
I'M JUST GONNA WAIT HERE ON STANDBY IN CASE ANYTHING HAPPENS TO FUJIMIYA-SAN, THAT'S ALL.
BADUM どき
BADUM どき
ガチャ
KACHAK
AH! SHE'S HERE!

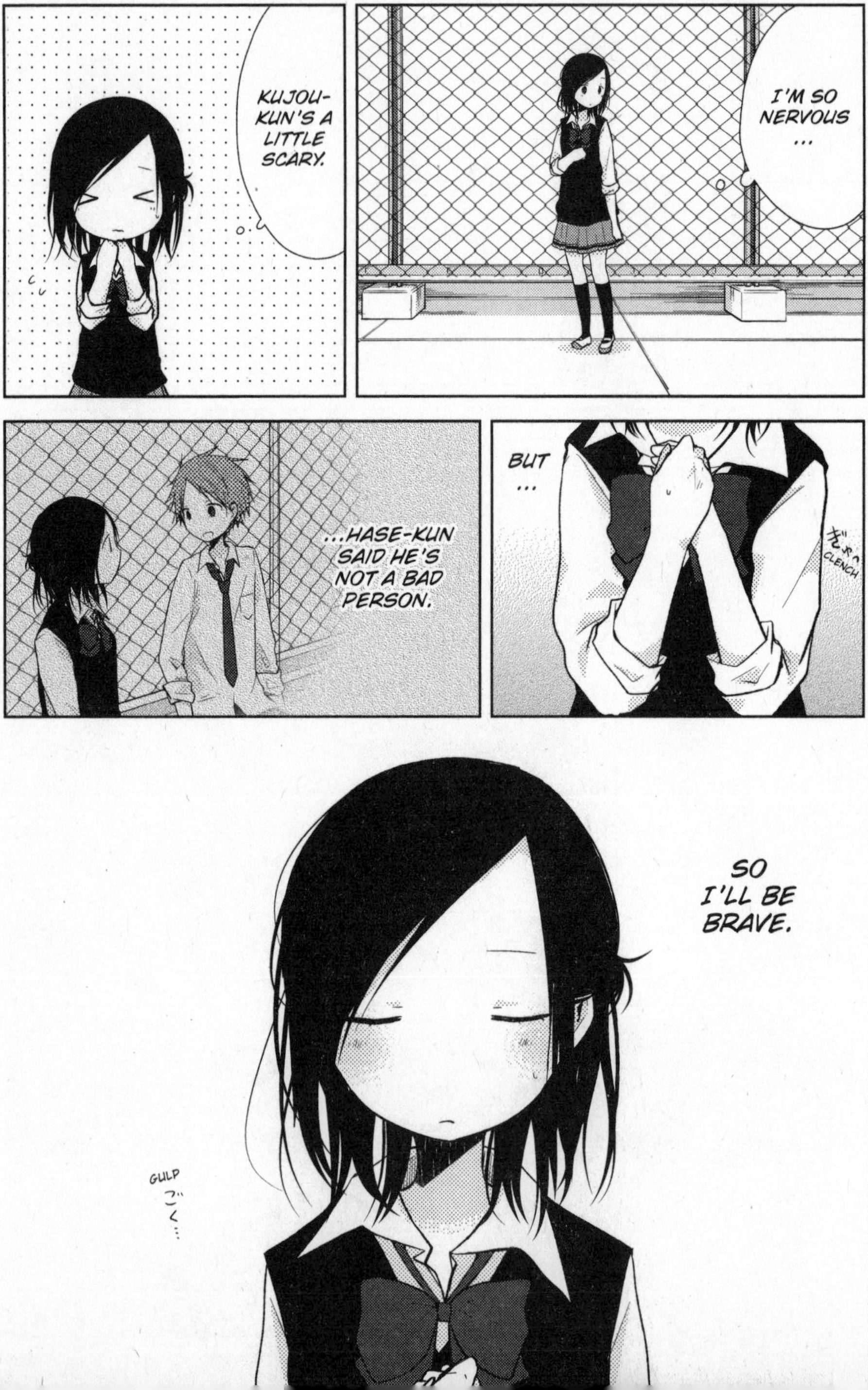
I'M SO NERVOUS ...
KUJOU-KUN'S A LITTLE SCARY.
BUT ...
CLENCH
...HASE-KUN SAID HE'S NOT A BAD PERSON.
SO I'LL BE BRAVE.
GULP
ごく…

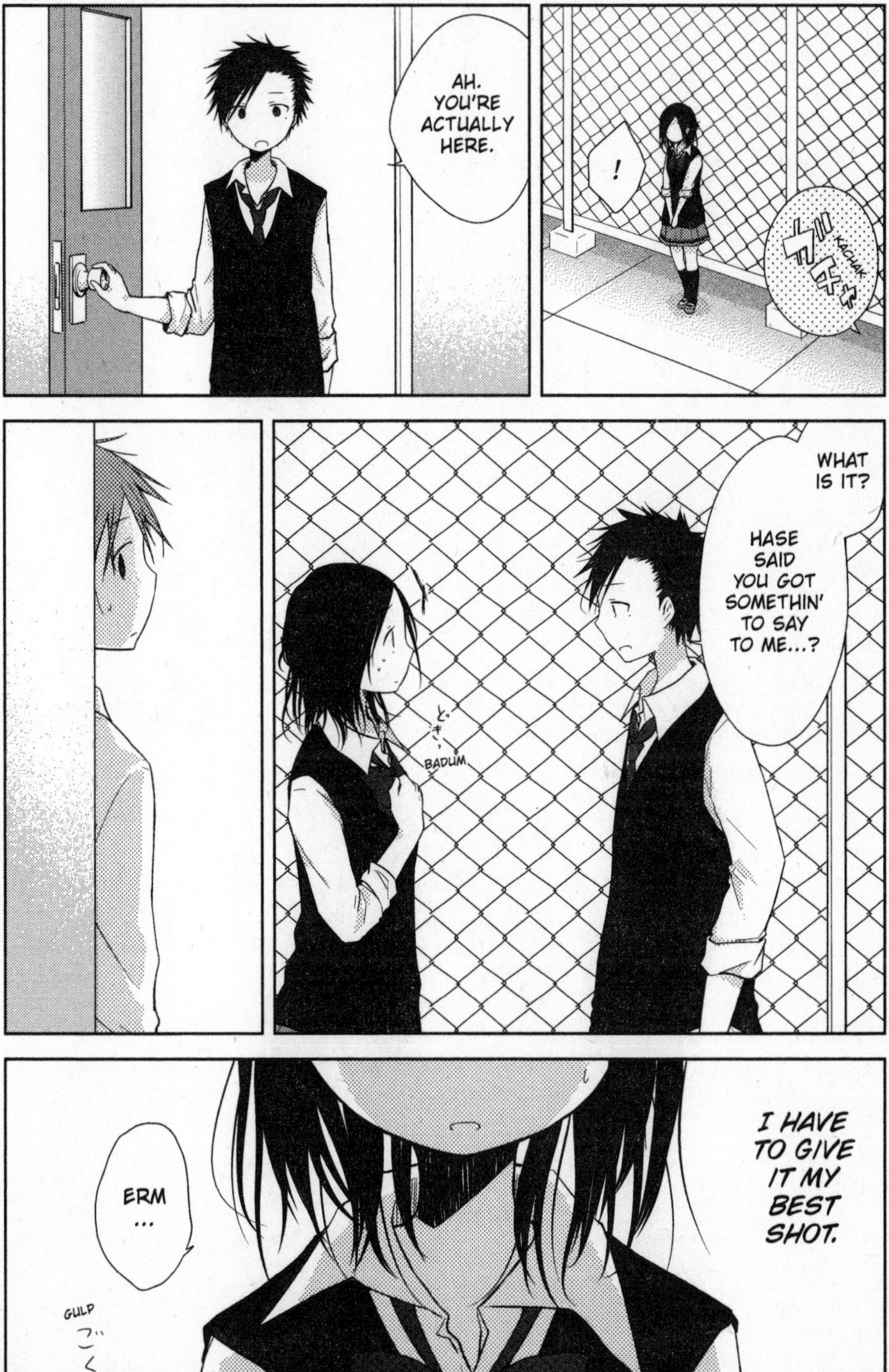
!
KACHAK
AH. YOU'RE ACTUALLY HERE.
WHAT IS IT?
HASE SAID YOU GOT SOMETHIN' TO SAY TO ME...?
どきっ
BADUM
I HAVE TO GIVE IT MY BEST SHOT.
ERM ...
GULP
ごく…

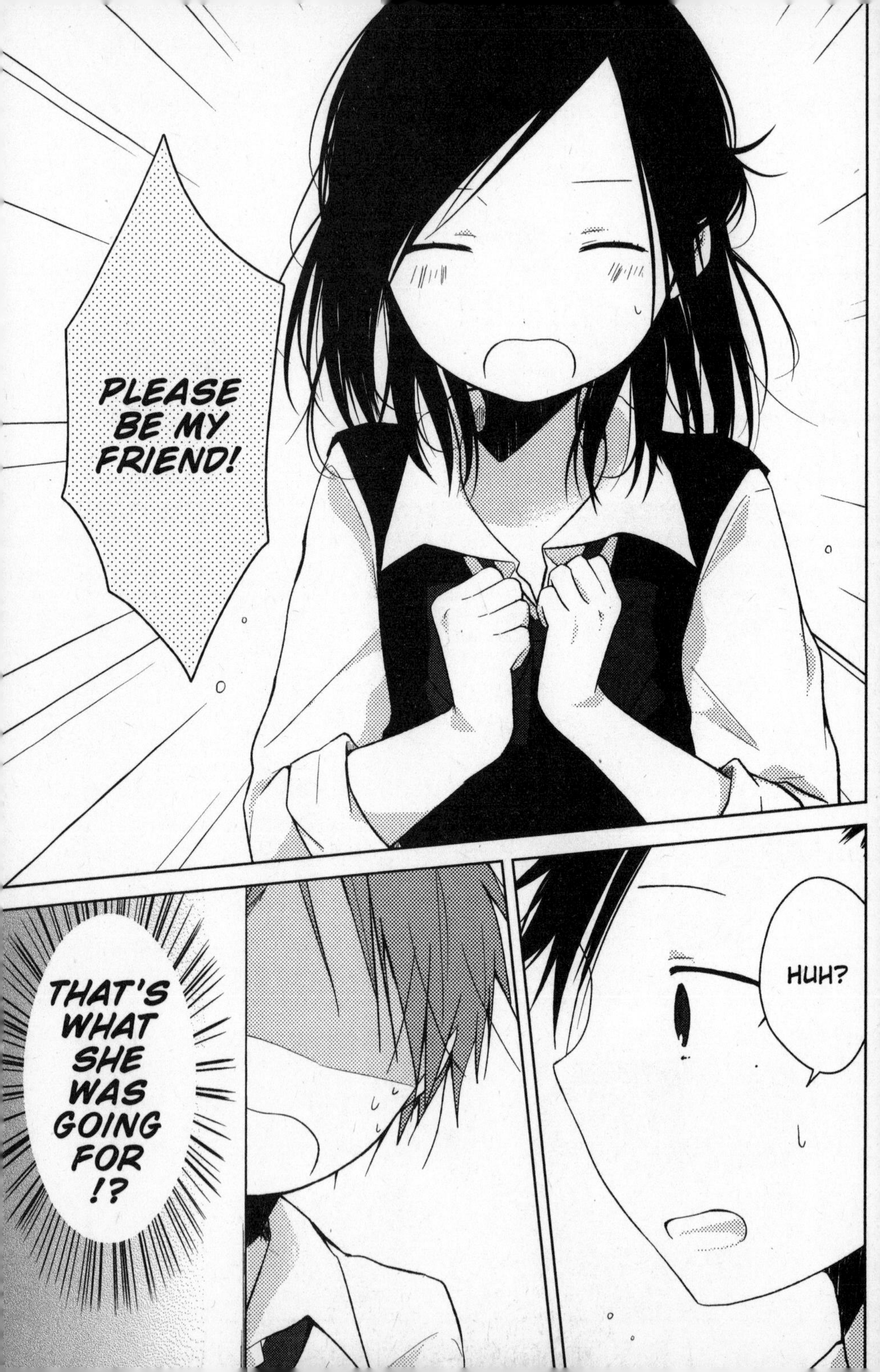
PLEASE BE MY FRIEND!
HUH?
THAT'S WHAT SHE WAS GOING FOR!?

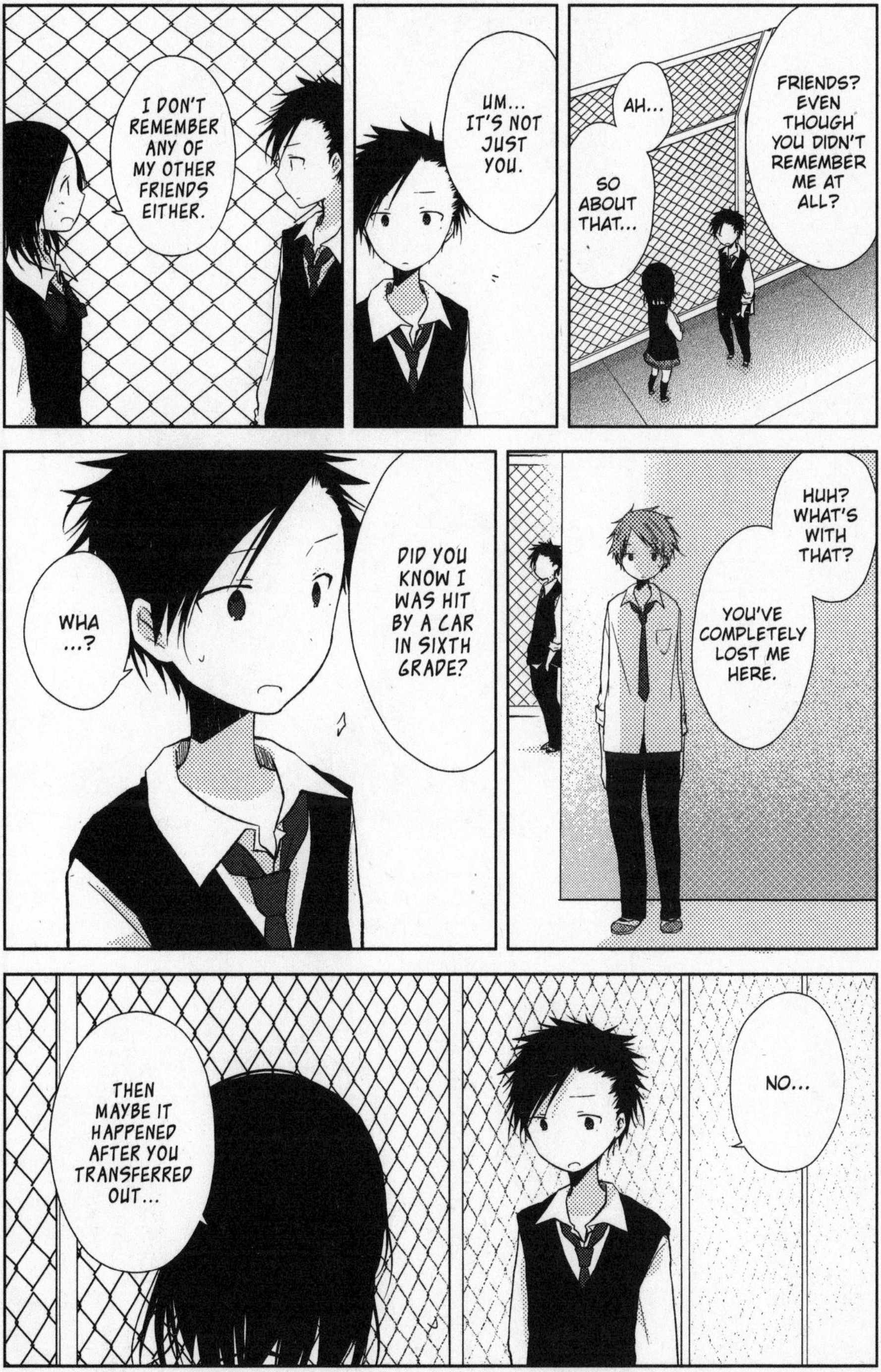
FRIENDS? EVEN THOUGH YOU DIDN'T REMEMBER ME AT ALL?
AH...
SO ABOUT THAT...
UM... IT'S NOT JUST YOU.
I DON'T REMEMBER ANY OF MY OTHER FRIENDS EITHER.
HUH? WHAT'S WITH THAT?
YOU'VE COMPLETELY LOST ME HERE.
DID YOU KNOW I WAS HIT BY A CAR IN SIXTH GRADE?
WHA...?
NO...
THEN MAYBE IT HAPPENED AFTER YOU TRANSFERRED OUT...

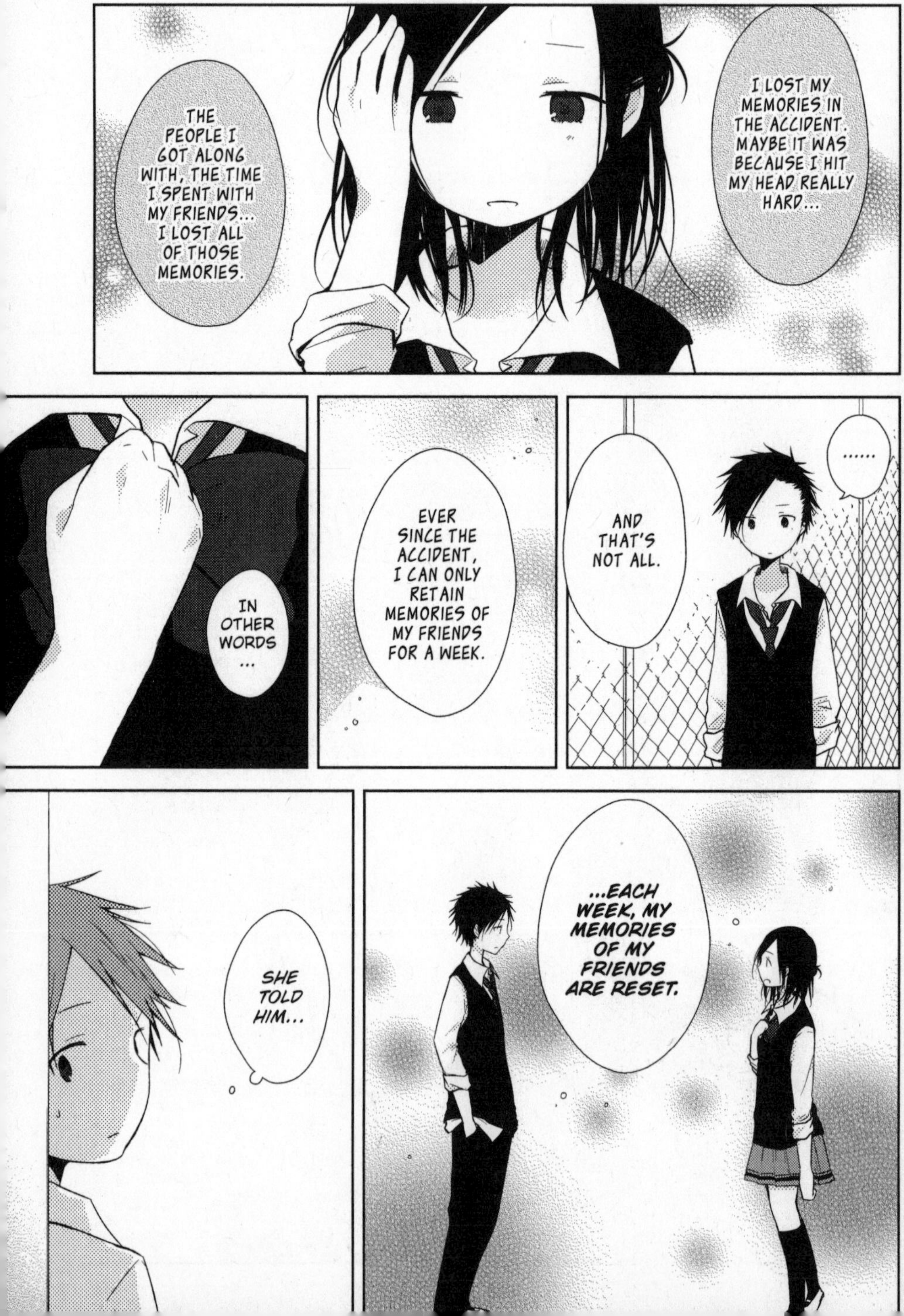
I LOST MY MEMORIES IN THE ACCIDENT. MAYBE IT WAS BECAUSE I HIT MY HEAD REALLY HARD...
THE PEOPLE I GOT ALONG WITH, THE TIME I SPENT WITH MY FRIENDS... I LOST ALL OF THOSE MEMORIES.
......
AND THAT'S NOT ALL.
EVER SINCE THE ACCIDENT, I CAN ONLY RETAIN MEMORIES OF MY FRIENDS FOR A WEEK.
IN OTHER WORDS ...
...EACH WEEK, MY MEMORIES OF MY FRIENDS ARE RESET.
SHE TOLD HIM...

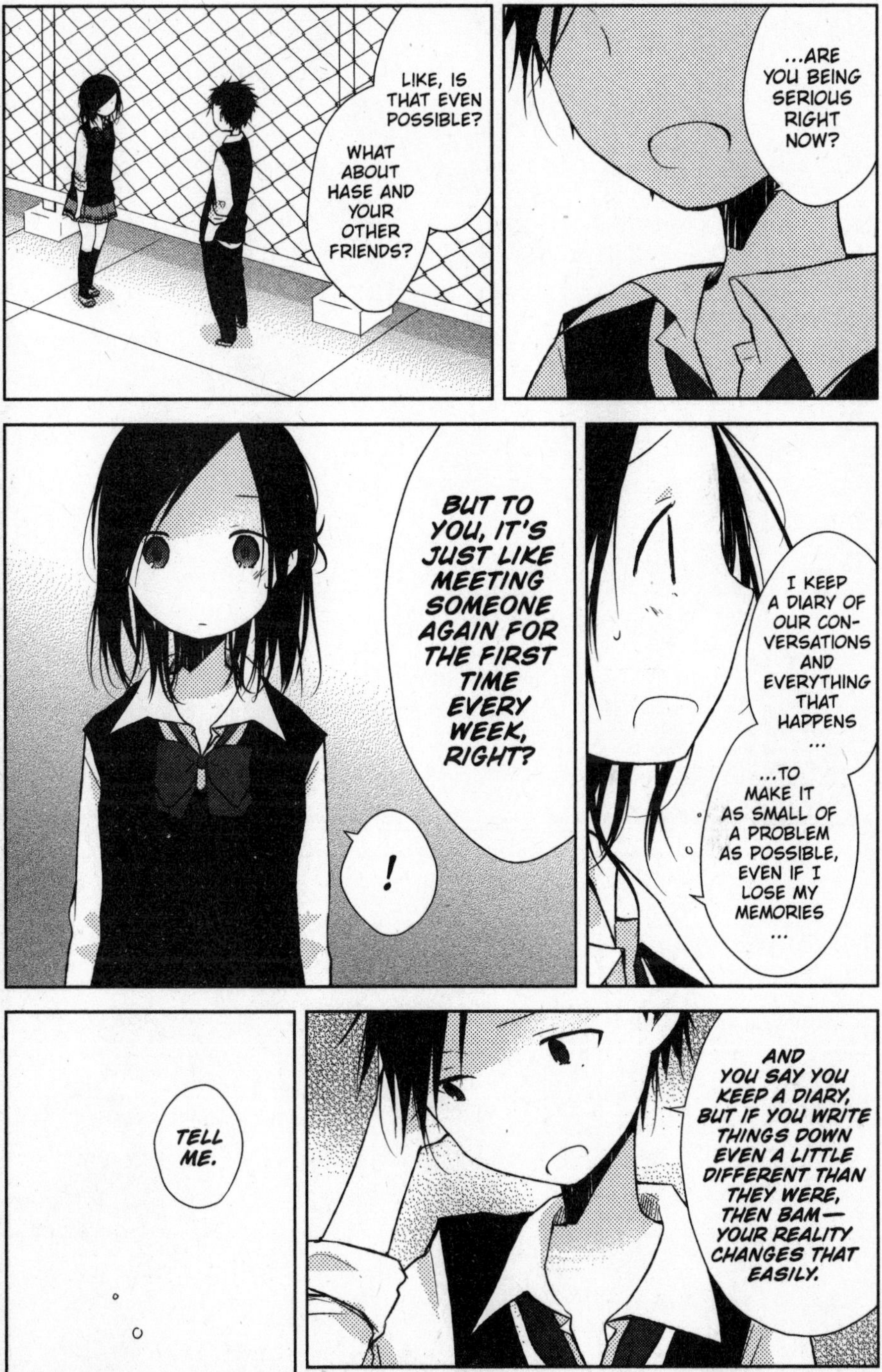
...ARE YOU BEING SERIOUS RIGHT NOW?
LIKE, IS THAT EVEN POSSIBLE?
WHAT ABOUT HASE AND YOUR OTHER FRIENDS?
I KEEP A DIARY OF OUR CON-VERSATIONS AND EVERYTHING THAT HAPPENS...
...TO MAKE IT AS SMALL OF A PROBLEM AS POSSIBLE, EVEN IF I LOSE MY MEMORIES...
BUT TO YOU, IT'S JUST LIKE MEETING SOMEONE AGAIN FOR THE FIRST TIME EVERY WEEK, RIGHT?
!
AND YOU SAY YOU KEEP A DIARY, BUT IF YOU WRITE THINGS DOWN EVEN A LITTLE DIFFERENT THAN THEY WERE, THEN BAM— YOUR REALITY CHANGES THAT EASILY.
TELL ME.

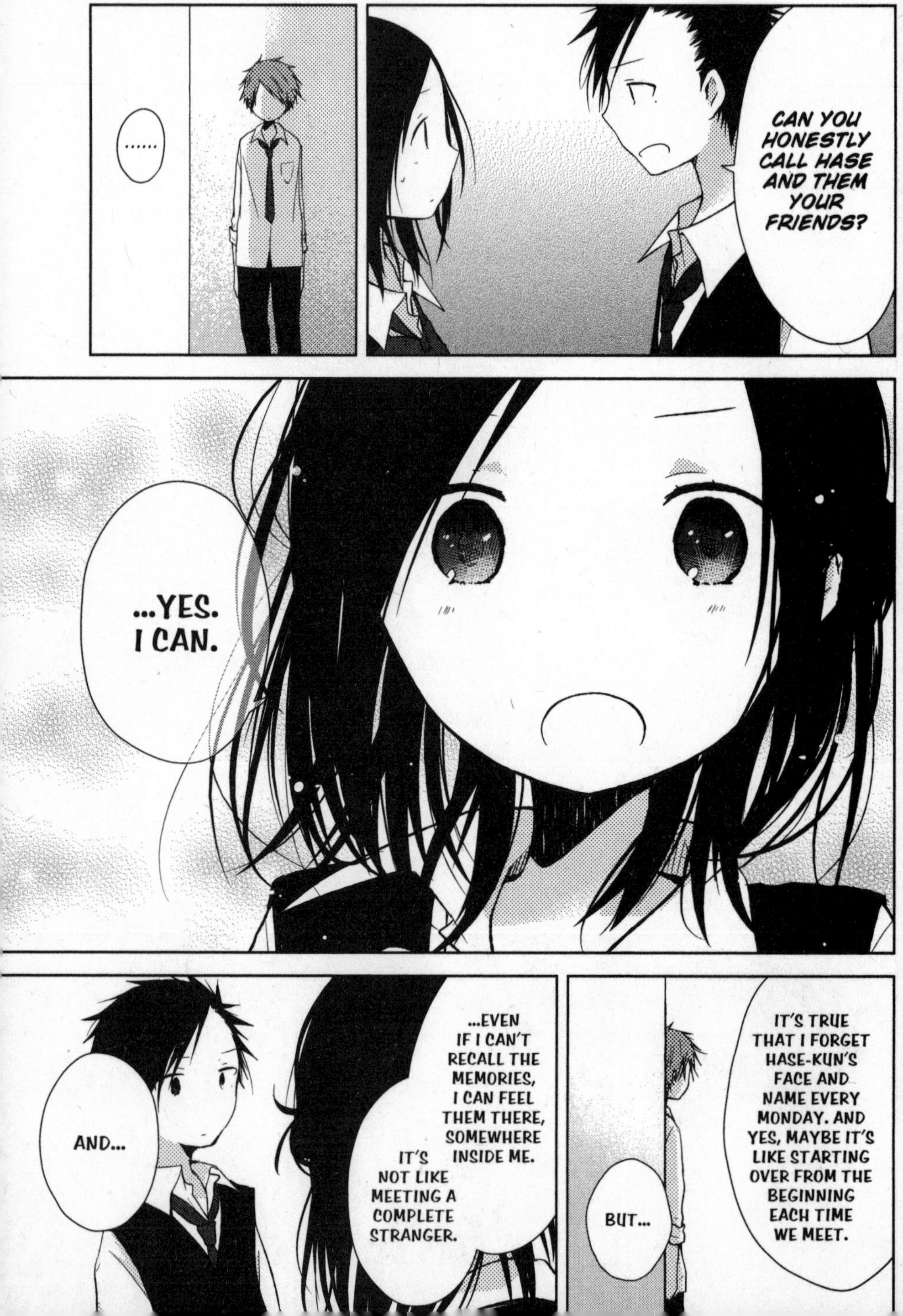
CAN YOU HONESTLY CALL HASE AND THEM YOUR FRIENDS?
......
...YES. I CAN.
IT'S TRUE THAT I FORGET HASE-KUN'S FACE AND NAME EVERY MONDAY. AND YES, MAYBE IT'S LIKE STARTING OVER FROM THE BEGINNING EACH TIME WE MEET.
BUT...
...EVEN IF I CAN'T RECALL THE MEMORIES, I CAN FEEL THEM THERE, SOMEWHERE INSIDE ME.
IT'S NOT LIKE MEETING A COMPLETE STRANGER.
AND...

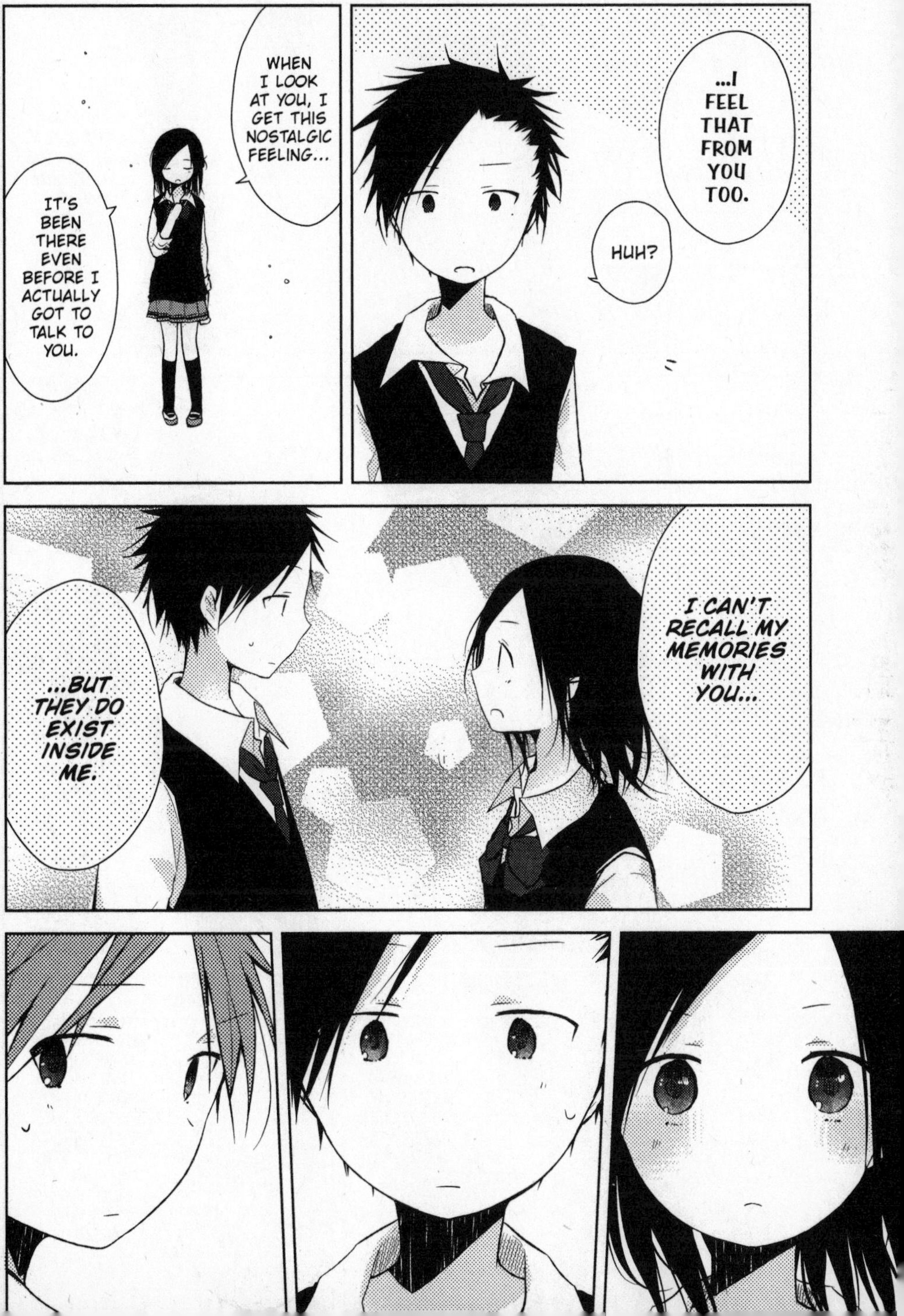
...I FEEL THAT FROM YOU TOO.
HUH?
WHEN I LOOK AT YOU, I GET THIS NOSTALGIC FEELING...
IT'S BEEN THERE EVEN BEFORE I ACTUALLY GOT TO TALK TO YOU.
I CAN'T RECALL MY MEMORIES WITH YOU...
...BUT THEY DO EXIST INSIDE ME.

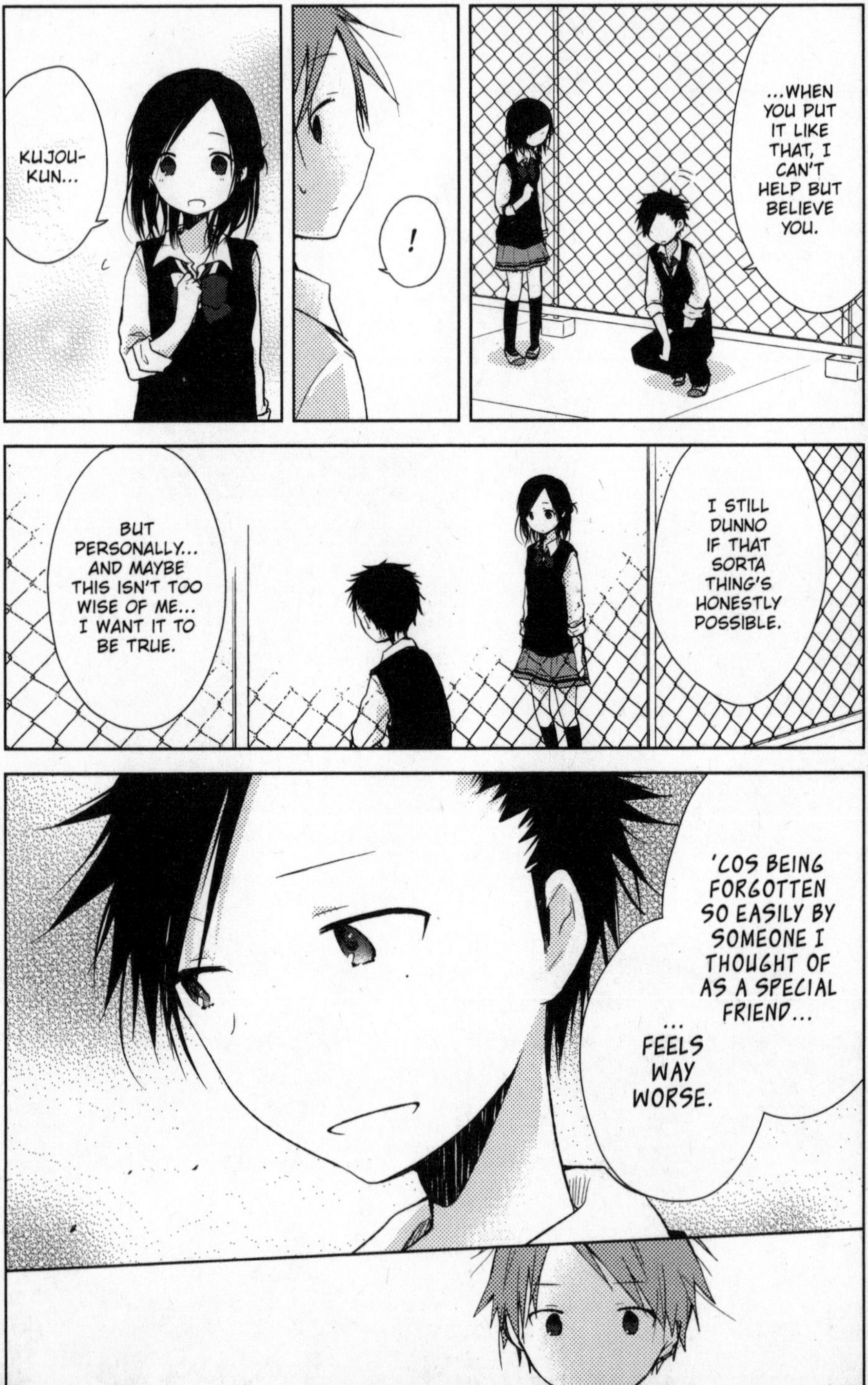
...WHEN YOU PUT IT LIKE THAT, I CAN'T HELP BUT BELIEVE YOU.
!
KUJOU-KUN...
I STILL DUNNO IF THAT SORTA THING'S HONESTLY POSSIBLE.
BUT PERSONALLY... AND MAYBE THIS ISN'T TOO WISE OF ME... I WANT IT TO BE TRUE.
'COS BEING FORGOTTEN SO EASILY BY SOMEONE I THOUGHT OF AS A SPECIAL FRIEND...
...FEELS WAY WORSE.

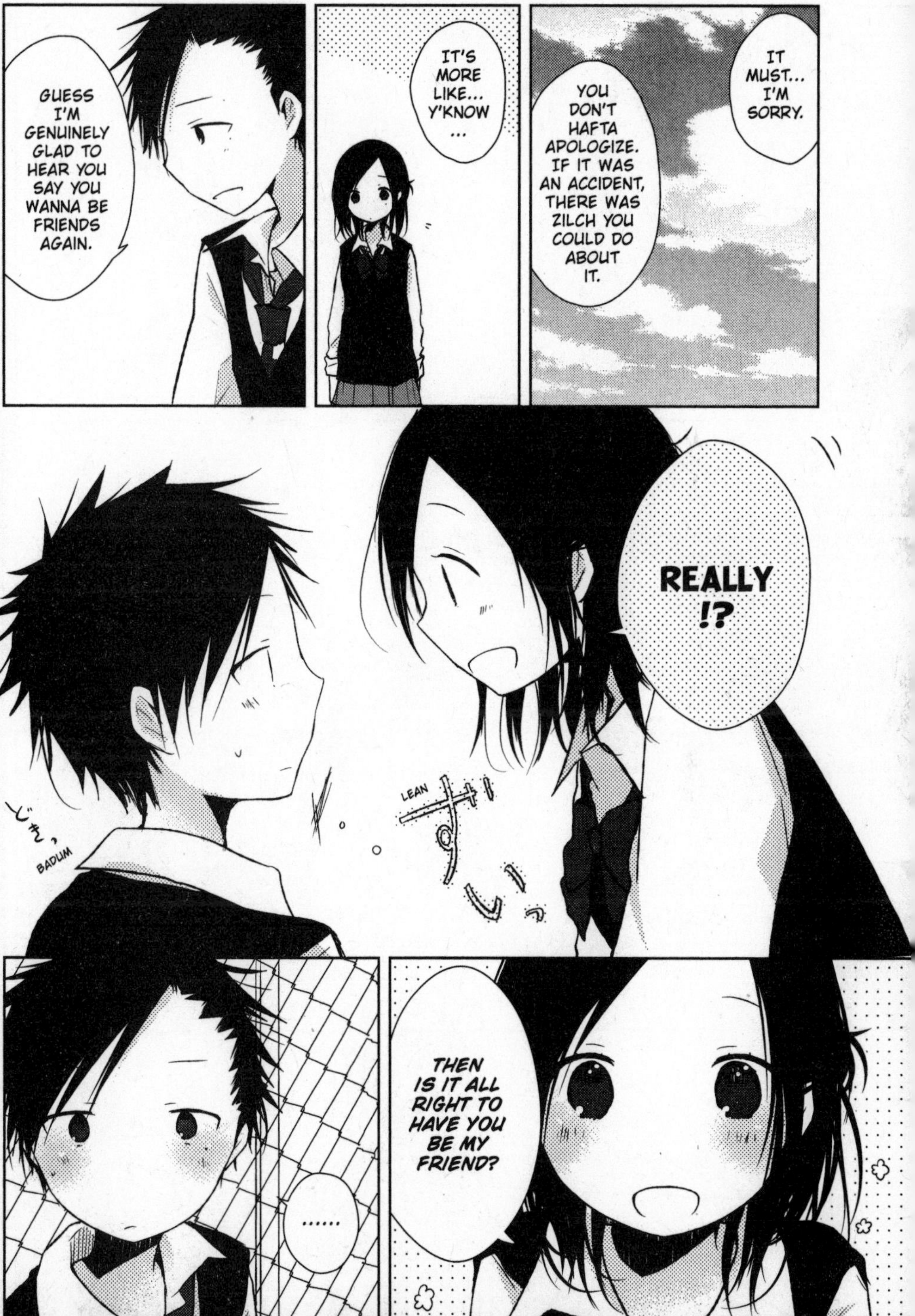
IT MUST... I'M SORRY.
YOU DON'T HAFTA APOLOGIZE. IF IT WAS AN ACCIDENT, THERE WAS ZILCH YOU COULD DO ABOUT IT.
IT'S MORE LIKE... Y'KNOW ...
GUESS I'M GENUINELY GLAD TO HEAR YOU SAY YOU WANNA BE FRIENDS AGAIN.
REALLY !?
LEAN
どき
BADUM
THEN IS IT ALL RIGHT TO HAVE YOU BE MY FRIEND?
......

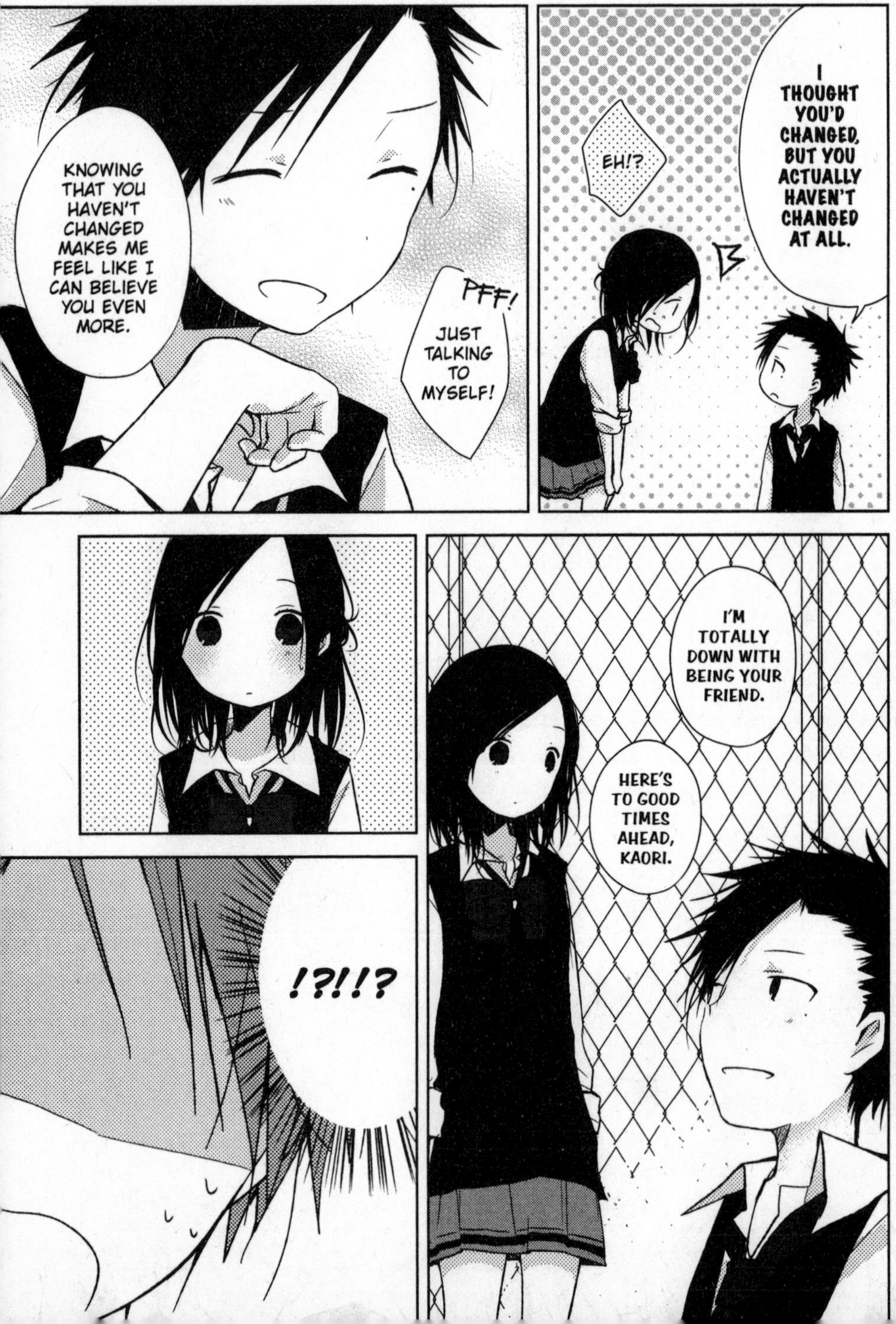
I THOUGHT YOU'D CHANGED, BUT YOU ACTUALLY HAVEN'T CHANGED AT ALL.
EH!?
KNOWING THAT YOU HAVEN'T CHANGED MAKES ME FEEL LIKE I CAN BELIEVE YOU EVEN MORE.
PFF!
JUST TALKING TO MYSELF!
I'M TOTALLY DOWN WITH BEING YOUR FRIEND.
HERE'S TO GOOD TIMES AHEAD, KAORI.
!?!!?

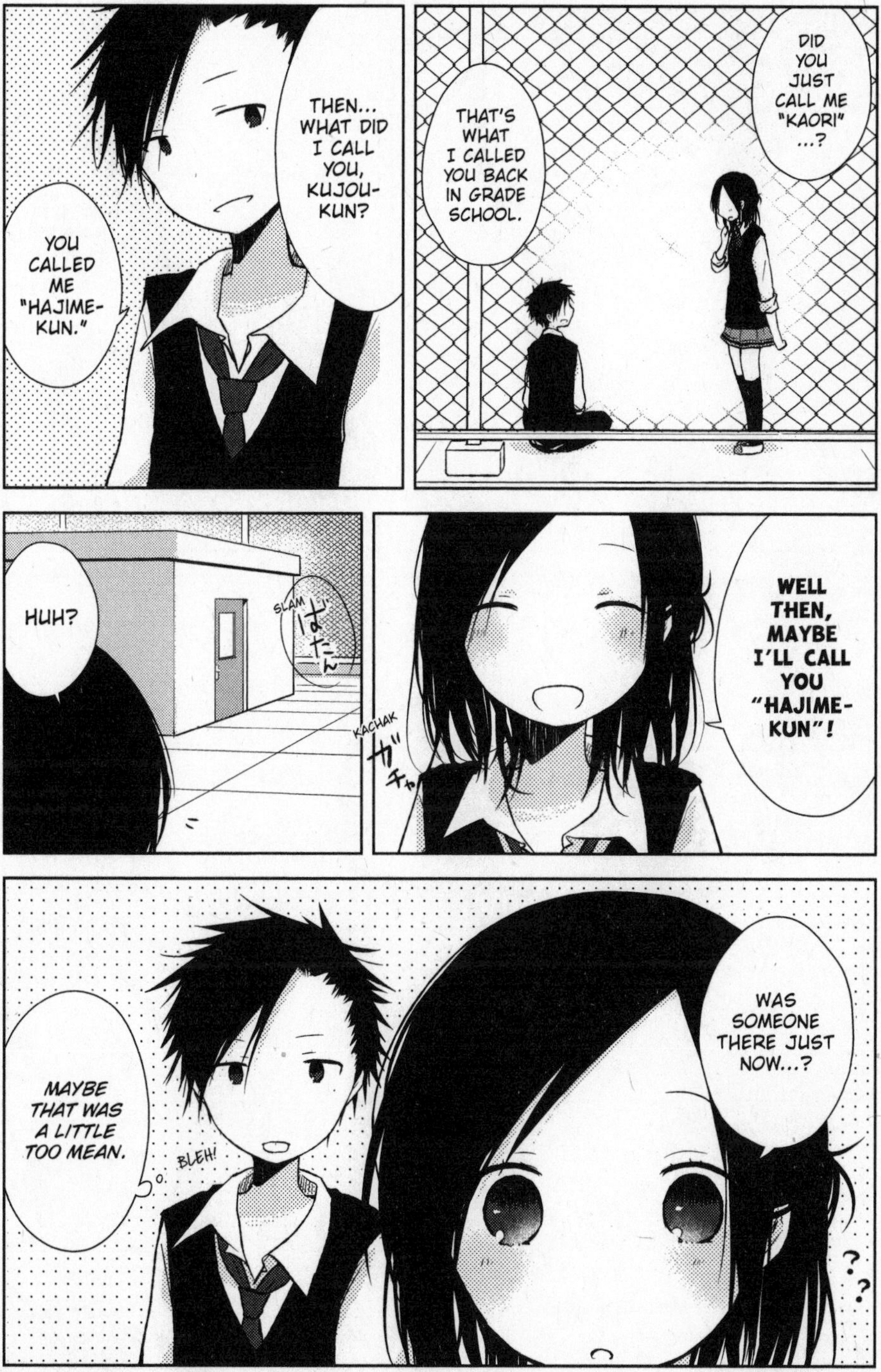
DID YOU JUST CALL ME "KAORI" ...?
THAT'S WHAT I CALLED YOU BACK IN GRADE SCHOOL.
THEN... WHAT DID I CALL YOU, KUJOU-KUN?
YOU CALLED ME "HAJIME-KUN."
WELL THEN, MAYBE I'LL CALL YOU "HAJIME-KUN"!
KACHAK
ガチャ
SLAM
ばたん
HUH?
WAS SOMEONE THERE JUST NOW...?
MAYBE THAT WAS A LITTLE TOO MEAN.
BLEH!

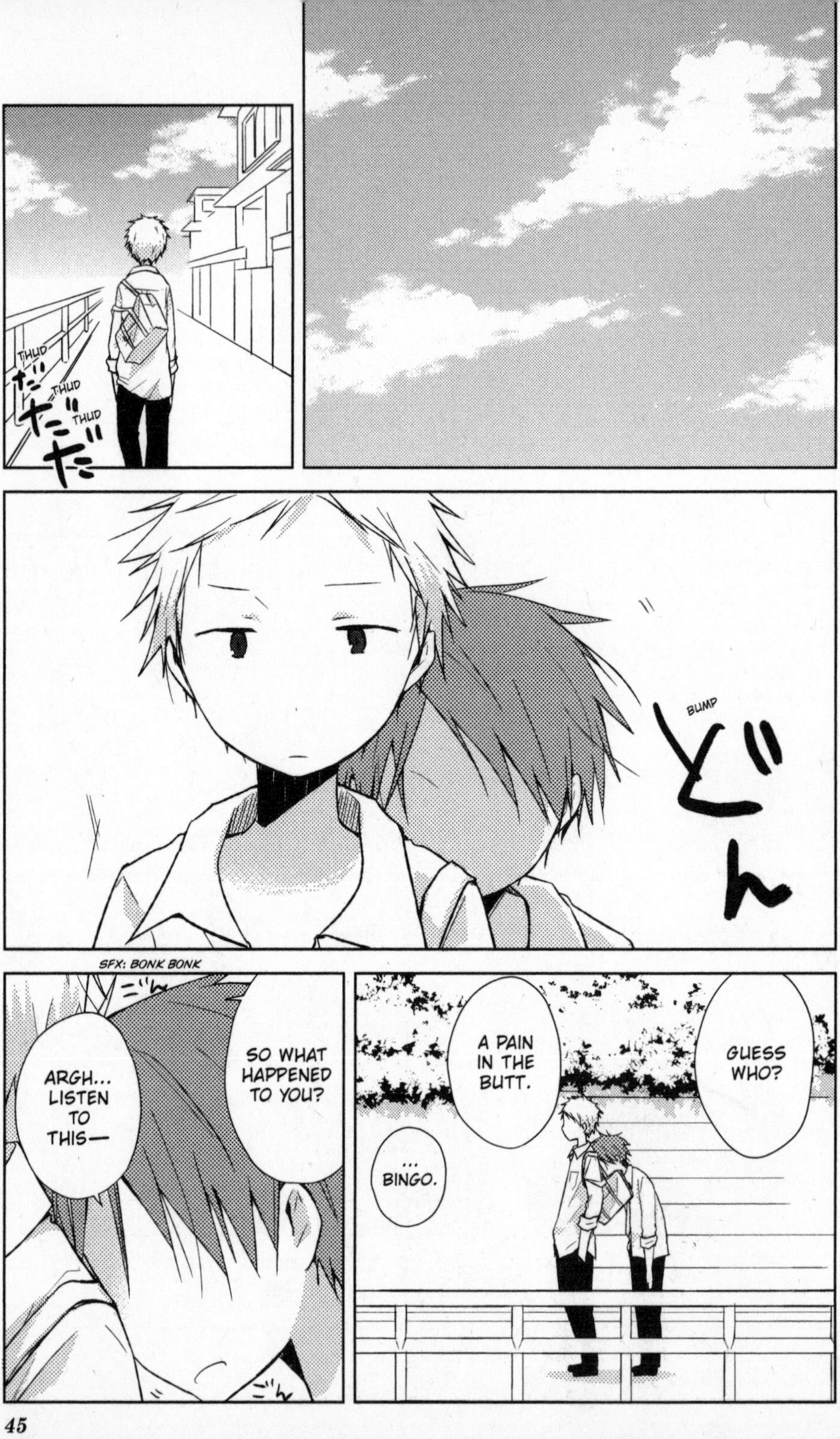
THUD
THUD
THUD
BUMP
GUESS WHO?
A PAIN IN THE BUTT.
...BINGO.
SFX: BONK BONK
SO WHAT HAPPENED TO YOU?
ARGH... LISTEN TO THIS—

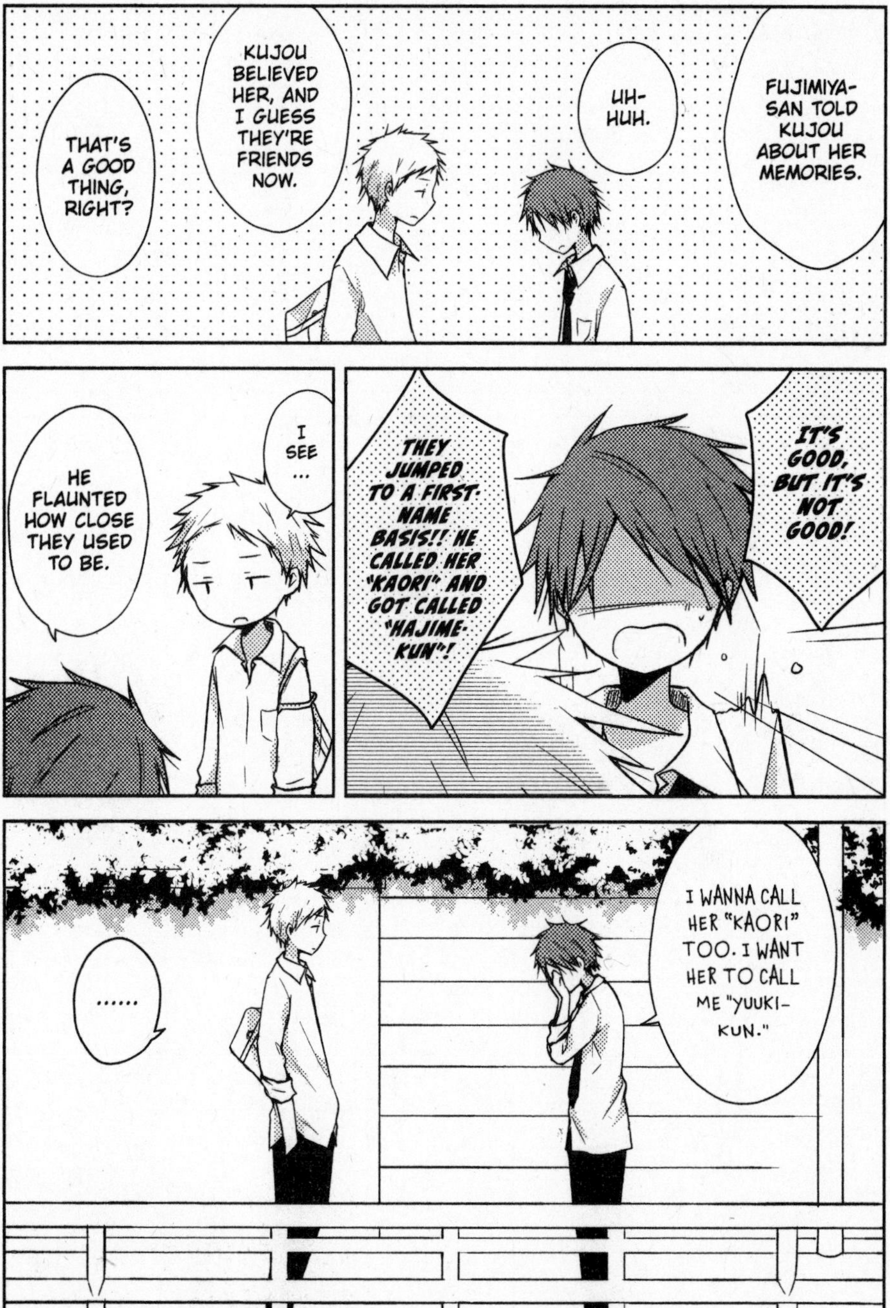
FUJIMIYA-SAN TOLD KUJOU ABOUT HER MEMORIES.
UH-HUH.
KUJOU BELIEVED HER, AND I GUESS THEY'RE FRIENDS NOW.
THAT'S A GOOD THING, RIGHT?
IT'S GOOD, BUT IT'S NOT GOOD!
THEY JUMPED TO A FIRST-NAME BASIS!! HE CALLED HER "KAORI" AND GOT CALLED "HAJIME-KUN"!
I SEE...
HE FLAUNTED HOW CLOSE THEY USED TO BE.
I WANNA CALL HER "KAORI" TOO. I WANT HER TO CALL ME "YUUKI-KUN."
......

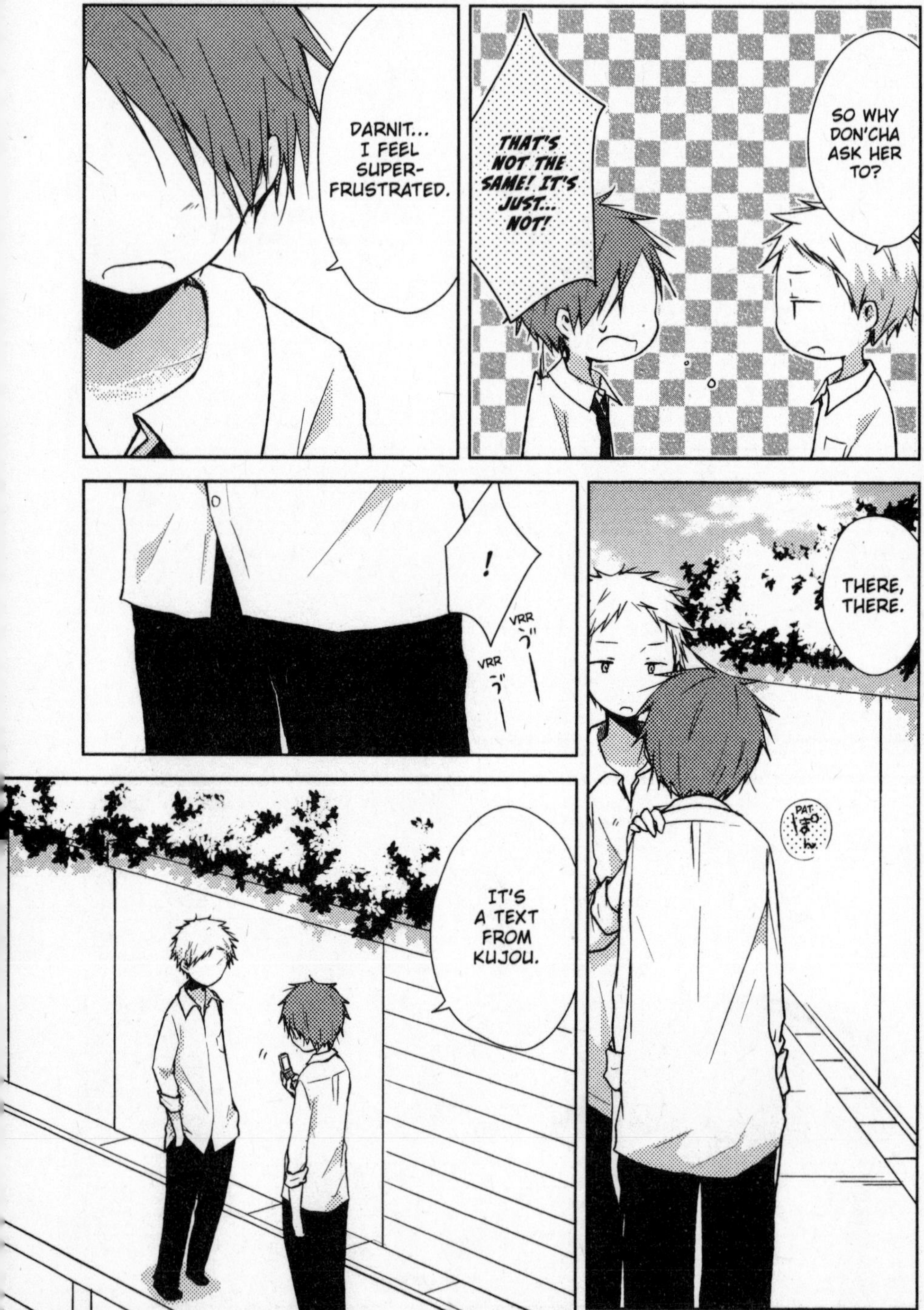
SO WHY DON'CHA ASK HER TO?
THAT'S NOT THE SAME! IT'S JUST... NOT!
DARNIT... I FEEL SUPER-FRUSTRATED.
THERE, THERE.
PAT
!
VRR
VRR
IT'S A TEXT FROM KUJOU.

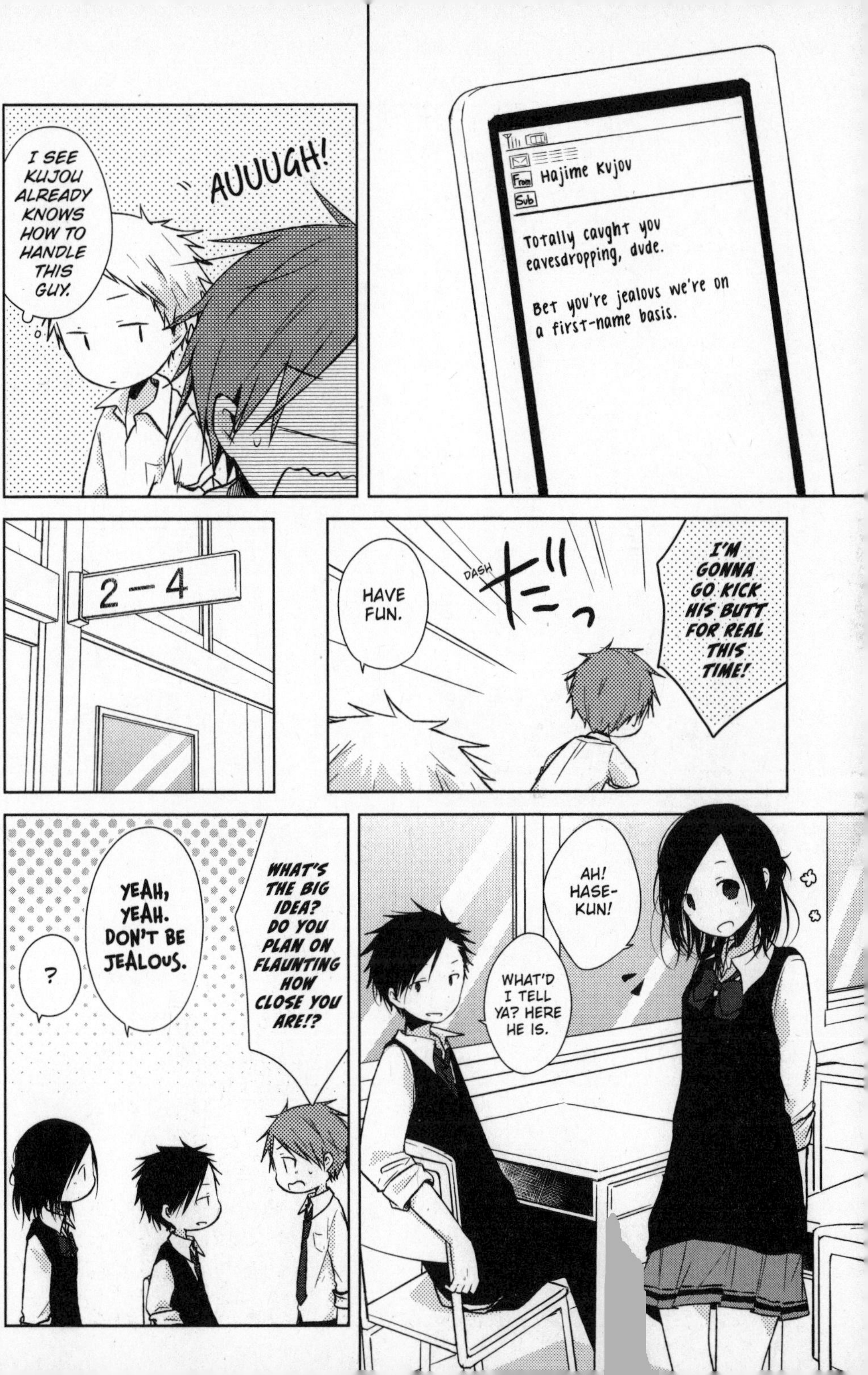
Hajime Kujou
Totally caught you eavesdropping, dude.
Bet you're jealous we're on a first-name basis.
AUUUGH!
I SEE KUJOU ALREADY KNOWS HOW TO HANDLE THIS GUY.
I'M GONNA GO KICK HIS BUTT FOR REAL THIS TIME!
DASH
HAVE FUN.
2-4
AH! HASE-KUN!
WHAT'D I TELL YA? HERE HE IS.
WHAT'S THE BIG IDEA? DO YOU PLAN ON FLAUNTING HOW CLOSE YOU ARE!?
YEAH, YEAH. DON'T BE JEALOUS.
?

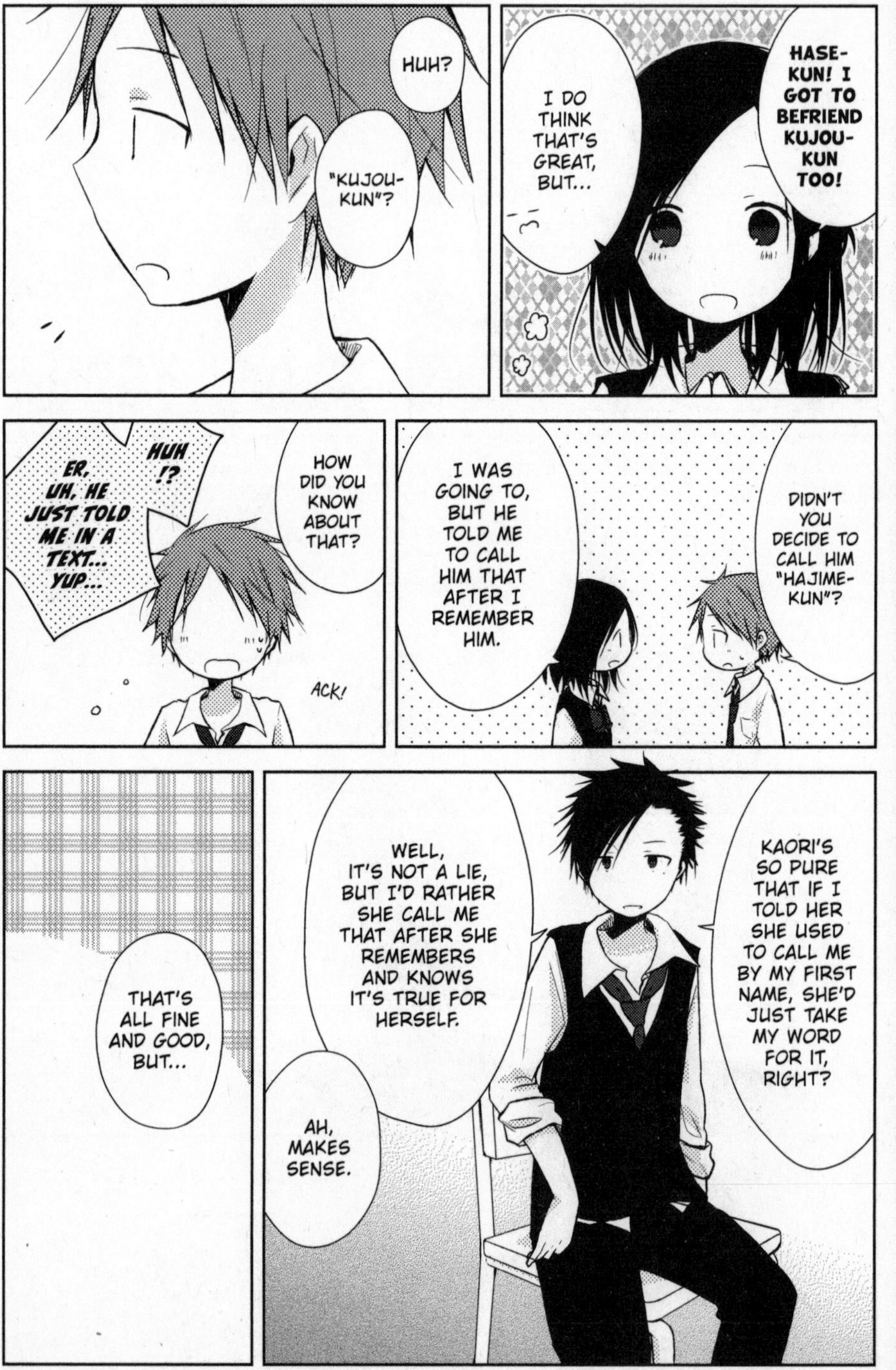
HASE-KUN! I GOT TO BEFRIEND KUJOU-KUN TOO!
I DO THINK THAT'S GREAT, BUT...
HUH?
"KUJOU-KUN"?
DIDN'T YOU DECIDE TO CALL HIM "HAJIME-KUN"?
I WAS GOING TO, BUT HE TOLD ME TO CALL HIM THAT AFTER I REMEMBER HIM.
HOW DID YOU KNOW ABOUT THAT?
HUH!?
ER, UH, HE JUST TOLD ME IN A TEXT... YUP...
ACK!
KAORI'S SO PURE THAT IF I TOLD HER SHE USED TO CALL ME BY MY FIRST NAME, SHE'D JUST TAKE MY WORD FOR IT, RIGHT?
WELL, IT'S NOT A LIE, BUT I'D RATHER SHE CALL ME THAT AFTER SHE REMEMBERS AND KNOWS IT'S TRUE FOR HERSELF.
AH, MAKES SENSE.
THAT'S ALL FINE AND GOOD, BUT...

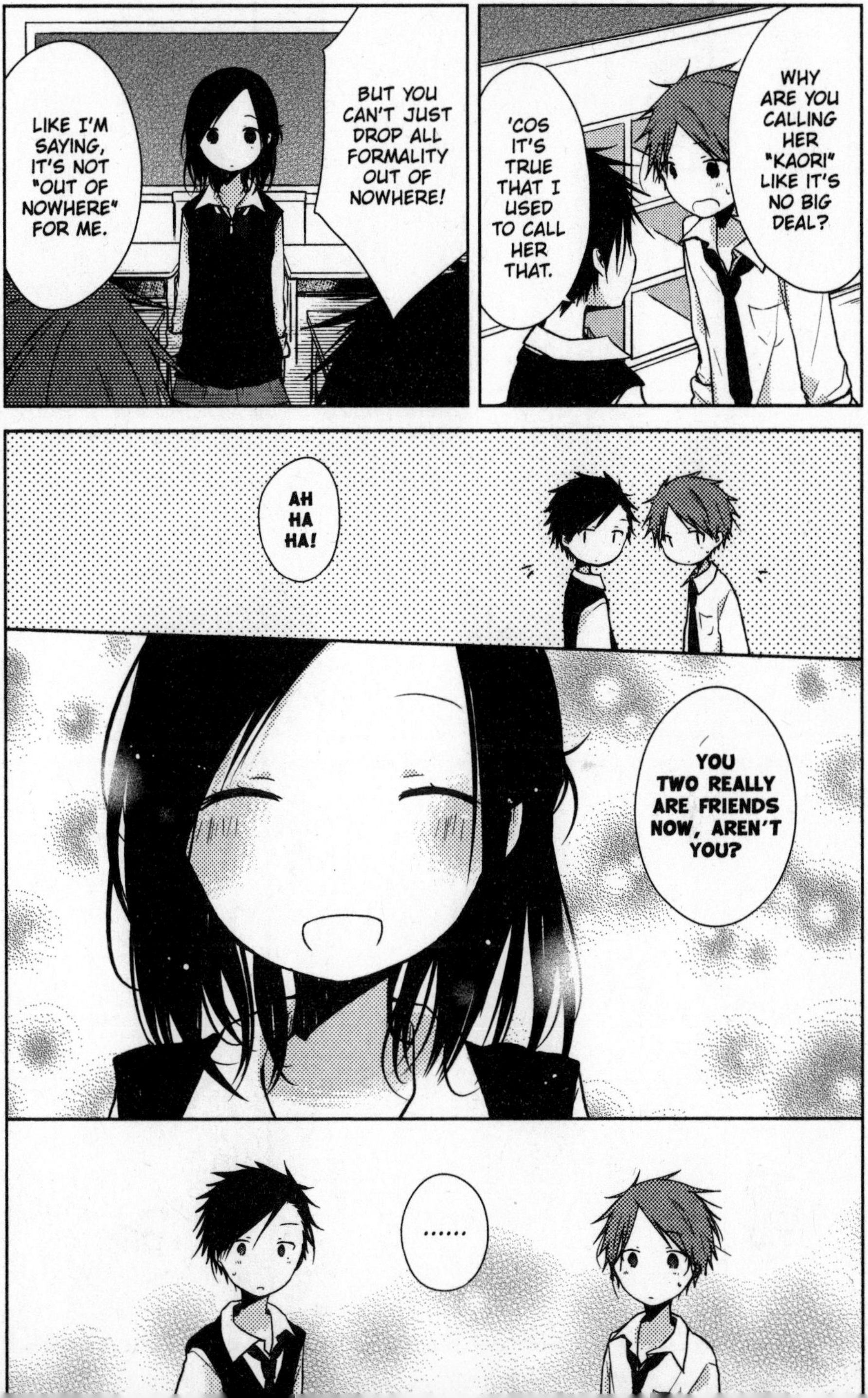
WHY ARE YOU CALLING HER "KAORI" LIKE IT'S NO BIG DEAL?
'COS IT'S TRUE THAT I USED TO CALL HER THAT.
BUT YOU CAN'T JUST DROP ALL FORMALITY OUT OF NOWHERE!
LIKE I'M SAYING, IT'S NOT "OUT OF NOWHERE" FOR ME.
AH HA HA!
YOU TWO REALLY ARE FRIENDS NOW, AREN'T YOU?
......

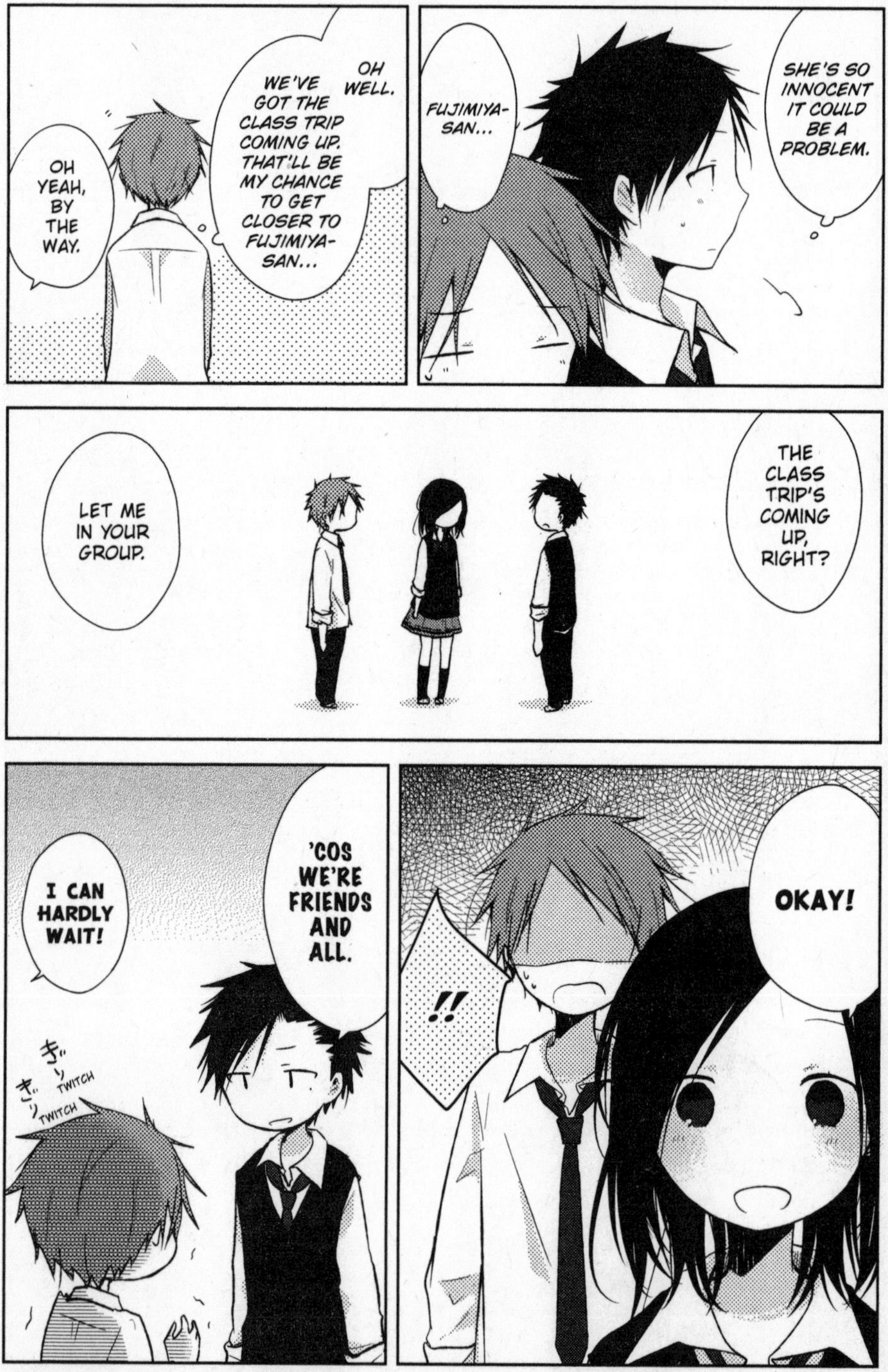
SHE'S SO INNOCENT IT COULD BE A PROBLEM.
FUJIMIYA-SAN...
OH WELL. WE'VE GOT THE CLASS TRIP COMING UP. THAT'LL BE MY CHANCE TO GET CLOSER TO FUJIMIYA-SAN...
OH YEAH, BY THE WAY.
THE CLASS TRIP'S COMING UP, RIGHT?
LET ME IN YOUR GROUP.
OKAY!
!!
'COS WE'RE FRIENDS AND ALL.
I CAN HARDLY WAIT!
ぎり TWITCH
ぎり TWITCH

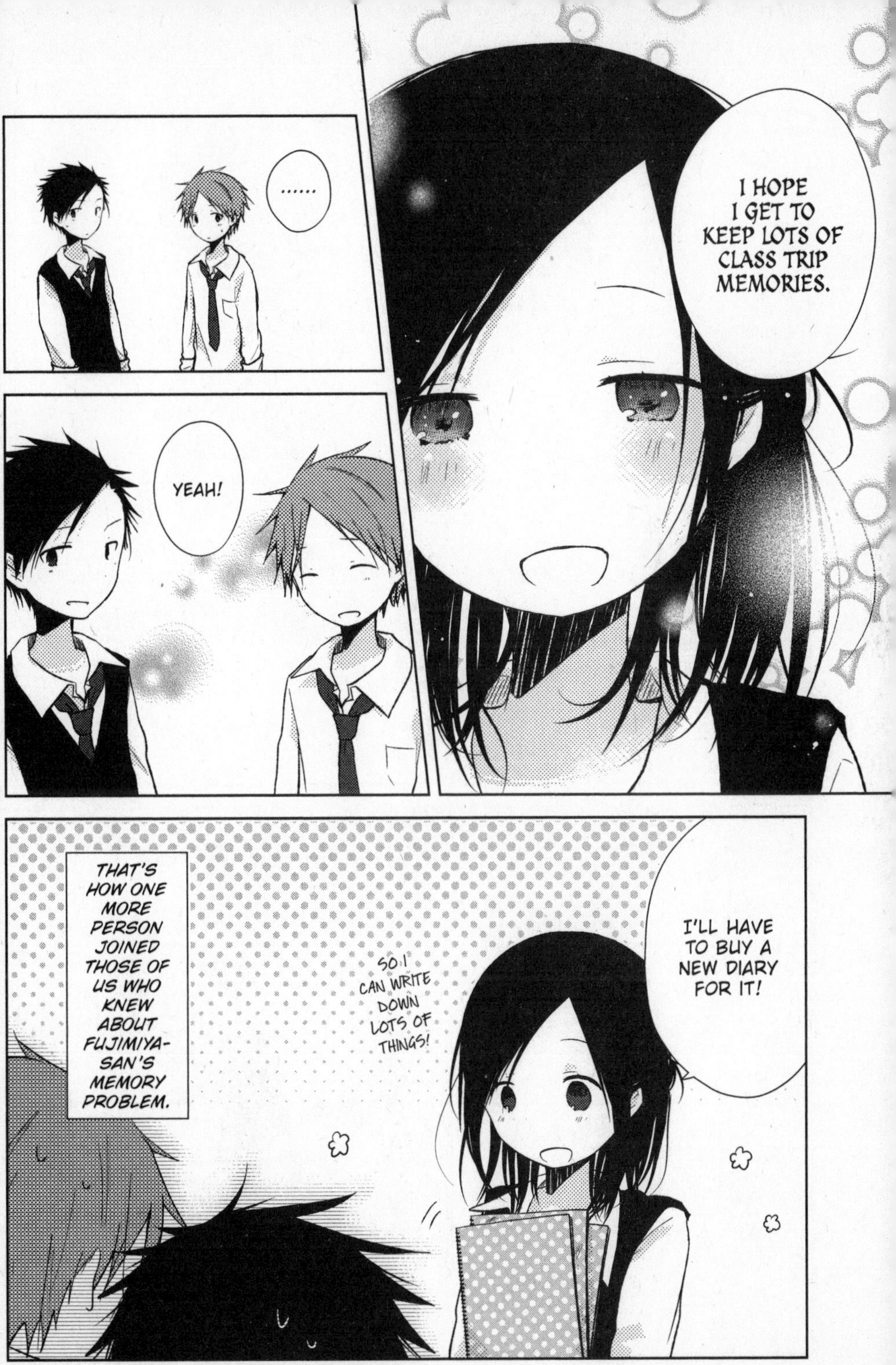
I HOPE I GET TO KEEP LOTS OF CLASS TRIP MEMORIES.
......
YEAH!
I'LL HAVE TO BUY A NEW DIARY FOR IT!
SO I CAN WRITE DOWN LOTS OF THINGS!
THAT'S HOW ONE MORE PERSON JOINED THOSE OF US WHO KNEW ABOUT FUJIMIYA-SAN'S MEMORY PROBLEM.

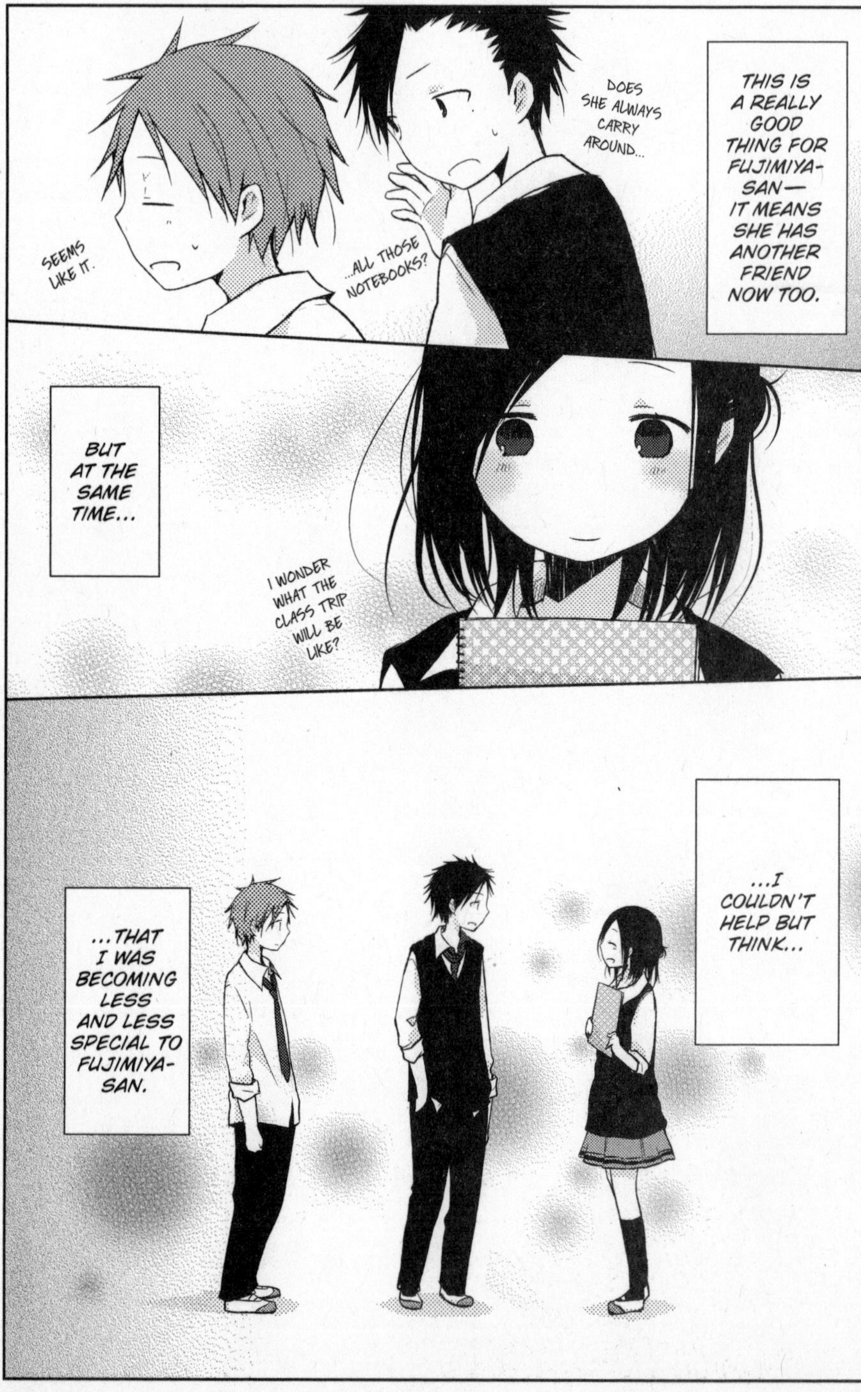
THIS IS A REALLY GOOD THING FOR FUJIMIYA-SAN—IT MEANS SHE HAS ANOTHER FRIEND NOW TOO.
DOES SHE ALWAYS CARRY AROUND...
...ALL THOSE NOTEBOOKS?
SEEMS LIKE IT.
I WONDER WHAT THE CLASS TRIP WILL BE LIKE?
BUT AT THE SAME TIME...
...I COULDN'T HELP BUT THINK...
...THAT I WAS BECOMING LESS AND LESS SPECIAL TO FUJIMIYA-SAN.

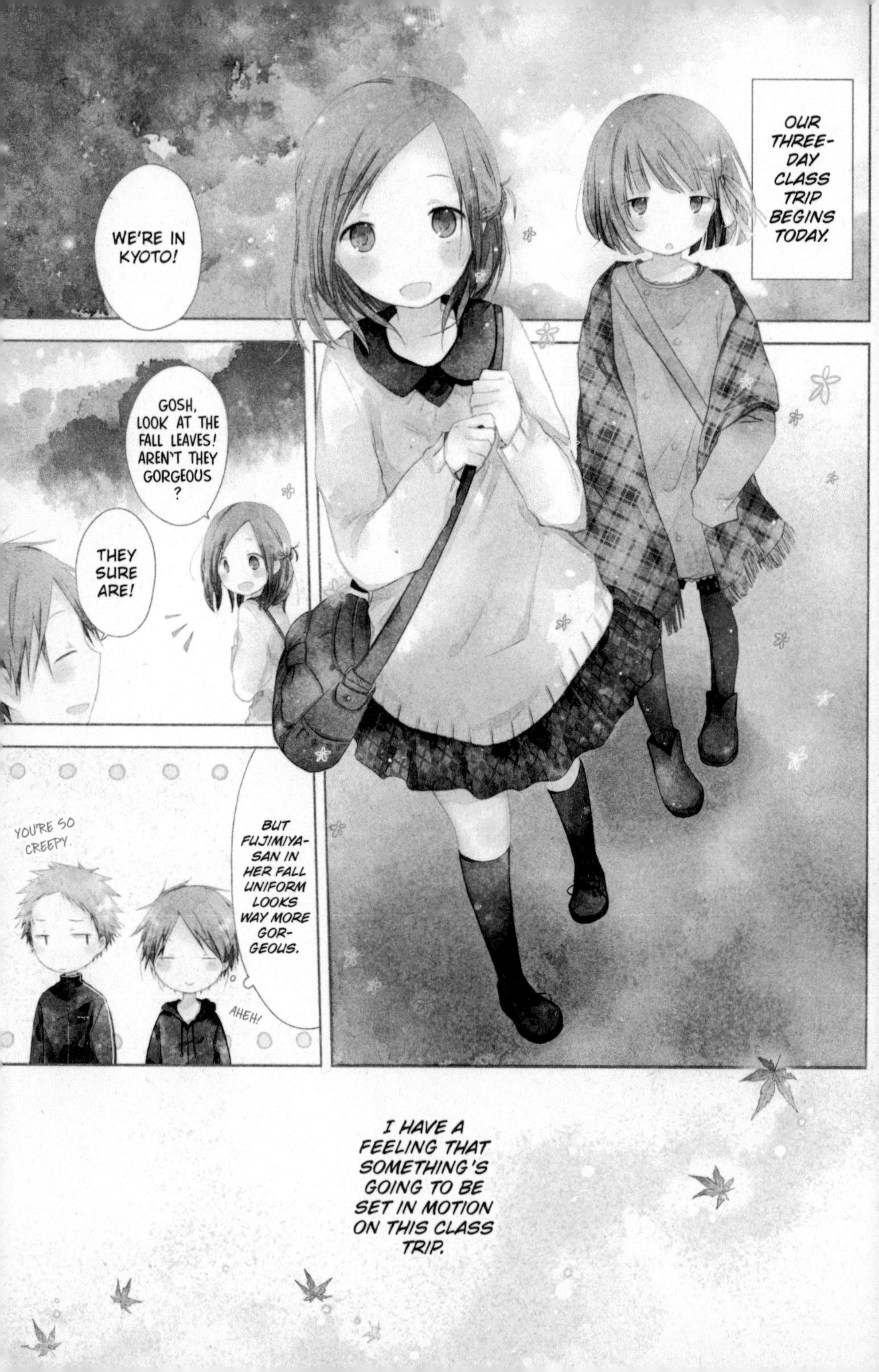
OUR THREE-DAY CLASS TRIP BEGINS TODAY.
WE'RE IN KYOTO!
GOSH, LOOK AT THE FALL LEAVES! AREN'T THEY GORGEOUS?
THEY SURE ARE!
BUT FUJIMIYA-SAN IN HER FALL UNIFORM LOOKS WAY MORE GORGEOUS.
AHEH!
YOU'RE SO CREEPY.
I HAVE A FEELING THAT SOMETHING'S GOING TO BE SET IN MOTION ON THIS CLASS TRIP.

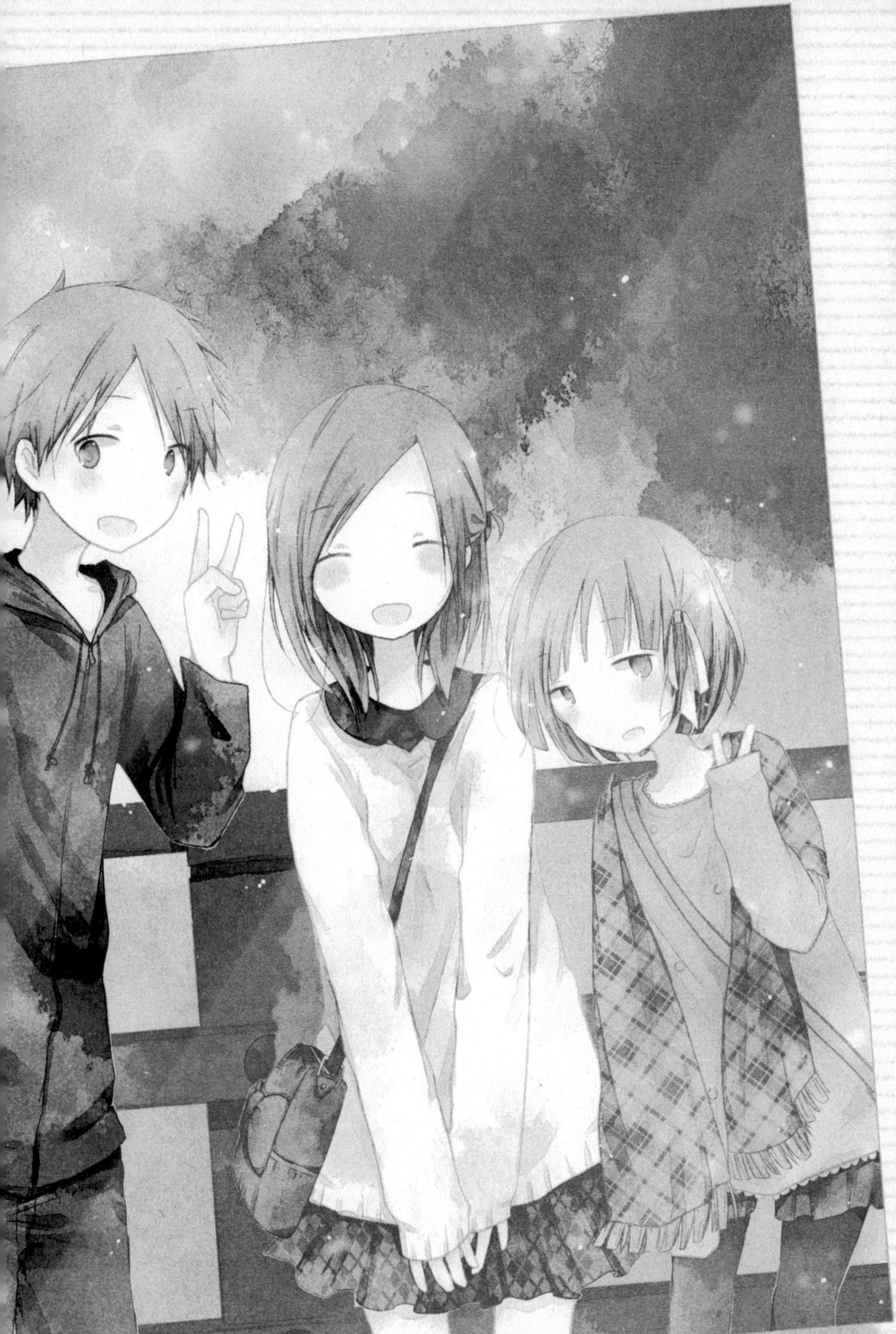

CHAPTER 24 FUSHIMI INARI MOSAIC

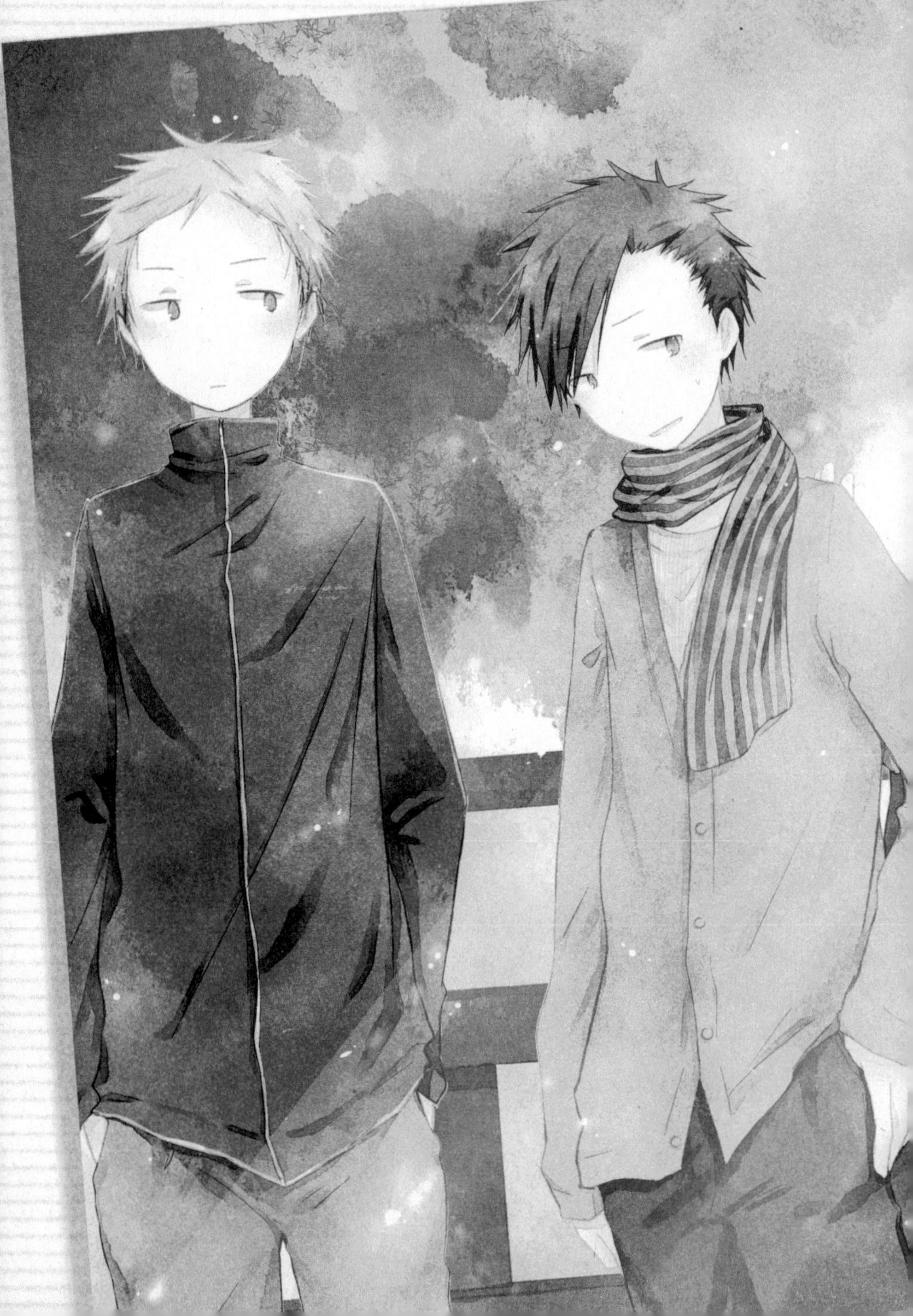

ONE WEEK FRIENDS

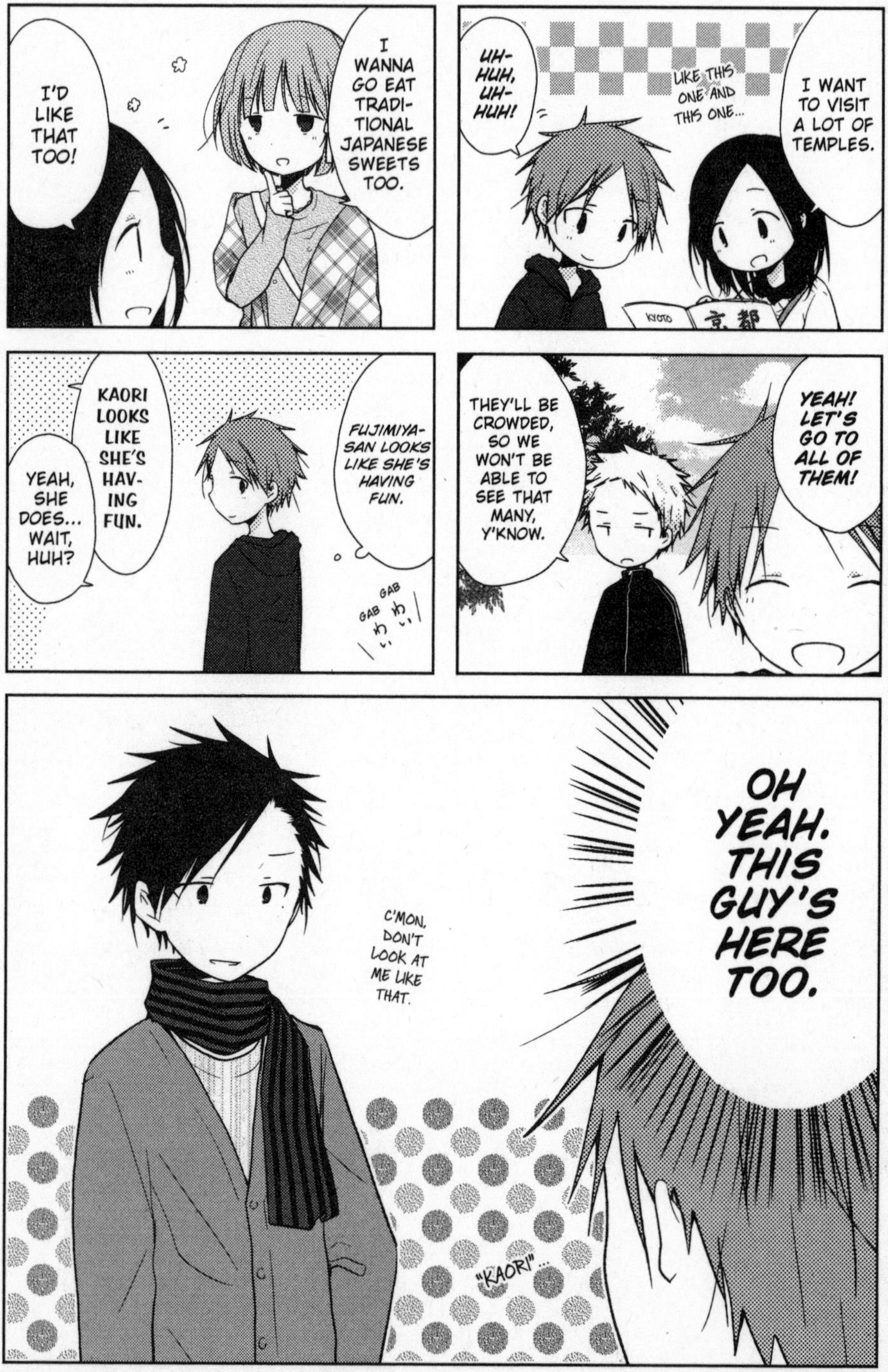
I WANT TO VISIT A LOT OF TEMPLES.
LIKE THIS ONE AND THIS ONE...
UH-HUH, UH-HUH!
KYOTO
京都
I WANNA GO EAT TRADITIONAL JAPANESE SWEETS TOO.
I'D LIKE THAT TOO!
YEAH! LET'S GO TO ALL OF THEM!
THEY'LL BE CROWDED, SO WE WON'T BE ABLE TO SEE THAT MANY, Y'KNOW.
FUJIMIYA-SAN LOOKS LIKE SHE'S HAVING FUN.
GAB GAB
KAORI LOOKS LIKE SHE'S HAVING FUN.
YEAH, SHE DOES... WAIT, HUH?
OH YEAH. THIS GUY'S HERE TOO.
C'MON, DON'T LOOK AT ME LIKE THAT.
"KAORI"...

EXCITED

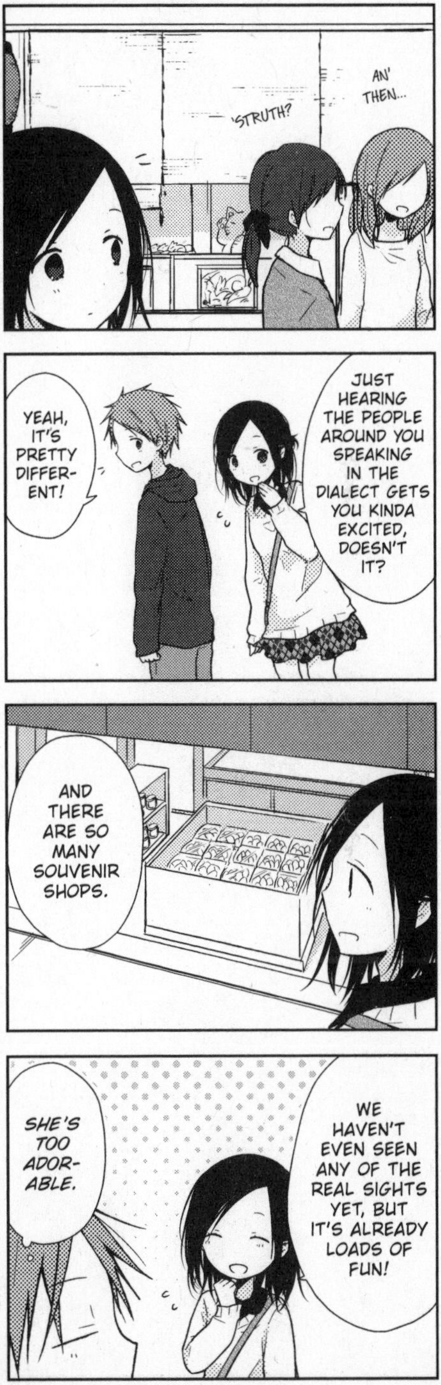
AN' THEN...
'STRUTH?
JUST HEARING THE PEOPLE AROUND YOU SPEAKING IN THE DIALECT GETS YOU KINDA EXCITED, DOESN'T IT?
YEAH, IT'S PRETTY DIFFERENT!
AND THERE ARE SO MANY SOUVENIR SHOPS.
WE HAVEN'T EVEN SEEN ANY OF THE REAL SIGHTS YET, BUT IT'S ALREADY LOADS OF FUN!
SHE'S TOO ADORABLE.

TEMPLE HOPPING

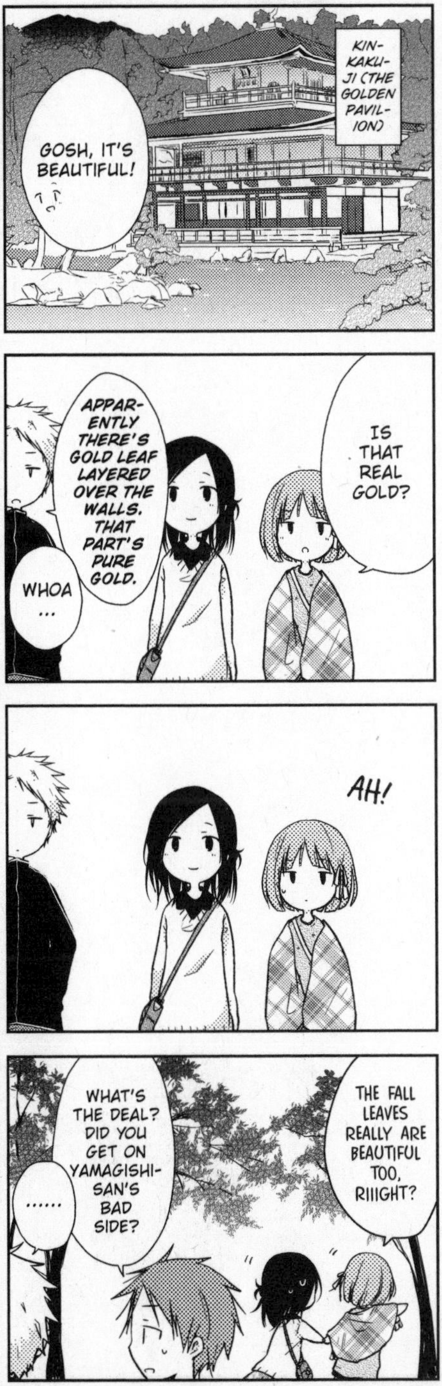
KINKAKUJI (THE GOLDEN PAVILION)
GOSH, IT'S BEAUTIFUL!
IS THAT REAL GOLD?
APPARENTLY THERE'S GOLD LEAF LAYERED OVER THE WALLS. THAT PART'S PURE GOLD.
WHOA...
AH!
THE FALL LEAVES REALLY ARE BEAUTIFUL TOO, RIIIGHT?
WHAT'S THE DEAL? DID YOU GET ON YAMAGISHI-SAN'S BAD SIDE?
......

REQUEST

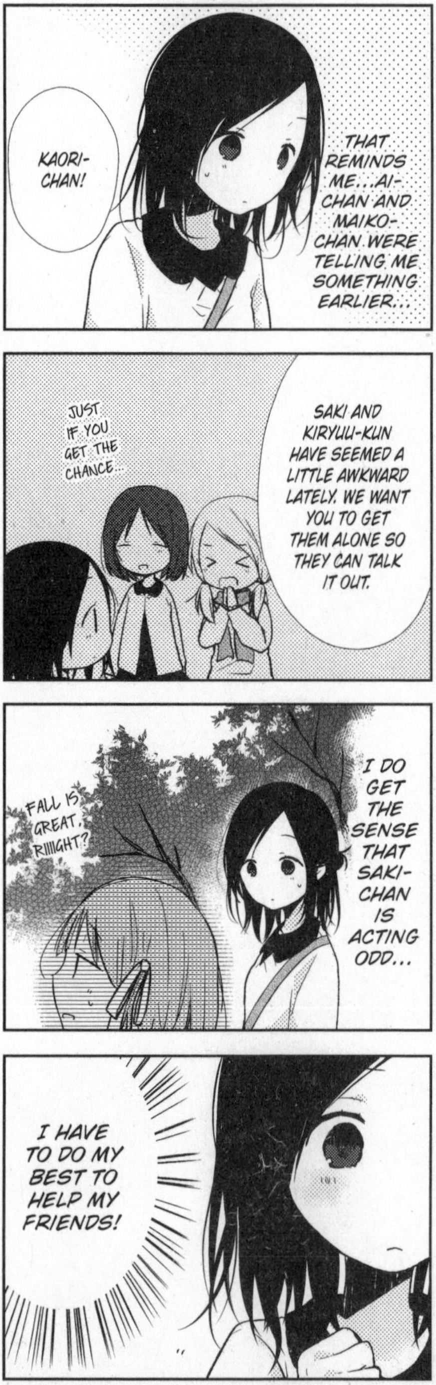

THAT REMINDS ME... AI-CHAN AND MAIKO-CHAN WERE TELLING ME SOMETHING EARLIER...
KAORI-CHAN!
SAKI AND KIRYUU-KUN HAVE SEEMED A LITTLE AWKWARD LATELY. WE WANT YOU TO GET THEM ALONE SO THEY CAN TALK IT OUT.
JUST IF YOU GET THE CHANCE...
I DO GET THE SENSE THAT SAKI-CHAN IS ACTING ODD...
FALL IS GREAT, RIIIIGHT?
I HAVE TO DO MY BEST TO HELP MY FRIENDS!

DOING HER BEST

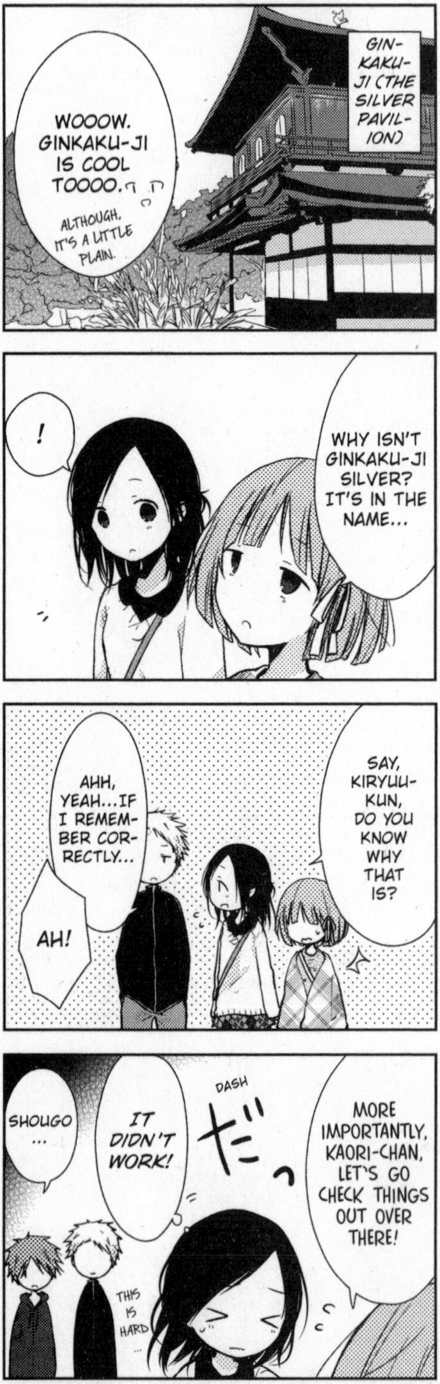

GIN-KAKU-JI (THE SILVER PAVILION)
WOOOW. GINKAKU-JI IS COOL TOOOO.
ALTHOUGH, IT'S A LITTLE PLAIN.
WHY ISN'T GINKAKU-JI SILVER? IT'S IN THE NAME...
!
SAY, KIRYUU-KUN, DO YOU KNOW WHY THAT IS?
AHH, YEAH...IF I REMEMBER CORRECTLY...
AH!
MORE IMPORTANTLY, KAORI-CHAN, LET'S GO CHECK THINGS OUT OVER THERE!
DASH
IT DIDN'T WORK!
SHOUGO...
THIS IS HARD...

DISCONTENT

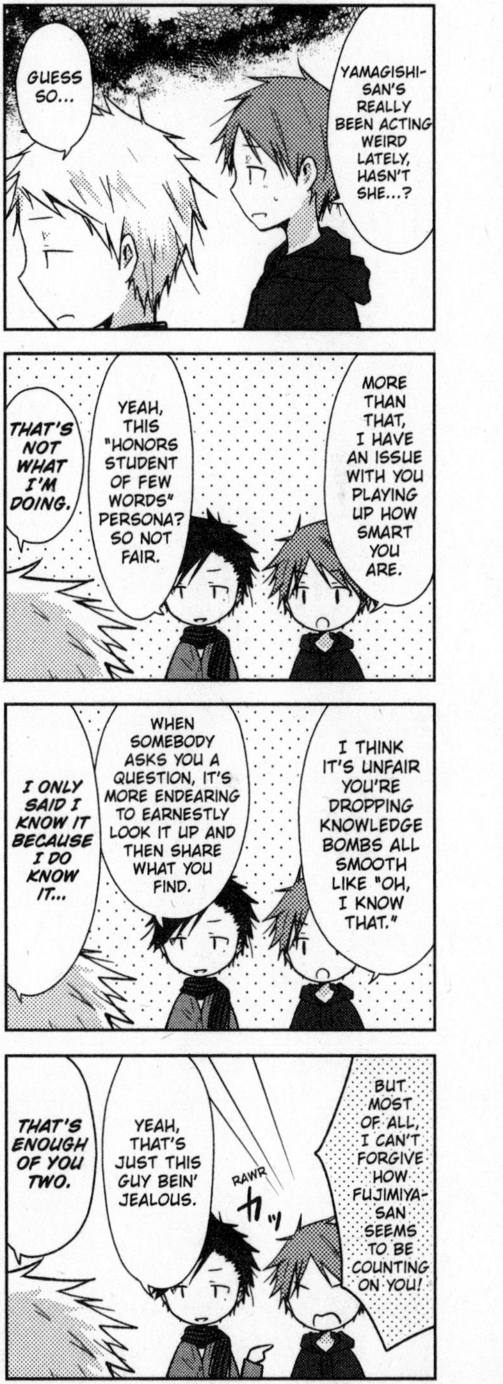
YAMAGISHI-SAN'S REALLY BEEN ACTING WEIRD LATELY, HASN'T SHE...?
GUESS SO...
MORE THAN THAT, I HAVE AN ISSUE WITH YOU PLAYING UP HOW SMART YOU ARE.
YEAH, THIS "HONORS STUDENT OF FEW WORDS" PERSONA? SO NOT FAIR.
THAT'S NOT WHAT I'M DOING.
I THINK IT'S UNFAIR YOU'RE DROPPING KNOWLEDGE BOMBS ALL SMOOTH LIKE "OH, I KNOW THAT."
WHEN SOMEBODY ASKS YOU A QUESTION, IT'S MORE ENDEARING TO EARNESTLY LOOK IT UP AND THEN SHARE WHAT YOU FIND.
I ONLY SAID I KNOW IT BECAUSE I DO KNOW IT...
BUT MOST OF ALL, I CAN'T FORGIVE HOW FUJIMIYA-SAN SEEMS TO BE COUNTING ON YOU!
RAWR
カッ
YEAH, THAT'S JUST THIS GUY BEIN' JEALOUS.
THAT'S ENOUGH OF YOU TWO.

HIGH PLACES

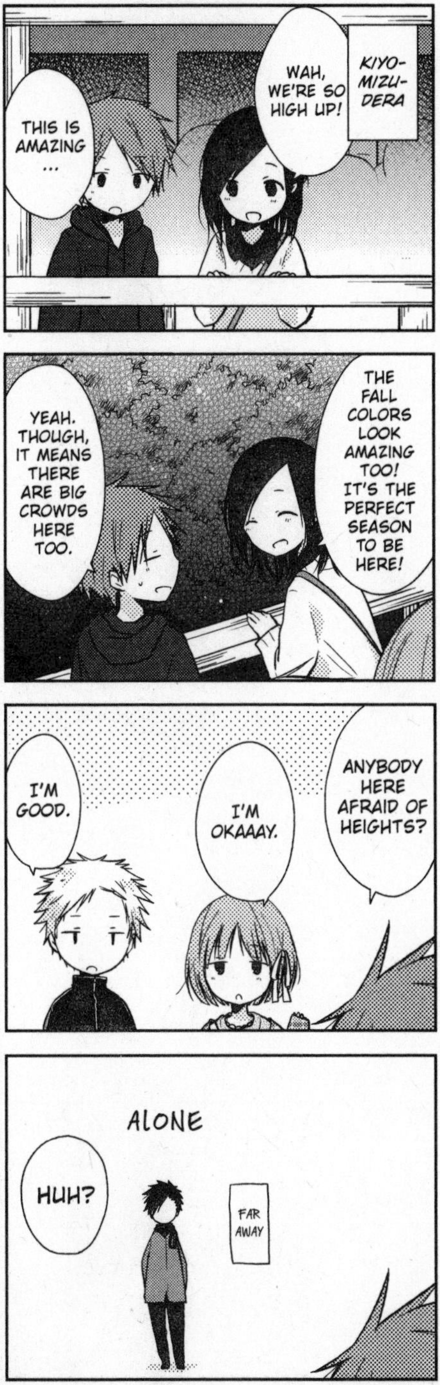
KIYO-MIZU-DERA
WAH, WE'RE SO HIGH UP!
THIS IS AMAZING ...
THE FALL COLORS LOOK AMAZING TOO! IT'S THE PERFECT SEASON TO BE HERE!
YEAH. THOUGH, IT MEANS THERE ARE BIG CROWDS HERE TOO.
ANYBODY HERE AFRAID OF HEIGHTS?
I'M OKAAAY.
I'M GOOD.
ALONE
FAR AWAY
HUH?

WEAKNESSES

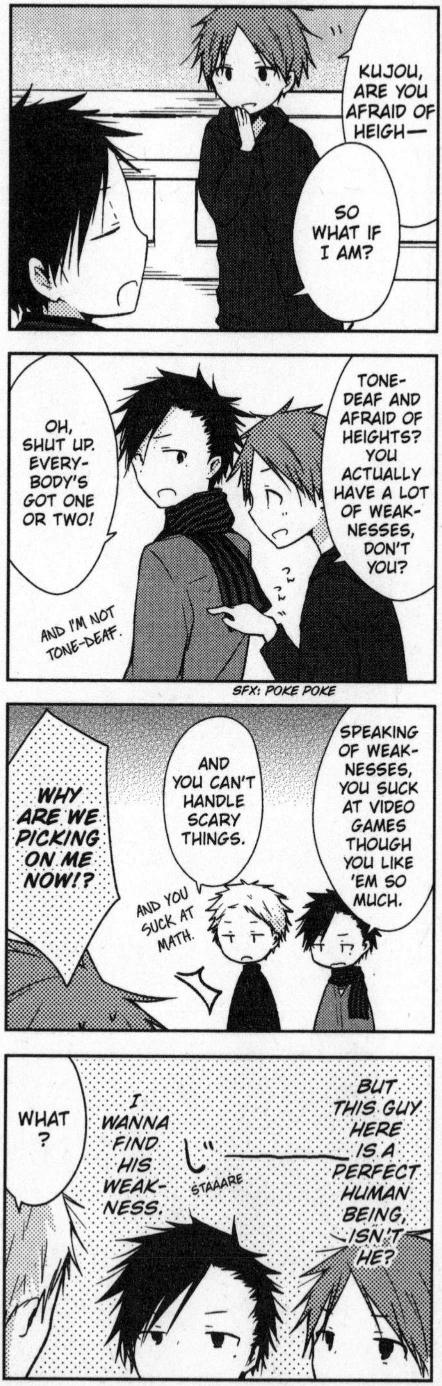
KUJOU, ARE YOU AFRAID OF HEIGH—
SO WHAT IF I AM?
TONE-DEAF AND AFRAID OF HEIGHTS? YOU ACTUALLY HAVE A LOT OF WEAKNESSES, DON'T YOU?
OH, SHUT UP. EVERYBODY'S GOT ONE OR TWO!
AND I'M NOT TONE-DEAF.
SFX: POKE POKE
SPEAKING OF WEAKNESSES, YOU SUCK AT VIDEO GAMES THOUGH YOU LIKE 'EM SO MUCH.
AND YOU CAN'T HANDLE SCARY THINGS.
AND YOU SUCK AT MATH.
WHY ARE WE PICKING ON ME NOW!?
BUT THIS GUY HERE IS A PERFECT HUMAN BEING, ISN'T HE?
STAAARE
I WANNA FIND HIS WEAKNESS.
WHAT?

WANT TO DO WHAT I CAN

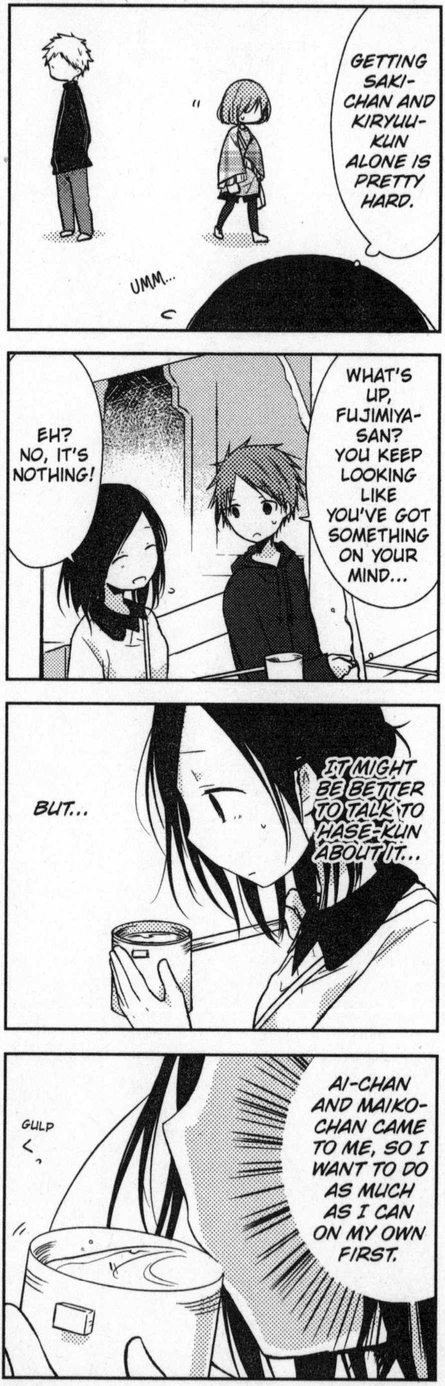
GETTING SAKI-CHAN AND KIRYUU-KUN ALONE IS PRETTY HARD.
UMM...
WHAT'S UP, FUJIMIYA-SAN? YOU KEEP LOOKING LIKE YOU'VE GOT SOMETHING ON YOUR MIND...
EH? NO, IT'S NOTHING!
IT MIGHT BE BETTER TO TALK TO HASE-KUN ABOUT IT...
BUT...
AI-CHAN AND MAIKO-CHAN CAME TO ME, SO I WANT TO DO AS MUCH AS I CAN ON MY OWN FIRST.
GULP

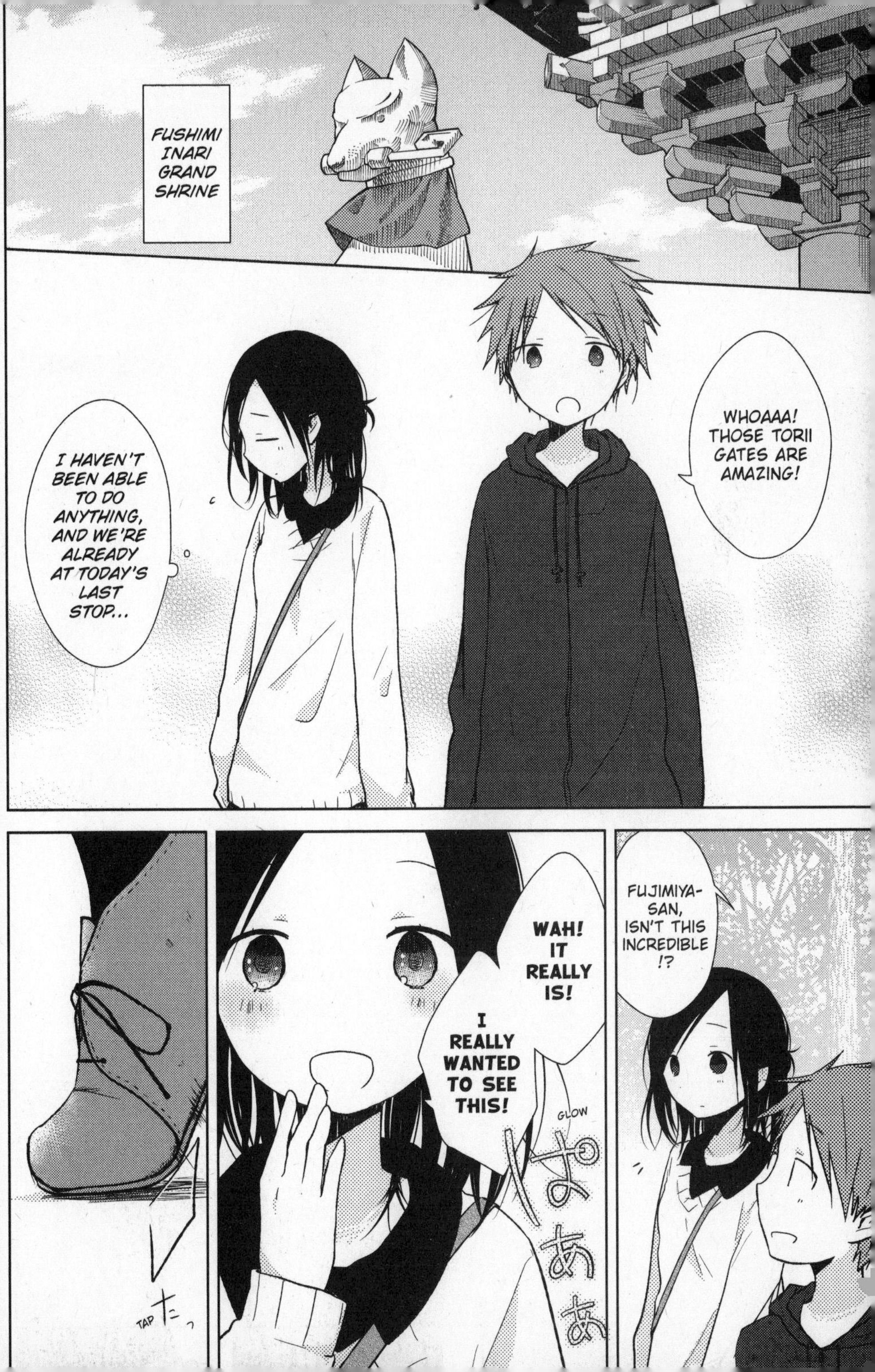
FUSHIMI INARI GRAND SHRINE
WHOAAA! THOSE TORII GATES ARE AMAZING!
I HAVEN'T BEEN ABLE TO DO ANYTHING, AND WE'RE ALREADY AT TODAY'S LAST STOP...
FUJIMIYA-SAN, ISN'T THIS INCREDIBLE!?
WAH! IT REALLY IS!
I REALLY WANTED TO SEE THIS!
GLOW
TAP

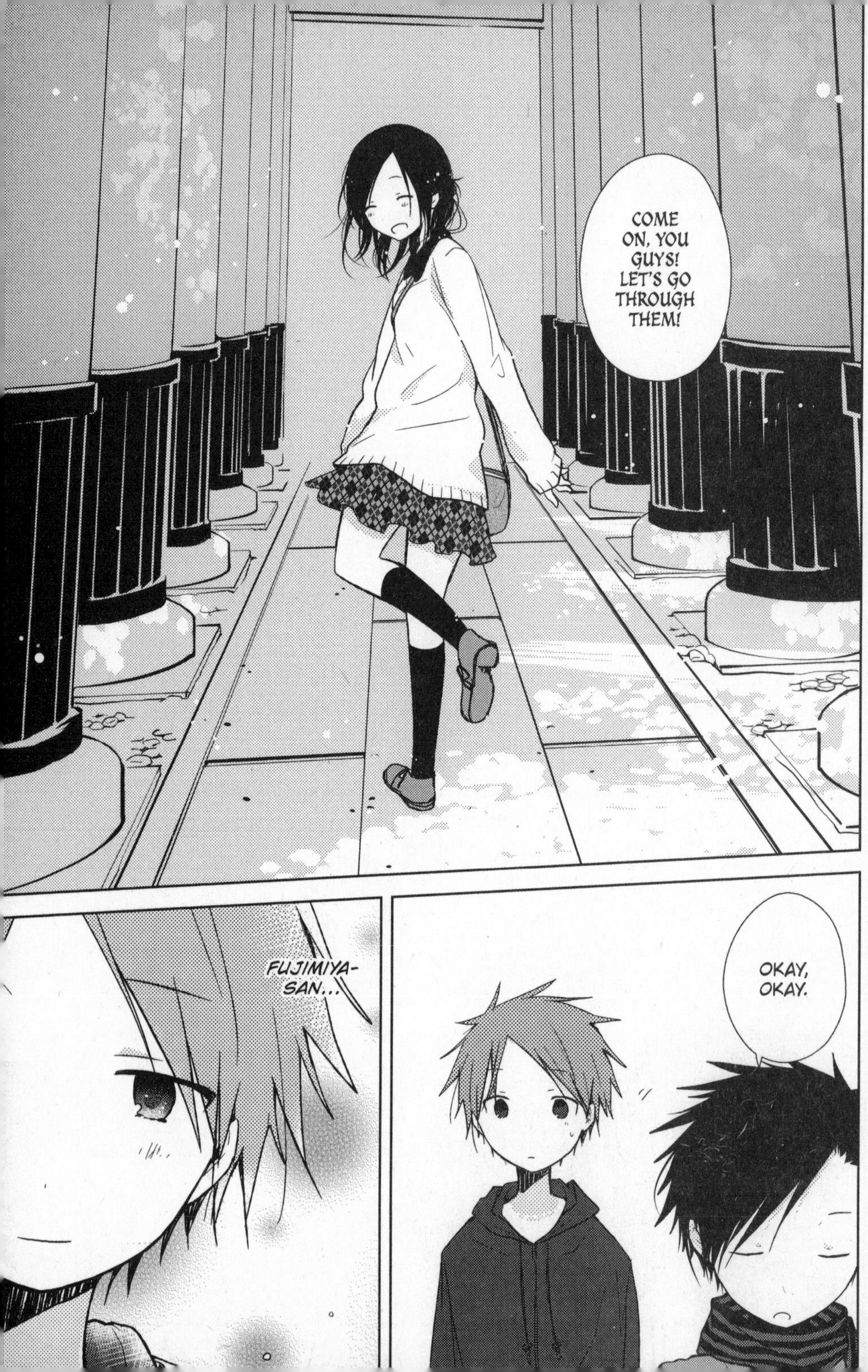
COME ON, YOU GUYS! LET'S GO THROUGH THEM!
OKAY, OKAY.
FUJIMIYA-SAN...

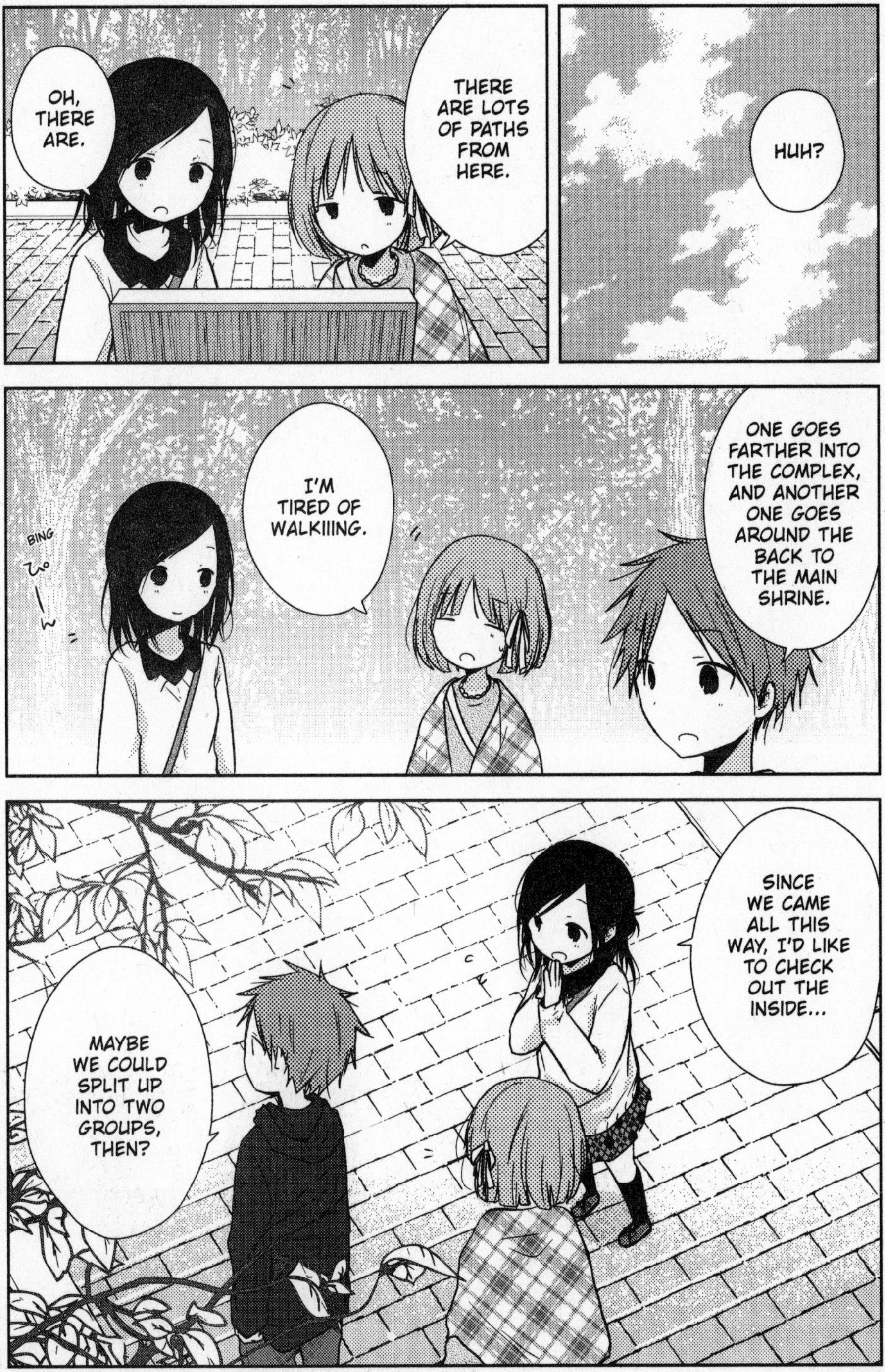
HUH?
THERE ARE LOTS OF PATHS FROM HERE.
OH, THERE ARE.
ONE GOES FARTHER INTO THE COMPLEX, AND ANOTHER ONE GOES AROUND THE BACK TO THE MAIN SHRINE.
I'M TIRED OF WALKIIING.
BING
SINCE WE CAME ALL THIS WAY, I'D LIKE TO CHECK OUT THE INSIDE...
MAYBE WE COULD SPLIT UP INTO TWO GROUPS, THEN?

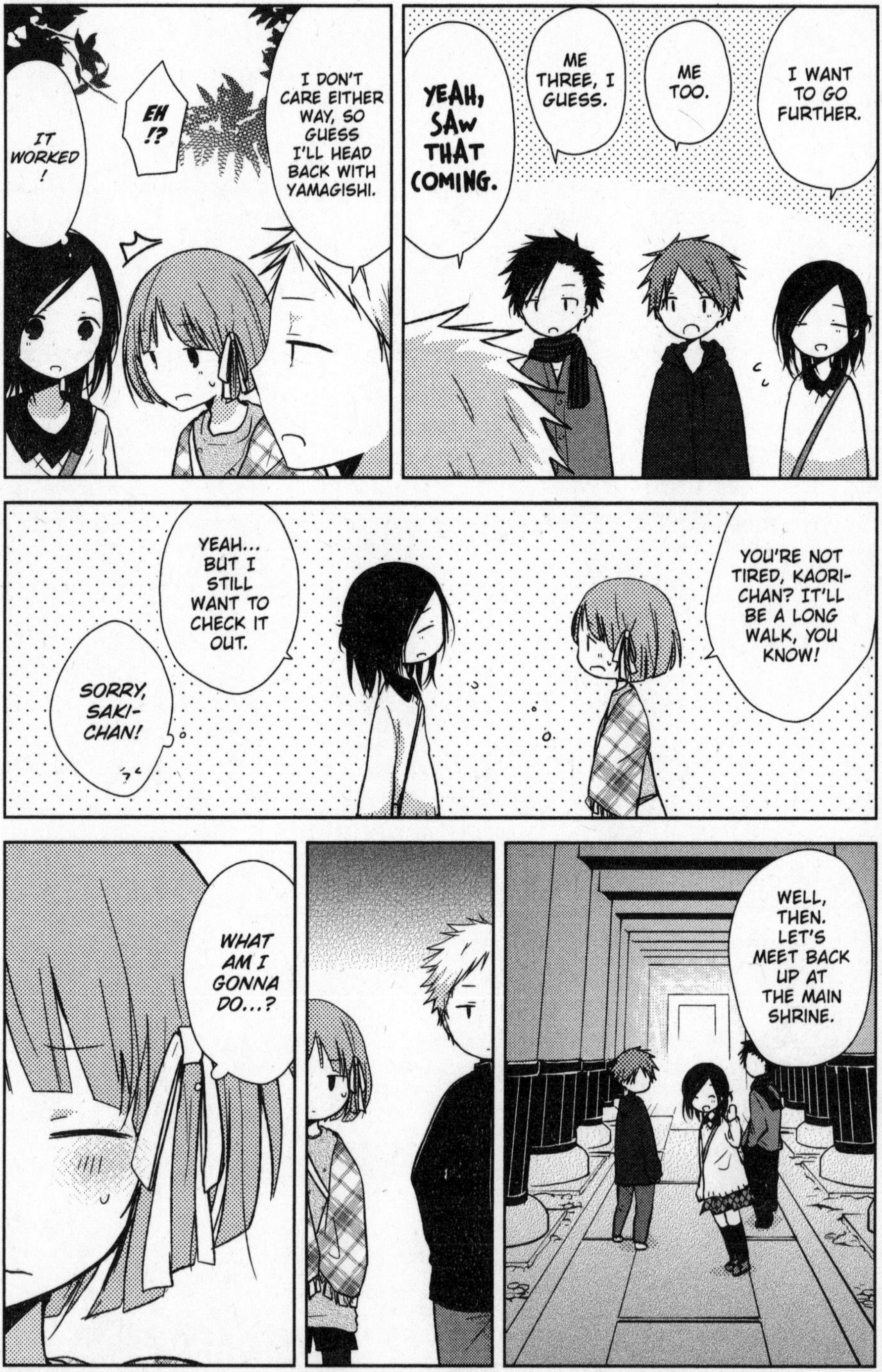
I WANT TO GO FURTHER.
ME TOO.
ME THREE, I GUESS.
YEAH, SAW THAT COMING.
I DON'T CARE EITHER WAY, SO GUESS I'LL HEAD BACK WITH YAMAGISHI.
EH !?
IT WORKED !
YOU'RE NOT TIRED, KAORI-CHAN? IT'LL BE A LONG WALK, YOU KNOW!
YEAH... BUT I STILL WANT TO CHECK IT OUT.
SORRY, SAKI-CHAN!
WELL, THEN. LET'S MEET BACK UP AT THE MAIN SHRINE.
WHAT AM I GONNA DO...?

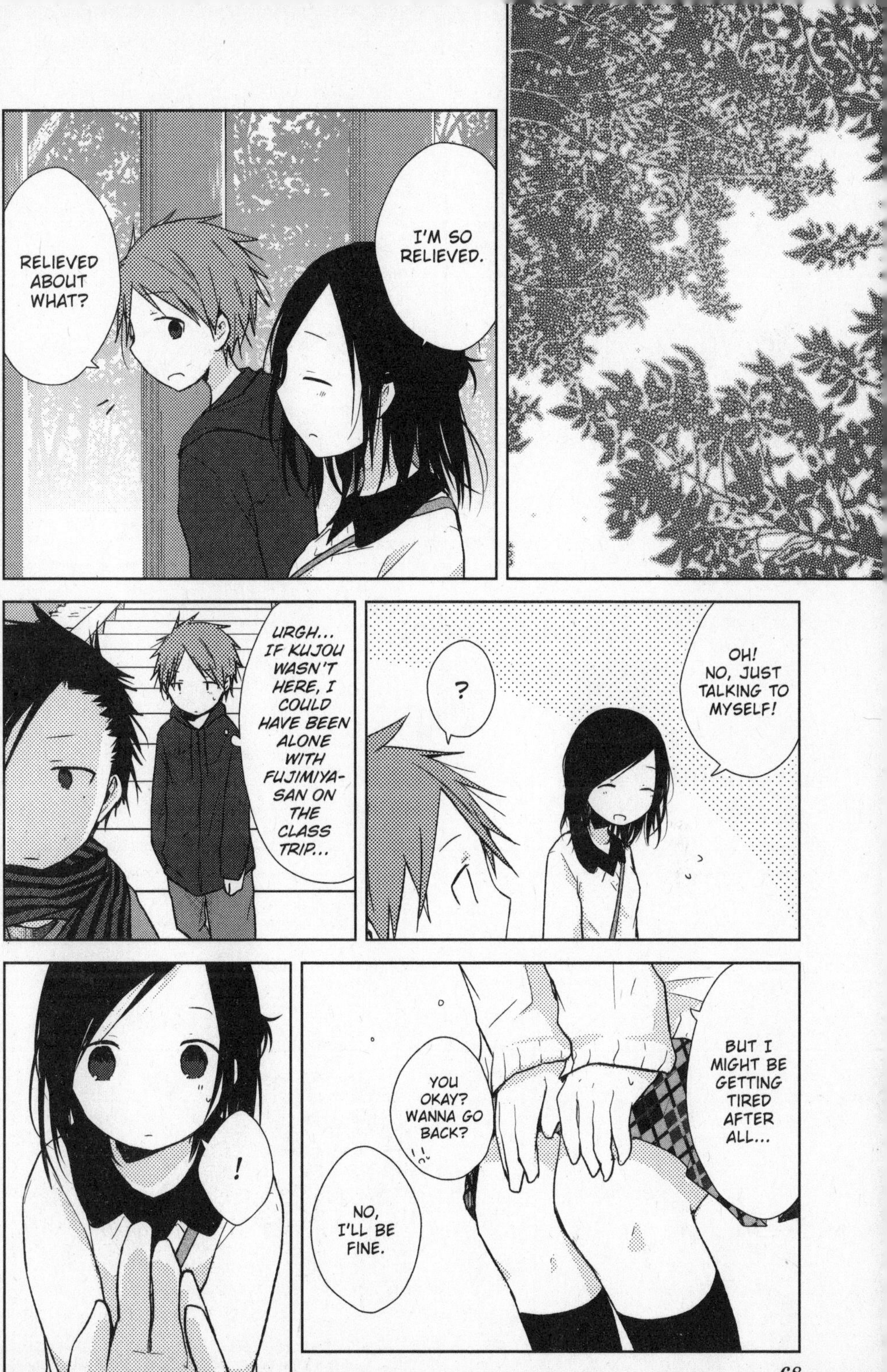
I'M SO RELIEVED.
RELIEVED ABOUT WHAT?
OH! NO, JUST TALKING TO MYSELF!
?
URGH... IF KUJOU WASN'T HERE, I COULD HAVE BEEN ALONE WITH FUJIMIYA-SAN ON THE CLASS TRIP...
BUT I MIGHT BE GETTING TIRED AFTER ALL...
YOU OKAY? WANNA GO BACK?
NO, I'LL BE FINE.
!

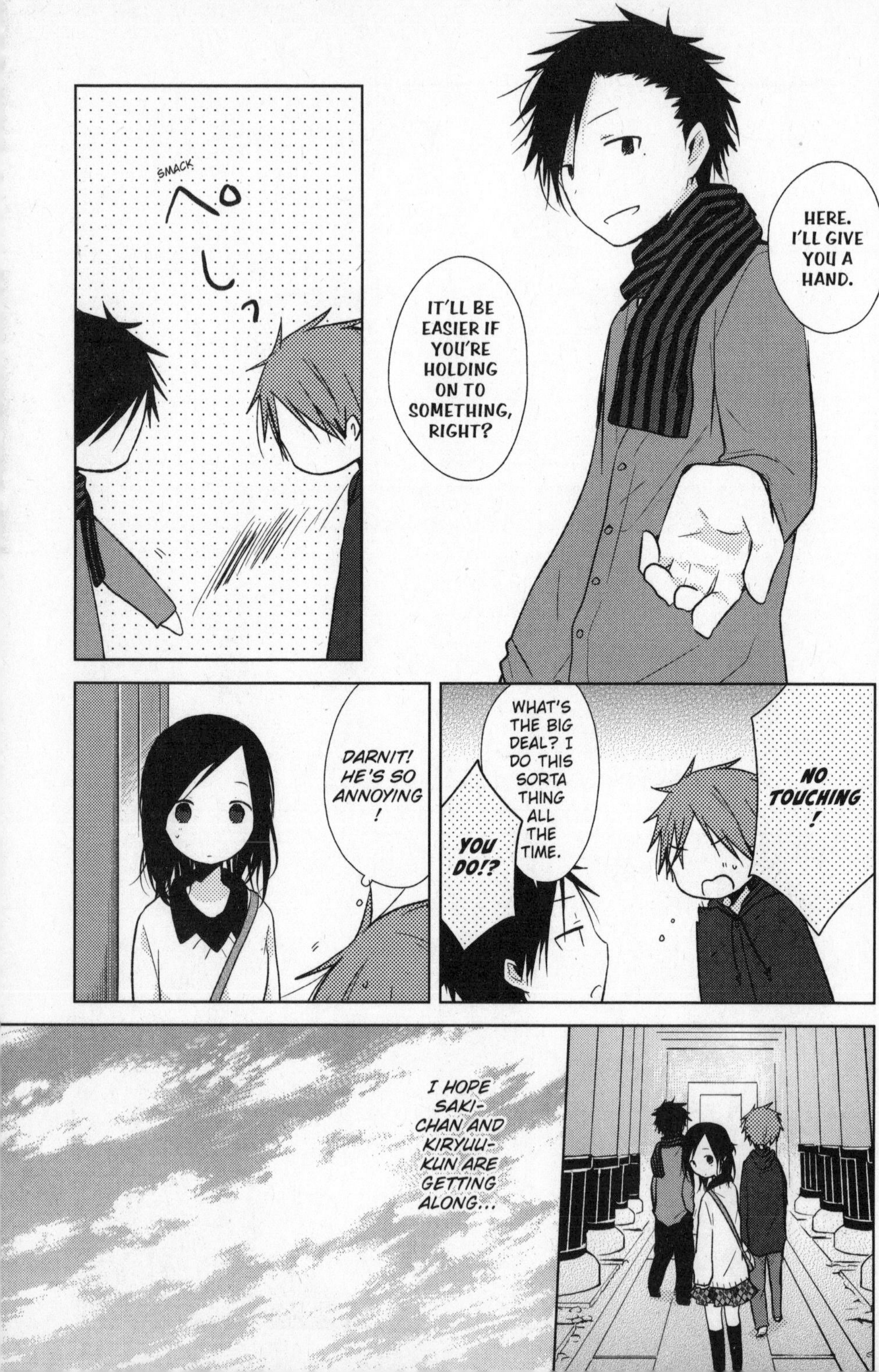
HERE. I'LL GIVE YOU A HAND.
IT'LL BE EASIER IF YOU'RE HOLDING ON TO SOMETHING, RIGHT?
SMACK
ぺしっ
NO TOUCHING!
WHAT'S THE BIG DEAL? I DO THIS SORTA THING ALL THE TIME.
YOU DO!?
DARNIT! HE'S SO ANNOYING!
I HOPE SAKI-CHAN AND KIRYUU-KUN ARE GETTING ALONG...

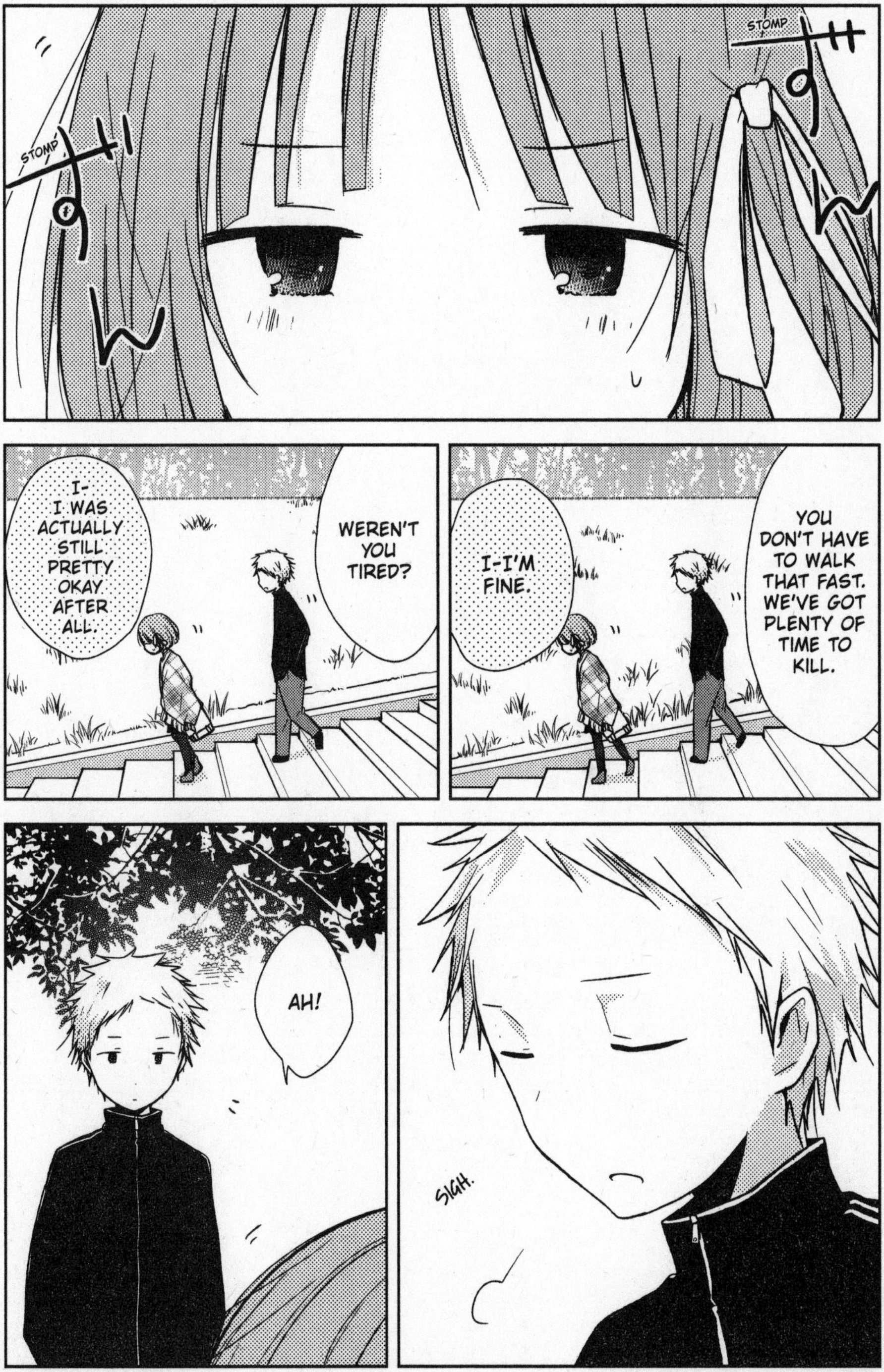
STOMP
STOMP
YOU DON'T HAVE TO WALK THAT FAST. WE'VE GOT PLENTY OF TIME TO KILL.
I-I'M FINE.
WEREN'T YOU TIRED?
I- I WAS ACTUALLY STILL PRETTY OKAY AFTER ALL.
SIGH.
AH!

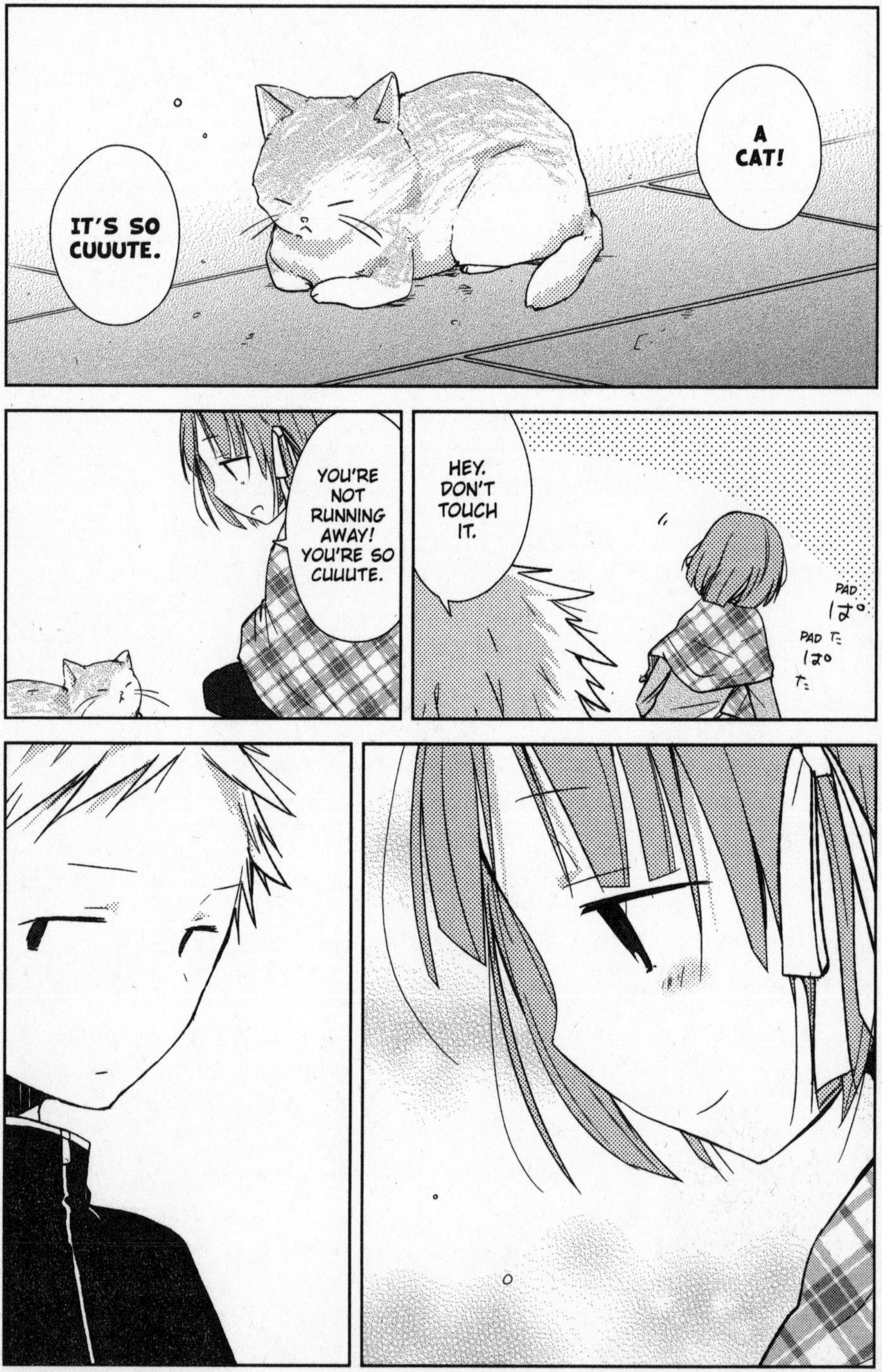
A CAT!
IT'S SO CUUUTE.
HEY. DON'T TOUCH IT.
PAD ぱた
PAD ぱた
YOU'RE NOT RUNNING AWAY! YOU'RE SO CUUUTE.

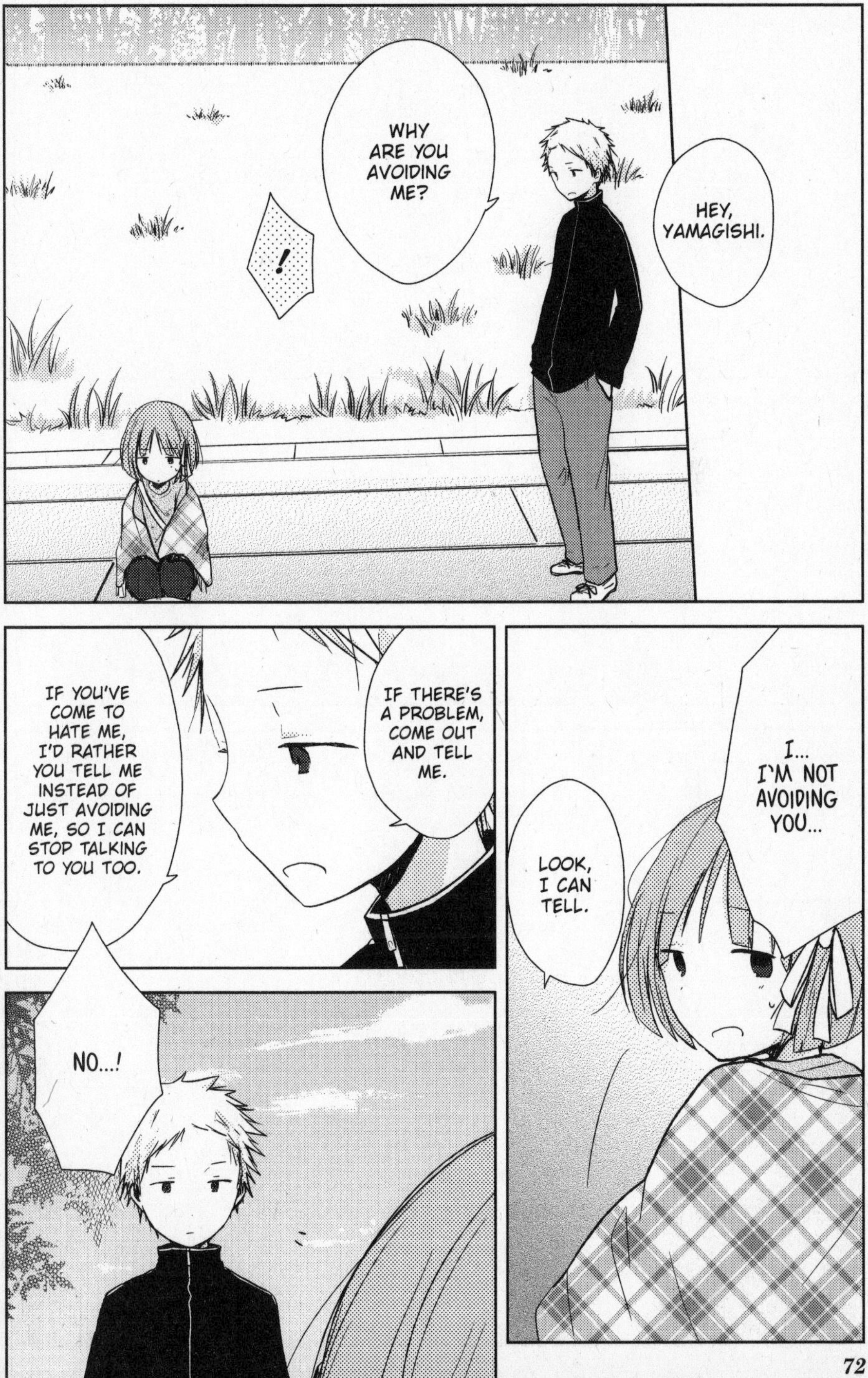
HEY, YAMAGISHI.
WHY ARE YOU AVOIDING ME?
!
I... I'M NOT AVOIDING YOU...
LOOK, I CAN TELL.
IF THERE'S A PROBLEM, COME OUT AND TELL ME.
IF YOU'VE COME TO HATE ME, I'D RATHER YOU TELL ME INSTEAD OF JUST AVOIDING ME, SO I CAN STOP TALKING TO YOU TOO.
NO...!

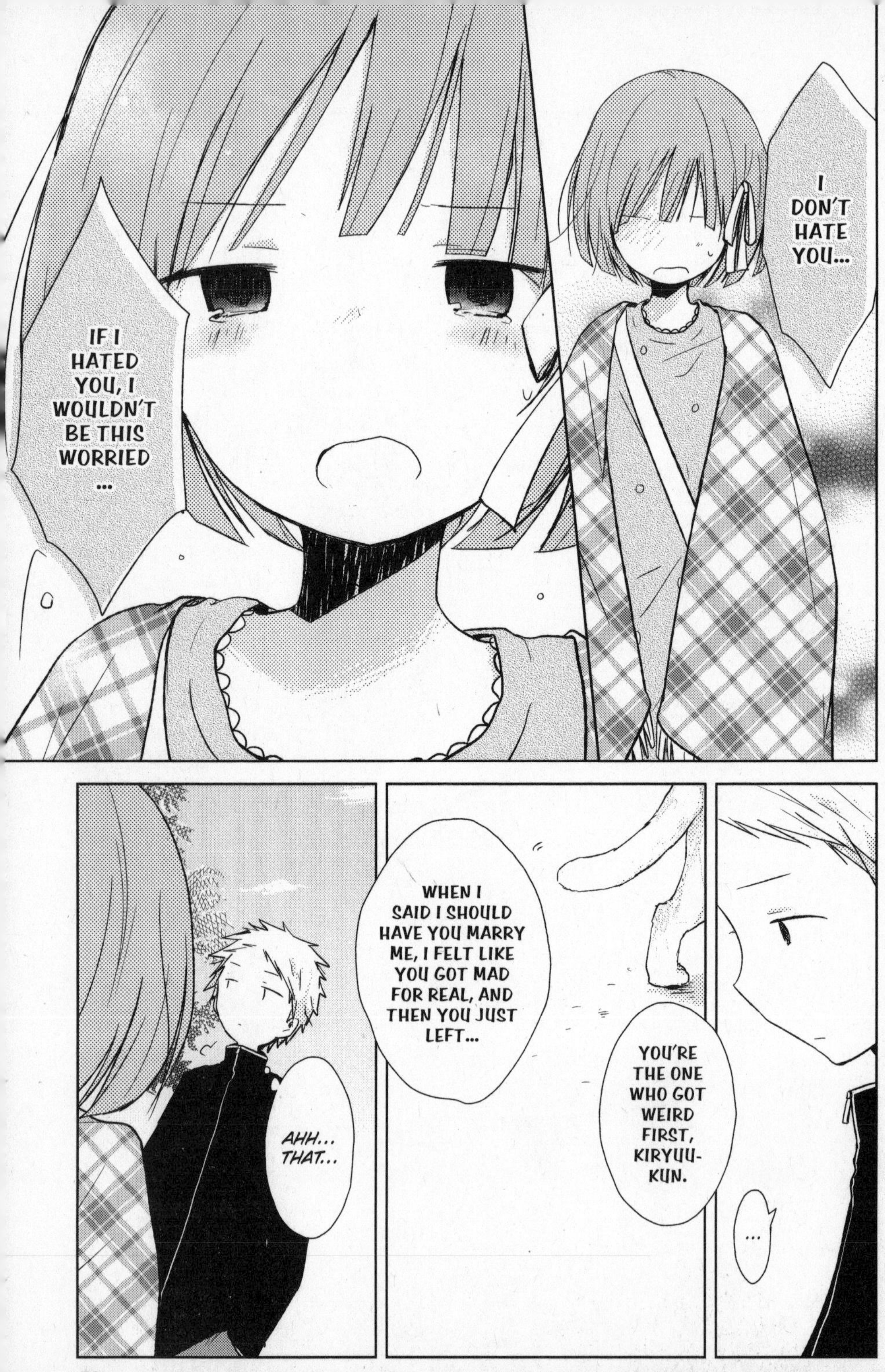
I DON'T HATE YOU...
IF I HATED YOU, I WOULDN'T BE THIS WORRIED ...
...
WHEN I SAID I SHOULD HAVE YOU MARRY ME, I FELT LIKE YOU GOT MAD FOR REAL, AND THEN YOU JUST LEFT...
YOU'RE THE ONE WHO GOT WEIRD FIRST, KIRYUU-KUN.
AHH... THAT...

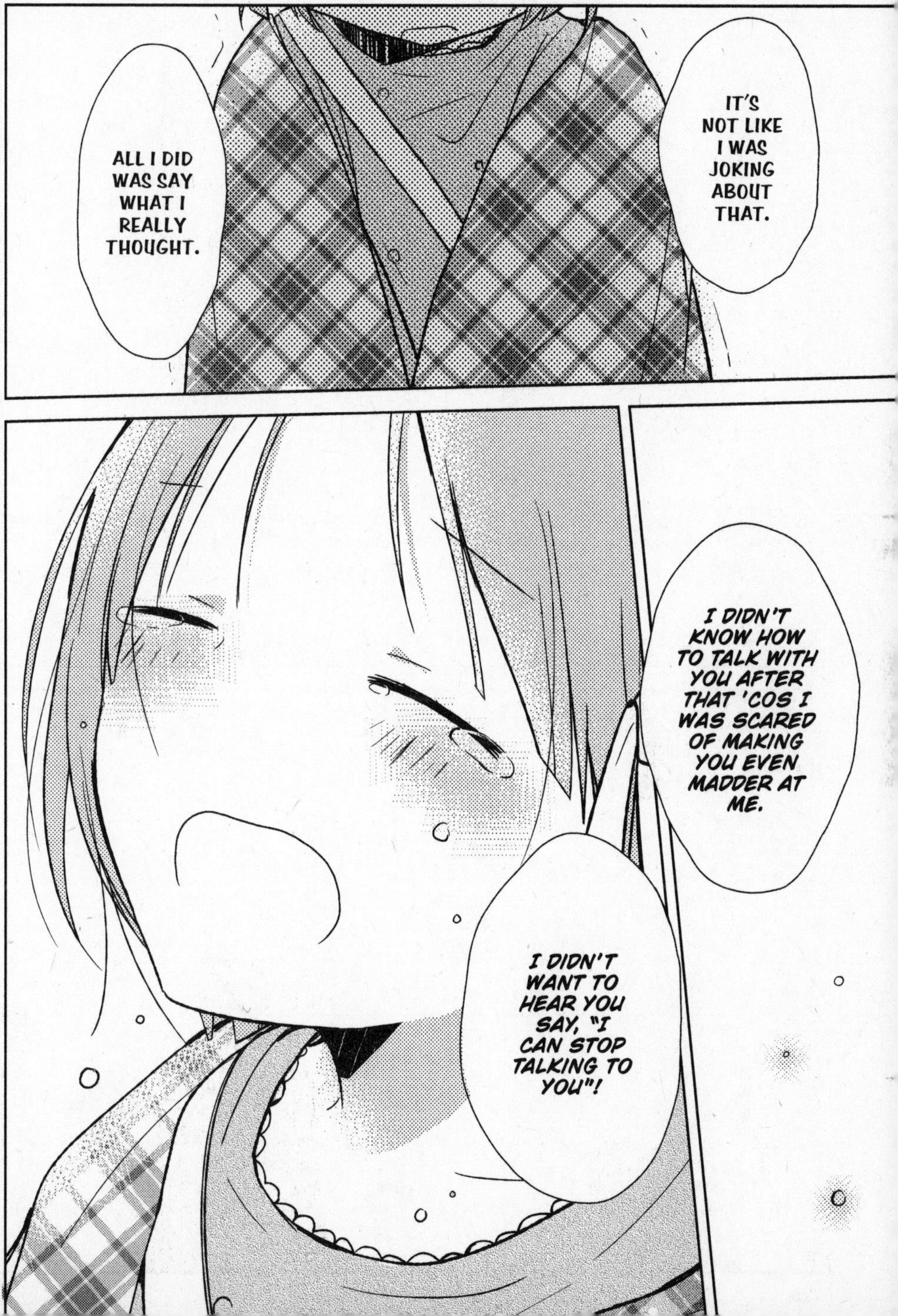
IT'S NOT LIKE I WAS JOKING ABOUT THAT.
ALL I DID WAS SAY WHAT I REALLY THOUGHT.
I DIDN'T KNOW HOW TO TALK WITH YOU AFTER THAT 'COS I WAS SCARED OF MAKING YOU EVEN MADDER AT ME.
I DIDN'T WANT TO HEAR YOU SAY, "I CAN STOP TALKING TO YOU"!

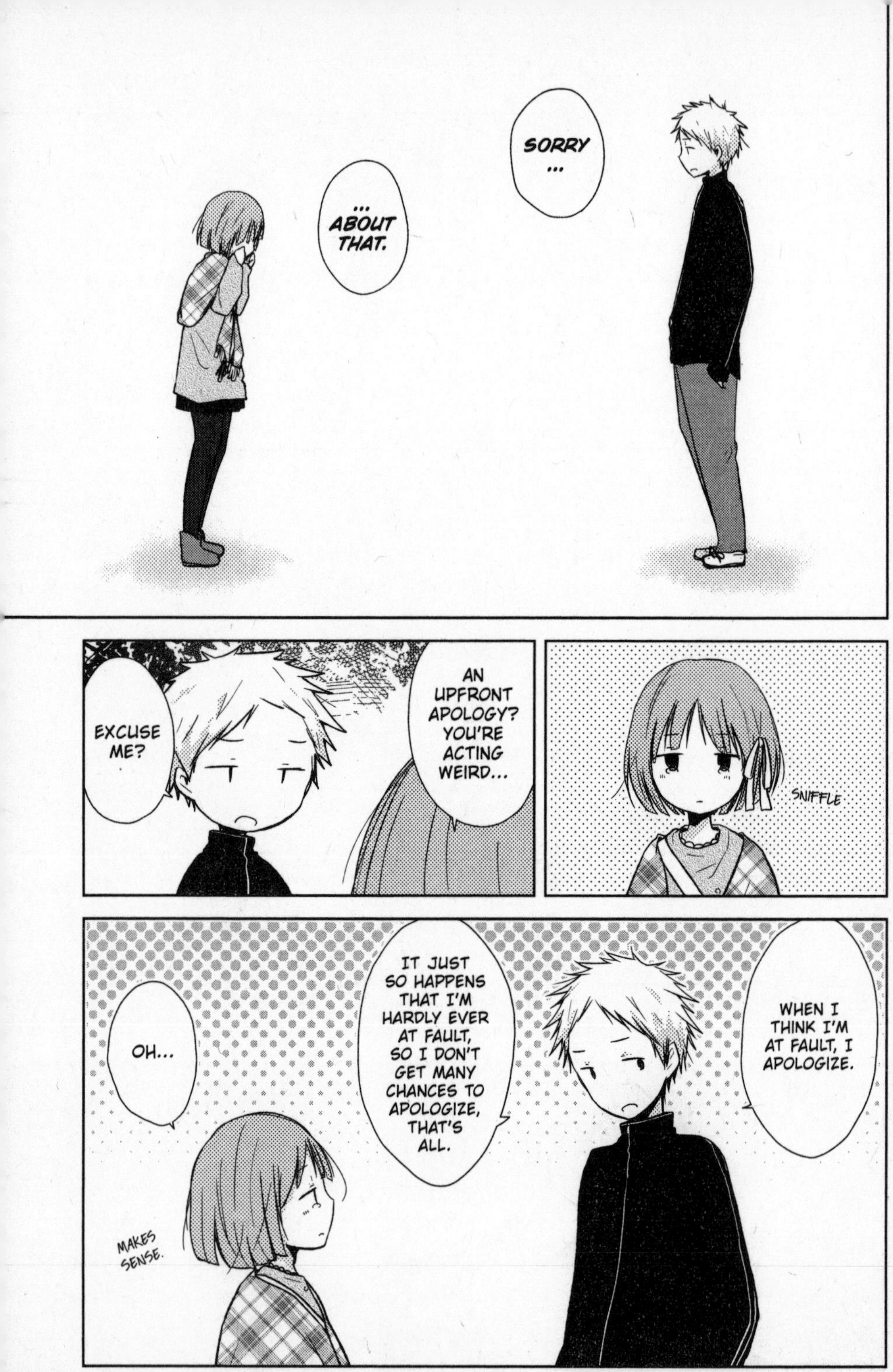
SORRY ...
... ABOUT THAT.
SNIFFLE
AN UPFRONT APOLOGY? YOU'RE ACTING WEIRD...
EXCUSE ME?
WHEN I THINK I'M AT FAULT, I APOLOGIZE.
IT JUST SO HAPPENS THAT I'M HARDLY EVER AT FAULT, SO I DON'T GET MANY CHANCES TO APOLOGIZE, THAT'S ALL.
OH...
MAKES SENSE.

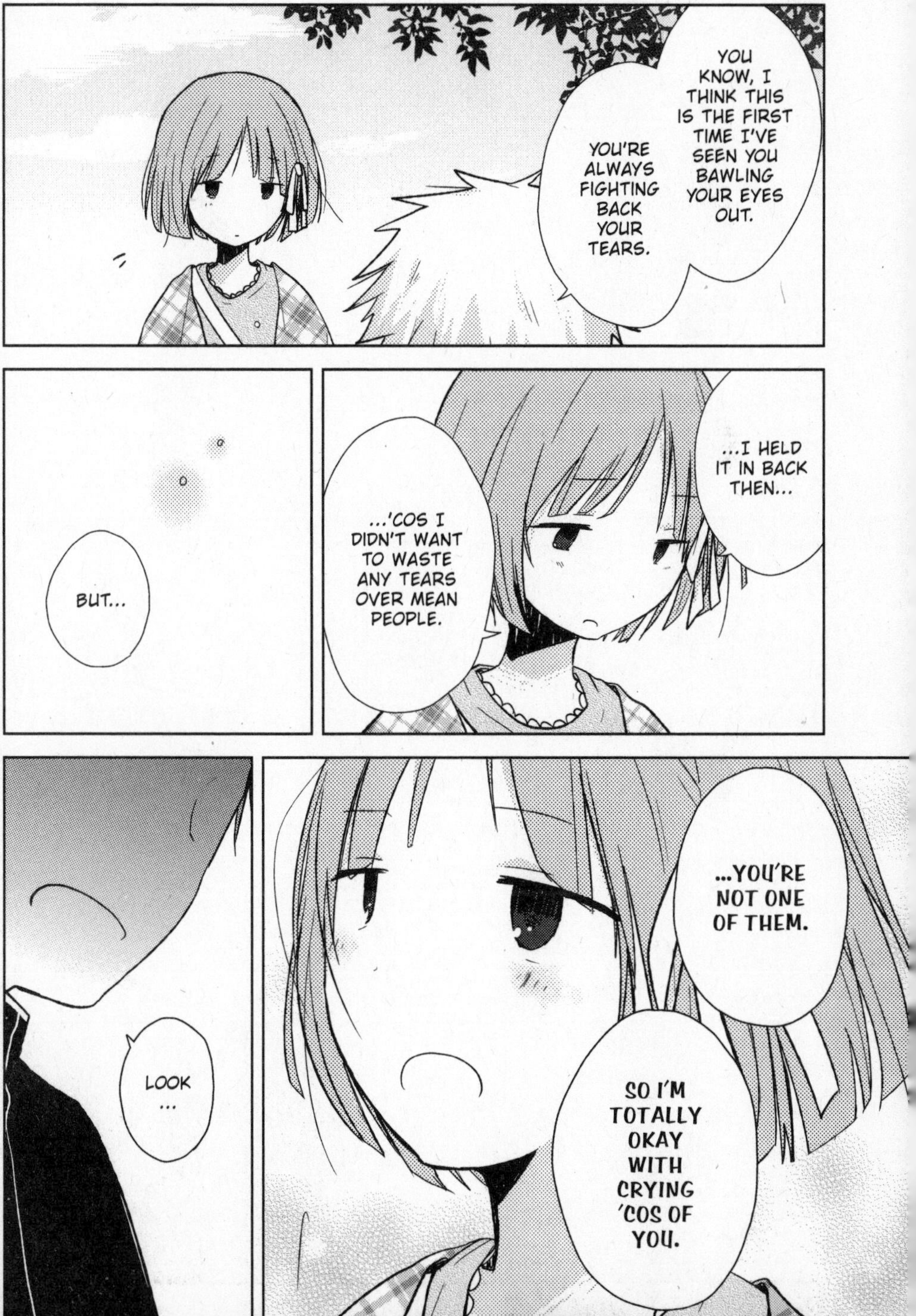
YOU KNOW, I THINK THIS IS THE FIRST TIME I'VE SEEN YOU BAWLING YOUR EYES OUT.
YOU'RE ALWAYS FIGHTING BACK YOUR TEARS.
...I HELD IT IN BACK THEN...
...'COS I DIDN'T WANT TO WASTE ANY TEARS OVER MEAN PEOPLE.
BUT...
...YOU'RE NOT ONE OF THEM.
SO I'M TOTALLY OKAY WITH CRYING 'COS OF YOU.
LOOK ...

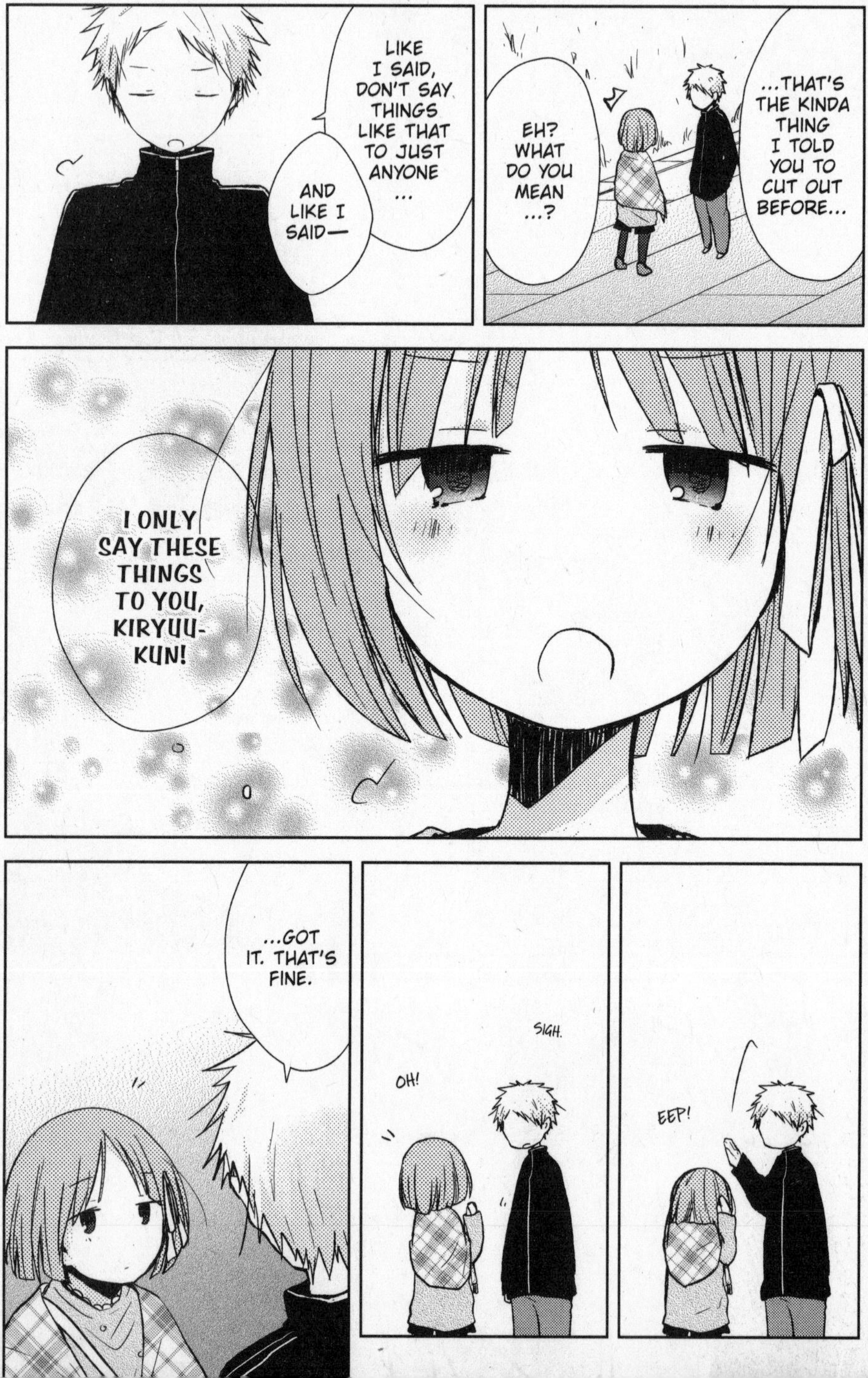
...THAT'S THE KINDA THING I TOLD YOU TO CUT OUT BEFORE...
EH? WHAT DO YOU MEAN ...?
LIKE I SAID, DON'T SAY THINGS LIKE THAT TO JUST ANYONE ...
AND LIKE I SAID—
I ONLY SAY THESE THINGS TO YOU, KIRYUU-KUN!
EEP!
SIGH.
OH!
...GOT IT. THAT'S FINE.

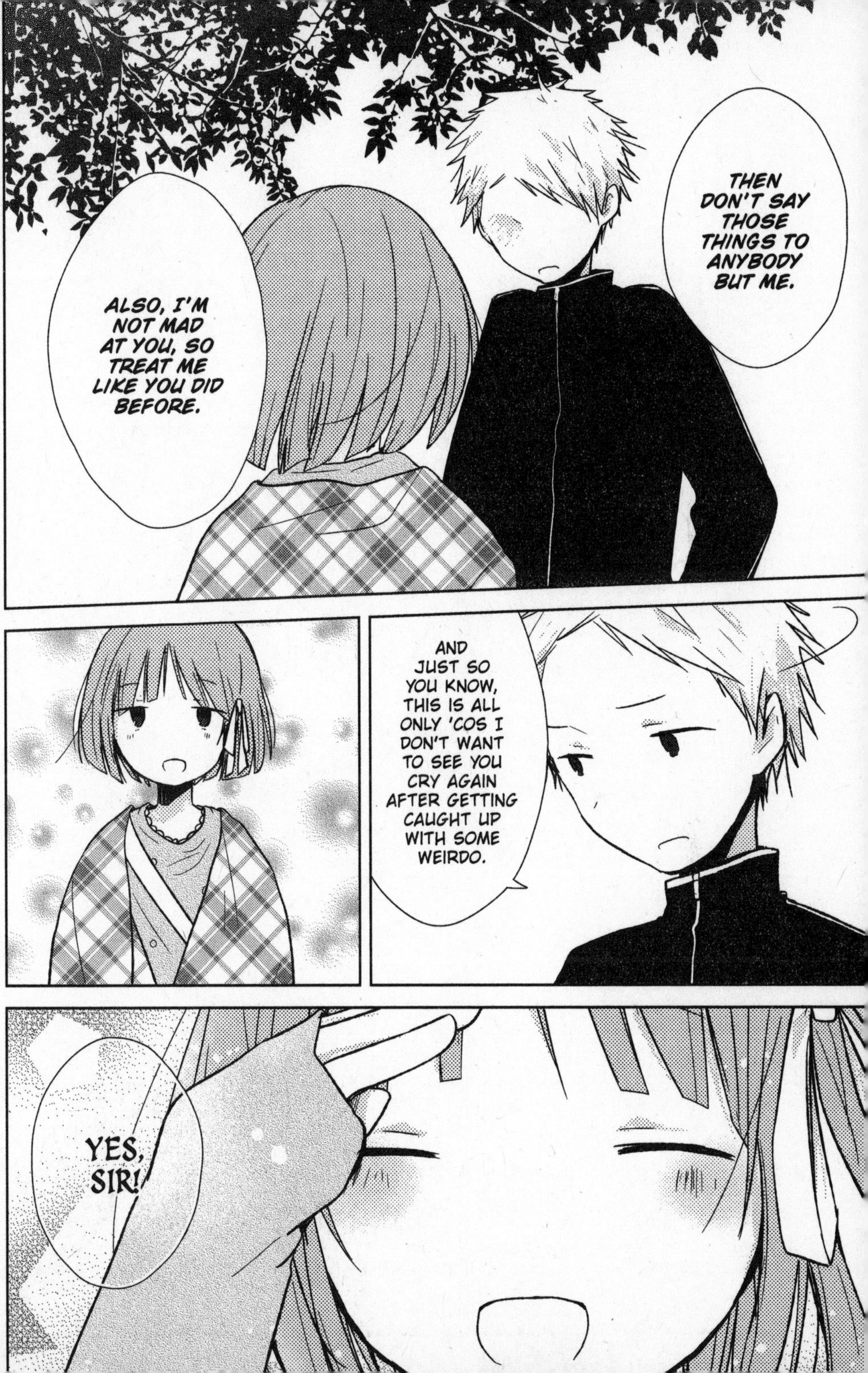
THEN DON'T SAY THOSE THINGS TO ANYBODY BUT ME.
ALSO, I'M NOT MAD AT YOU, SO TREAT ME LIKE YOU DID BEFORE.
AND JUST SO YOU KNOW, THIS IS ALL ONLY 'COS I DON'T WANT TO SEE YOU CRY AGAIN AFTER GETTING CAUGHT UP WITH SOME WEIRDO.
YES, SIR!

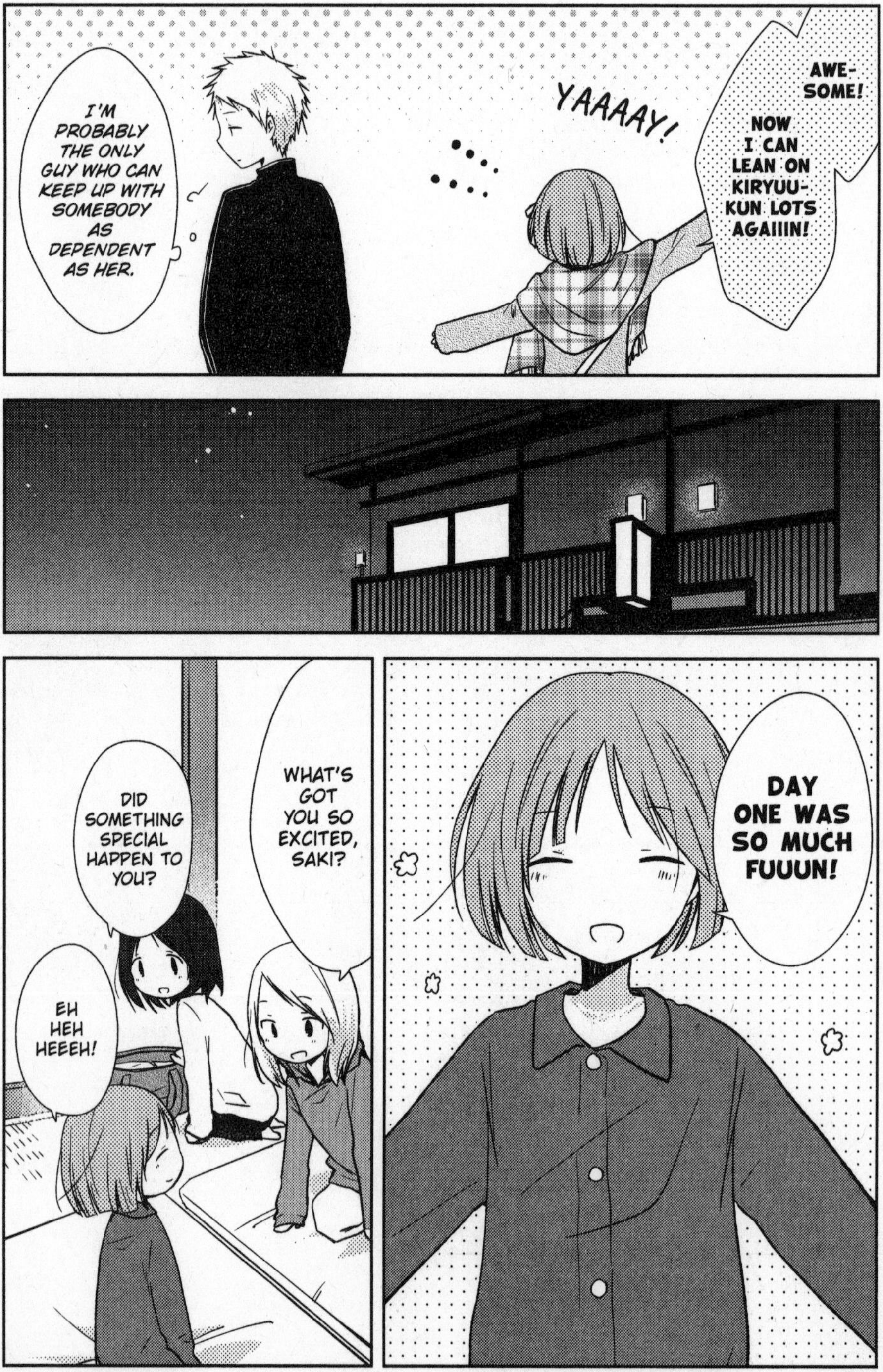
AWE-SOME! NOW I CAN LEAN ON KIRYUU-KUN LOTS AGAIIIN!
YAAAAY!
...
I'M PROBABLY THE ONLY GUY WHO CAN KEEP UP WITH SOMEBODY AS DEPENDENT AS HER.
DAY ONE WAS SO MUCH FUUUN!
WHAT'S GOT YOU SO EXCITED, SAKI?
DID SOMETHING SPECIAL HAPPEN TO YOU?
EH HEH HEEEH!

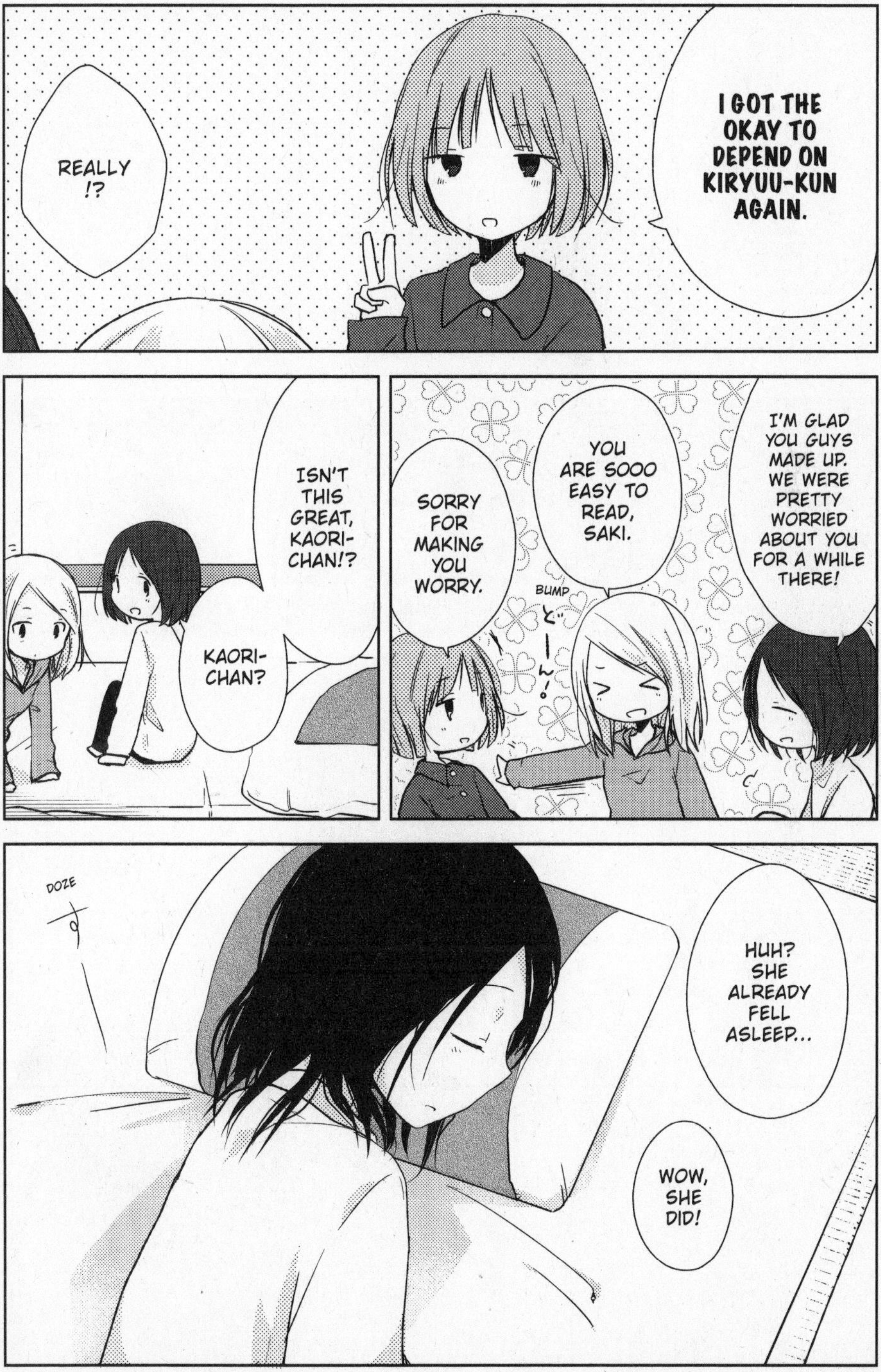
I GOT THE OKAY TO DEPEND ON KIRYUU-KUN AGAIN.
REALLY !?
I'M GLAD YOU GUYS MADE UP. WE WERE PRETTY WORRIED ABOUT YOU FOR A WHILE THERE!
YOU ARE SOOO EASY TO READ, SAKI.
BUMP
SORRY FOR MAKING YOU WORRY.
ISN'T THIS GREAT, KAORI-CHAN!?
KAORI-CHAN?
HUH? SHE ALREADY FELL ASLEEP...
WOW, SHE DID!
DOZE

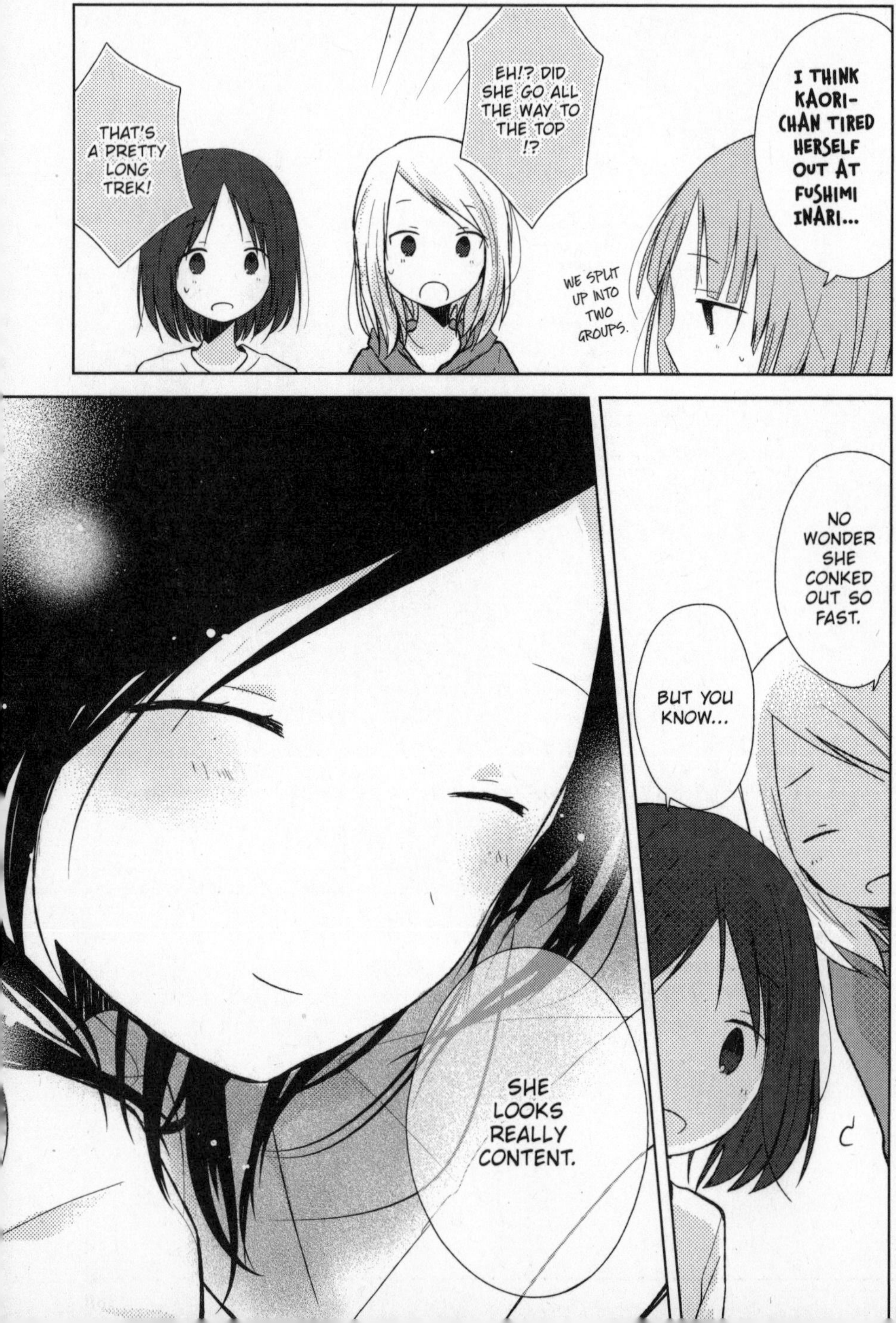
I THINK KAORI-CHAN TIRED HERSELF OUT AT FUSHIMI INARI...
WE SPLIT UP INTO TWO GROUPS.
EH!? DID SHE GO ALL THE WAY TO THE TOP !?
THAT'S A PRETTY LONG TREK!
NO WONDER SHE CONKED OUT SO FAST.
BUT YOU KNOW...
SHE LOOKS REALLY CONTENT.

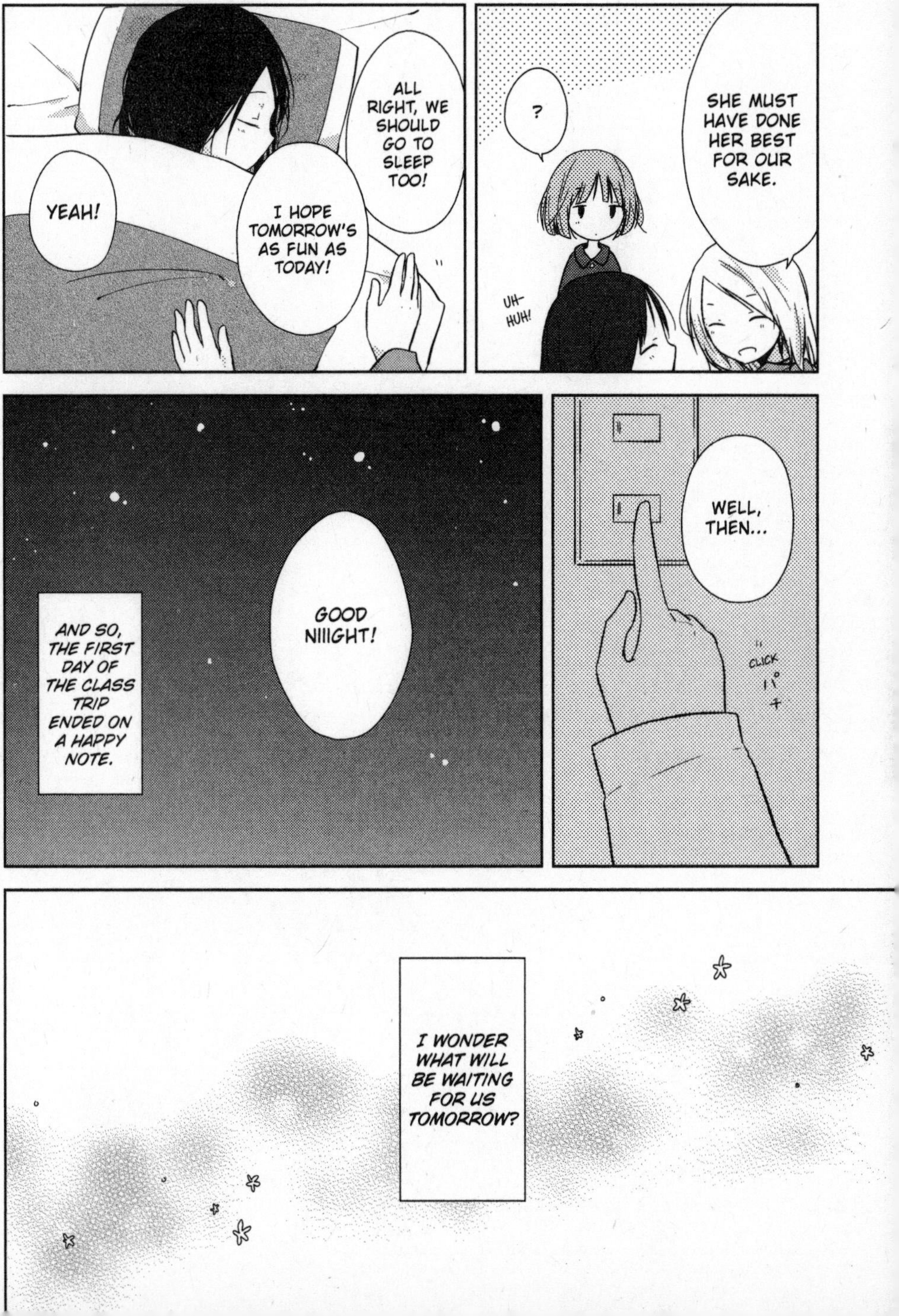
SHE MUST HAVE DONE HER BEST FOR OUR SAKE.
?
UH-HUH!
ALL RIGHT, WE SHOULD GO TO SLEEP TOO!
I HOPE TOMORROW'S AS FUN AS TODAY!
YEAH!
WELL, THEN...
CLICK
パチ
GOOD NIIIGHT!
AND SO, THE FIRST DAY OF THE CLASS TRIP ENDED ON A HAPPY NOTE.
I WONDER WHAT WILL BE WAITING FOR US TOMORROW?

EEP!
SIGH.
OH!

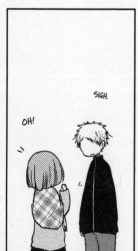

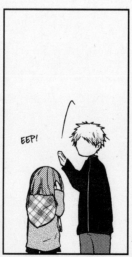

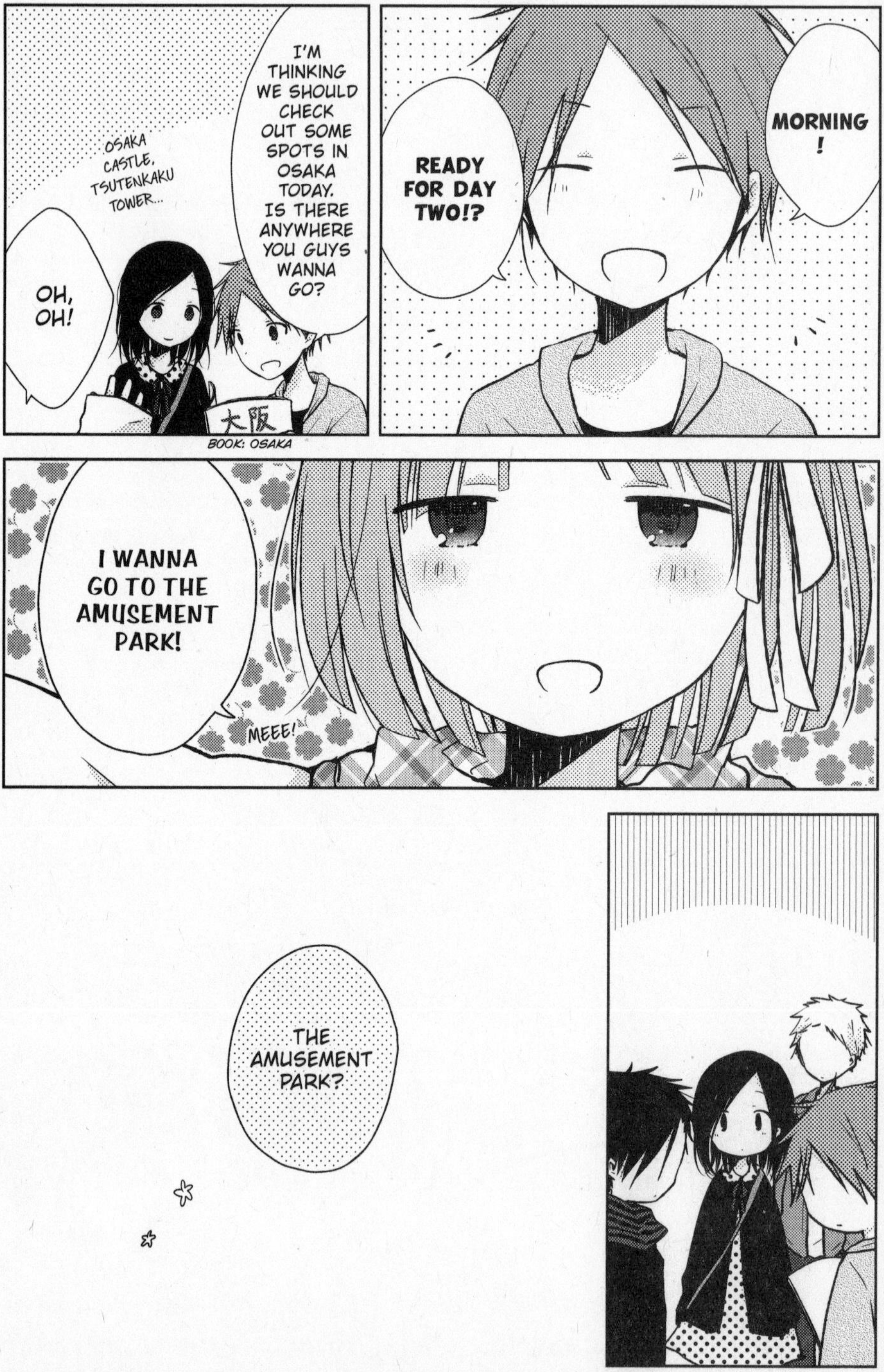
MORNING!
READY FOR DAY TWO!?
I'M THINKING WE SHOULD CHECK OUT SOME SPOTS IN OSAKA TODAY. IS THERE ANYWHERE YOU GUYS WANNA GO?
OSAKA CASTLE, TSUTENKAKU TOWER...
OH, OH!
大阪
BOOK: OSAKA
I WANNA GO TO THE AMUSEMENT PARK!
MEEE!
THE AMUSEMENT PARK?

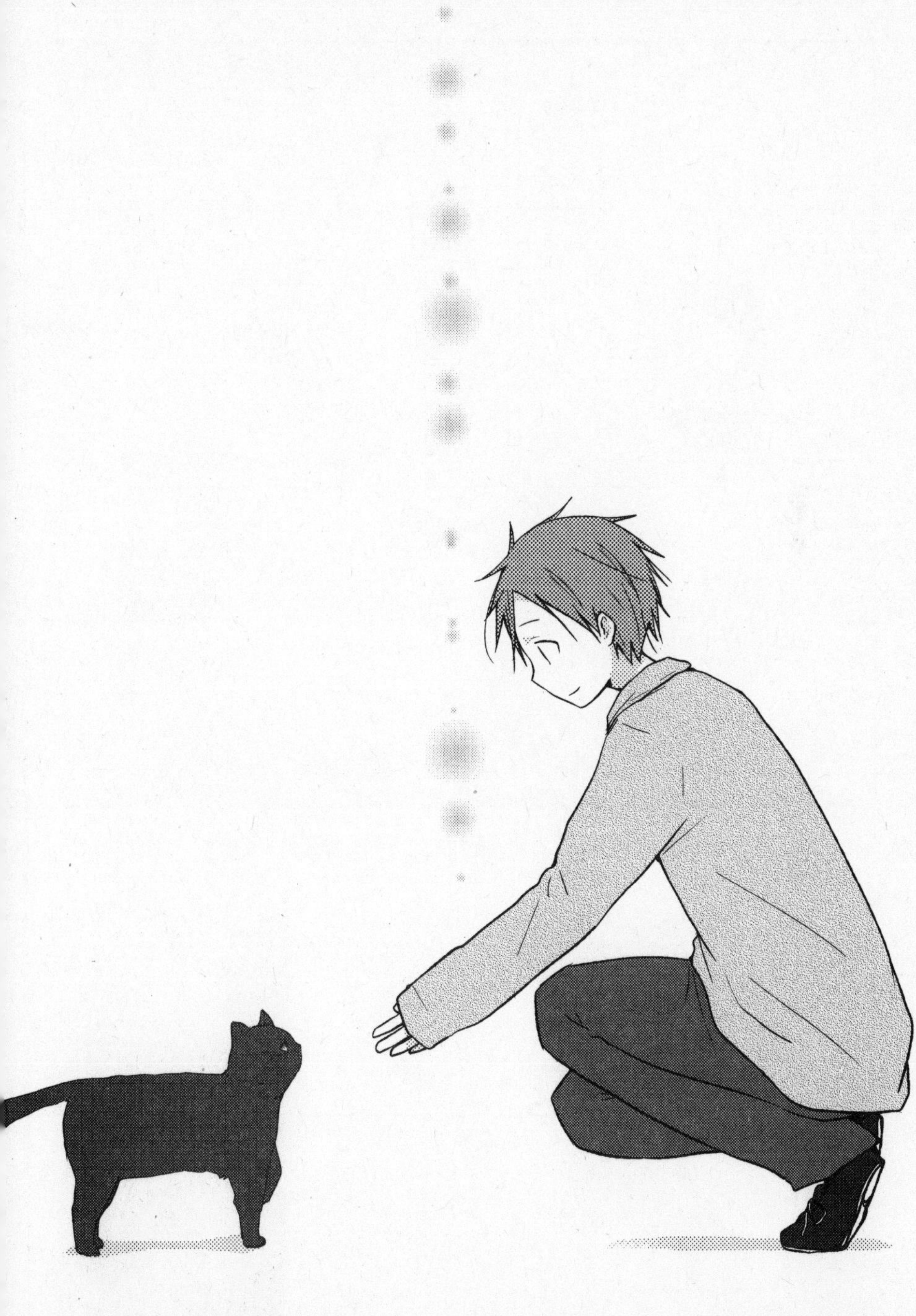

CHAPTER 25 WHAT ARE WE GOING TO BE ANYWAY?

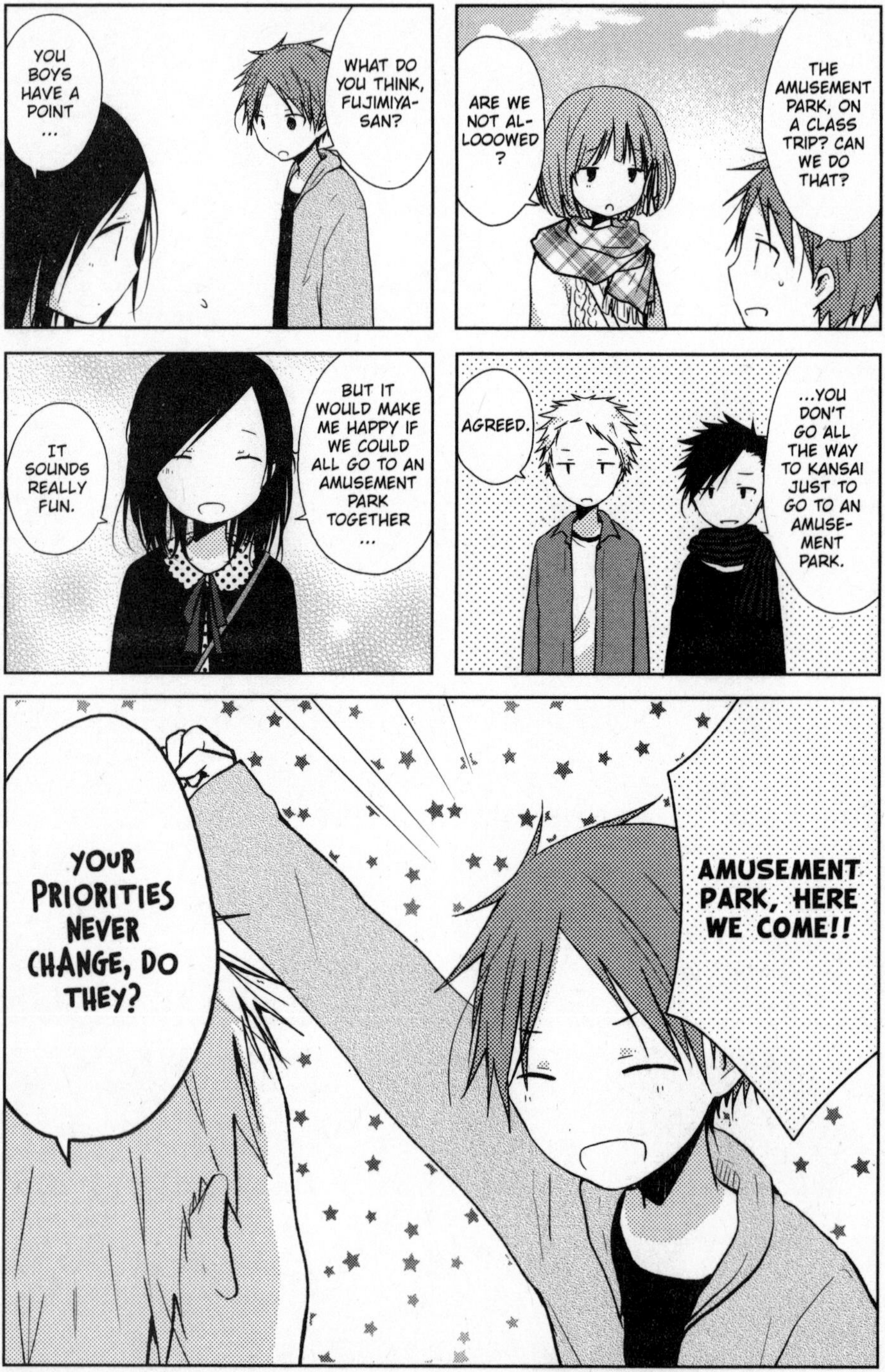
THE AMUSEMENT PARK, ON A CLASS TRIP? CAN WE DO THAT?
ARE WE NOT AL-LOOOWED?
WHAT DO YOU THINK, FUJIMIYA-SAN?
YOU BOYS HAVE A POINT ...
...YOU DON'T GO ALL THE WAY TO KANSAI JUST TO GO TO AN AMUSE-MENT PARK.
AGREED.
BUT IT WOULD MAKE ME HAPPY IF WE COULD ALL GO TO AN AMUSEMENT PARK TOGETHER ...
IT SOUNDS REALLY FUN.
AMUSEMENT PARK, HERE WE COME!!
YOUR PRIORITIES NEVER CHANGE, DO THEY?

LONGING

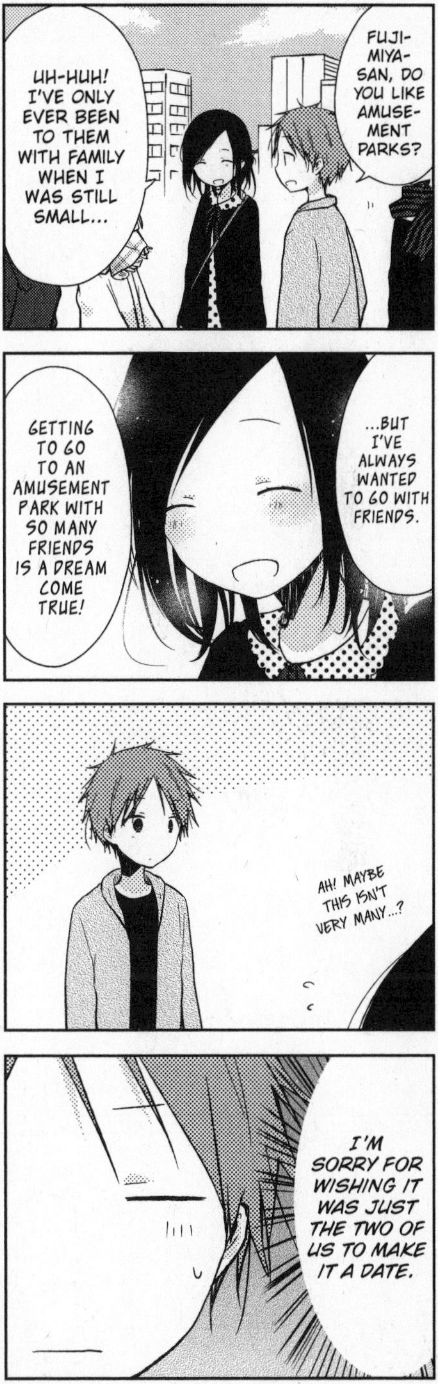
FUJI-MIYA-SAN, DO YOU LIKE AMUSEMENT PARKS?
UH-HUH! I'VE ONLY EVER BEEN TO THEM WITH FAMILY WHEN I WAS STILL SMALL...
...BUT I'VE ALWAYS WANTED TO GO WITH FRIENDS.
GETTING TO GO TO AN AMUSEMENT PARK WITH SO MANY FRIENDS IS A DREAM COME TRUE!
AH! MAYBE THIS ISN'T VERY MANY...?
I'M SORRY FOR WISHING IT WAS JUST THE TWO OF US TO MAKE IT A DATE.

GROUP SIZE

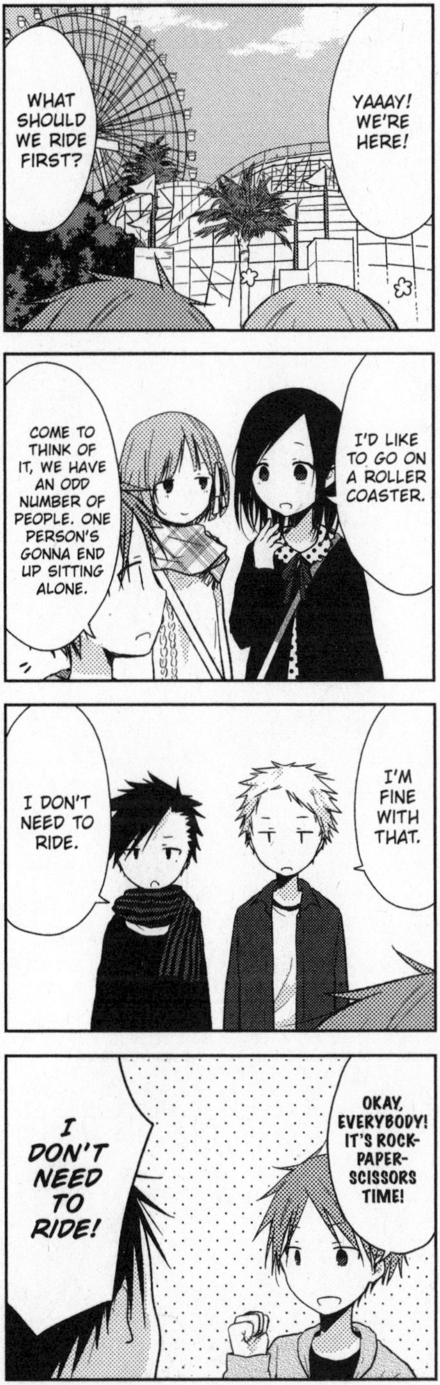
YAAAY! WE'RE HERE!
WHAT SHOULD WE RIDE FIRST?
I'D LIKE TO GO ON A ROLLER COASTER.
COME TO THINK OF IT, WE HAVE AN ODD NUMBER OF PEOPLE. ONE PERSON'S GONNA END UP SITTING ALONE.
I'M FINE WITH THAT.
I DON'T NEED TO RIDE.
OKAY, EVERYBODY! IT'S ROCK-PAPER-SCISSORS TIME!
I DON'T NEED TO RIDE!

ROLLER COASTER

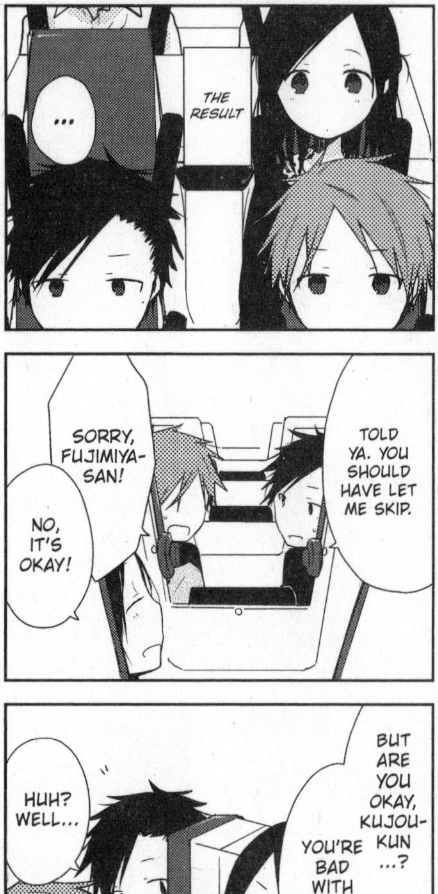
THE RESULT
...
TOLD YA. YOU SHOULD HAVE LET ME SKIP.
SORRY, FUJIMIYA-SAN!
NO, IT'S OKAY!
BUT ARE YOU OKAY, KUJOU-KUN ...?
YOU'RE BAD WITH HEIGHTS, RIGHT ...?
HUH? WELL...
IT'S NOT LIKE I CAN'T HANDLE ANY HEIGHTS AT ALL. I'M COOL.
DON'T PUSH YOURSELF, OKAY?
THIS ISN'T MUCH FUN SOMEHOW ...

JERK

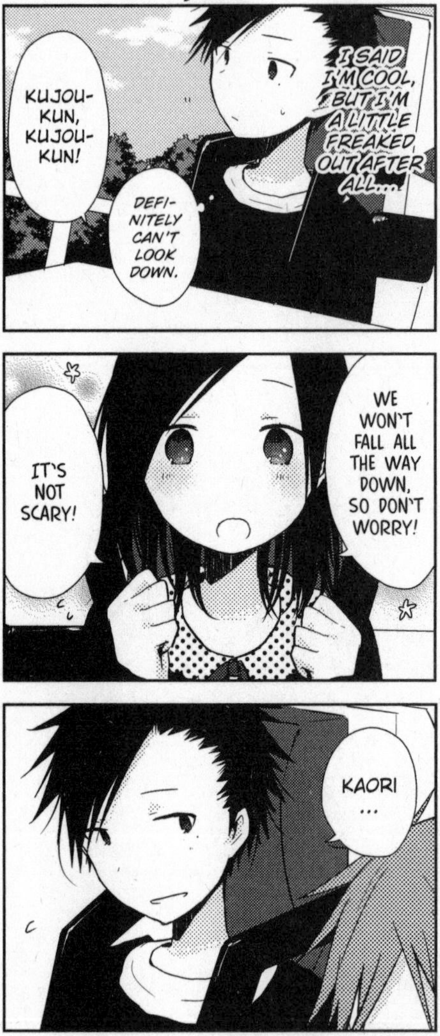
I SAID I'M COOL, BUT I'M A LITTLE FREAKED OUT AFTER ALL...
KUJOU-KUN, KUJOU-KUN!
DEFINITELY CAN'T LOOK DOWN.
WE WON'T FALL ALL THE WAY DOWN, SO DON'T WORRY!
IT'S NOT SCARY!
KAORI ...
WE'RE SO GONNA FALL.
DUDE, YOU'RE A JERK.

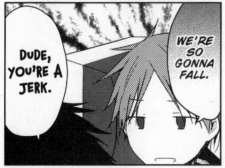

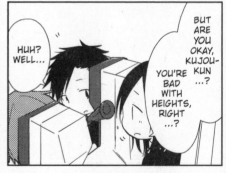

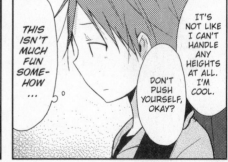

PEER PRESSURE

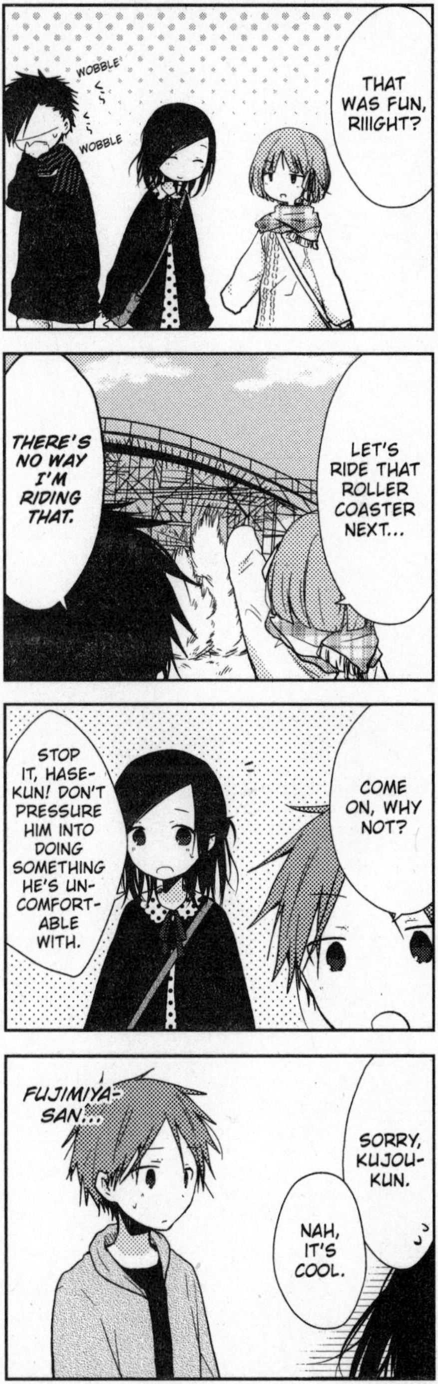
THAT WAS FUN, RIIIGHT?
WOBBLE
WOBBLE
LET'S RIDE THAT ROLLER COASTER NEXT...
THERE'S NO WAY I'M RIDING THAT.
COME ON, WHY NOT?
STOP IT, HASE-KUN! DON'T PRESSURE HIM INTO DOING SOMETHING HE'S UN-COMFORT-ABLE WITH.
SORRY, KUJOU-KUN.
NAH, IT'S COOL.
FUJIMIYA-SAN...

EVERYBODY

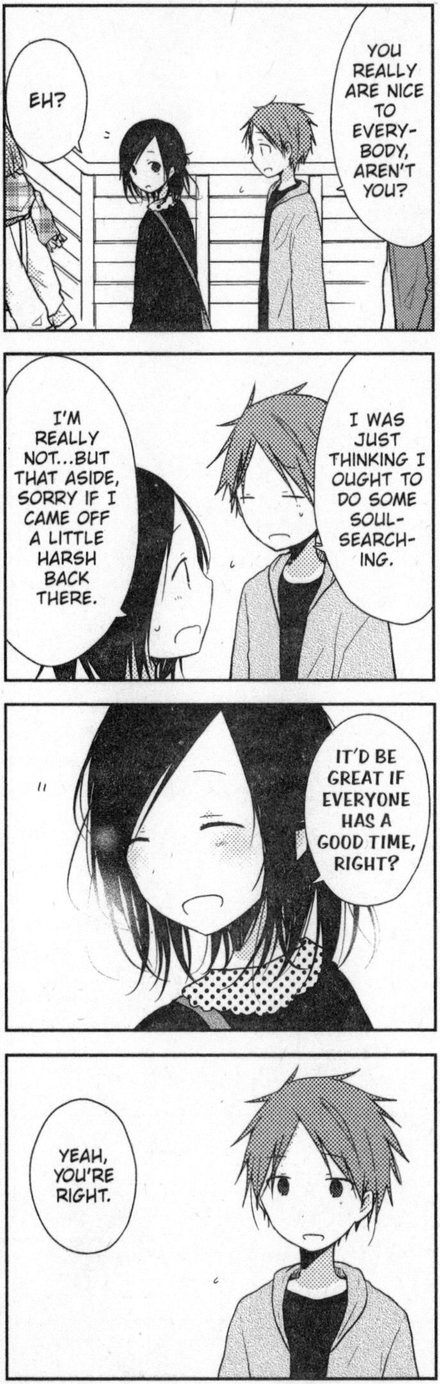
YOU REALLY ARE NICE TO EVERY-BODY, AREN'T YOU?
EH?
I WAS JUST THINKING I OUGHT TO DO SOME SOUL-SEARCH-ING.
I'M REALLY NOT...BUT THAT ASIDE, SORRY IF I CAME OFF A LITTLE HARSH BACK THERE.
IT'D BE GREAT IF EVERYONE HAS A GOOD TIME, RIGHT?
YEAH, YOU'RE RIGHT.

BROODING

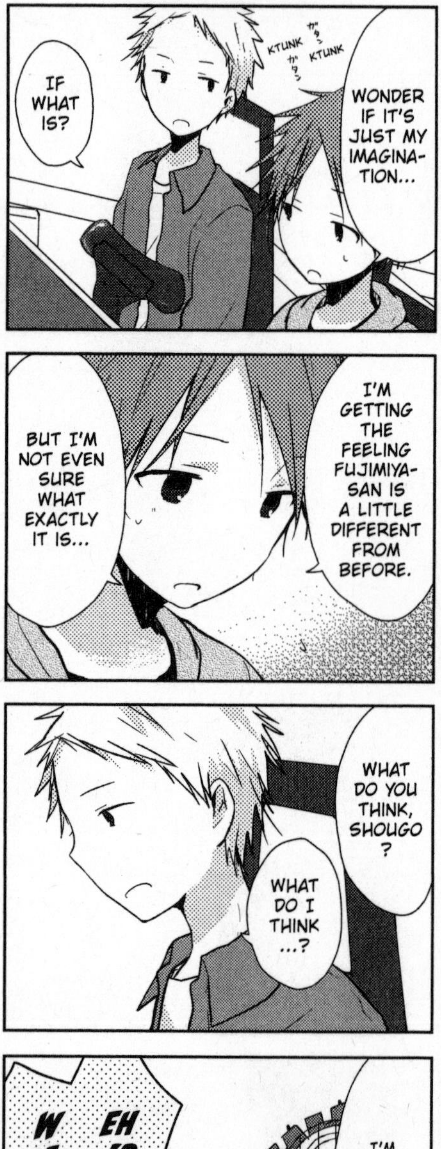
WONDER IF IT'S JUST MY IMAGINATION...
KTUNK KTUNK
IF WHAT IS?
I'M GETTING THE FEELING FUJIMIYA-SAN IS A LITTLE DIFFERENT FROM BEFORE.
BUT I'M NOT EVEN SURE WHAT EXACTLY IT IS...
WHAT DO YOU THINK, SHOUGO?
WHAT DO I THINK ...?
I'M THINKING WE'RE ABOUT TO DROP.
EH!?
WAAAAAH!

HE'S THE SAME AS ALWAYS TOO

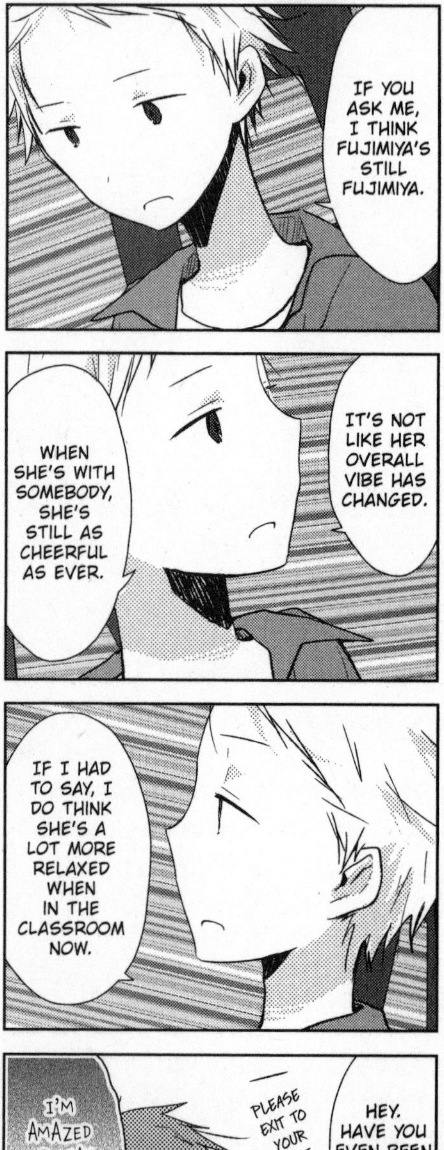
IF YOU ASK ME, I THINK FUJIMIYA'S STILL FUJIMIYA.
IT'S NOT LIKE HER OVERALL VIBE HAS CHANGED.
WHEN SHE'S WITH SOMEBODY, SHE'S STILL AS CHEERFUL AS EVER.
IF I HAD TO SAY, I DO THINK SHE'S A LOT MORE RELAXED WHEN IN THE CLASSROOM NOW.
HEY. HAVE YOU EVEN BEEN LISTENING?
PLEASE EXIT TO YOUR LEFT.
I'M AMAZED YOU CAN TALK SO CALMLY EVEN WHILE FALLING.
I COULDN'T HEAR YOU!

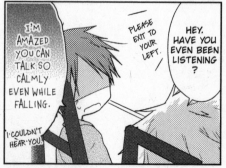

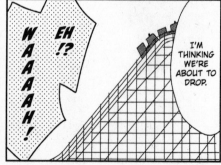

DANGEROUS TEACUPS

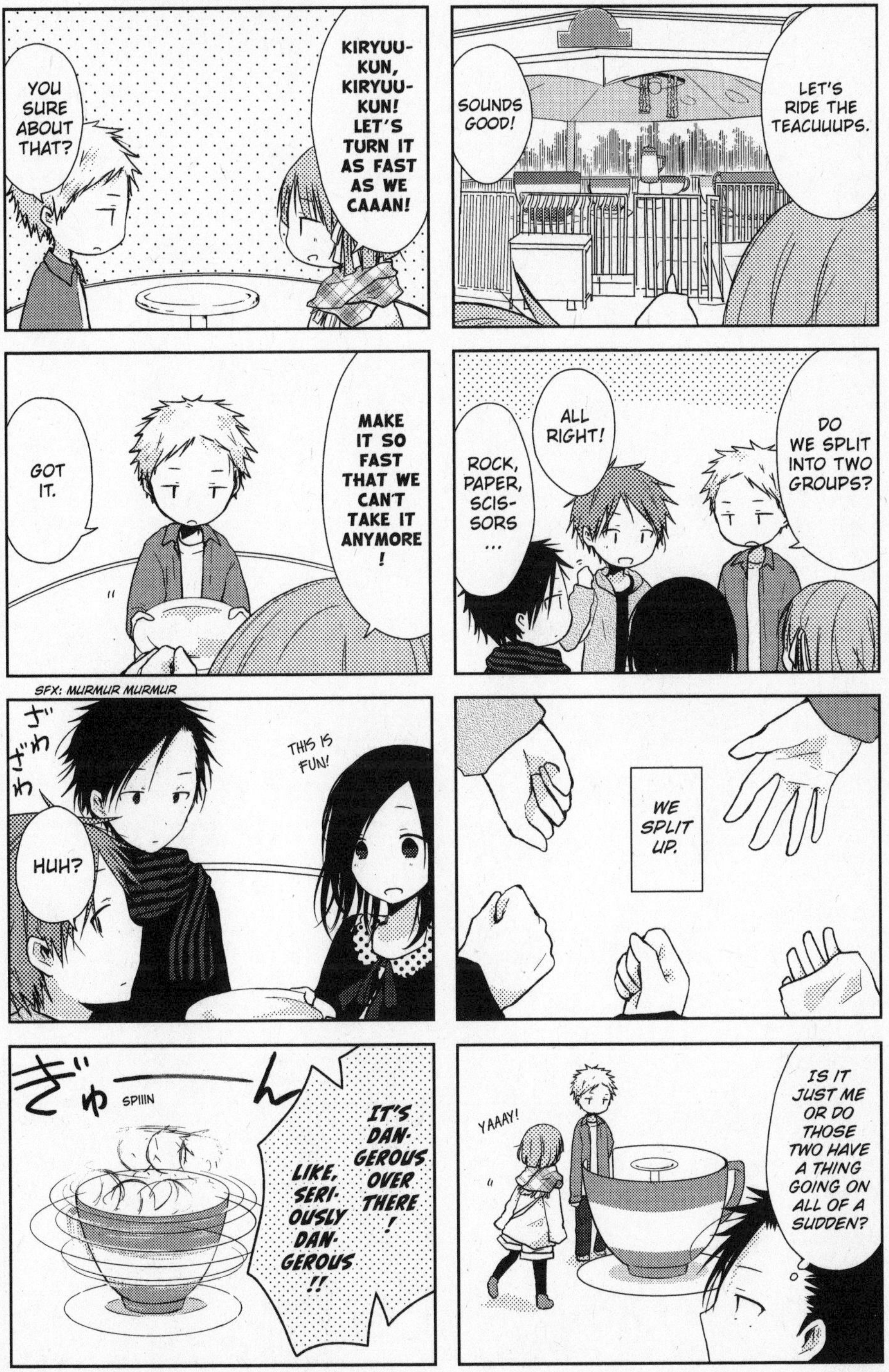

LET'S RIDE THE TEACUUUPS.
SOUNDS GOOD!
DO WE SPLIT INTO TWO GROUPS?
ALL RIGHT!
ROCK, PAPER, SCIS-SORS ...
WE SPLIT UP.
IS IT JUST ME OR DO THOSE TWO HAVE A THING GOING ON ALL OF A SUDDEN?
YAAAY!
KIRYUU-KUN, KIRYUU-KUN! LET'S TURN IT AS FAST AS WE CAAAN!
YOU SURE ABOUT THAT?
MAKE IT SO FAST THAT WE CAN'T TAKE IT ANYMORE!
GOT IT.
SFX: MURMUR MURMUR
ざわざわ
THIS IS FUN!
HUH?
ぎゅーーん
SPIIIN
IT'S DAN-GEROUS OVER THERE!
LIKE, SERI-OUSLY DAN-GEROUS!!

SPIIIN

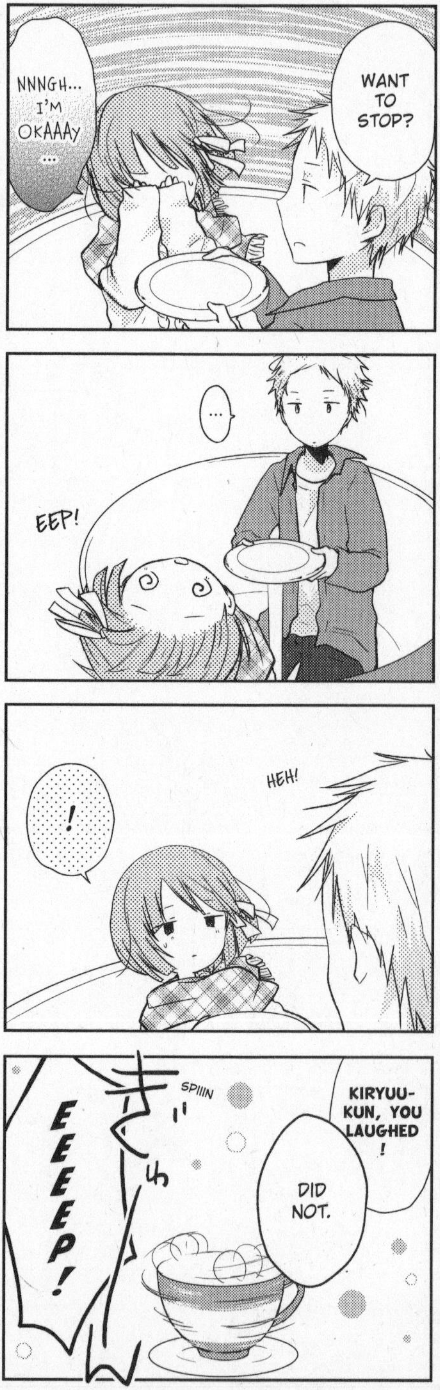
WANT TO STOP?
NNNGH... I'M OKAAAy ...
...
EEP!
HEH!
!
KIRYUU-KUN, YOU LAUGHED!
DID NOT.
SPIIIN
EEEEEP!

SEND-OFF

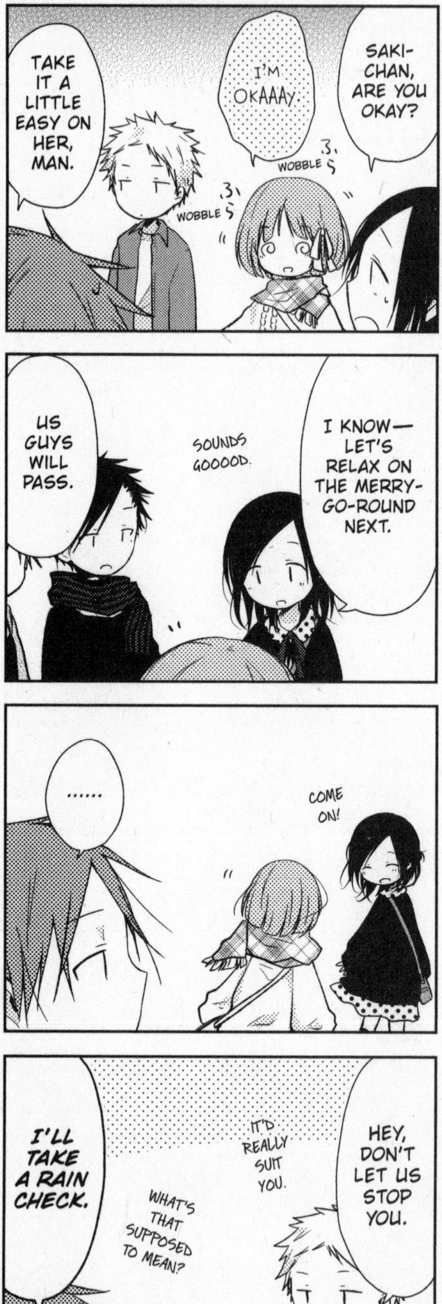
SAKI-CHAN, ARE YOU OKAY?
I'M OKAAAy.
WOBBLE
WOBBLE
TAKE IT A LITTLE EASY ON HER, MAN.
I KNOW—LET'S RELAX ON THE MERRY-GO-ROUND NEXT.
SOUNDS GOOOOD.
US GUYS WILL PASS.
COME ON!
......
HEY, DON'T LET US STOP YOU.
IT'D REALLY SUIT YOU.
WHAT'S THAT SUPPOSED TO MEAN?
I'LL TAKE A RAIN CHECK.

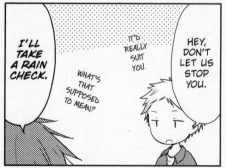

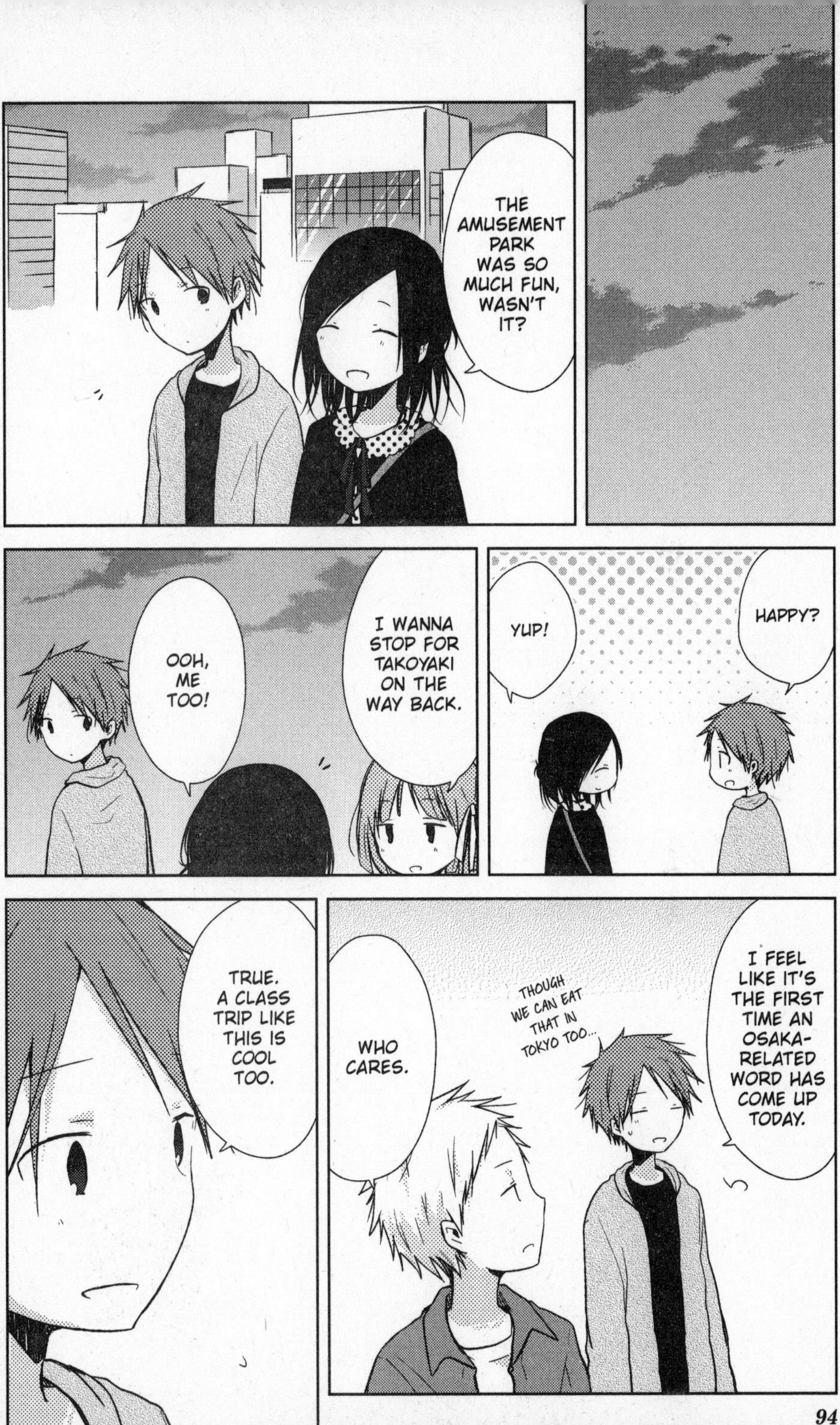
THE AMUSEMENT PARK WAS SO MUCH FUN, WASN'T IT?
HAPPY?
YUP!
I WANNA STOP FOR TAKOYAKI ON THE WAY BACK.
OOH, ME TOO!
I FEEL LIKE IT'S THE FIRST TIME AN OSAKA-RELATED WORD HAS COME UP TODAY.
THOUGH WE CAN EAT THAT IN TOKYO TOO...
WHO CARES.
TRUE. A CLASS TRIP LIKE THIS IS COOL TOO.

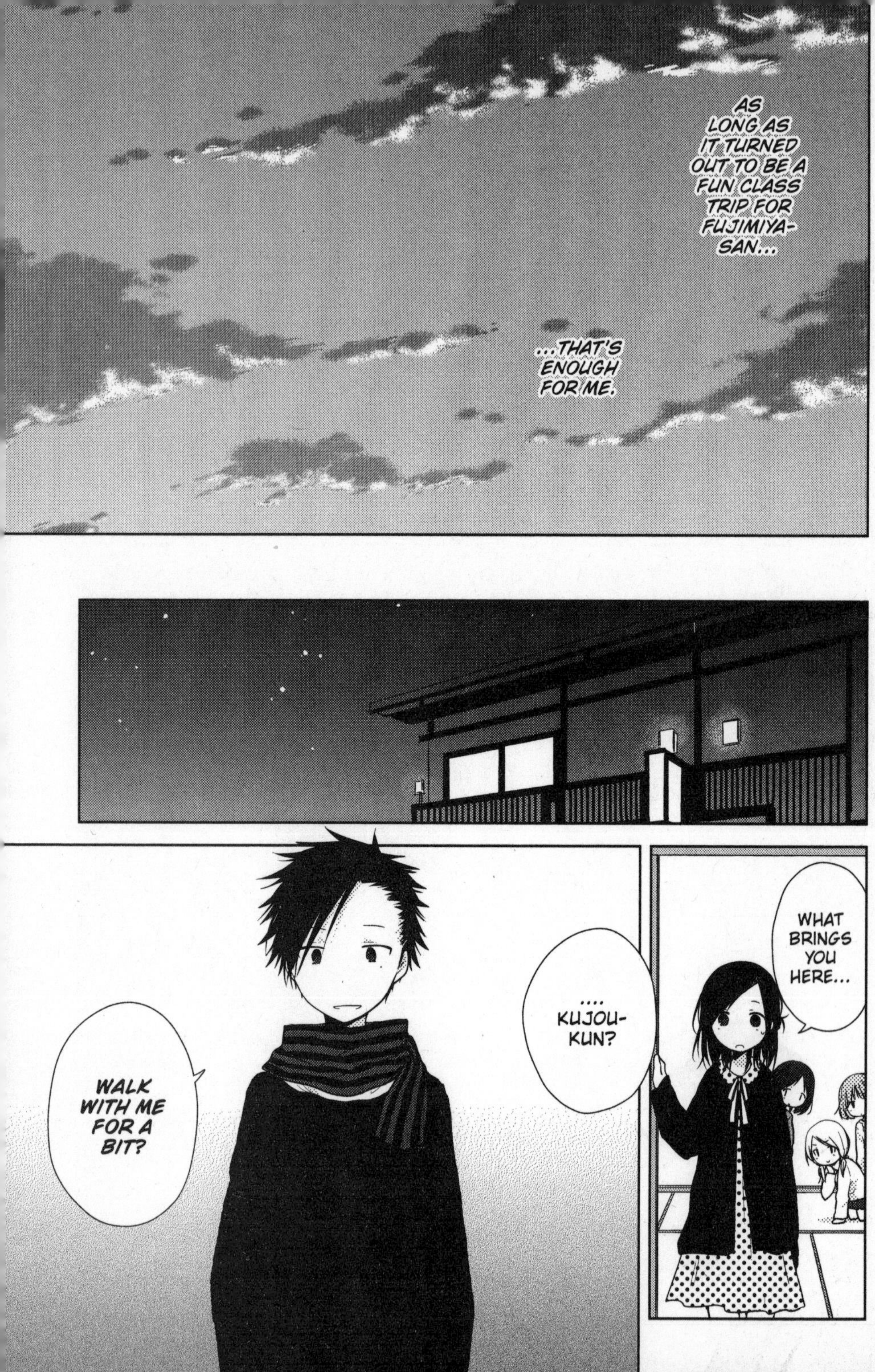
AS LONG AS IT TURNED OUT TO BE A FUN CLASS TRIP FOR FUJIMIYA-SAN...
...THAT'S ENOUGH FOR ME.
WHAT BRINGS YOU HERE...
....KUJOU-KUN?
WALK WITH ME FOR A BIT?

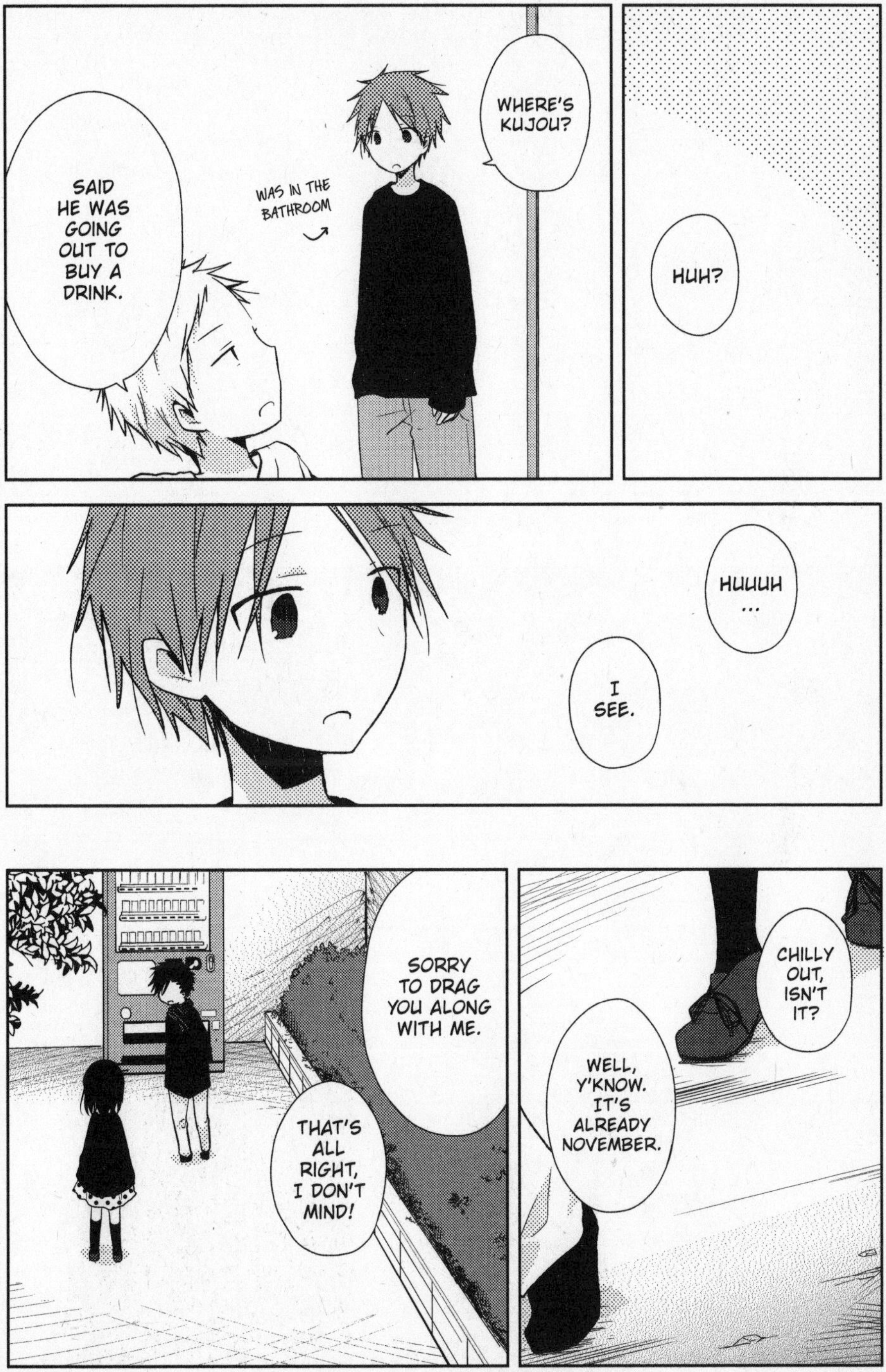
HUH?
WHERE'S KUJOU?
SAID HE WAS GOING OUT TO BUY A DRINK.
WAS IN THE BATHROOM
HUUUH...
I SEE.
CHILLY OUT, ISN'T IT?
WELL, Y'KNOW. IT'S ALREADY NOVEMBER.
SORRY TO DRAG YOU ALONG WITH ME.
THAT'S ALL RIGHT, I DON'T MIND!

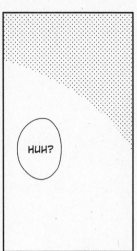

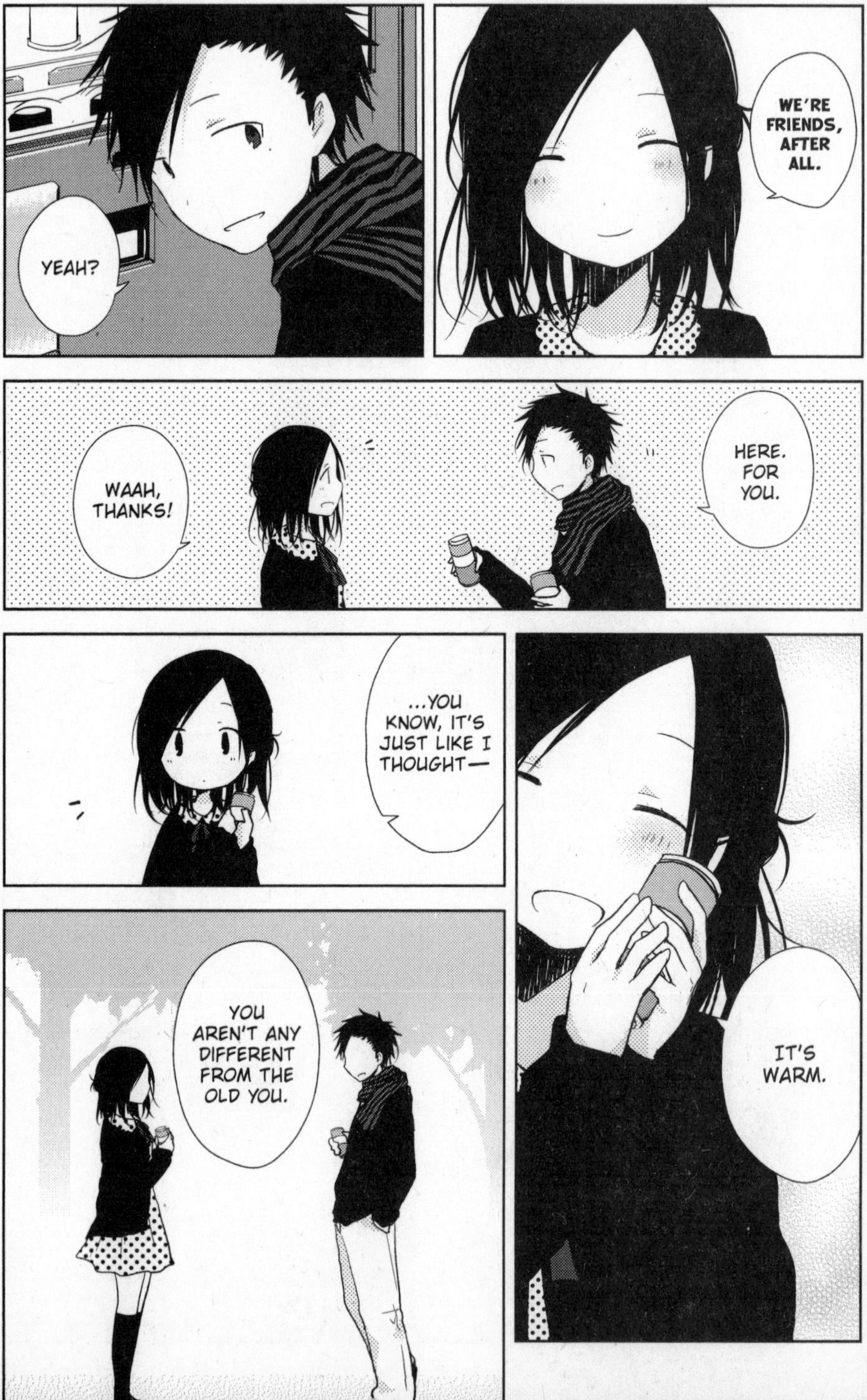
WE'RE FRIENDS, AFTER ALL.
YEAH?
HERE. FOR YOU.
WAAH, THANKS!
IT'S WARM.
...YOU KNOW, IT'S JUST LIKE I THOUGHT—
YOU AREN'T ANY DIFFERENT FROM THE OLD YOU.

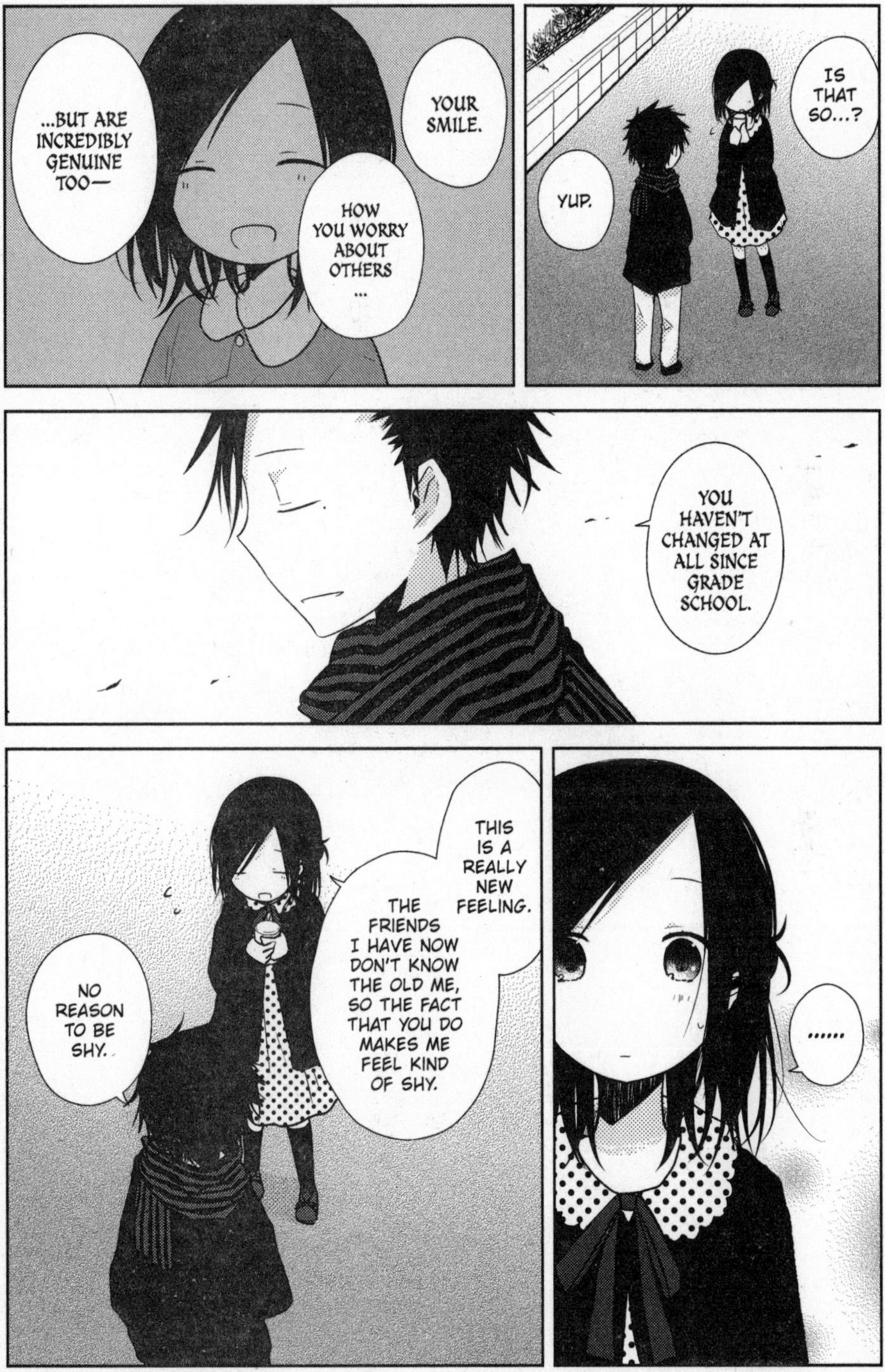
IS THAT SO...?
YUP.
YOUR SMILE.
HOW YOU WORRY ABOUT OTHERS ...
...BUT ARE INCREDIBLY GENUINE TOO—
YOU HAVEN'T CHANGED AT ALL SINCE GRADE SCHOOL.
......
THIS IS A REALLY NEW FEELING.
THE FRIENDS I HAVE NOW DON'T KNOW THE OLD ME, SO THE FACT THAT YOU DO MAKES ME FEEL KIND OF SHY.
NO REASON TO BE SHY.

I WAS HONESTLY RELIEVED YOU HADN'T CHANGED.
I'M GLAD I GOT TO MEET YOU AGAIN, KAORI.
... YEAH.
I'M REALLY GLAD I GOT TO BECOME YOUR FRIEND AGAIN TOO, KUJOU-KUN.

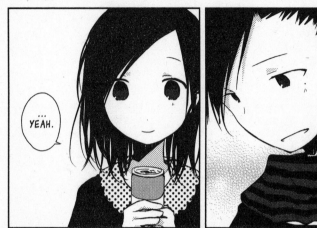

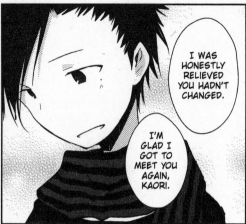

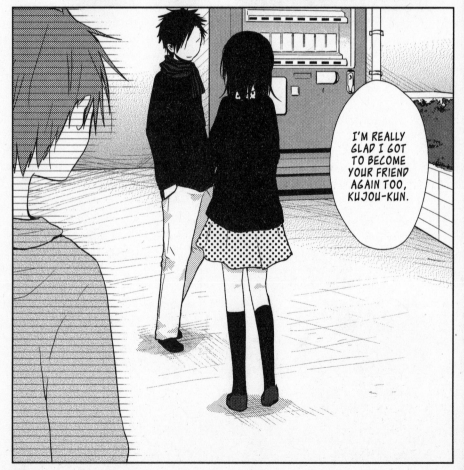

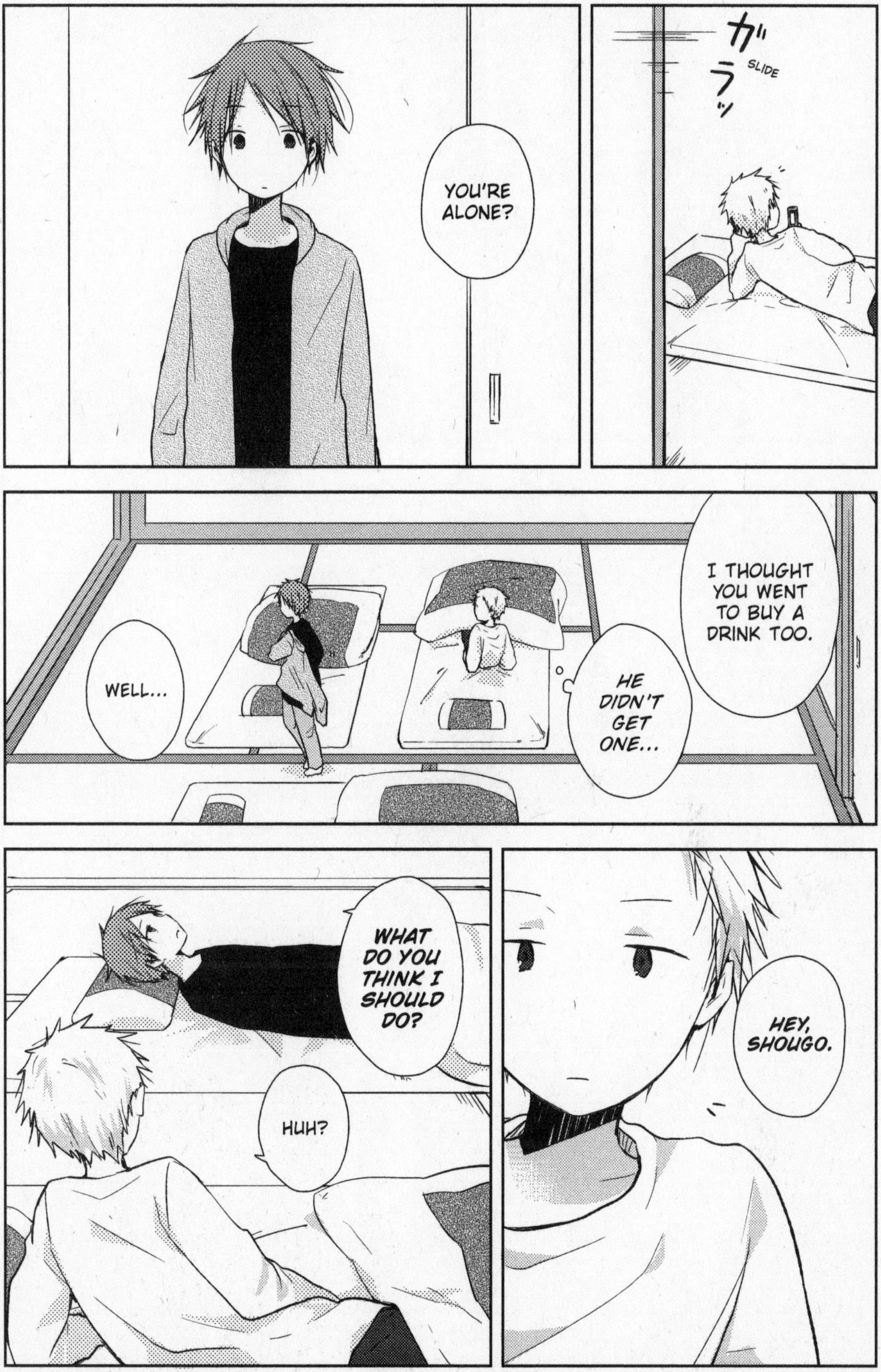
ガラッ
SLIDE
YOU'RE ALONE?
I THOUGHT YOU WENT TO BUY A DRINK TOO.
HE DIDN'T GET ONE...
WELL...
HEY, SHOUGO.
WHAT DO YOU THINK I SHOULD DO?
HUH?

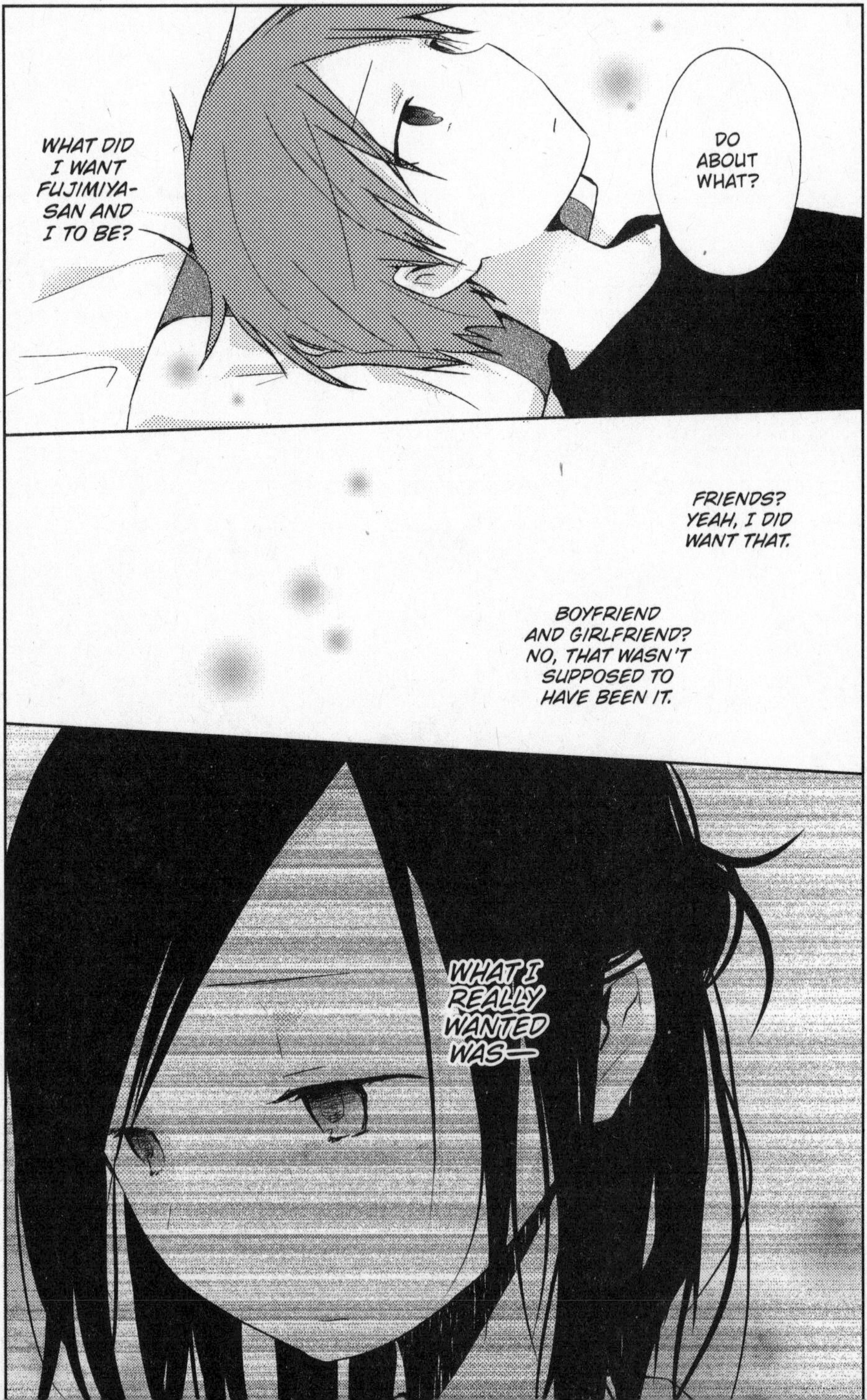
DO ABOUT WHAT?
WHAT DID I WANT FUJIMIYA-SAN AND I TO BE?
FRIENDS? YEAH, I DID WANT THAT.
BOYFRIEND AND GIRLFRIEND? NO, THAT WASN'T SUPPOSED TO HAVE BEEN IT.
WHAT I REALLY WANTED WAS—

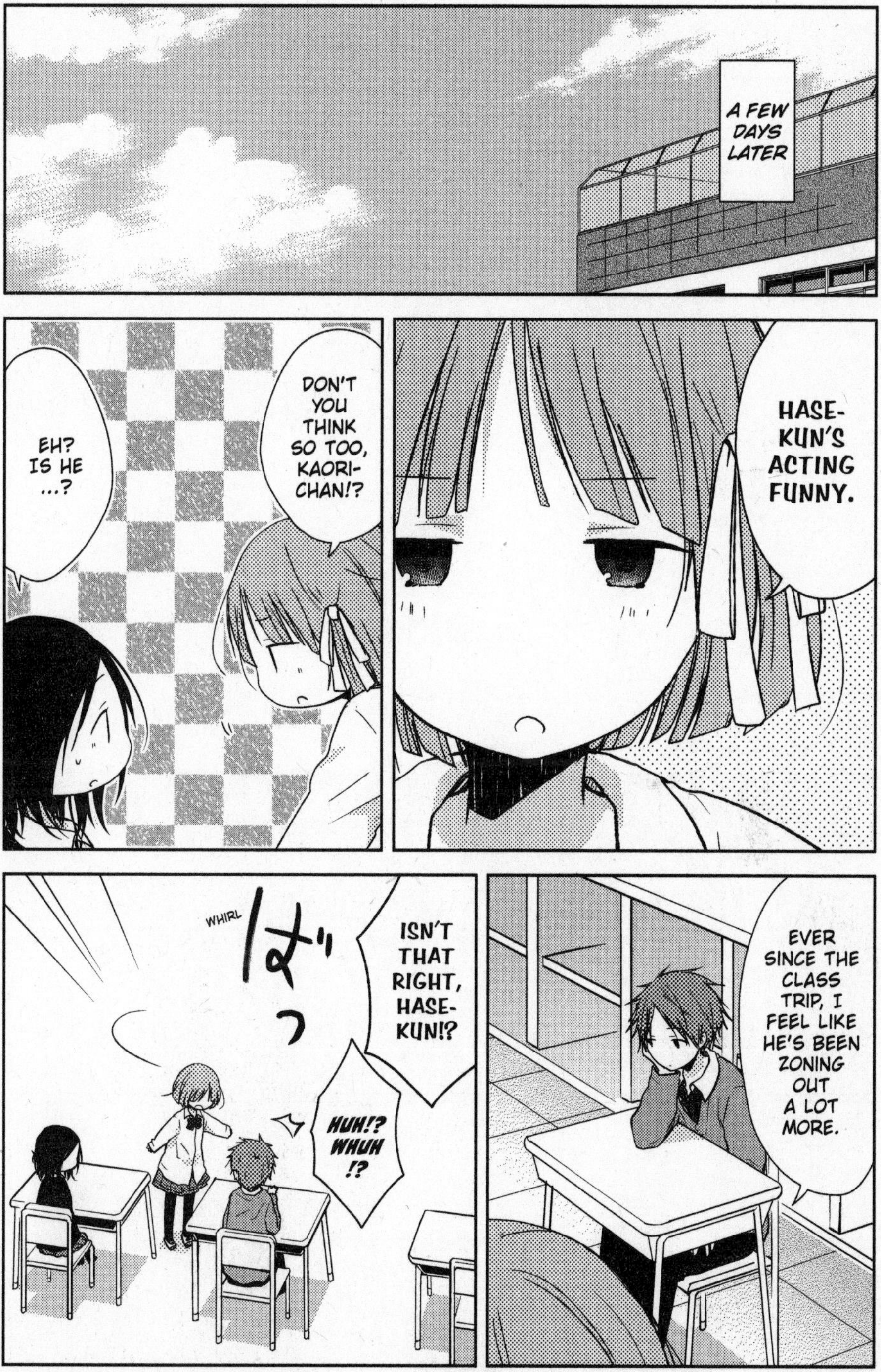
A FEW DAYS LATER
HASE-KUN'S ACTING FUNNY.
DON'T YOU THINK SO TOO, KAORI-CHAN!?
EH? IS HE ...?
EVER SINCE THE CLASS TRIP, I FEEL LIKE HE'S BEEN ZONING OUT A LOT MORE.
ばっ
WHIRL
ISN'T THAT RIGHT, HASE-KUN!?
HUH!? WHUH!?

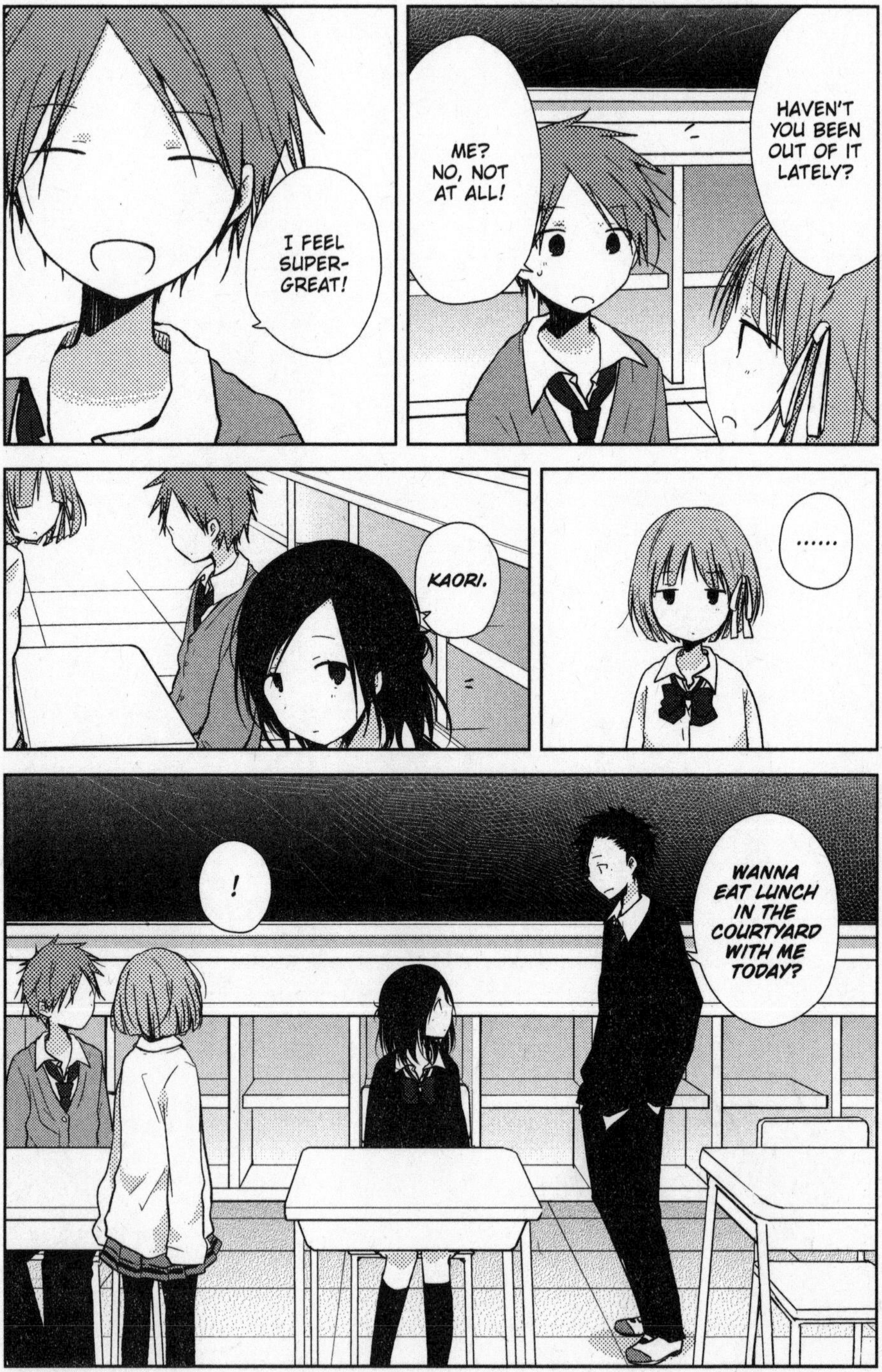
HAVEN'T YOU BEEN OUT OF IT LATELY?
ME? NO, NOT AT ALL!
I FEEL SUPER-GREAT!
......
KAORI.
WANNA EAT LUNCH IN THE COURTYARD WITH ME TODAY?
!

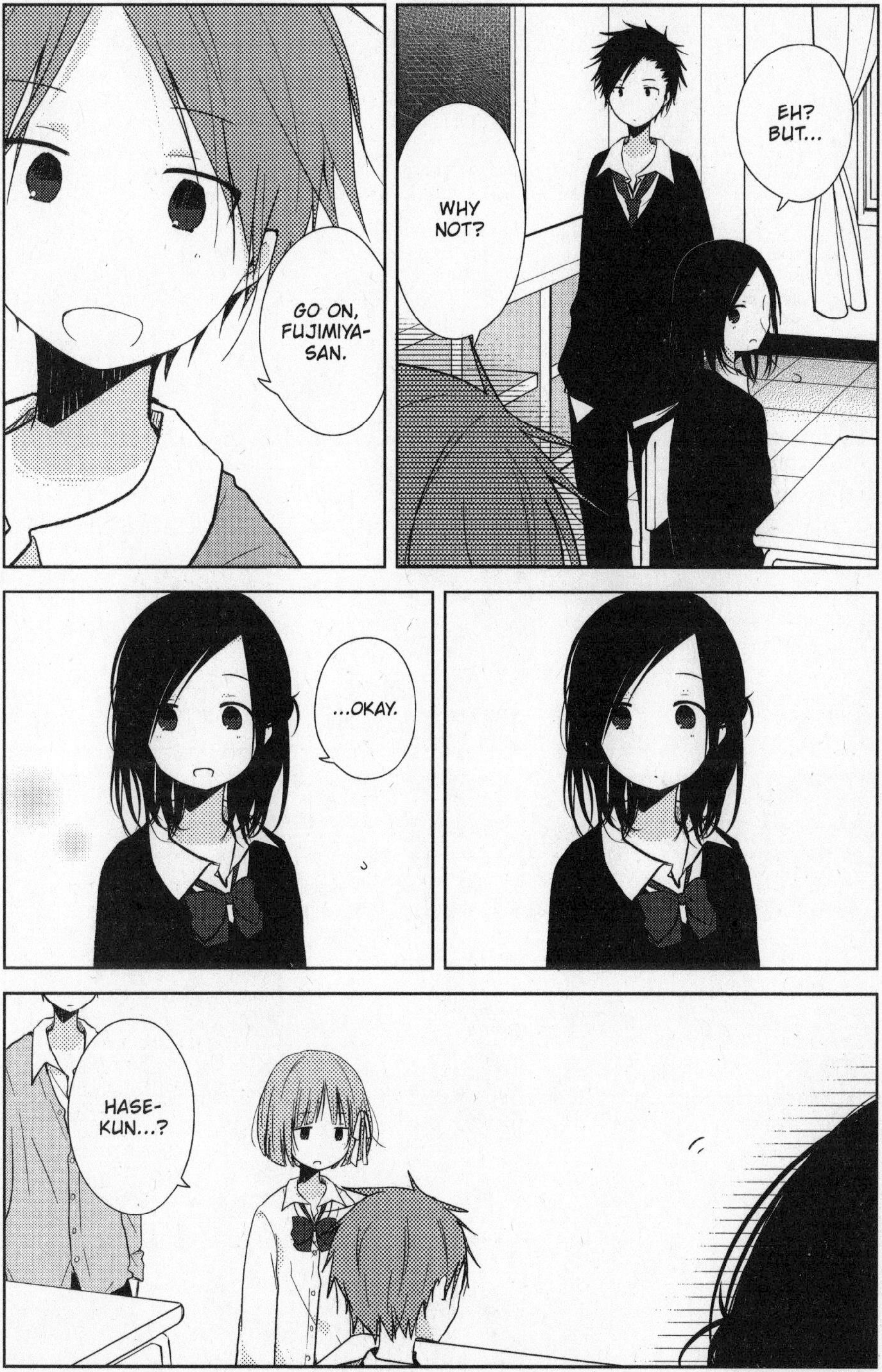
EH? BUT...
WHY NOT?
GO ON, FUJIMIYA-SAN.
...OKAY.
HASE-KUN...?

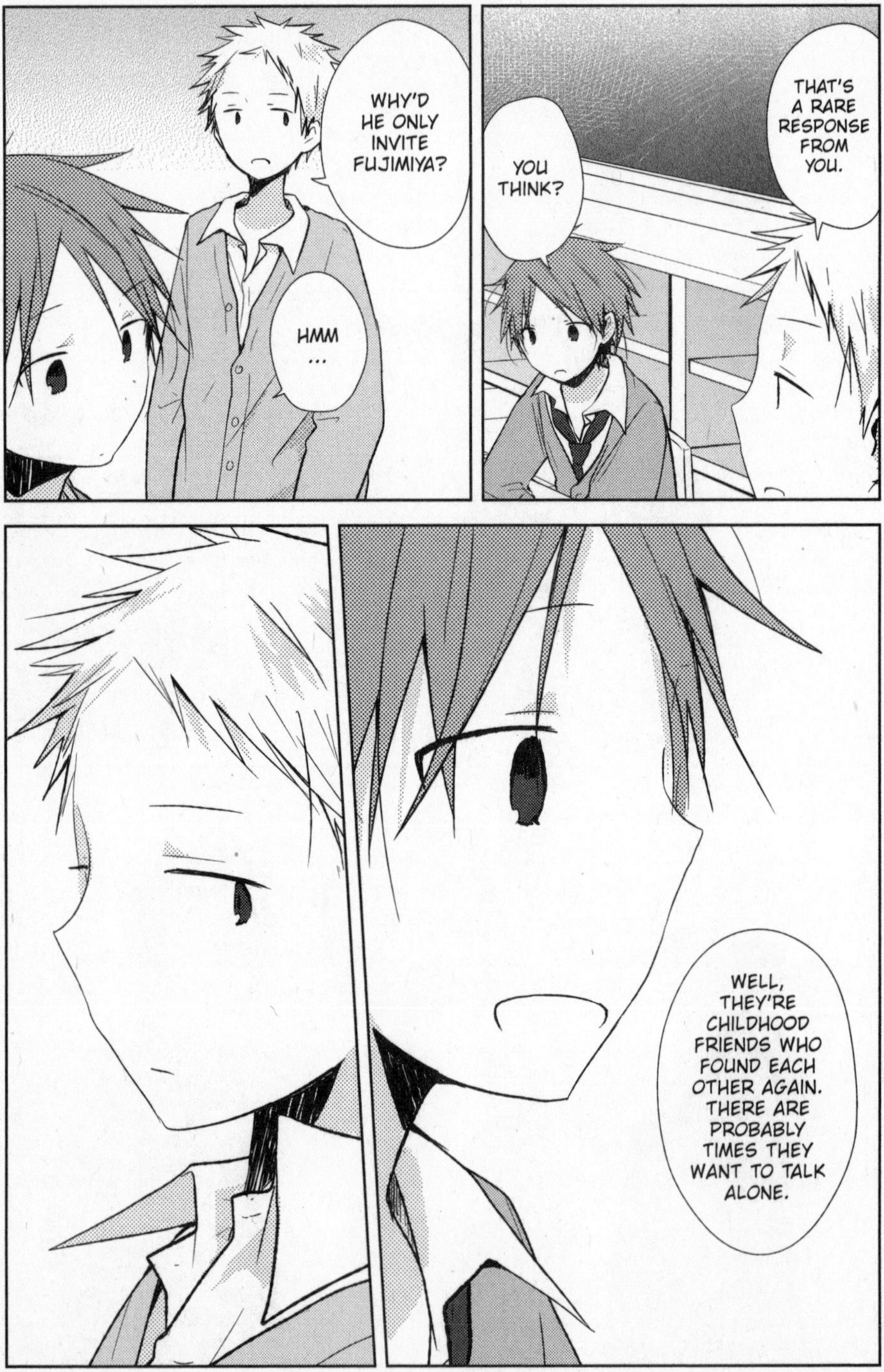
THAT'S A RARE RESPONSE FROM YOU.
YOU THINK?
WHY'D HE ONLY INVITE FUJIMIYA?
HMM ...
WELL, THEY'RE CHILDHOOD FRIENDS WHO FOUND EACH OTHER AGAIN. THERE ARE PROBABLY TIMES THEY WANT TO TALK ALONE.

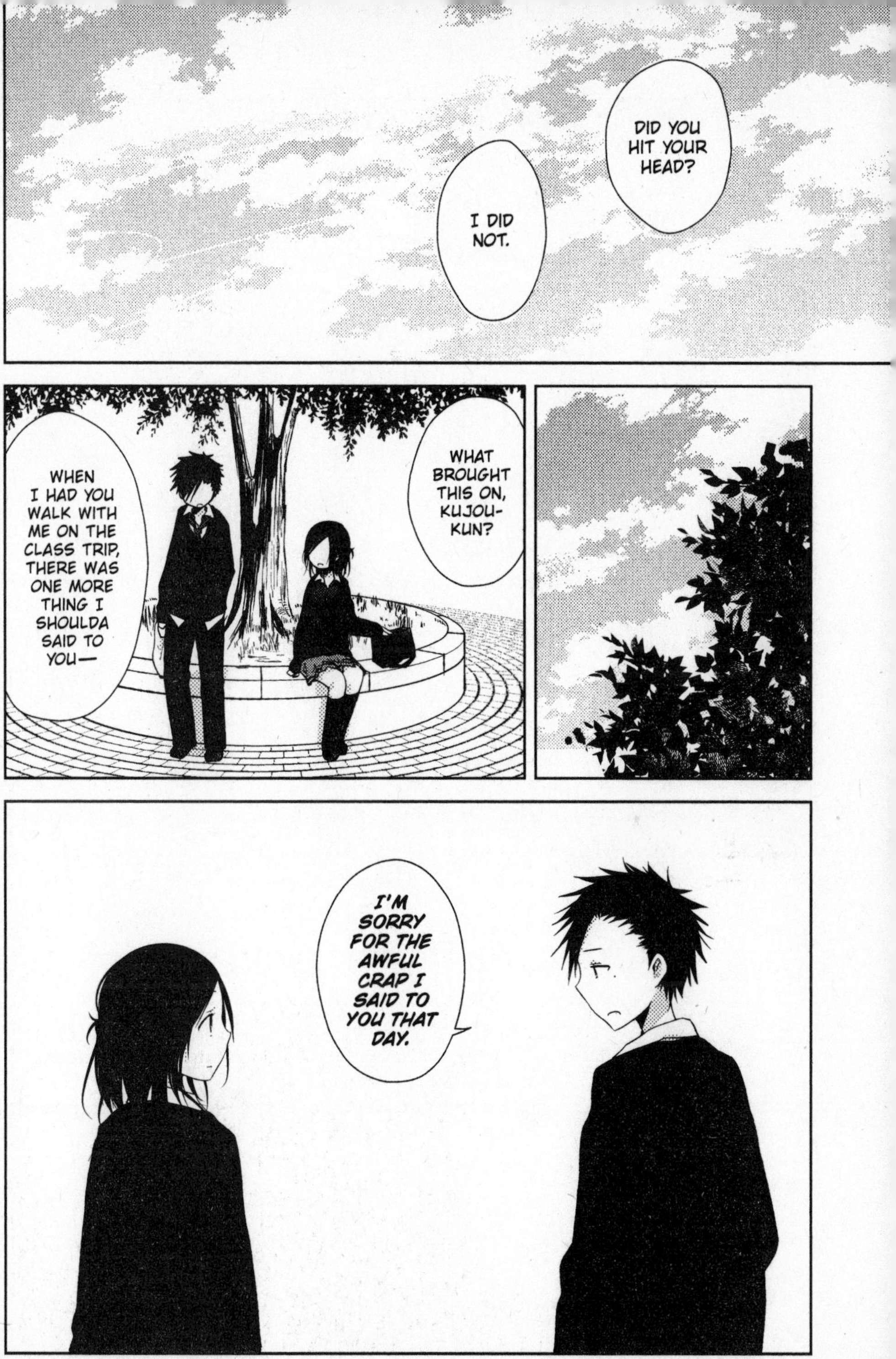
DID YOU HIT YOUR HEAD?
I DID NOT.
WHAT BROUGHT THIS ON, KUJOU-KUN?
WHEN I HAD YOU WALK WITH ME ON THE CLASS TRIP, THERE WAS ONE MORE THING I SHOULDA SAID TO YOU—
I'M SORRY FOR THE AWFUL CRAP I SAID TO YOU THAT DAY.

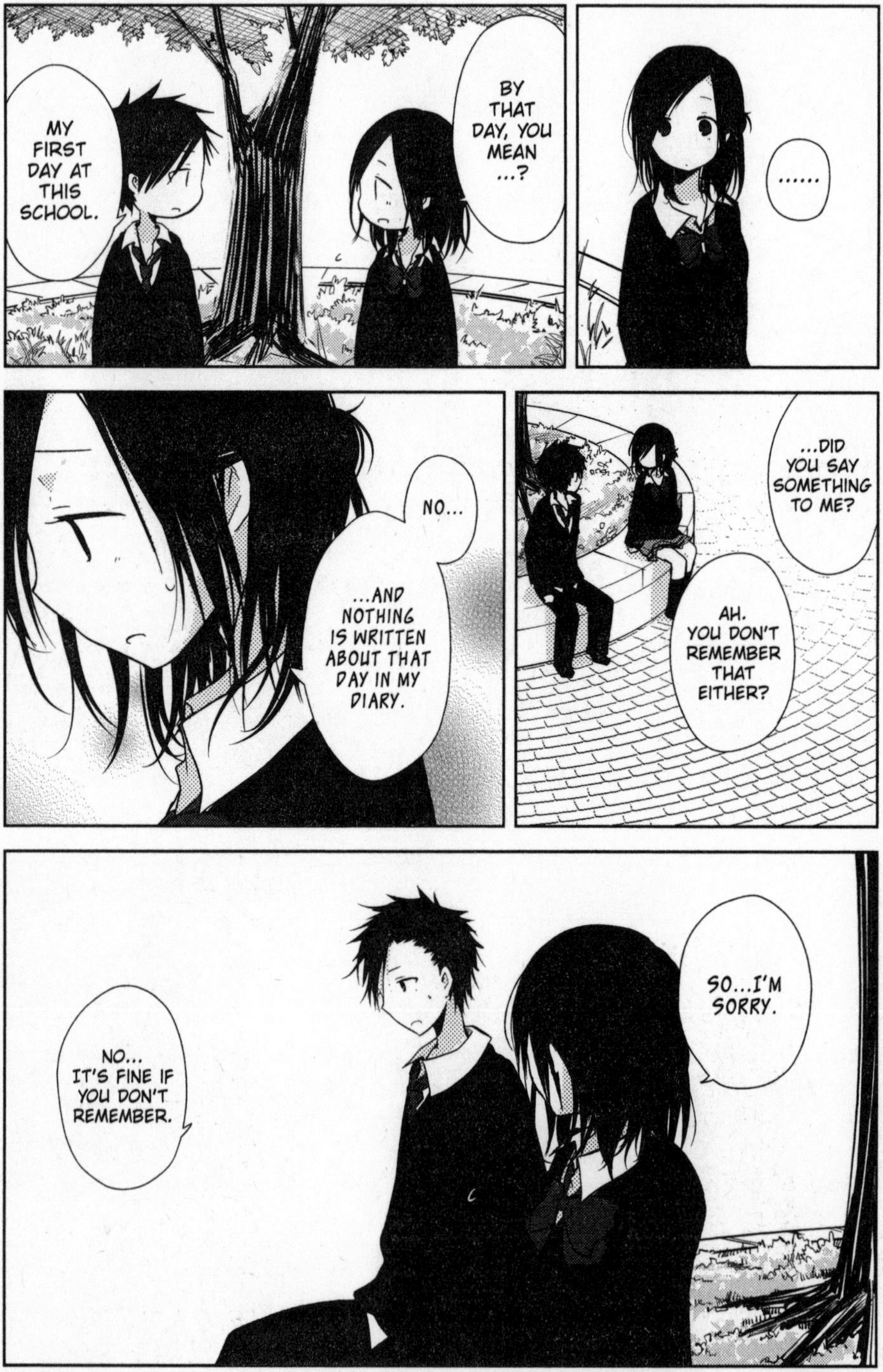
......
BY THAT DAY, YOU MEAN ...?
MY FIRST DAY AT THIS SCHOOL.
...DID YOU SAY SOMETHING TO ME?
AH. YOU DON'T REMEMBER THAT EITHER?
NO...
...AND NOTHING IS WRITTEN ABOUT THAT DAY IN MY DIARY.
SO...I'M SORRY.
NO... IT'S FINE IF YOU DON'T REMEMBER.

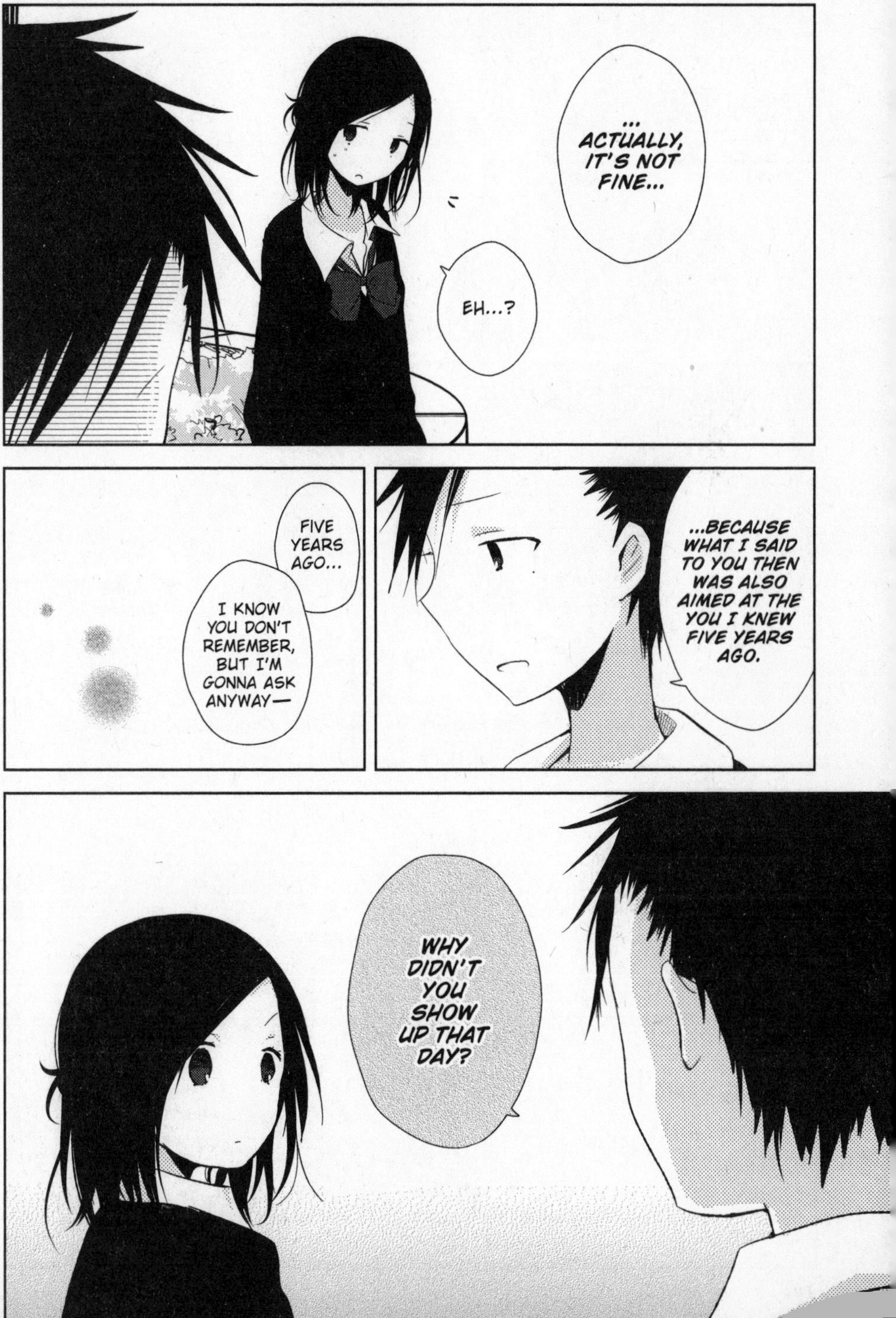
...ACTUALLY, IT'S NOT FINE...
EH...?
...BECAUSE WHAT I SAID TO YOU THEN WAS ALSO AIMED AT THE YOU I KNEW FIVE YEARS AGO.
FIVE YEARS AGO...
I KNOW YOU DON'T REMEMBER, BUT I'M GONNA ASK ANYWAY—
WHY DIDN'T YOU SHOW UP THAT DAY?

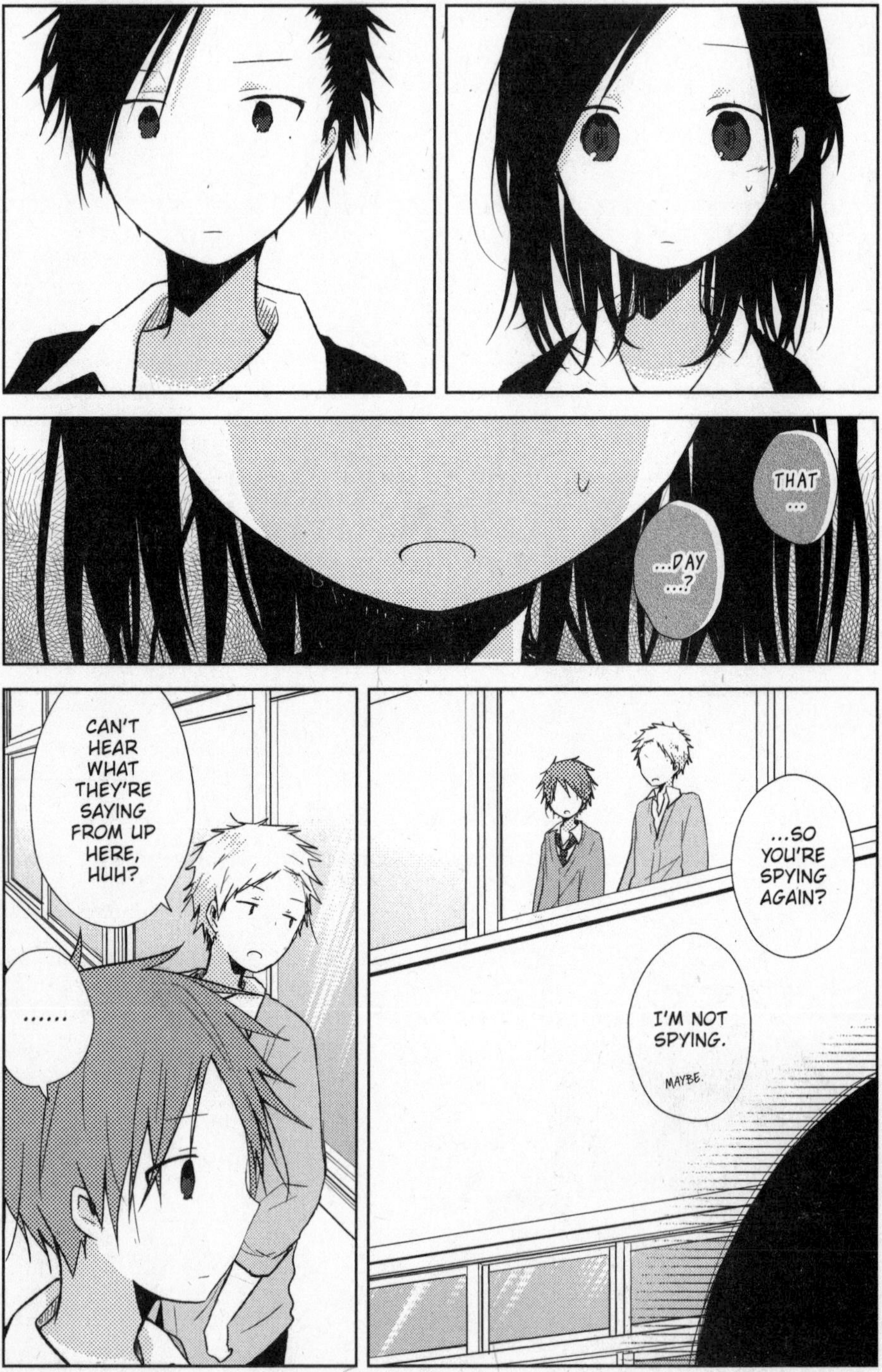
THAT ...
...DAY ...?
...SO YOU'RE SPYING AGAIN?
I'M NOT SPYING.
MAYBE.
CAN'T HEAR WHAT THEY'RE SAYING FROM UP HERE, HUH?
......

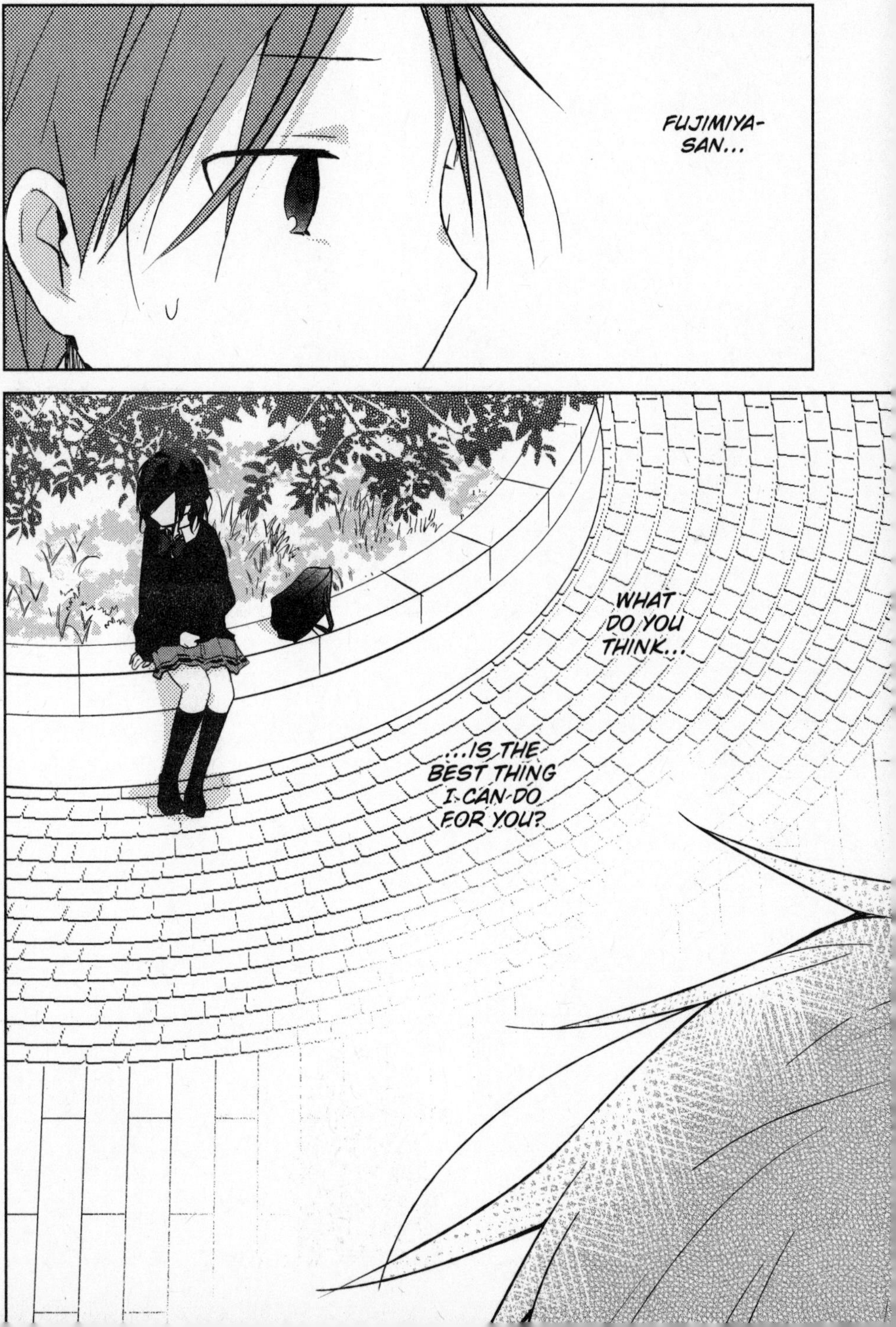
FUJIMIYA-SAN...
WHAT DO YOU THINK...
...IS THE BEST THING I CAN DO FOR YOU?

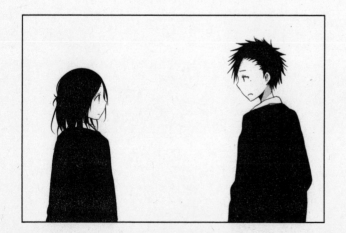

TRANSLATION NOTES

COMMON HONORIFICS

No honorific: Indicates familiarity or closeness; if used without permission or reason, addressing someone in this manner would constitute an insult.

-san: The Japanese equivalent of Mr./Mrs./Miss. If a situation calls for politeness, this is the fail-safe honorific.

-kun: Used most often when referring to boys, this indicates affection or familiarity. Occasionally used by older men among their peers, but it may also be used by anyone referring to a person of lower standing.

-chan: An affectionate honorific indicating familiarity used mostly in reference to girls; also used in reference to cute persons or animals of either gender.

-sensei: A respectful term for teachers, artists, or high-level professionals.

nee: Japanese equivalent to "older sis."
nii: Japanese equivalent to "older bro."

PAGE 8

Not only is **Hajime**'s given name written as the kanji character for "one," the first character in his family name is "nine."

Japanese children are sometimes named with numbers in their names according to the order in which they're born, so Hajime's name would be more fitting for a firstborn son.

PAGE 55

Kyoto, capital city of Kyoto Prefecture, is a common high school class-trip destination. It is located in the Kansai region (the southern-central region on Japan's main island, Honshu). The city is a historic capital of Japan (from 794 to 1869) and is considered a cultural center of the country.

PAGE 56

Fushimi Inari Grand Shrine is famous for its rows of thousands of *torii* gates. Located at the base of a mountain, it also has long trails up the mountain to smaller shrines.

PAGE 60

Kinkaku-ji ("Temple of the Golden Pavilion"), completed in 1397, was a villa bought by shogun Ashikaga Yoshimitsu and turned into a Zen temple upon his death. The pavilion is coated in gold-leaf gilding, giving it a striking look.

PAGE 61

Ginkaku-ji ("Temple of the Silver Pavilion") is a Zen Buddhist temple that was originally built as a place of rest for shogun Ashikaga Yoshimasa (1436–1490). It was supposed to be covered in silver foil, thus the name, but was left incomplete upon Yoshimasa's death. Ginkaku-ji is actually based off of Kinkaku-ji (Yoshimitsu was Yoshimasa's grandfather).

PAGE 62

Kiyomizu-dera is a Buddhist temple founded in 778. Kaori and friends are looking out from the temple's famous hillside veranda.

PAGE 64

Torii are gateways that mark the entrance to sacred ground. They're usually found at the entrance to Shinto shrines and are usually painted a striking red.

PAGE 85

Osaka, capital of Osaka Prefecture in the Kansai region, is Japan's second-largest metropolitan area.

Osaka Castle, one of Japan's most famous landmarks, was built from 1583 to 1597.

Tsutenkaku Tower (meaning "Tower Reaching Heaven") is another Osaka landmark, famous for its neon lights. The tower was originally built in 1912 and later rebuilt in 1956.

PAGE 94

Takoyaki (fried batter balls with octopus bits) is a popular fast-food option in Japan that's especially associated with the Kansai region and Osaka.

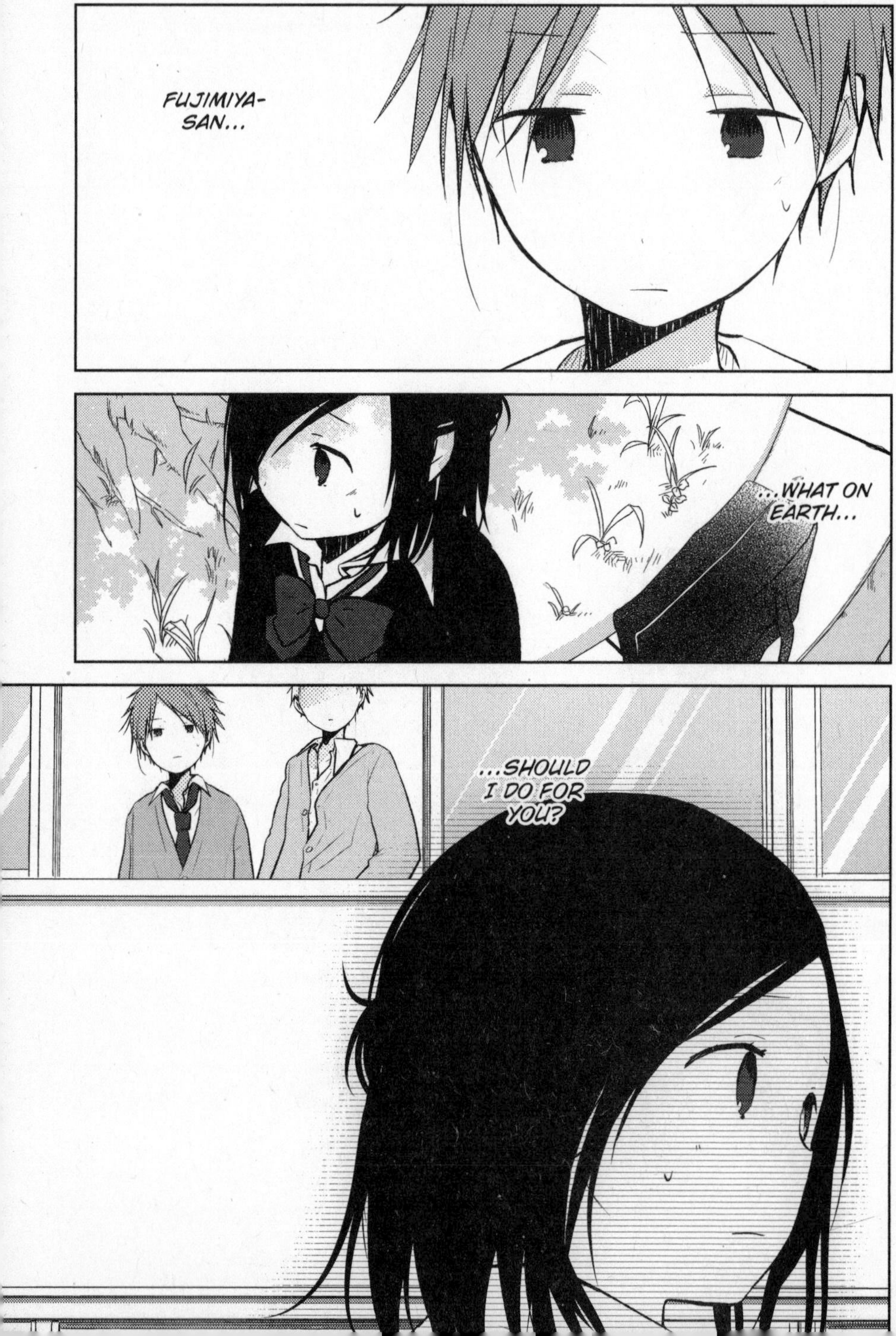
FUJIMIYA-SAN...
...WHAT ON EARTH...
...SHOULD I DO FOR YOU?

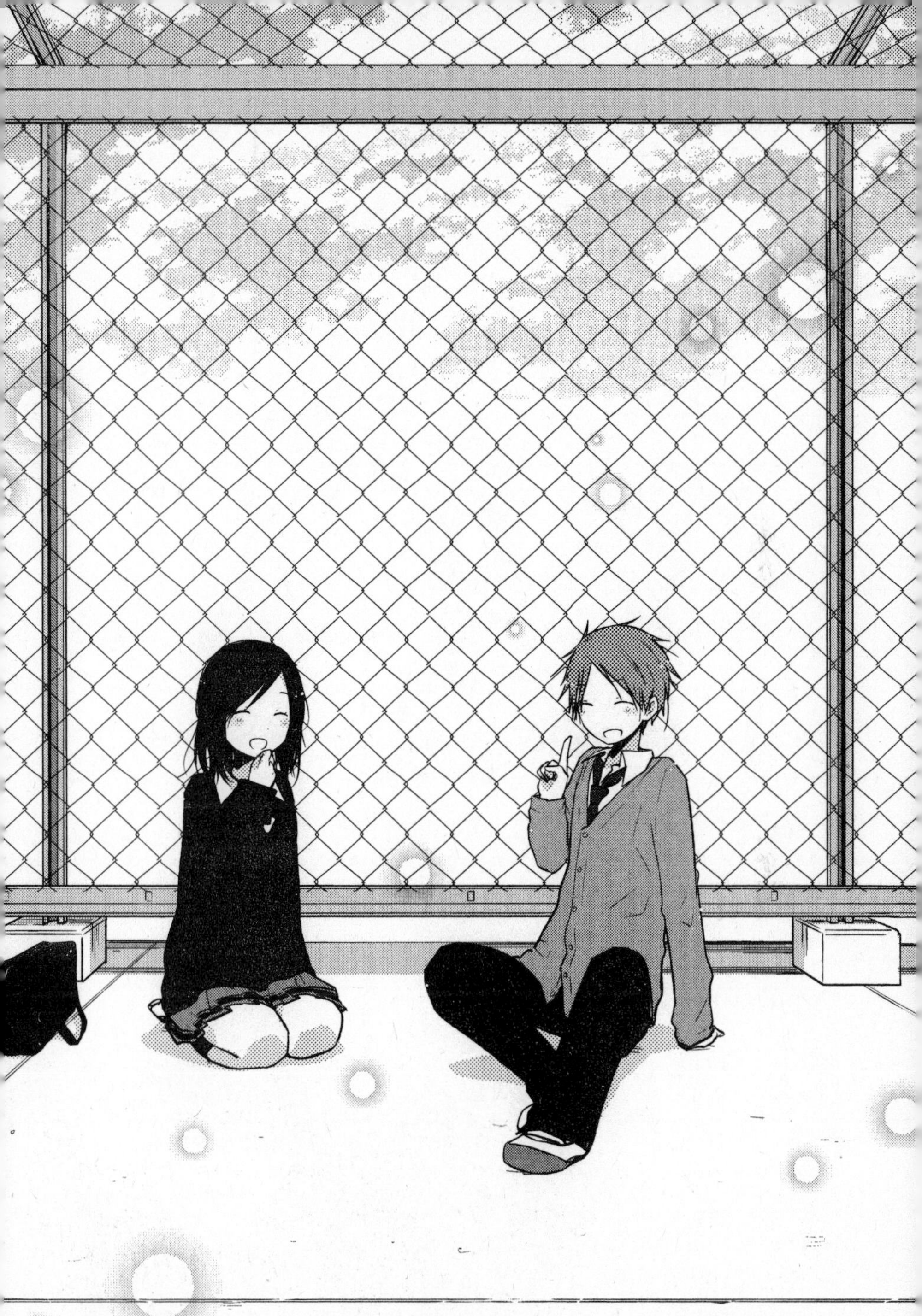

CHAPTER 26 ar^{n-1} INFINITELY CLOSE TO ZERO

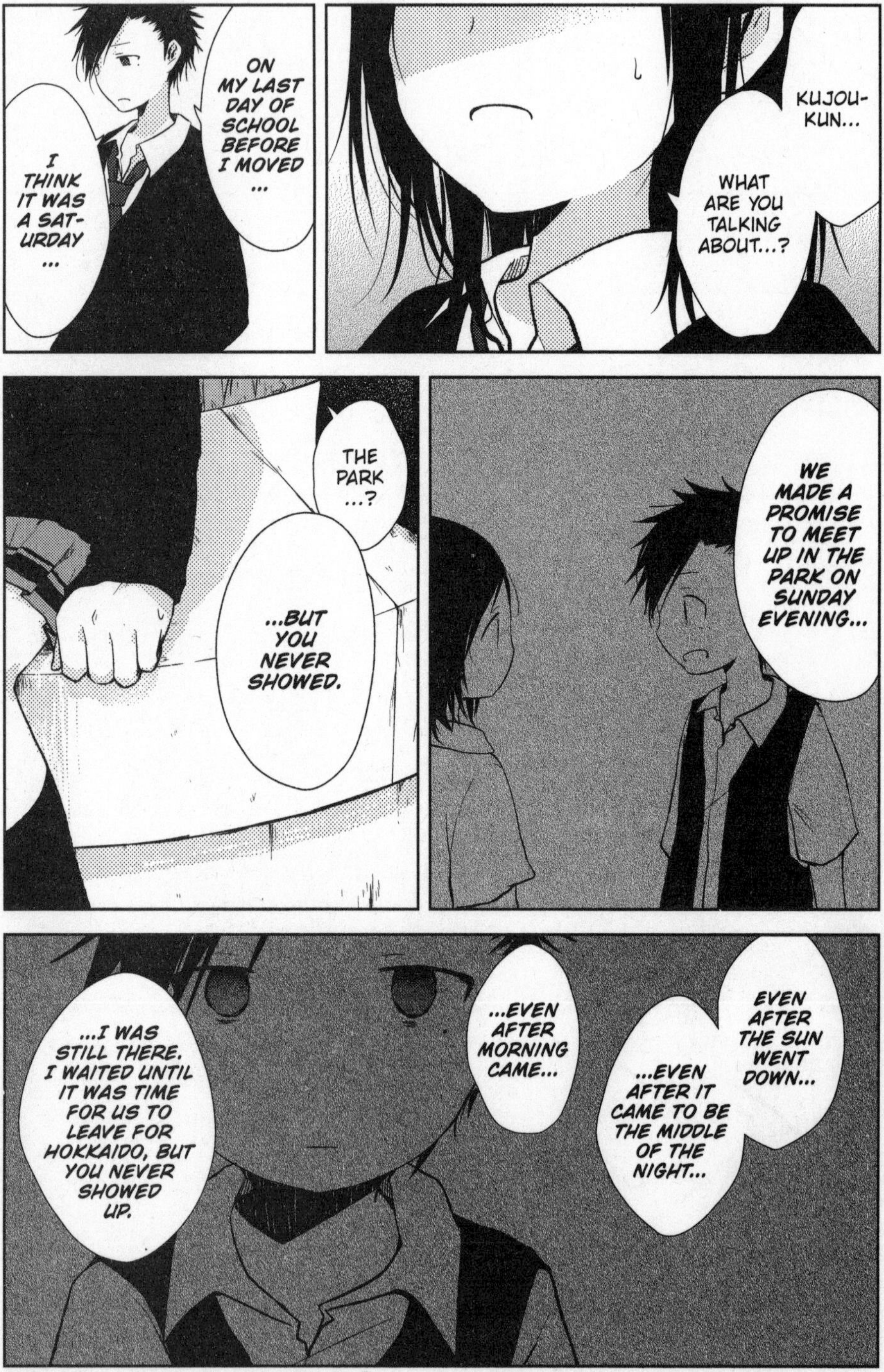
KUJOU-KUN...
WHAT ARE YOU TALKING ABOUT...?
ON MY LAST DAY OF SCHOOL BEFORE I MOVED...
I THINK IT WAS A SATURDAY...
WE MADE A PROMISE TO MEET UP IN THE PARK ON SUNDAY EVENING...
THE PARK...?
...BUT YOU NEVER SHOWED.
EVEN AFTER THE SUN WENT DOWN...
...EVEN AFTER IT CAME TO BE THE MIDDLE OF THE NIGHT...
...EVEN AFTER MORNING CAME...
...I WAS STILL THERE. I WAITED UNTIL IT WAS TIME FOR US TO LEAVE FOR HOKKAIDO, BUT YOU NEVER SHOWED UP.

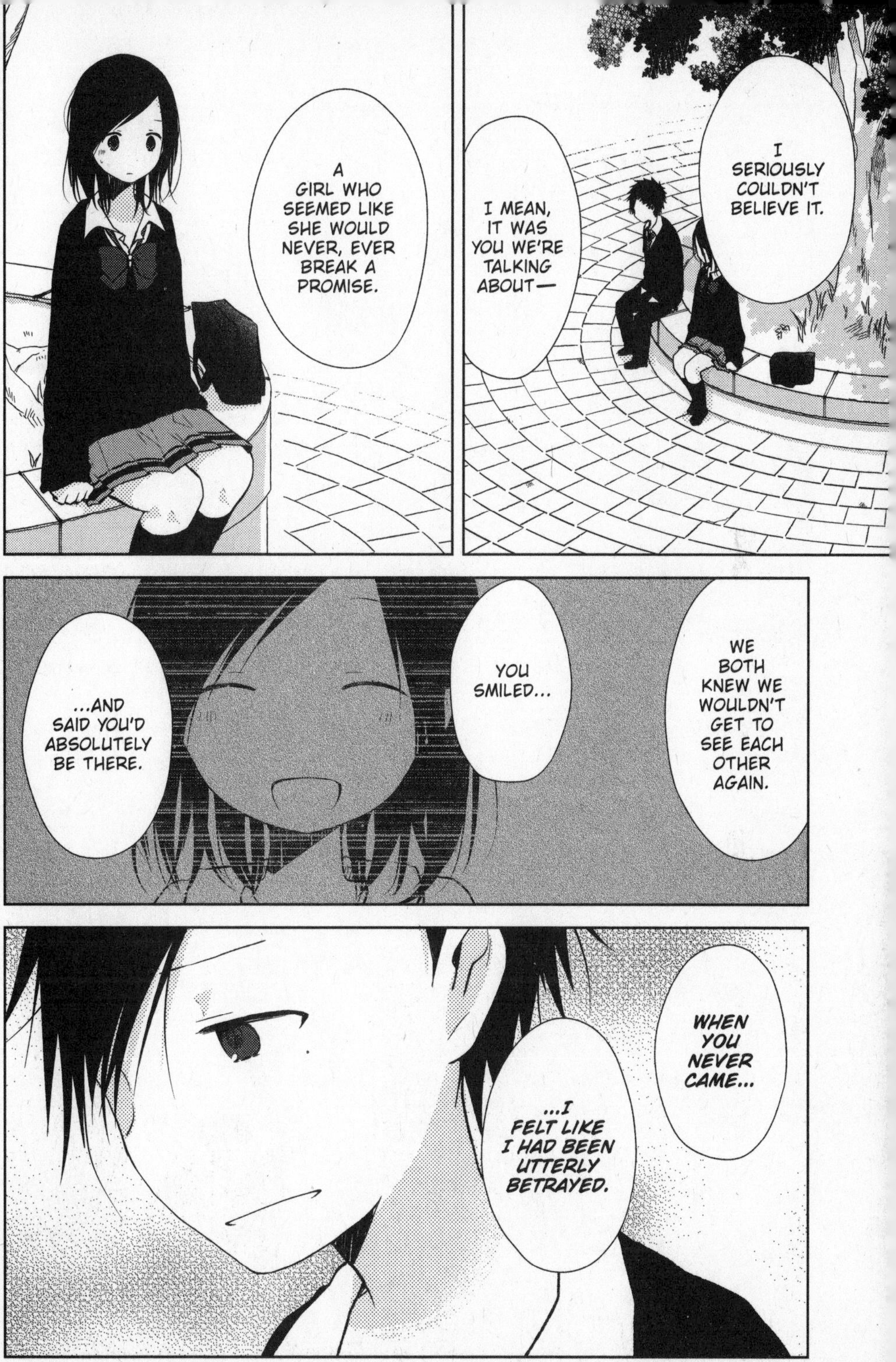
I SERIOUSLY COULDN'T BELIEVE IT.
I MEAN, IT WAS YOU WE'RE TALKING ABOUT—
A GIRL WHO SEEMED LIKE SHE WOULD NEVER, EVER BREAK A PROMISE.
WE BOTH KNEW WE WOULDN'T GET TO SEE EACH OTHER AGAIN.
YOU SMILED...
...AND SAID YOU'D ABSOLUTELY BE THERE.
WHEN YOU NEVER CAME...
...I FELT LIKE I HAD BEEN UTTERLY BETRAYED.

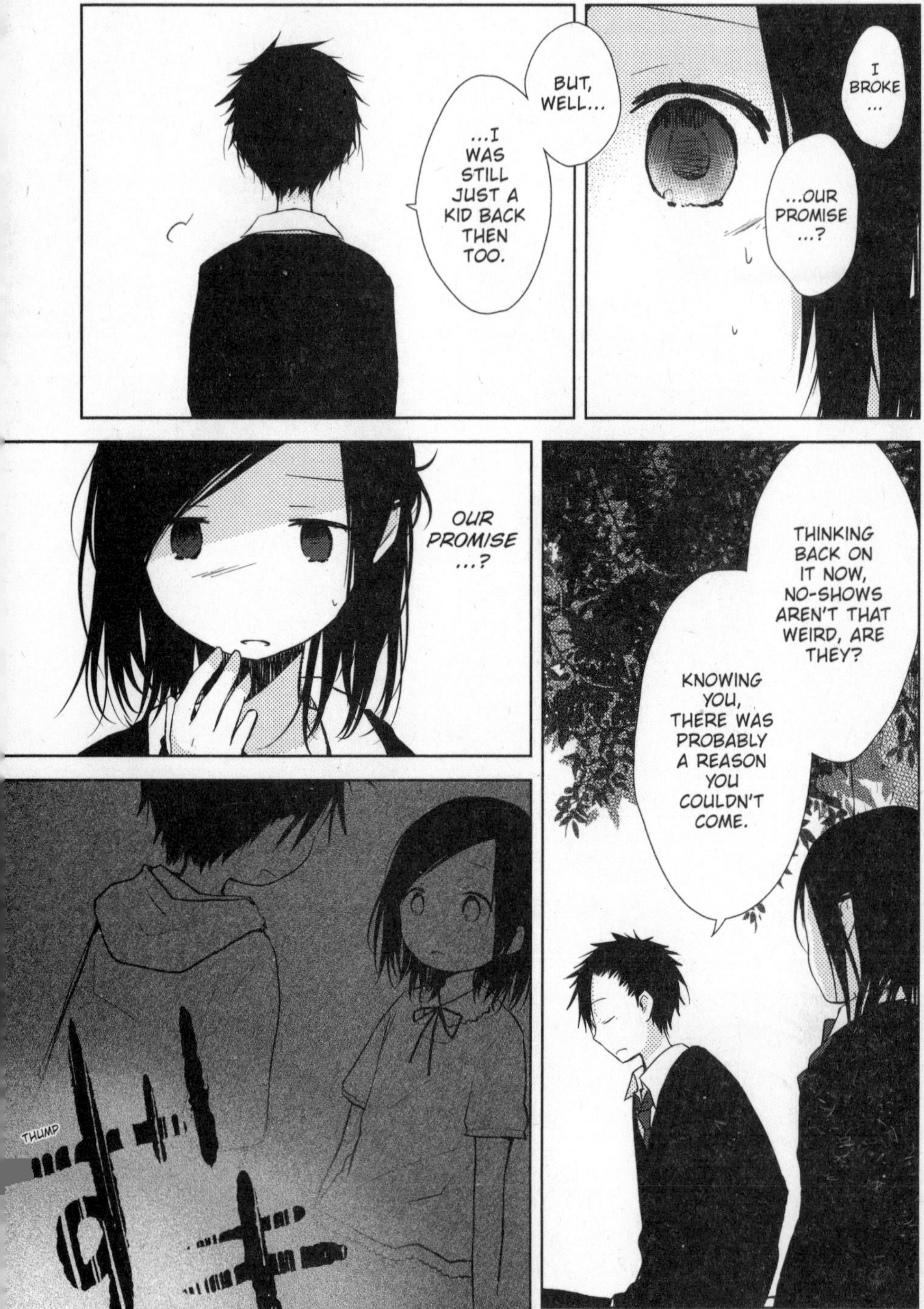
I BROKE ...
...OUR PROMISE ...?
BUT, WELL...
...I WAS STILL JUST A KID BACK THEN TOO.
THINKING BACK ON IT NOW, NO-SHOWS AREN'T THAT WEIRD, ARE THEY?
KNOWING YOU, THERE WAS PROBABLY A REASON YOU COULDN'T COME.
OUR PROMISE ...?
THUMP

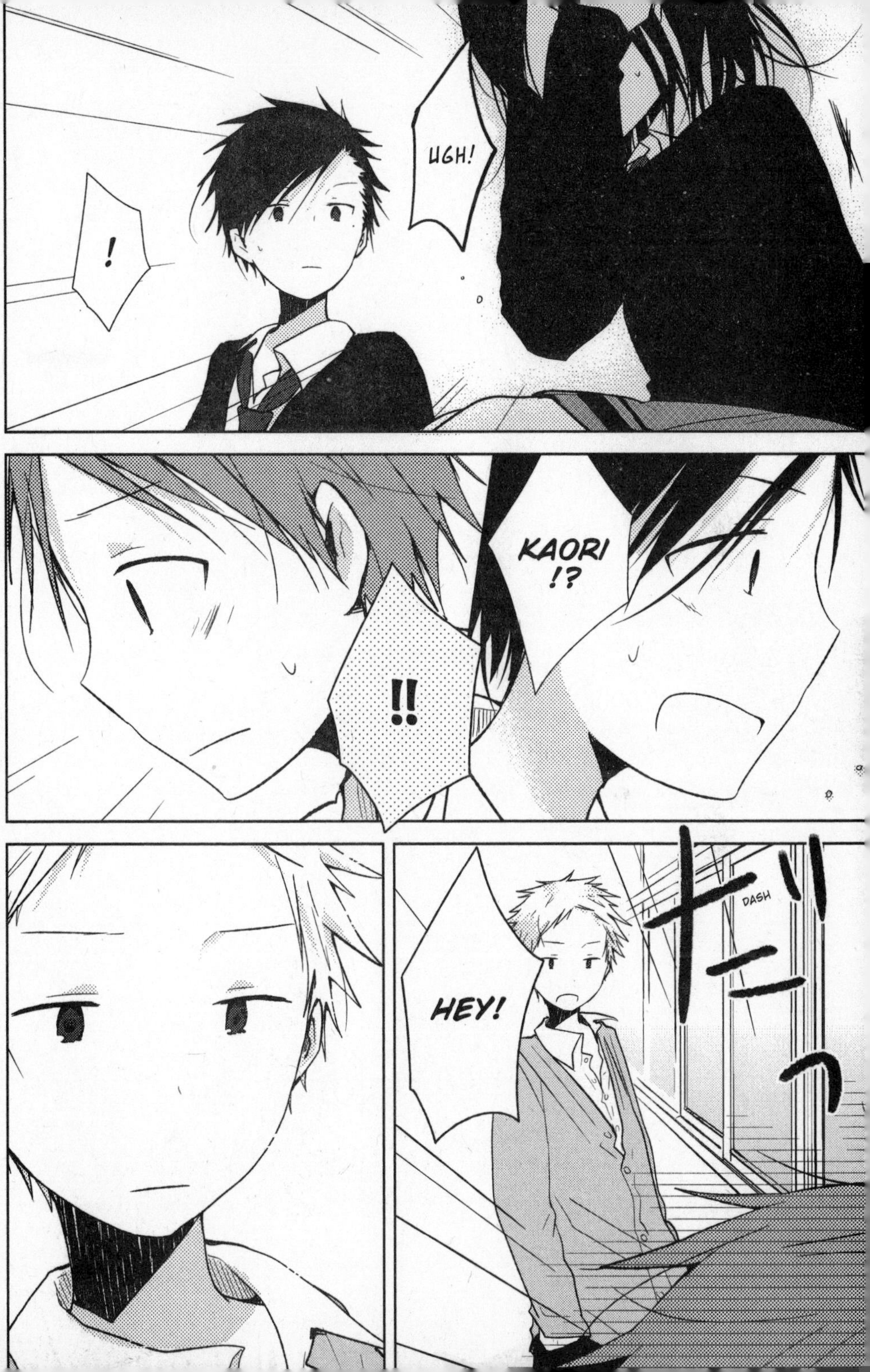
UGH!
!
KAORI !?
!!
DASH
HEY!

IT... HURTS ...
ARE YOU OKAY !?
HUFF!
HUFF!
NO... I...
I DIDN'T BETRAY YOU...
YEAH, YOU'RE RIGHT... YOU MUST HAVE HAD SOME REASON FOR NOT BEING THERE.
I... DID... GO...
HUH? WHAT?
I WENT... BUT...
I CAN'T HEAR Y...
TELL ME.

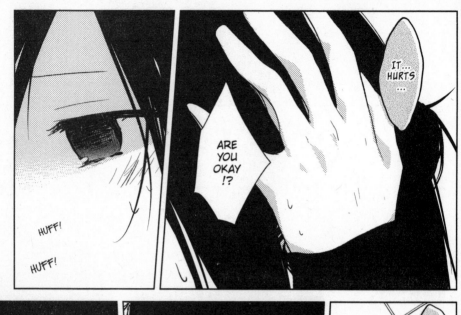

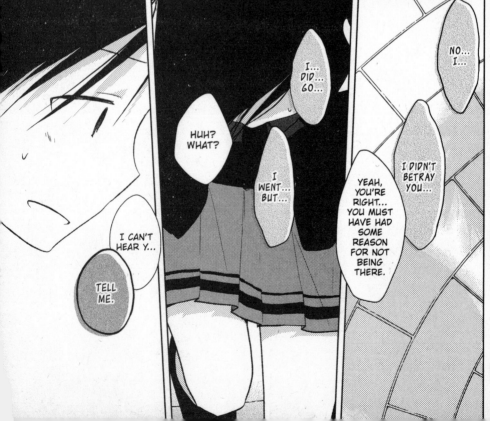

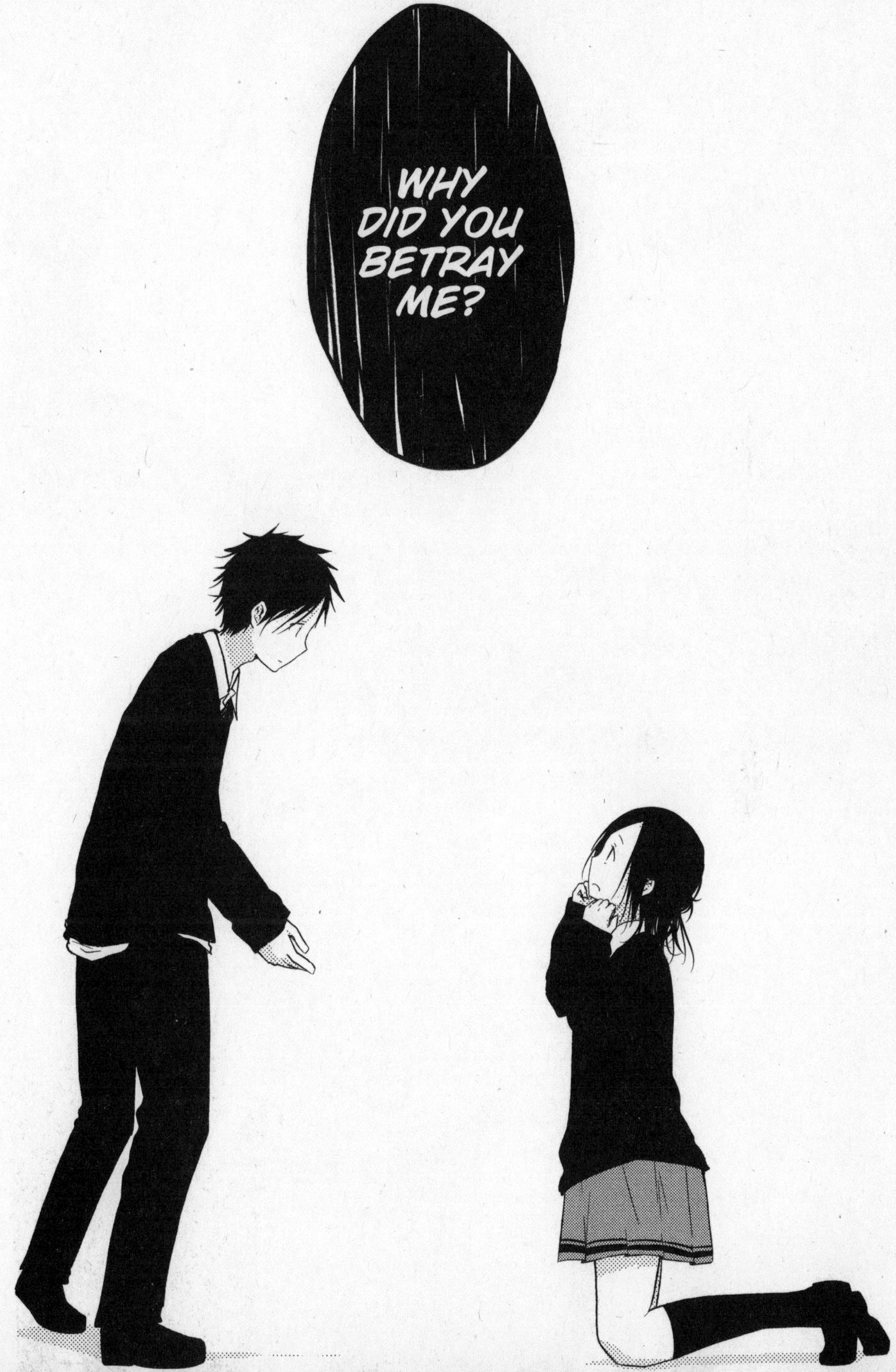
WHY DID YOU BETRAY ME?

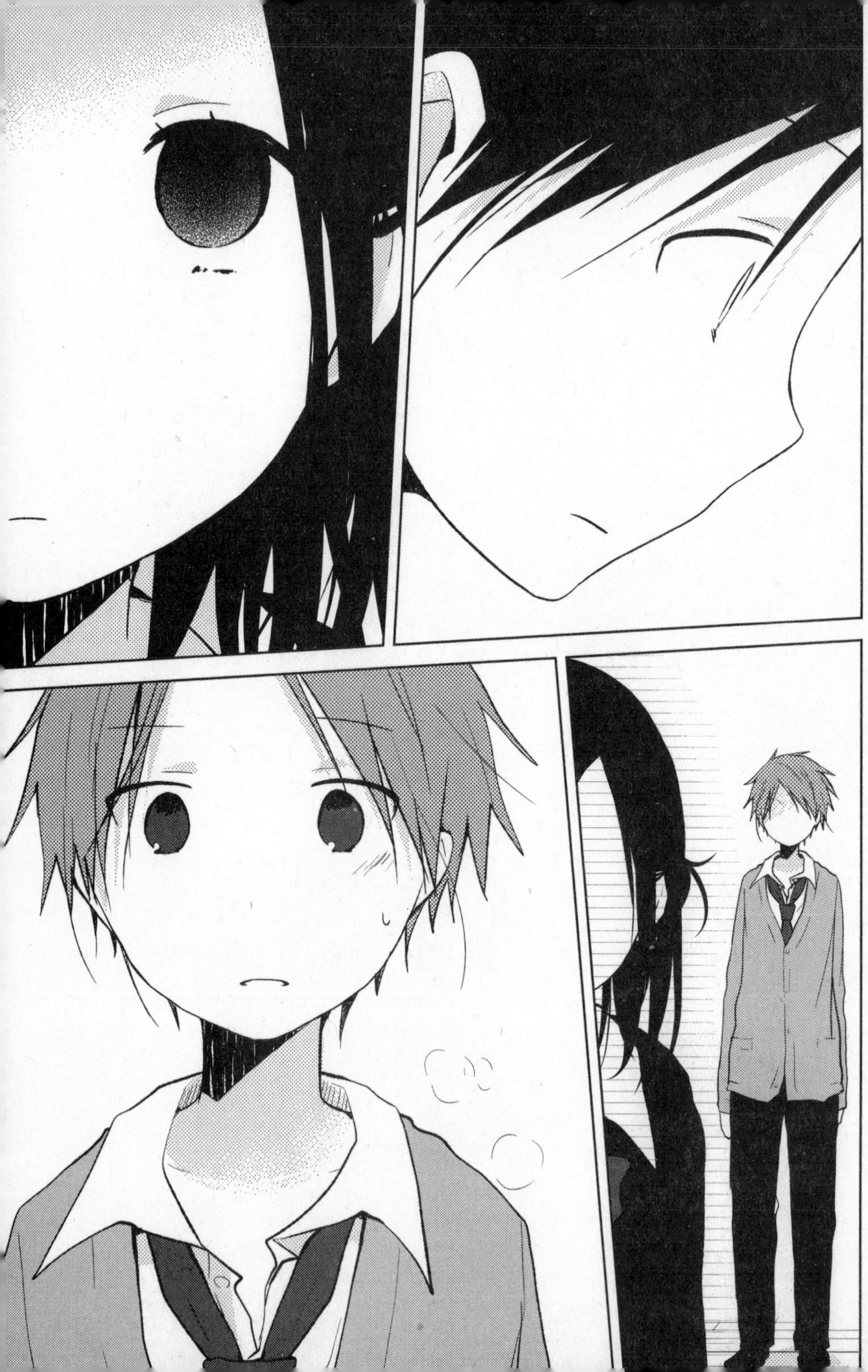

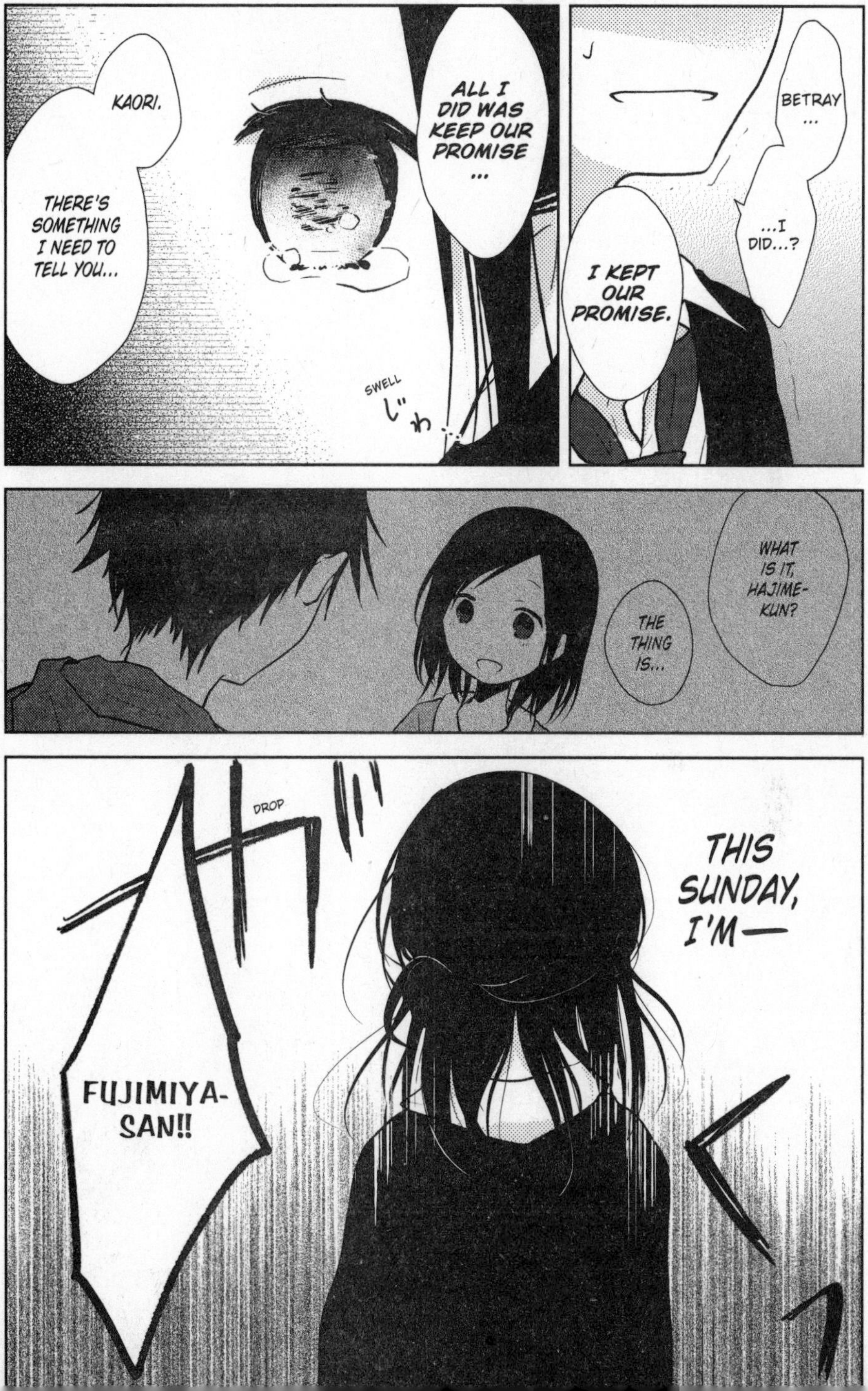
BETRAY ...
...I DID...?
I KEPT OUR PROMISE.
ALL I DID WAS KEEP OUR PROMISE ...
KAORI.
THERE'S SOMETHING I NEED TO TELL YOU...
SWELL
じわ
WHAT IS IT, HAJIME-KUN?
THE THING IS...
THIS SUNDAY, I'M—
DROP
FUJIMIYA-SAN!!

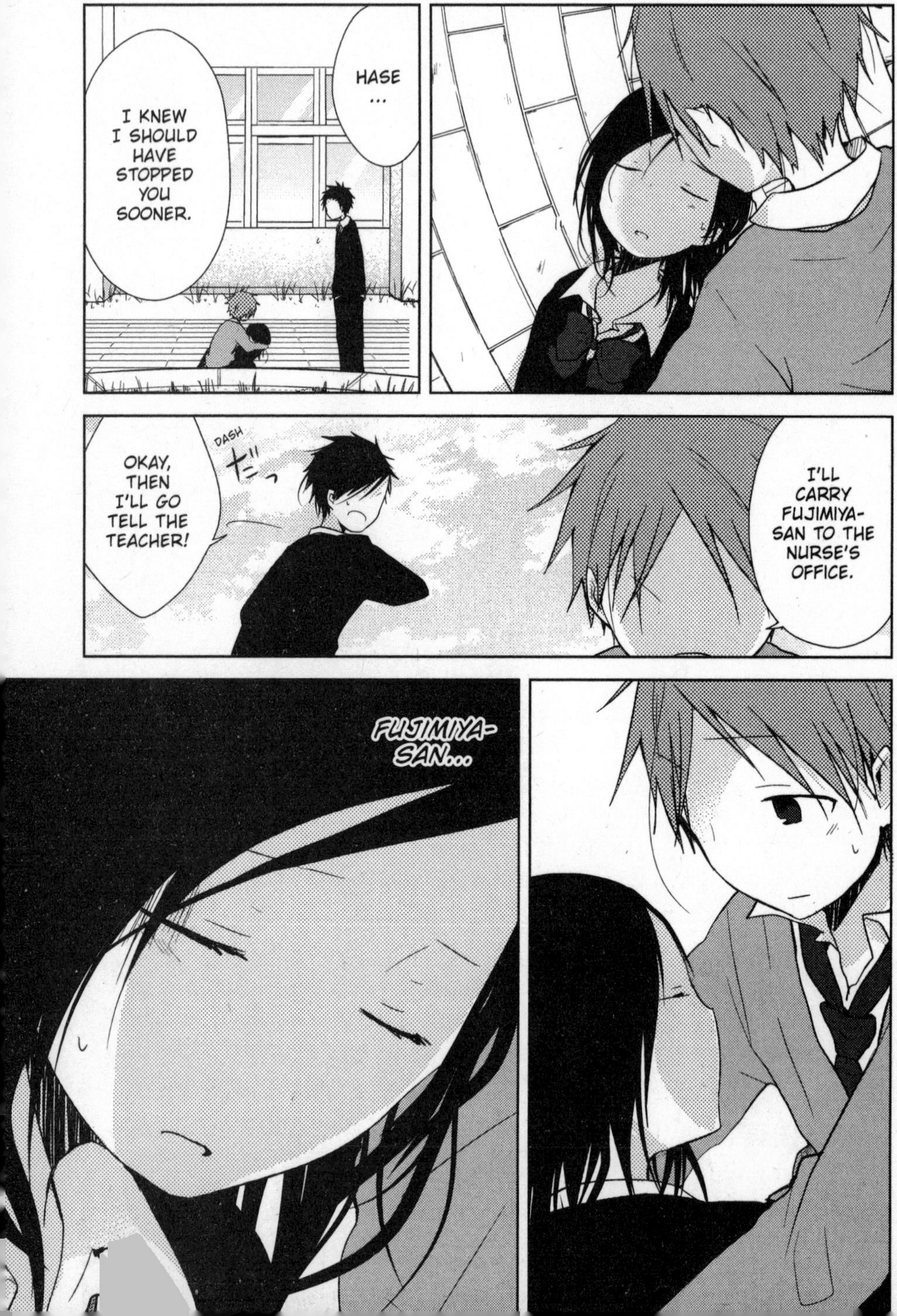
HASE...
I KNEW I SHOULD HAVE STOPPED YOU SOONER.
I'LL CARRY FUJIMIYA-SAN TO THE NURSE'S OFFICE.
DASH
OKAY, THEN I'LL GO TELL THE TEACHER!
FUJIMIYA-SAN...

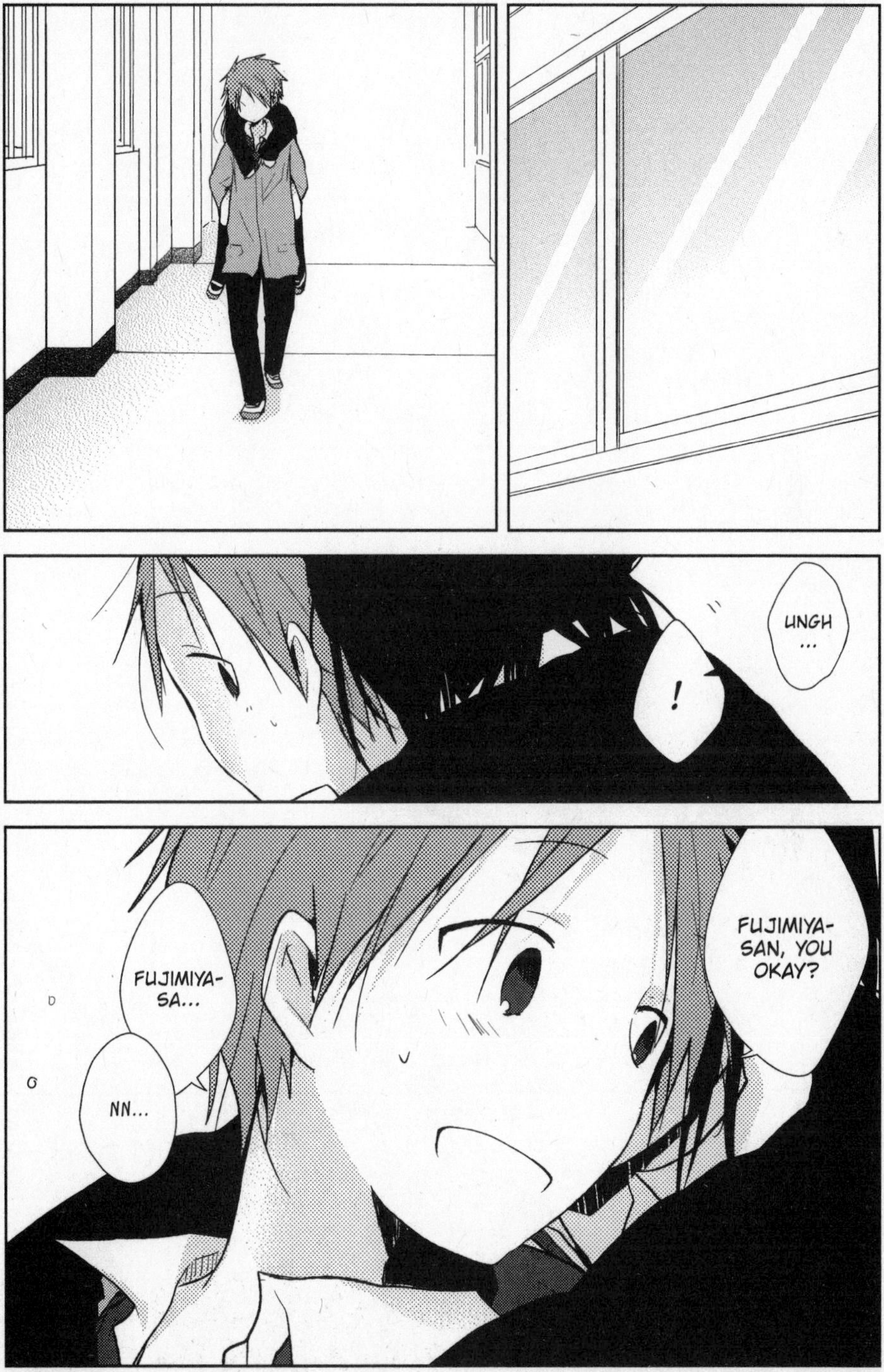
UNGH ...
!
FUJIMIYA-SAN, YOU OKAY?
FUJIMIYA-SA...
NN...

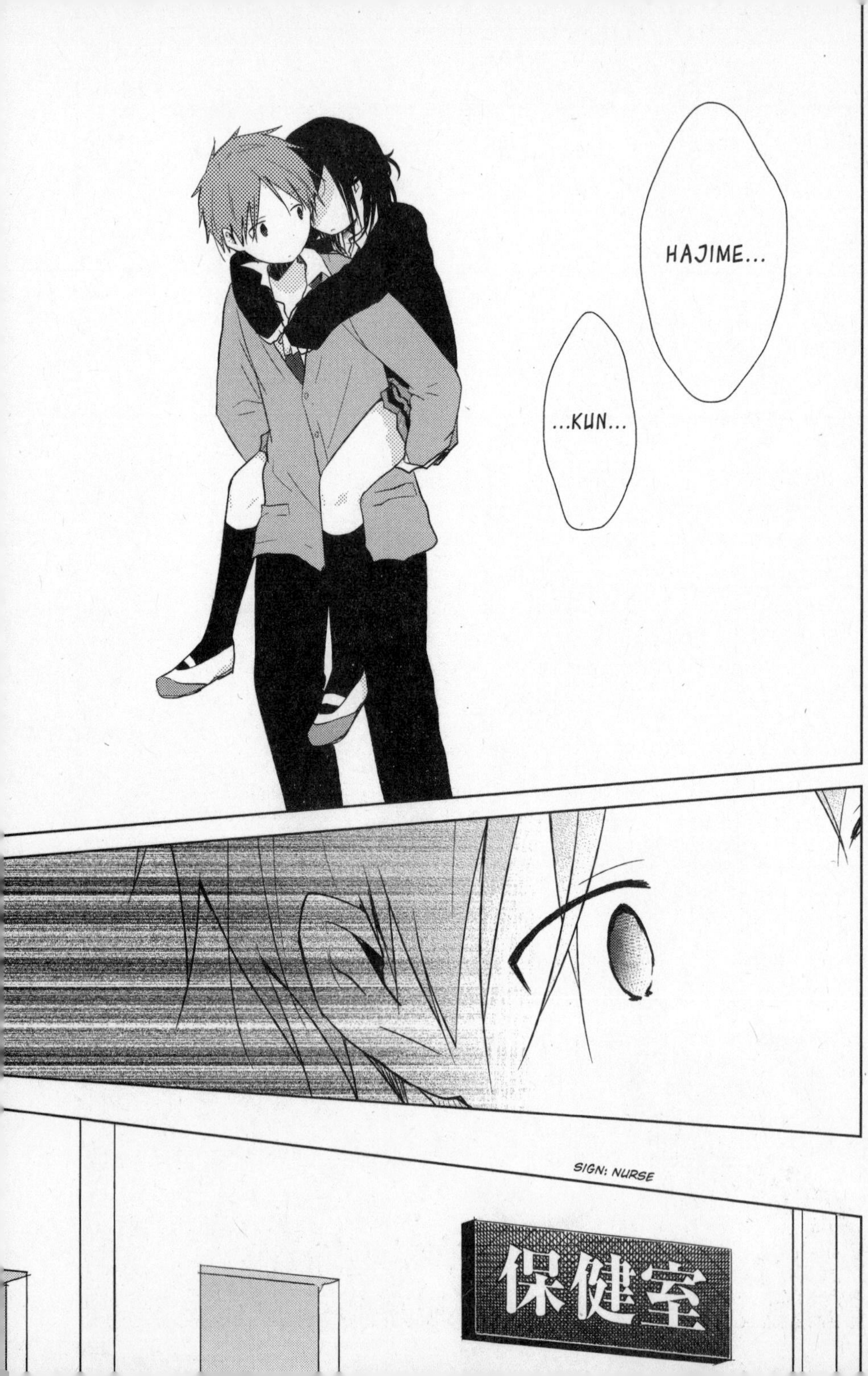
HAJIME...
...KUN...
SIGN: NURSE
保健室

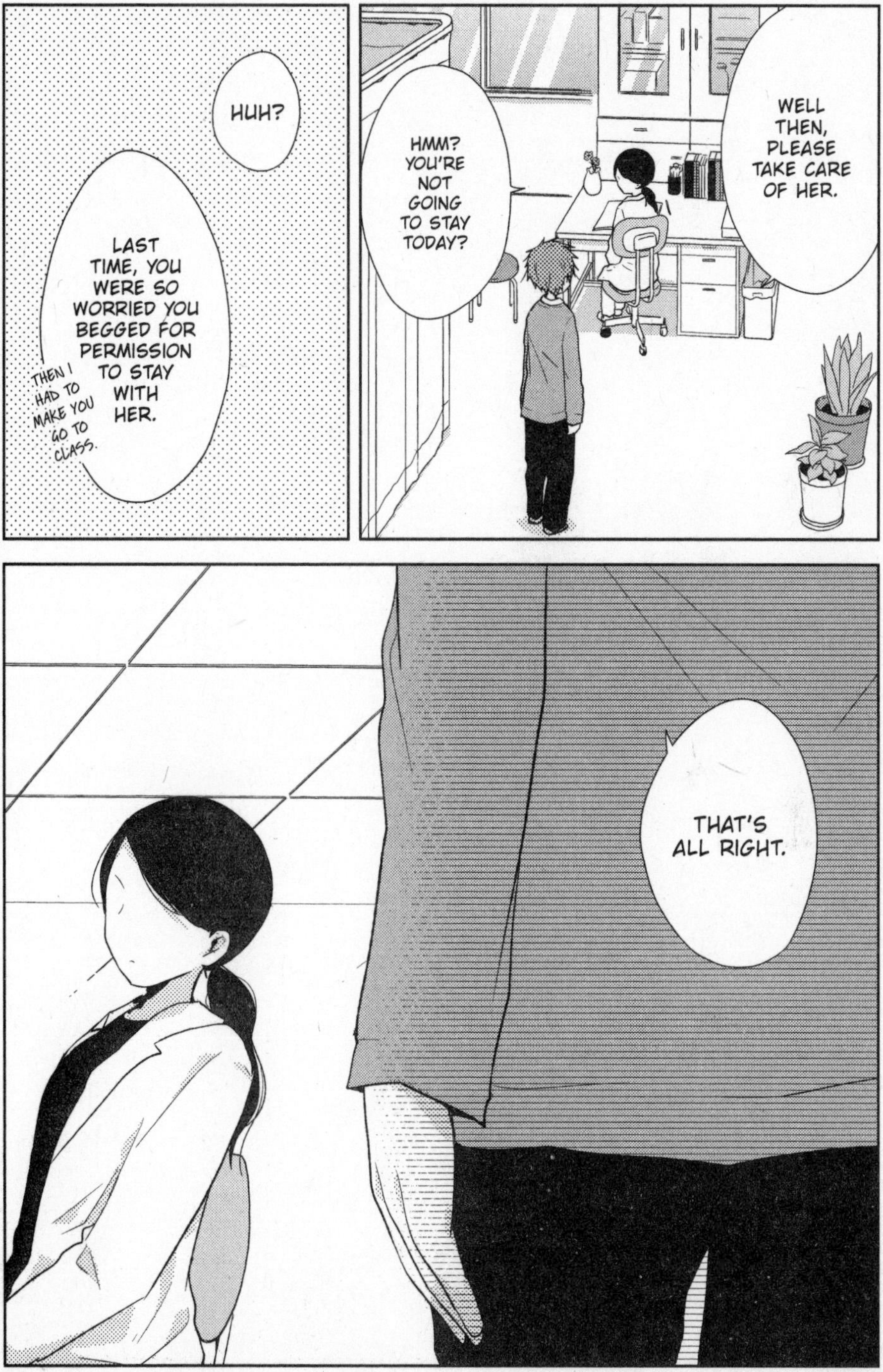
WELL THEN, PLEASE TAKE CARE OF HER.
HMM? YOU'RE NOT GOING TO STAY TODAY?
HUH?
LAST TIME, YOU WERE SO WORRIED YOU BEGGED FOR PERMISSION TO STAY WITH HER.
THEN I HAD TO MAKE YOU GO TO CLASS.
THAT'S ALL RIGHT.

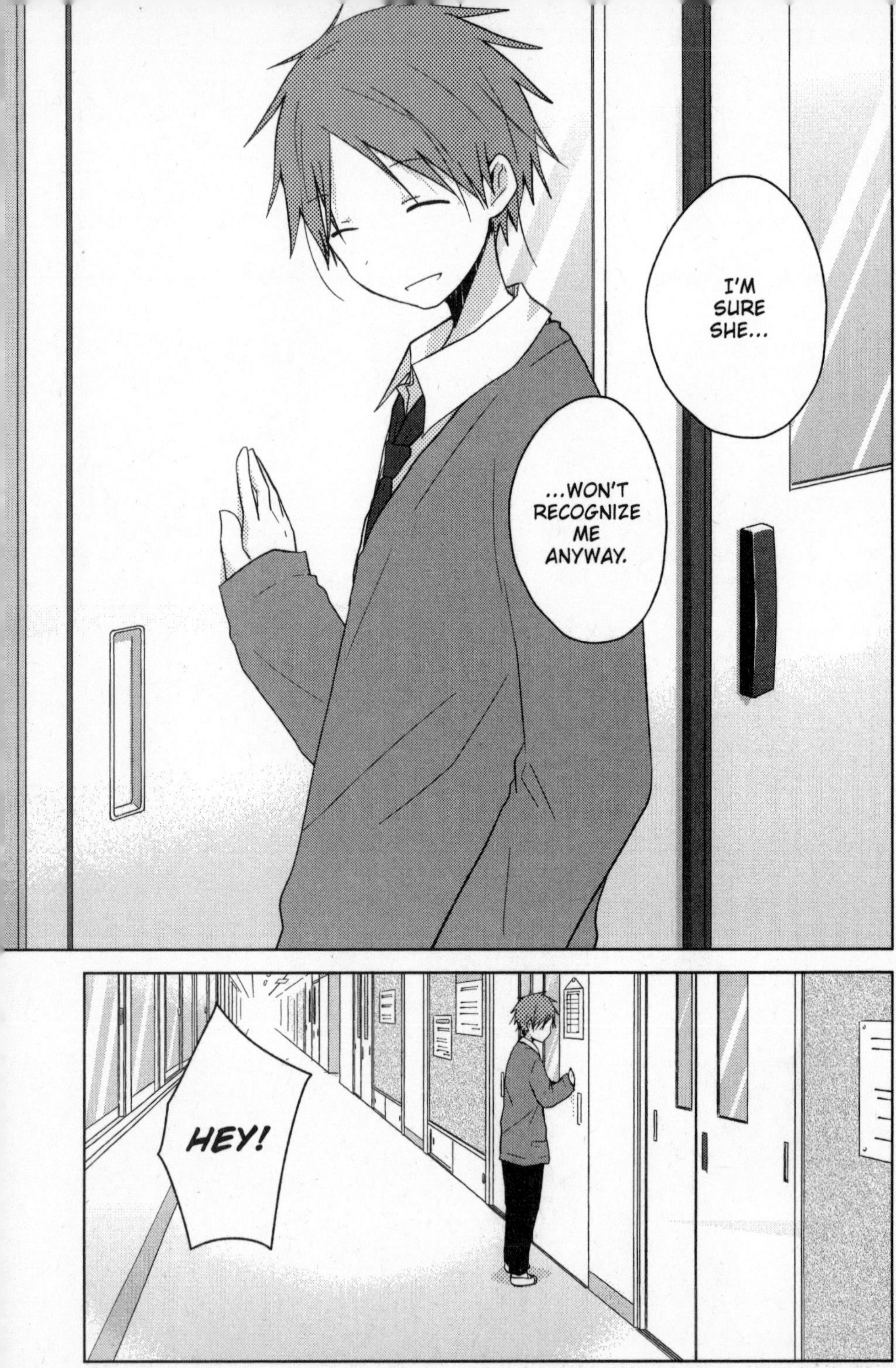
I'M SURE SHE...
...WON'T RECOGNIZE ME ANYWAY.
HEY!

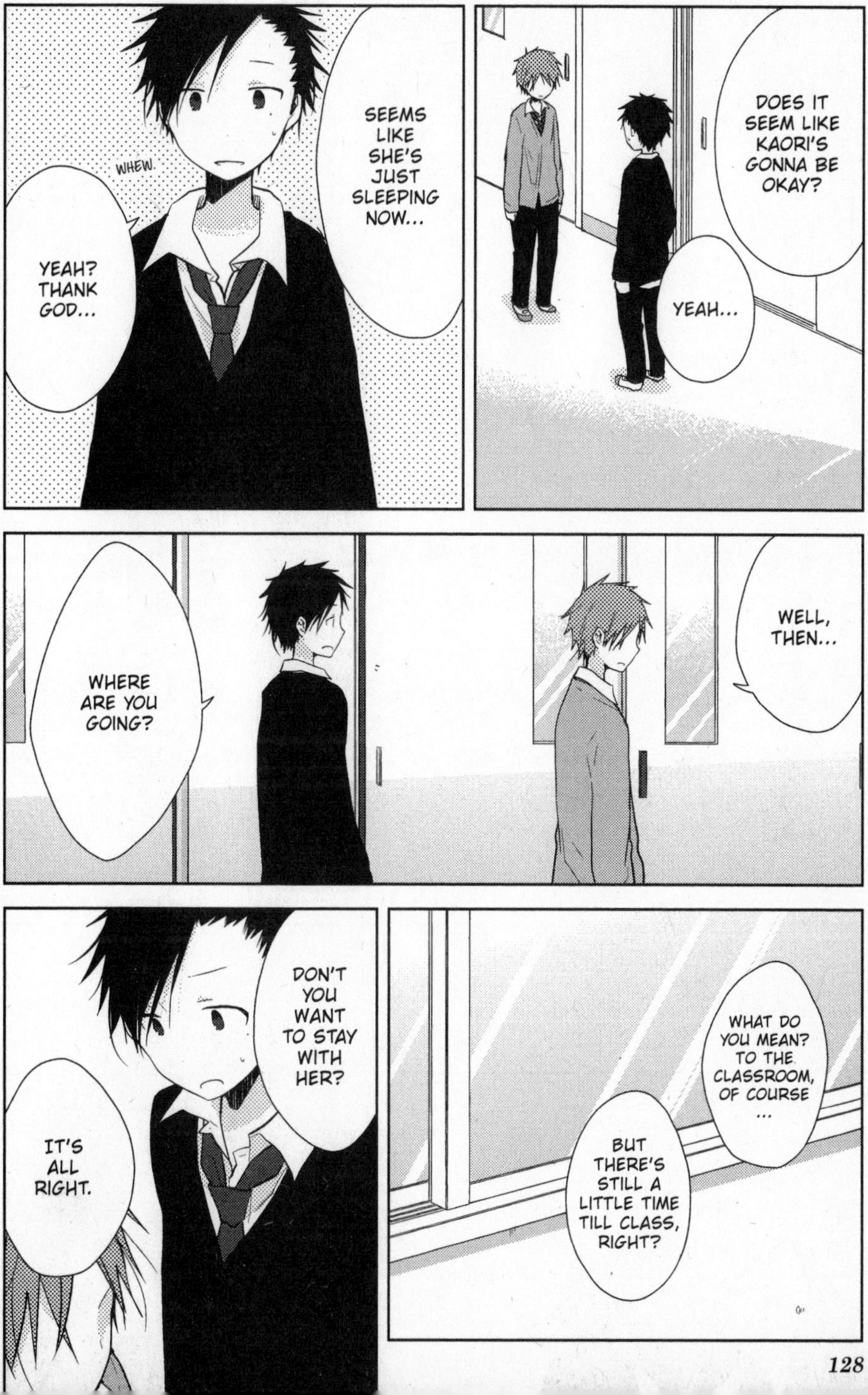
DOES IT SEEM LIKE KAORI'S GONNA BE OKAY?
YEAH...
SEEMS LIKE SHE'S JUST SLEEPING NOW...
WHEW.
YEAH? THANK GOD...
WELL, THEN...
WHERE ARE YOU GOING?
WHAT DO YOU MEAN? TO THE CLASSROOM, OF COURSE...
BUT THERE'S STILL A LITTLE TIME TILL CLASS, RIGHT?
DON'T YOU WANT TO STAY WITH HER?
IT'S ALL RIGHT.

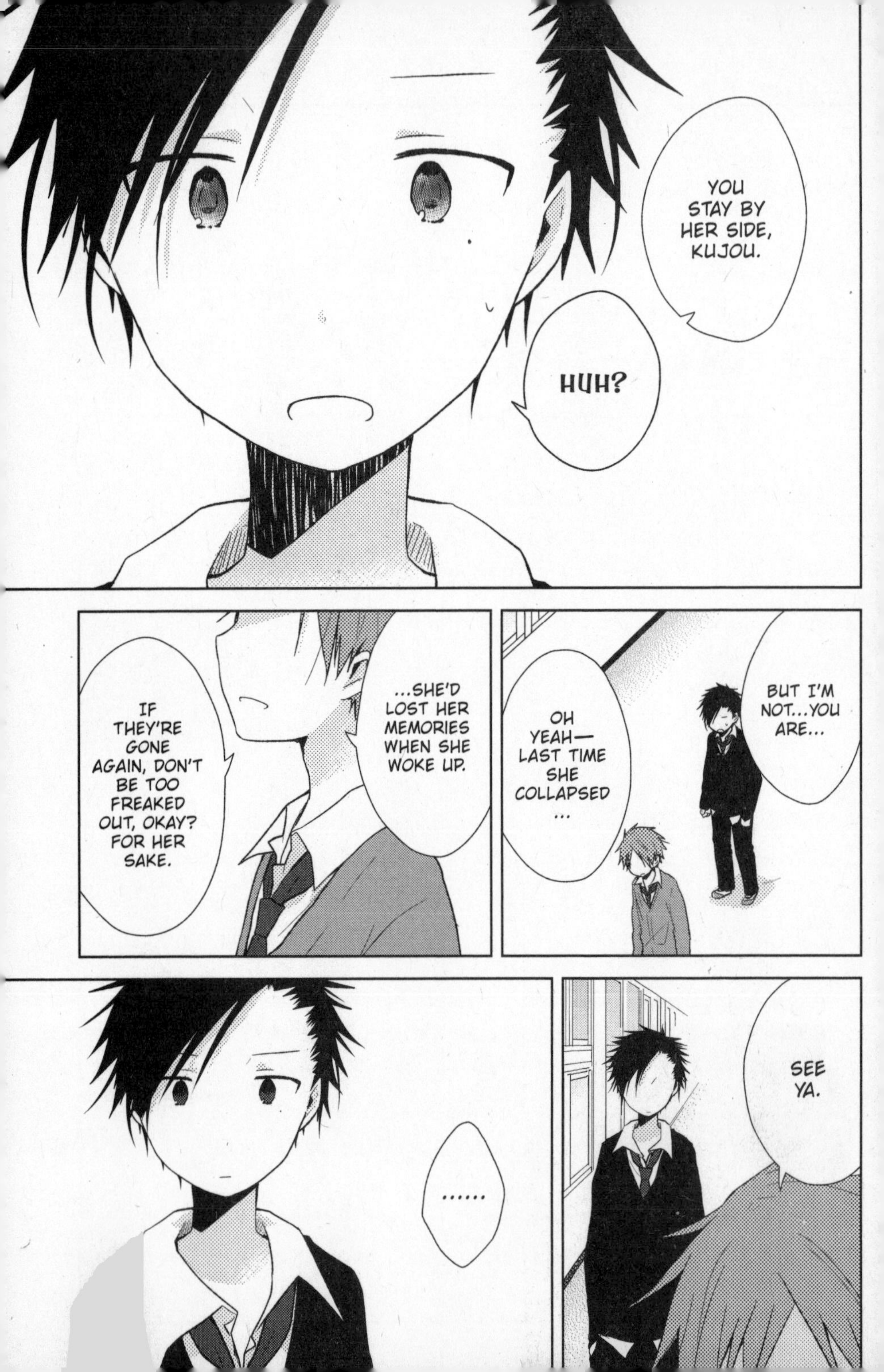
YOU STAY BY HER SIDE, KUJOU.
HUH?
BUT I'M NOT...YOU ARE...
OH YEAH—LAST TIME SHE COLLAPSED...
...SHE'D LOST HER MEMORIES WHEN SHE WOKE UP.
IF THEY'RE GONE AGAIN, DON'T BE TOO FREAKED OUT, OKAY? FOR HER SAKE.
SEE YA.
......

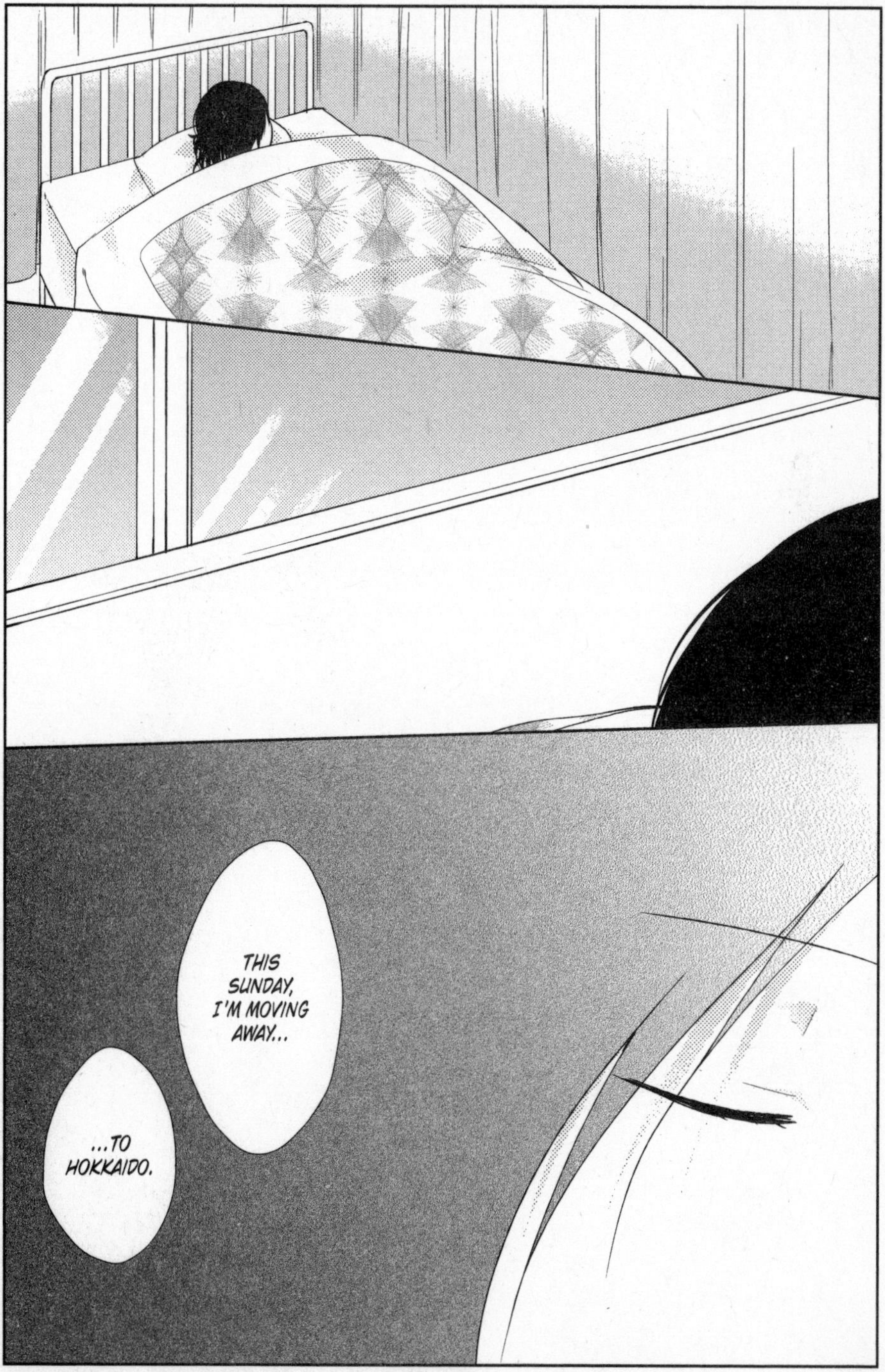
THIS SUNDAY, I'M MOVING AWAY...
...TO HOKKAIDO.

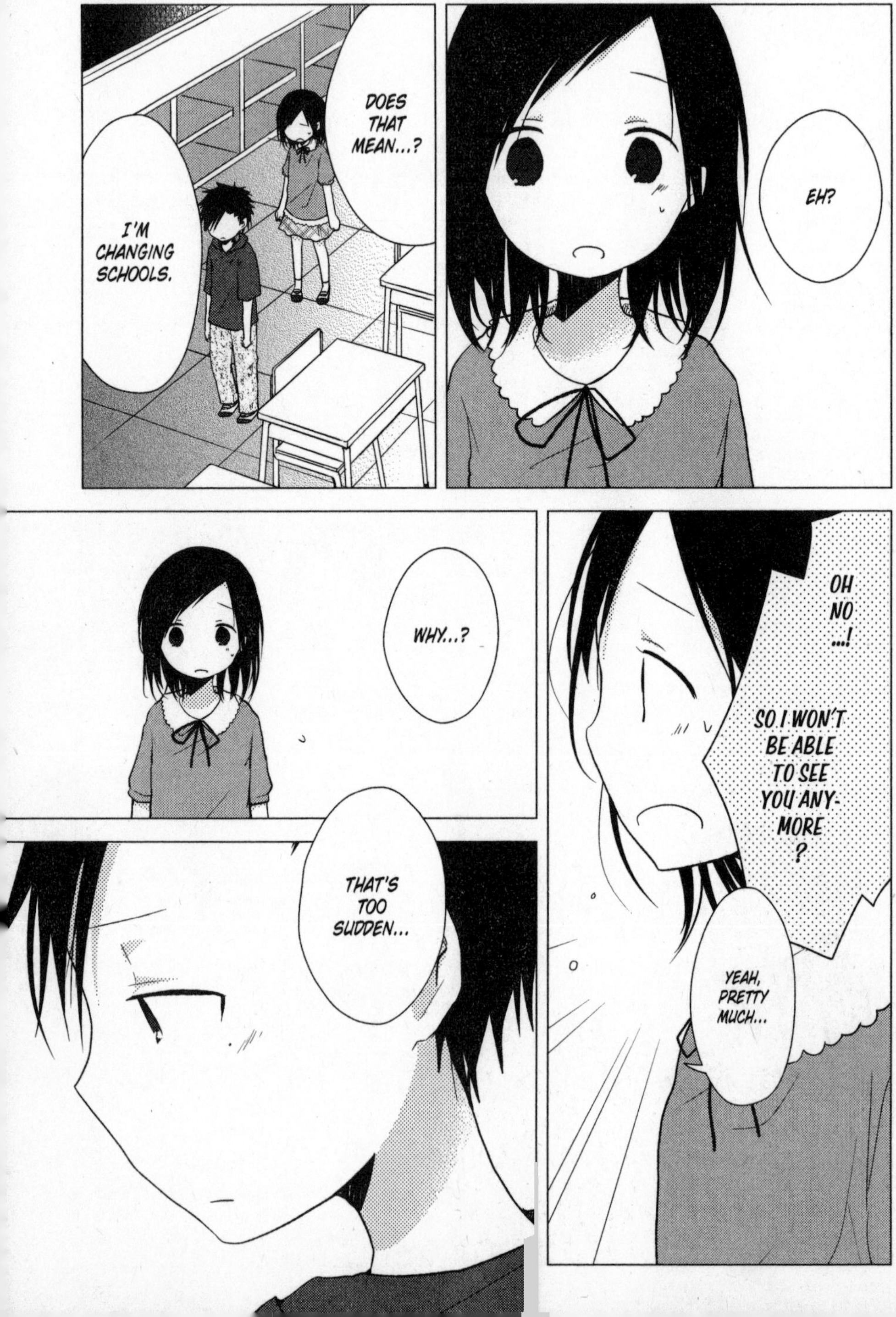
EH?
DOES THAT MEAN...?
I'M CHANGING SCHOOLS.
OH NO ...!
SO I WON'T BE ABLE TO SEE YOU ANY-MORE ?
YEAH, PRETTY MUCH...
WHY...?
THAT'S TOO SUDDEN...

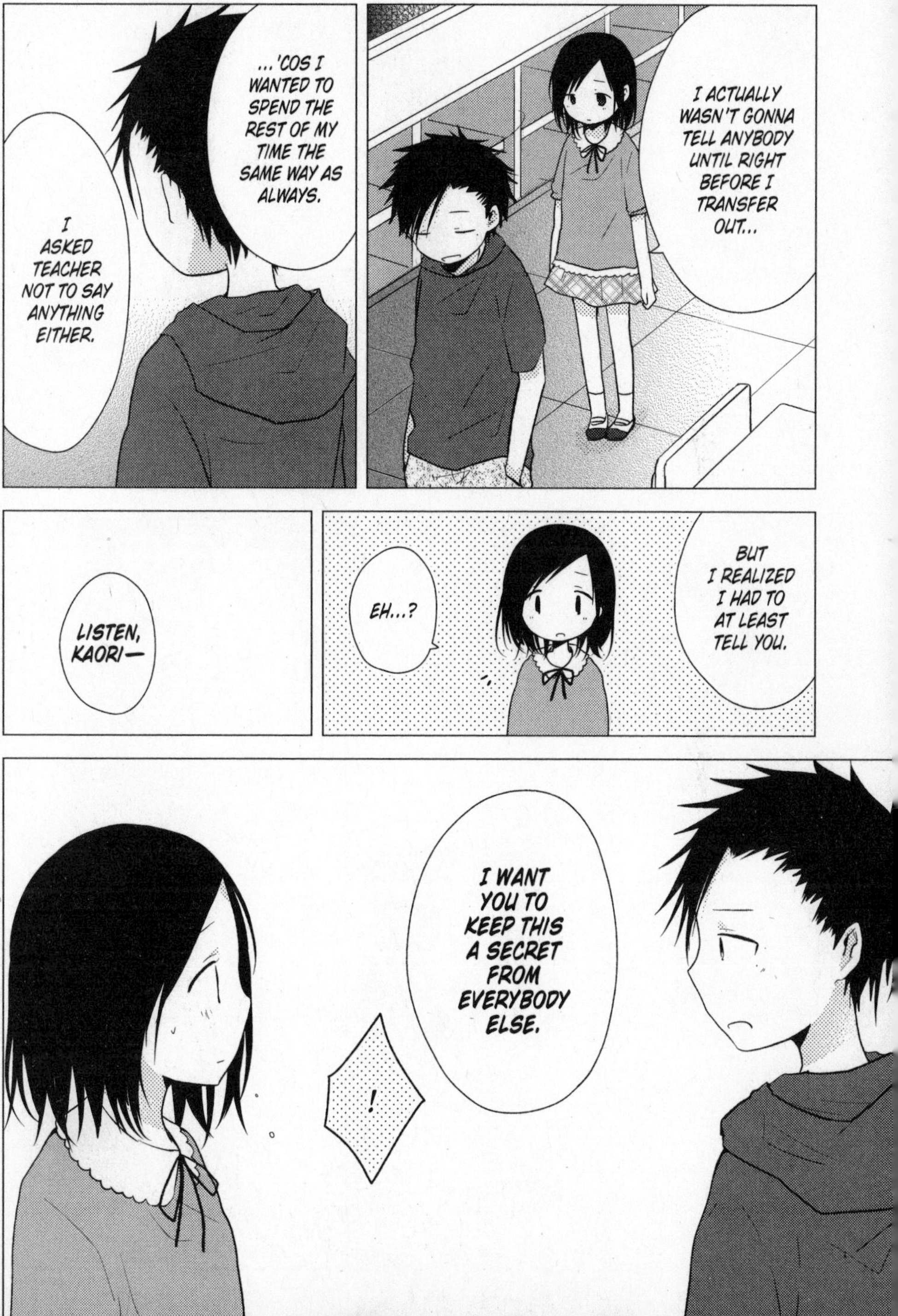
I ACTUALLY WASN'T GONNA TELL ANYBODY UNTIL RIGHT BEFORE I TRANSFER OUT...
...'COS I WANTED TO SPEND THE REST OF MY TIME THE SAME WAY AS ALWAYS.
I ASKED TEACHER NOT TO SAY ANYTHING EITHER.
BUT I REALIZED I HAD TO AT LEAST TELL YOU.
EH...?
LISTEN, KAORI—
I WANT YOU TO KEEP THIS A SECRET FROM EVERYBODY ELSE.
!

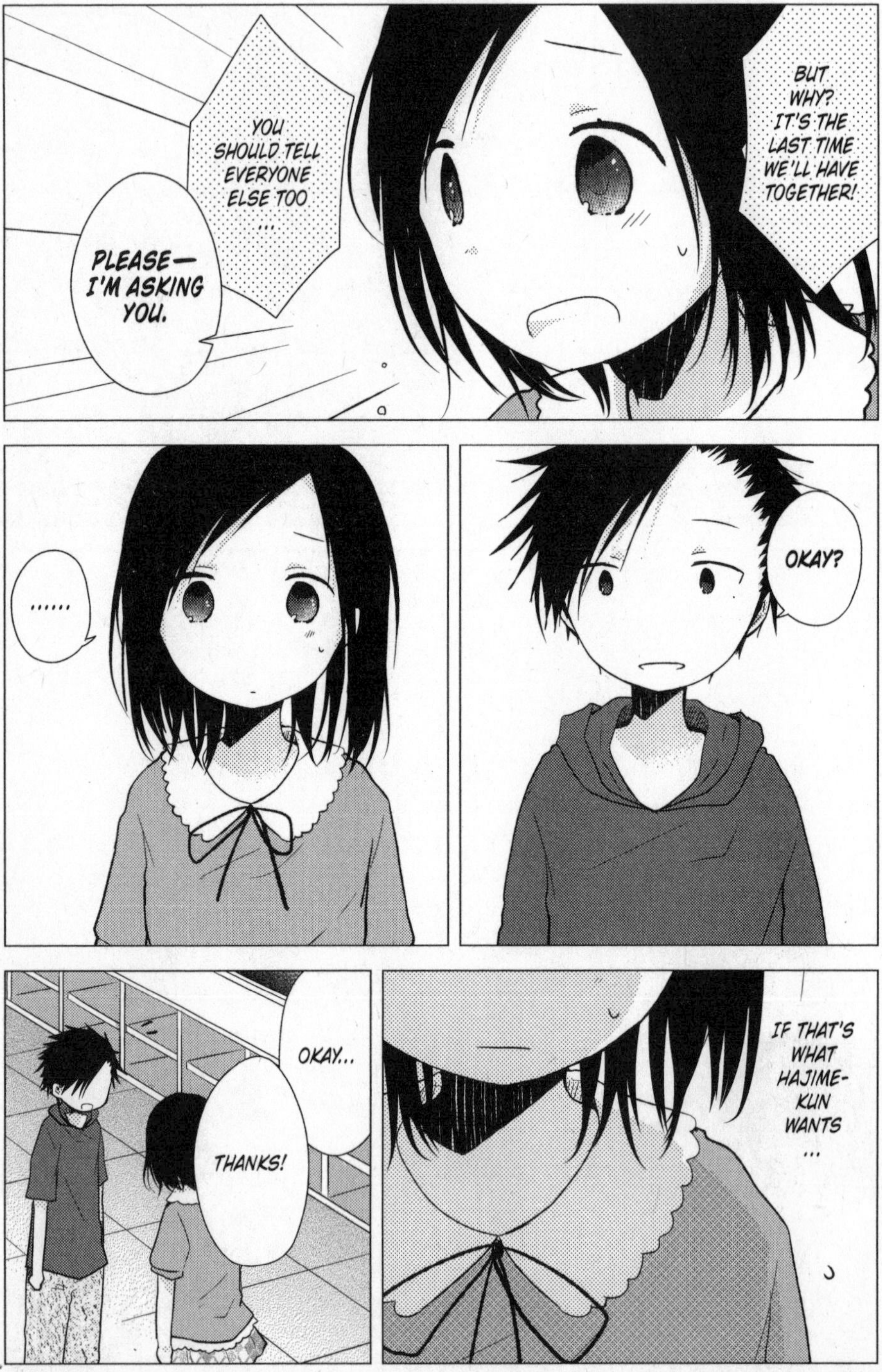
BUT WHY? IT'S THE LAST TIME WE'LL HAVE TOGETHER!
YOU SHOULD TELL EVERYONE ELSE TOO ...
PLEASE— I'M ASKING YOU.
OKAY?
......
IF THAT'S WHAT HAJIME-KUN WANTS ...
OKAY...
THANKS!

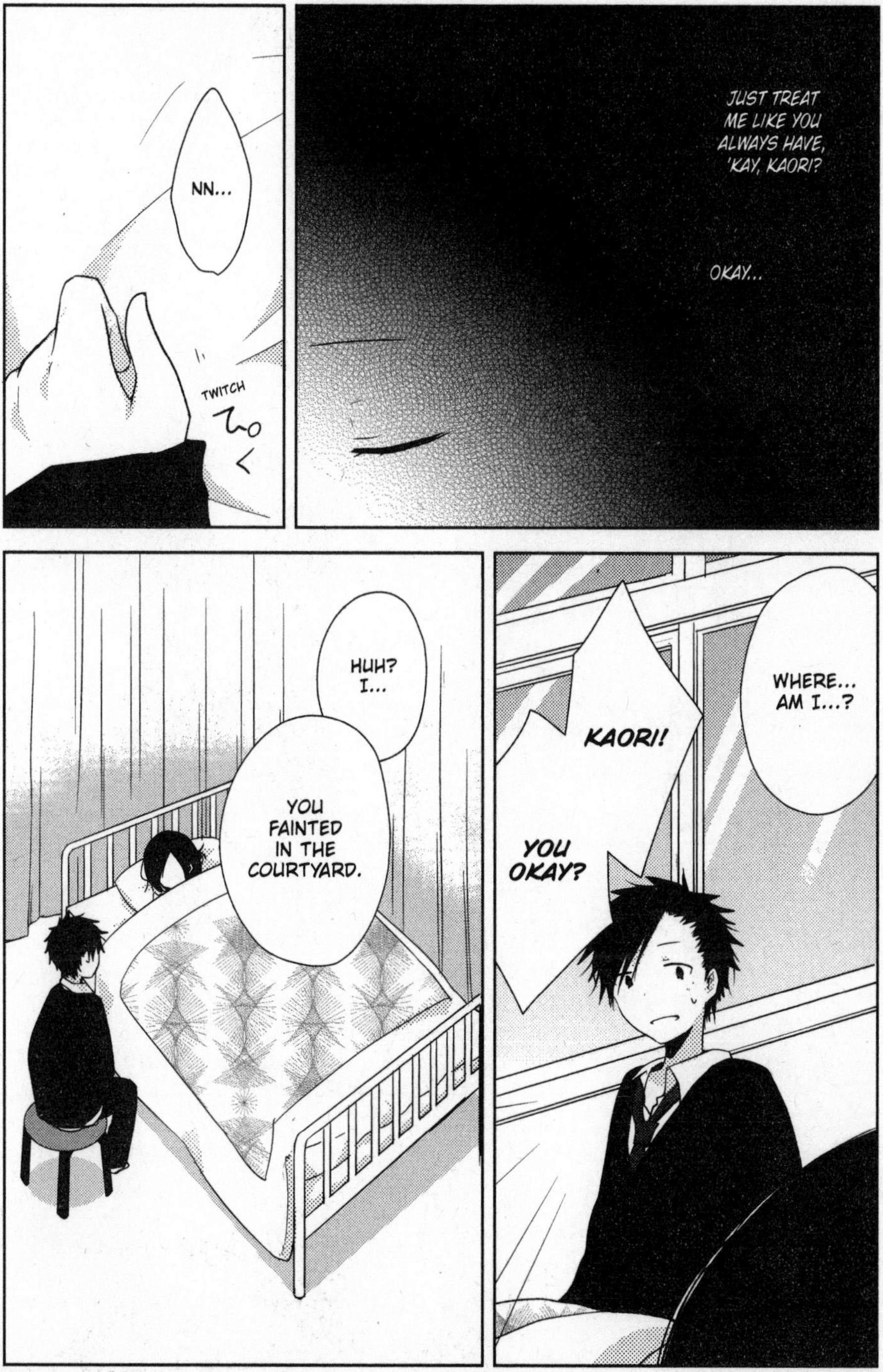
JUST TREAT ME LIKE YOU ALWAYS HAVE, 'KAY, KAORI?
OKAY...
NN...
TWITCH
WHERE... AM I...?
KAORI!
YOU OKAY?
HUH? I...
YOU FAINTED IN THE COURTYARD.

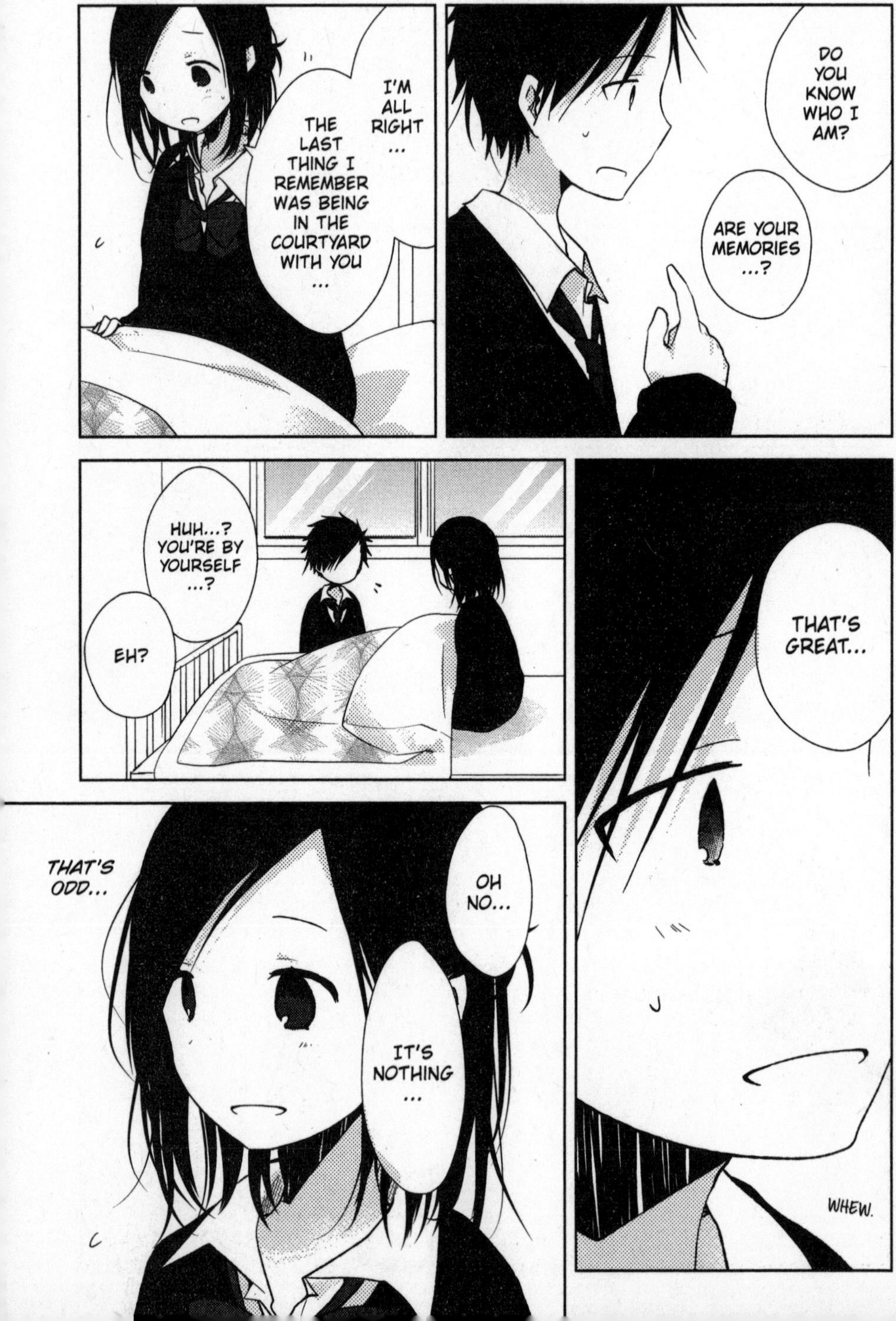
DO YOU KNOW WHO I AM?
ARE YOUR MEMORIES ...?
I'M ALL RIGHT ...
THE LAST THING I REMEMBER WAS BEING IN THE COURTYARD WITH YOU ...
THAT'S GREAT...
WHEW.
HUH...? YOU'RE BY YOURSELF ...?
EH?
OH NO...
IT'S NOTHING ...
THAT'S ODD...

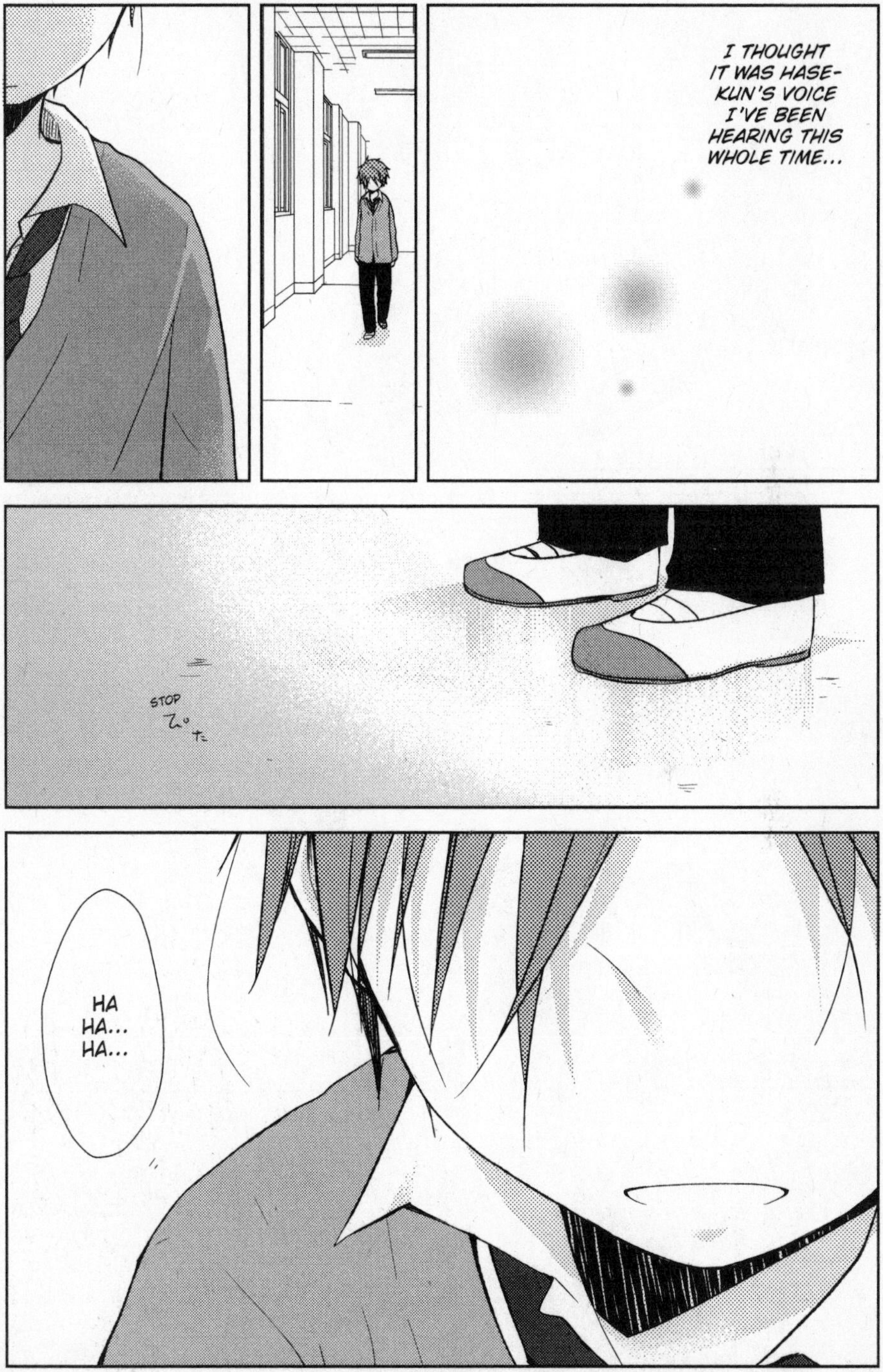
I THOUGHT IT WAS HASE-KUN'S VOICE I'VE BEEN HEARING THIS WHOLE TIME...
STOP
HA HA... HA...

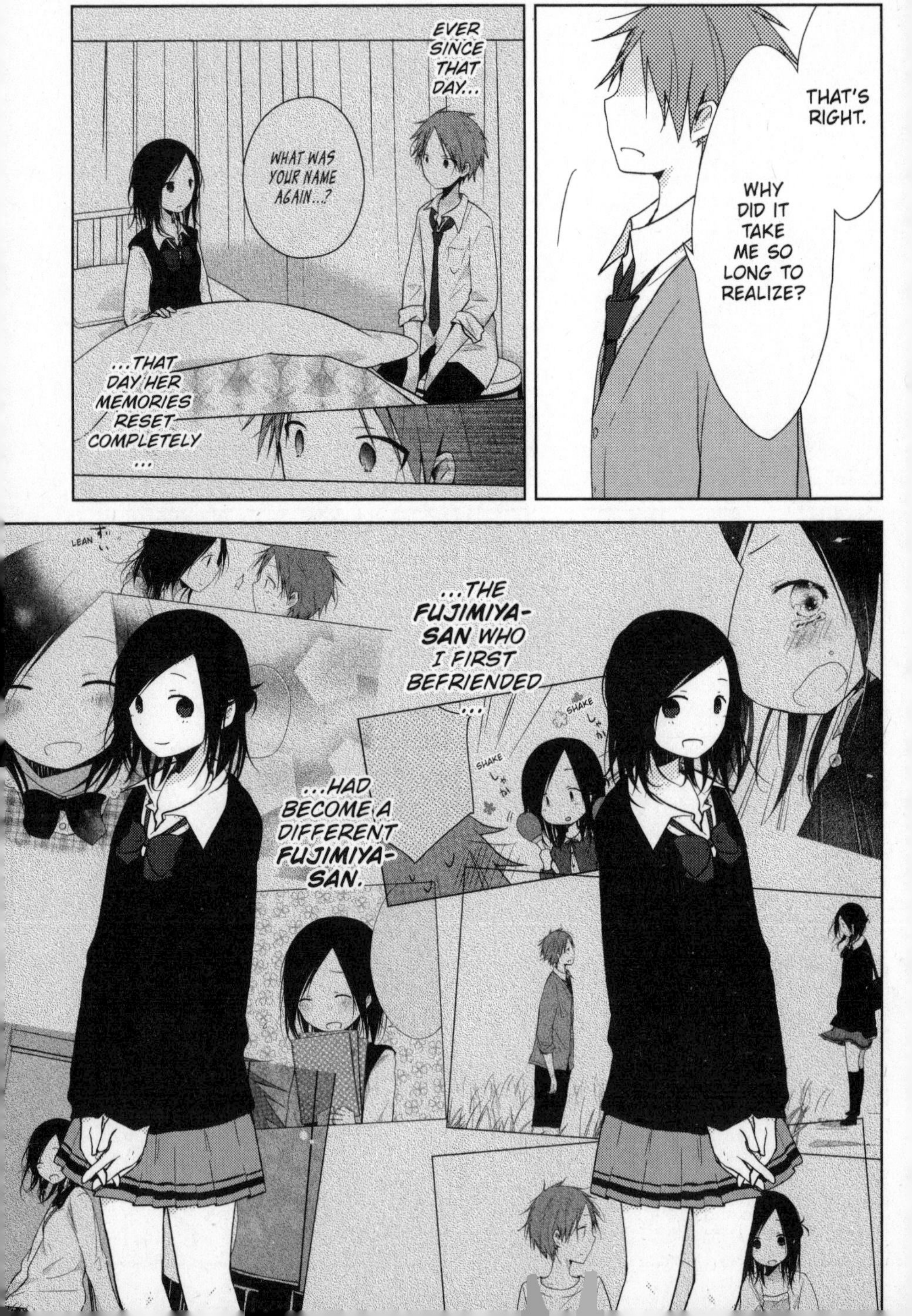
THAT'S RIGHT.
WHY DID IT TAKE ME SO LONG TO REALIZE?
EVER SINCE THAT DAY...
WHAT WAS YOUR NAME AGAIN...?
...THAT DAY HER MEMORIES RESET COMPLETELY...
SHAKE
SHAKE
...THE FUJIMIYA-SAN WHO I FIRST BEFRIENDED...
...HAD BECOME A DIFFERENT FUJIMIYA-SAN.
LEAN

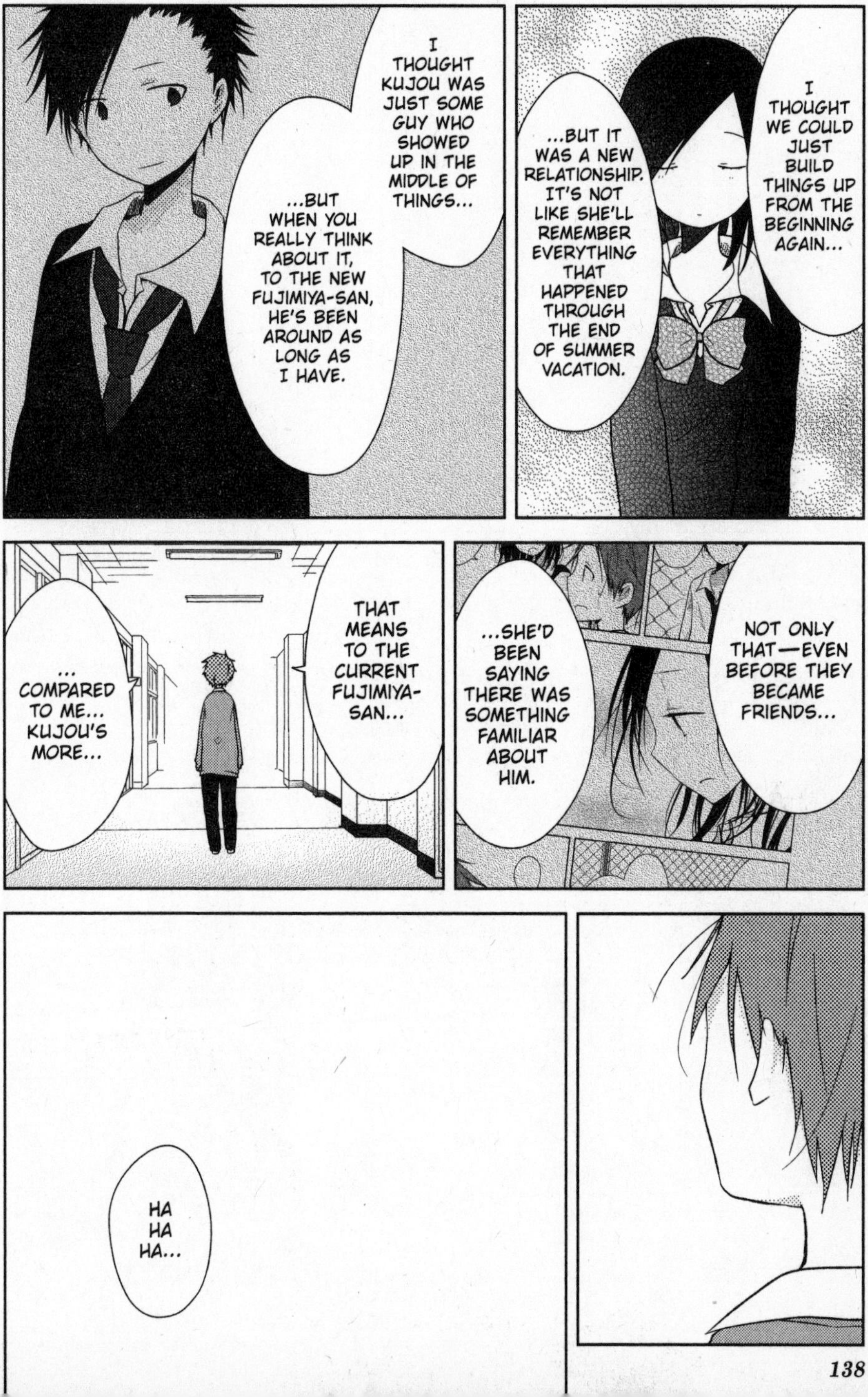
I THOUGHT WE COULD JUST BUILD THINGS UP FROM THE BEGINNING AGAIN...
...BUT IT WAS A NEW RELATIONSHIP. IT'S NOT LIKE SHE'LL REMEMBER EVERYTHING THAT HAPPENED THROUGH THE END OF SUMMER VACATION.
I THOUGHT KUJOU WAS JUST SOME GUY WHO SHOWED UP IN THE MIDDLE OF THINGS...
...BUT WHEN YOU REALLY THINK ABOUT IT, TO THE NEW FUJIMIYA-SAN, HE'S BEEN AROUND AS LONG AS I HAVE.
NOT ONLY THAT—EVEN BEFORE THEY BECAME FRIENDS...
...SHE'D BEEN SAYING THERE WAS SOMETHING FAMILIAR ABOUT HIM.
THAT MEANS TO THE CURRENT FUJIMIYA-SAN...
... COMPARED TO ME... KUJOU'S MORE...
HA HA HA...

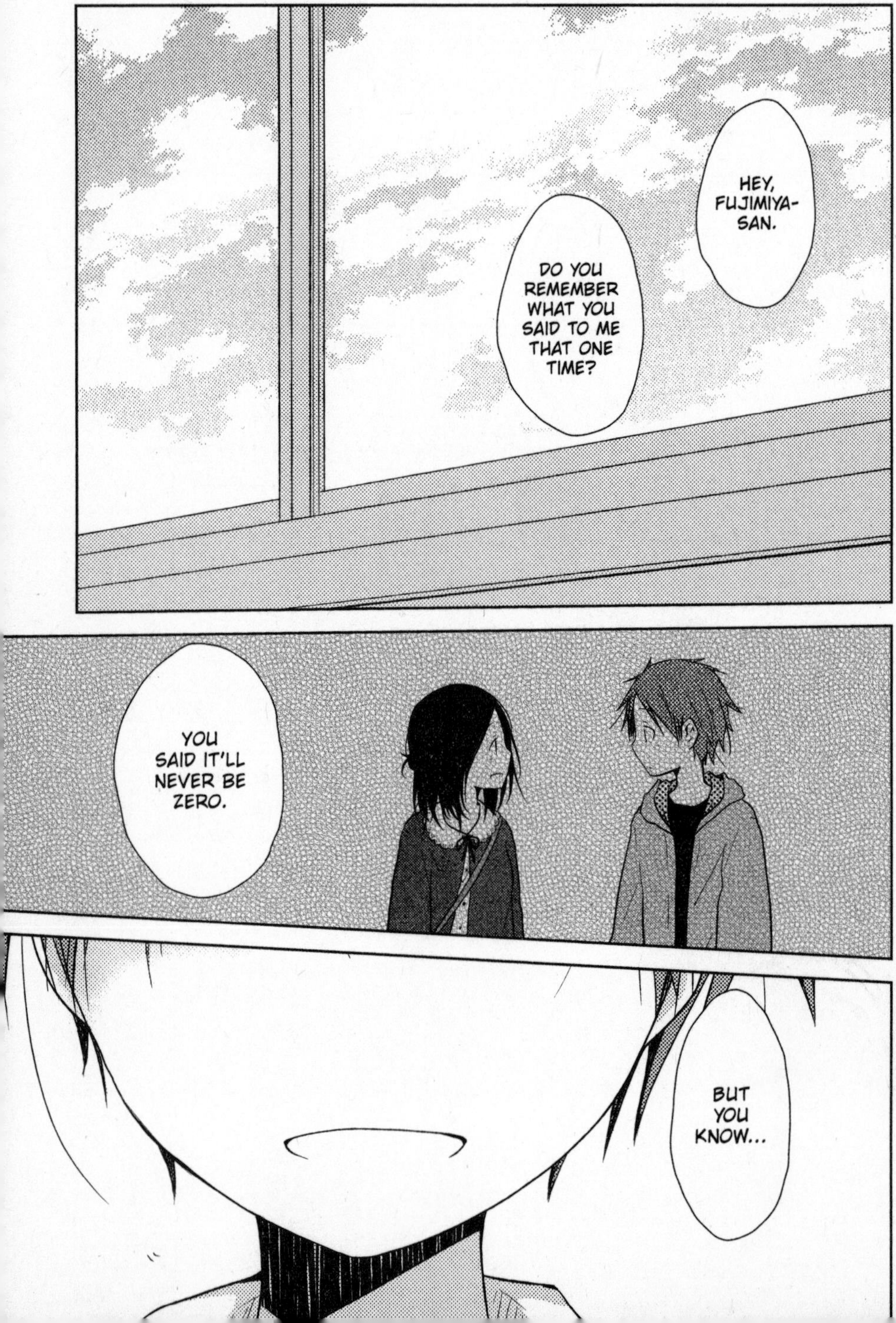
HEY, FUJIMIYA-SAN.
DO YOU REMEMBER WHAT YOU SAID TO ME THAT ONE TIME?
YOU SAID IT'LL NEVER BE ZERO.
BUT YOU KNOW...

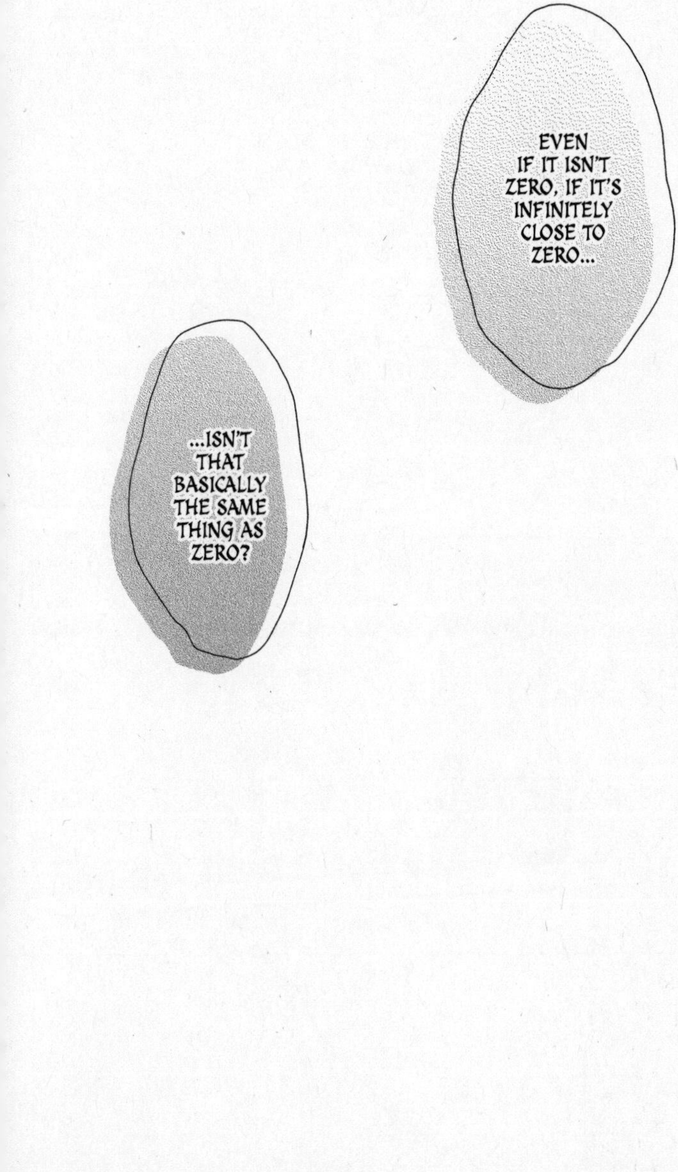
EVEN IF IT ISN'T ZERO, IF IT'S INFINITELY CLOSE TO ZERO...
...ISN'T THAT BASICALLY THE SAME THING AS ZERO?

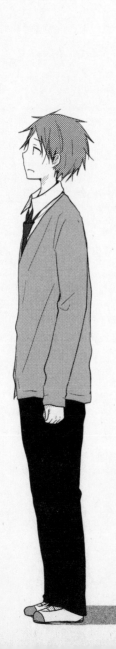

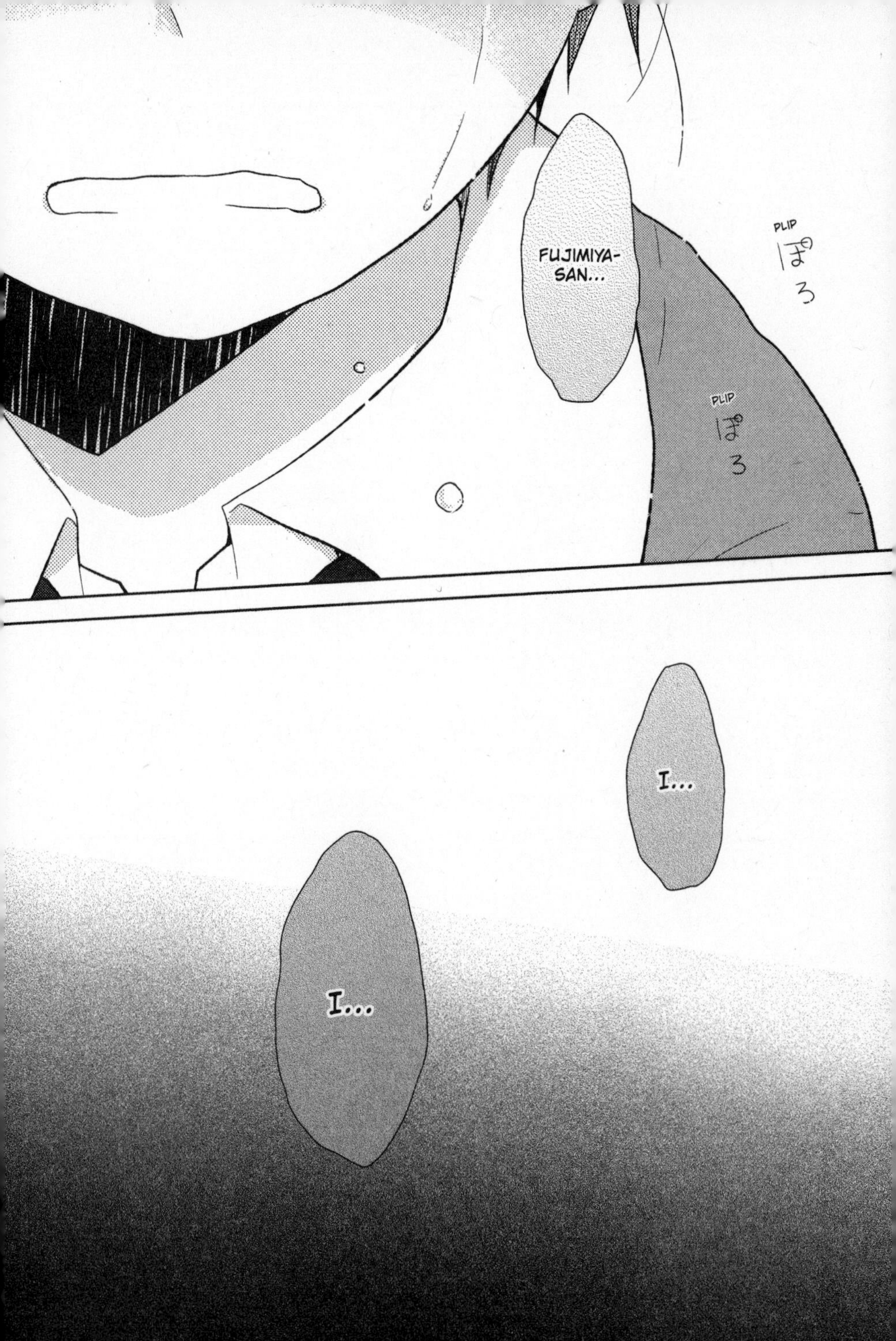
PLIP
ぽろ
FUJIMIYA-SAN...
PLIP
ぽろ
I...
I...

ONE WEEK FRIENDS 5 END

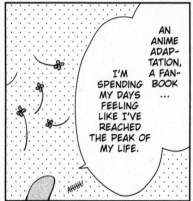

HELLO. IT'S ME, MATCHA HAZUKI.
WE'RE AT VOLUME 5. I'M SHOCKED.
FIVE?
FIVE!
AN ANIME ADAPTATION, A FANBOOK ...
I'M SPENDING MY DAYS FEELING LIKE I'VE REACHED THE PEAK OF MY LIFE.
AHHH!
I'VE ALWAYS LIKED LIVING A QUIET LIFE, SO MY HEART CAN'T KEEP UP WITH THIS SITUATION, AND SOMETIMES I START TO WANT TO DISAPPEAR ...
TIME TO DISAPPEAR.
YES, THAT'S WHAT I'LL DO.
SHMMM
...BUT SINCE I HAVE VARIOUS JOBS TO DO SUCCESSIVELY, I'M JUST BARELY MANAGING NOT TO DISAPPEAR.
DON'T LET MY CONFESSION WORRY YOU— I'M GOING TO KEEP DOING MY BEST.
I HOPE WE'LL SEE YOU FOR THE NEXT VOLUME TOO!
special thanks
MY EDITOR MATH-SAN FRIED TUNA-SAN
URUSHIHARA-SAN SANBOU-SAN ALL MY FRIENDS & FAMILY
EVERYONE CONNECTED TO THE BOOK

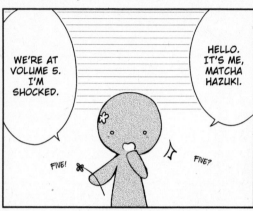

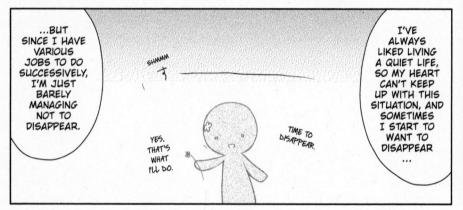

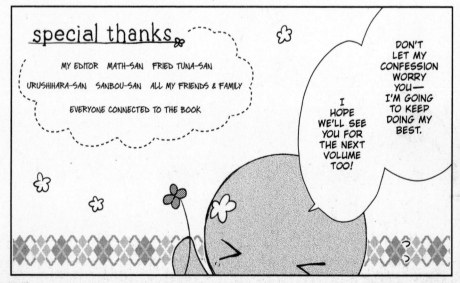

IT'S
ALL RIGHT.
I'LL DO
WHATEVER
YOU WANT TO
DO TODAY.

DON'T
STRAIN
YOURSELF.

ARE
YOU
GIVING
UP...

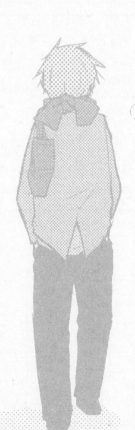

I WONDER HOW
FUJIMIYA-SAN
WANTS TO SPEND
CHRISTMAS...?

ONE WEEK FRIENDS 6 COMING IN SPRING 2019

AW YEAH! IT'S DUET TIME!!

WE'LL CONTINUE TO BE FRIENDS.

IT'S REALLY COLD.

...ON FUJIMIYA-SAN?

THANKS FOR BEING MY FRIEND.

I THINK THE FIRST PLACE THE TWO OF US HUNG OUT WAS AT KARAOKE.

CHRISTMAS... HUH...?

NEXT ONE WEEK FRIENDS...

I CAN'T GAUGE A SENSE OF DISTANCE THAT'S JUST RIGHT.

ONE WEEK FRIENDS

MATCHA HAZUKI

W9-AOK-230

11/2019

Translation/Adaptation: Amanda Haley

Lettering: Bianca Pistillo

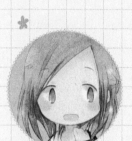

This book is a work of fiction. Names, characters, places, and incidents are the product of the author's imagination or are used fictitiously. Any resemblance to actual events, locales, or persons, living or dead, is coincidental.

ONE WEEK FRIENDS Volume 5 ©2014 Matcha Hazuki/ SQUARE ENIX CO., LTD. First published in Japan in 2014 by SQUARE ENIX CO., LTD. English translation rights arranged with SQUARE ENIX CO., LTD. and Yen Press, LLC through Tuttle-Mori Agency, Inc.

English translation © 2018 by SQUARE ENIX CO., LTD.

Yen Press, LLC supports the right to free expression and the value of copyright. The purpose of copyright is to encourage writers and artists to produce the creative works that enrich our culture.

The scanning, uploading, and distribution of this book without permission is a theft of the author's intellectual property. If you would like permission to use material from the book (other than for review purposes), please contact the publisher. Thank you for your support of the author's rights.

Yen Press
1290 Avenue of the Americas
New York, NY 10104

Visit us at yenpress.com
facebook.com/yenpress
twitter.com/yenpress
yenpress.tumblr.com
instagram.com/yenpress

First Yen Press Edition: December 2018

Yen Press is an imprint of Yen Press, LLC.
The Yen Press name and logo are trademarks of Yen Press, LLC.

The publisher is not responsible for websites (or their content) that are not owned by the publisher.

Library of Co

ISBNs: 978-0
        978-0

10 9 8 7 6

WOR

Printed in the United States of America

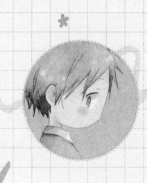

PALM BEACH COUNTY
LIBRARY SYSTEM
3650 Summit Boulevard
West Palm Beach, FL 33406-4198

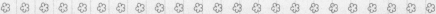